KING'

"Maurice Broaddus has a
the flavor of the streets
journey grounded in a gritty reality so compelling
that you'll swear these characters must live in your
own city. Put this on your must-read list!"

Bran
CORE

DISCARDED BY
URBANA FREE LIBRARY

The Urbana Free Library

To renew materials call
217-367-4057

"This is
recomm
in urb
attention."
Civilian Reader

"This book is a triumph. Maurice Broaddus has
created a masterpiece of original, compelling and
thought-provoking   drama,   irresistible   and

	DATE DUE	

King Maker
The Knights of Breton Court vol.I

Orgy of Souls
(novella, with Wrath James White)

Devil's Marionette
(novella)

Dark Faith
(editor)

MAURICE BROADDUS

King's Justice

THE KNIGHTS OF BRETON COURT
VOL. II

ANGRY
ROBOT

ANGRY ROBOT
A member of the Osprey Group

Lace Market House,
54-56 High Pavement,
Nottingham
NG1 1HW, UK

www.angryrobotbooks.com
Dragon rising

Originally published in the UK by Angry Robot 2011
First American paperback printing 2011

Distributed in the United States by Random House, Inc., New York

ISBN 978-0-85766-082-4

Printed in the United States of America

9 8 7 6 5 4 3 2 1

To Sally, Reese, and Malcolm,
as well as the kids and staff at Outreach Inc.

THE PLAYERS

The Crews

Breton Crew Folks	*Phoenix Apartment People*
Colvin	Rellik (Gavain Orkney)
Mulysa (Rondell Cheldric)	Garlan
Broyn DeForest	Bo "The Boars" Little
Melle	Lamont "Rok" Walters
Noles	

The Clients

Preston "Prez" Wilcox
Tristan Drust
Isabel "Iz" Cornwall

The Police

Capt. Octavia Burke
Det. Lee McCarrell
Det. Cantrell Williams

The Rogues

Omarosa
Naptown Red
Dred, Baylon

The Knights

King James White
Lott Carey
Wayne Orkney
Mcrlc
Lady G (Vere)
Rhianna Perkins
Percy

PROLOGUE

The ebon hole of the storm drain some called Cat's Eye Tunnel. A thin stream of water trickled down the center of the concrete tube, its sides not quite dry to the touch. Ignoring the faint smells of algae and waste, the boys crawled for what felt like quite a ways in the damp, dark pipe. Their ears strained against the shadows, past the faraway *plink-plink plinks* of water dripping somewhere further down the line. Nor was there any mistaking the skritching sounds.

"Rats!" a voice yelled in the dark.

"Oh, snap!" another called out.

Gavain and his younger brothers scrambled on all fours, sloshing through the brackish water, rushing towards the light of the opening until they tumbled out of the pipe. Piling onto one another, they formed a twelve-limbed beast that writhed in its own laughter. Gary and Rath were practically twins: the way their momma raised them. It was easier on the budget and it simplified fights if they both wore the same outfits. Gary, six, bright-eyed and innocent, idolized Gavain. Though a little bigger than Gary and only five years old, Rath had a potty mouth that sailors envied. Both had the scrawny physique of angry twigs. Their youngest brother, Wayne, stayed home with their mother. Sick again.

"Get your butt out my face." Gary shoved Rath.

"Who yelled 'rats'?" Gavain asked.

"Gary."

"Get that bad boy," Gavain said, knowing full well that it was actually he who had made the scratching sound. "Let's kick his li'l butt."

Gavain scooped Gary up and tossed him easily over his shoulder. He smacked his little brother's butt a couple of times, over Gary's playful squeals of "no" and "stop", before letting Rath get a piece. Gavain, nine and a half, felt a generation older than the other two. Tallest in his class, with the same weedy thinness of his brothers, Gavain loved both of them, but – in his heart of hearts, in that shadowed place where all secrets lay fallow – he admitted to being partial to Gary. The boy's unquestioning, unflinching idolization helped, but it was more the simple, no, innocent way that Gary approached the world. Gavain envied him his purity and wished just for a moment he could reclaim any sense of his own.

After letting Gary tumble from his grasp, Gavain leaned back against the grassy creek embankment to stare at the clouds. The thin creek divided their housing complex, Breton Court, from the rest of the neighborhood. Some days, it was the same sad stretch of trilling water serving as a receptacle for collecting trash. Other days the creek seemed to stretch out into infinity, an event horizon of adventure and mystery. Today it was both.

They laid on the grass of the sloping hill. The rear fences of houses caged Dobermans and Rottweilers, who barked incessantly at their presence. From their hillside vantage point, they could see all of Breton Court. Gavain liked this spot, the wide creek separating Breton Court from the residential neighborhood. He'd been chased by bullies through the court, his rare black face in the area too tempting a target for the white thugs. His speed kept him out of harm's way for a long time. Then, nearly cornered, he turned and dashed toward the creek. He leapt its breadth, landing flush on the other side. It was as if he crossed a border check and the bullies didn't have their papers in order. A natural dividing line.

"Look what I found." Rath held up a bent piece of discarded metal pipe.

"Here's another piece." Gary first held his pipe to his eye, scanning the neighborhood like it was a telescope before mounting it on his shoulder, like a bazooka. "Boom."

"Yeah, c'mon, we've got to kill our enemies," Rath declared.

Gavain watched the two of them scamper toward the overpass the creek ran under. Stifling heat thickened the air, making it akin to breathing steam. His brothers pantomimed shooting at the unsuspecting cars as they drove past. He meandered after them, just in time to break up the inevitable. No matter how much or how little money they had, no matter what school they attended, no matter which doors opened and closed for them in the maze of opportunities life afforded, boys would be boys.

"I said I was going to blow that one up." Rath swung his pipe at Gary.

Gavain separated them. Forgetting who he was for a moment, they turned at him with a feral grimace. "Don't hit me with that," Gavain said in an unmistakable, no longer playing, tone. "F'real. I ain't playing with you."

The sternness of Gavain's voice shocked them back to their senses. Rath slunk a short distance away, pouting, before contenting himself to shoot at more unsuspecting cars, unhindered by his distracted brother. The dreamy, distant stare – which so often filled Gary's eyes – signaled him drifting into his imagination. Whatever thoughts occupied his mind in that moment would find their way back to his little stack of "his papers" at home. Not quite a journal, more like a collection of stories and daydreams that he chronicled, such as his comic strips with doodles in each corner that depicted two superheroes fighting when he flipped the pages.

"'Mother, may I go out to swim?'/'Yes my darling daughter./Hang your clothes on an alder limb/And don't go near the water.'" Gary sang, dragging the length of pipe behind him.

"You little bitch!" Rath chased after him, in his half-stalking lope which indicated a mood to bully or get into mischief. He knew he was the tougher of the two. He hated the softness his brother had and hoped to toughen him up. It was either that or spend the bulk of his days as his brother's shadow protector. Which, all told, he didn't mind too much.

"Watch your mouth!" Gavain yelled.

"All right… preacher."

Preacher. The word spat at him with the venom of an ill-considered epithet. Gavain loved going to church, especially Sunday School. His class was small, so the teacher lavished extra attention on him; easy to do with an eager student. So, at his instigation, the brothers often played church, building blanket cathedrals in the living room. Gavain recited his favorite Old Testament stories (Noah, Moses, Jonah) and led songs while his brothers amened and sang along, happy just to be playing any variation of forts with him. They all knew it would only be a matter of time before his friends claimed him and he spent his days running around with them instead of spending time with his little brothers. At nine, the call of the streets beckoned with its siren song.

"Momma used to sing that to me," Gary said.

"Cause she thinks you're a girl. She still tucks you in too," Rath said. Gary lowered his head, with a splash of shame as if hit with too close a truth, obviously too sensitive to play insult games with Rath. He always took them too personally and hated the idea of hurting people for amusement.

"I know where we can go." Gavain changed topics, speaking more under his breath than to anyone in particular.

"Shut up." Gary had pretty much exhausted his comebacks in one shot.

"No, you shut up," Rath retorted.

Gavain stage-sighed. "Forget it. I'm going without either of you. I don't have time to babysit, no how."

It didn't matter who said what, the apologies rang with the same cheery melody, a chorus of "Wait up, Gavain" and "Yeah, we're sorry." Whenever they turned on him, or even got too out of line, the simple threat of abandoning them was usually enough to straighten things out. Gavain reveled in the adulation that bordered on respect and the power that accompanied it. He smiled a wan, yet victorious, smile.

"Where we going?" Gary asked.

"To the lake," Gavain said.

"But that's so far."

"We're almost there already." Gavain's tone didn't invite debate.

"Quit whinin', you can't come anyway. You too little," Rath said.

"Momma said I could go with you," Gary whispered.

Their momma's parting words slowed Gavain's steps. *Look after your little brothers.* "Fine. C'mon then."

The trio followed a trail known only to Gavain. This marked the first time he had taken them to his special spot. He retreated there to read, and think, be by himself, away from his brothers and the responsibilities of them. Though they only lived two miles from the park, Gavain had deemed his brothers too young to make the trip before; now they walked along the creek bed, its low flow revealed slippery rocks under the late afternoon sun.

Across from the Indianapolis Colts training facility, Eagle Creek Park, a national reserve spread out in open invitation. A brief traipse through the woods allowed the boys to bypass both the main gate (with its honor box: fifty cents for walk-in visitors to the park) and the ranger stations along the main roads (police, even wanna-be police, was still police). When they reached the old rusted-out fence, he knew that they neared their final destination. Long gashes, wounds of age and curious teenagers, marred the evenness of the links. Gavain pushed back the torn bit of fence barring their path. Flecks of rust painted his hand orange as he pushed through the low-lying branches occluding the dirt-worn and matted grass that served as their walkway.

His spot was a natural alcove of shore and trees, as if a giant mouth had taken a bite out of the park forest and backwashed sand. Dark sand, far from sun-bleached, lined the small inlet as waves lapped against it. The tree line dropped off sharply at the water, skeins of roots revealed by erosion. A tire on a rope hung in forlorn innocence from an old tree whose branches shaded a good chunk of their spot. Constructed to launch canoes before it dawned on the bureaucrats running the park to do so near the main beach and charge people for the privilege, the rickety boat launch bobbed on tires. Testing its mildewed boards, Gavain imagined himself walking the plank of a dilapidated pirate ship. The sun glinted from the water, its shards of light held Gary and Rath in rapt attention.

"You sure it's all right to be here?" Gary asked in an almost awe-struck whisper. "We didn't bring any clothes to swim in. Or towels."

"Damn, fool. You know momma wouldn't let us go swimming," Rath said.

"Just swim in your underwear. It'll dry out on the way home," Gavain reassured him with a smile.

That was all the encouragement the boys needed, shucking their clothes over near the tree roots and running to the water's edge. Warm gusts of wind blew towards them; tiny, lazy waves sloshed against the shoreline. The alcove lay around the bend from the main beach, like a forgotten part of the park, fenced off (or fenced in) to keep people from wandering off. With the occasional boat horn belching in the distance, he knew they weren't alone. On such a beautiful picnicking day, the beach proper had to be crowded and all the shelters full.

However, nary a sound drifted into their alcove.

A strong breeze rushed off the water. It was

downright frigid in the shadows where Gavain watched the boys play. They wobbled on slick rocks, their arms flailing to steady their balance as they acted out kung fu movies. Gavain already regretted letting them watch *The Five Deadly Venoms*. Discarded in their frolic, the branches piled at the dock. He feared that he'd have to confiscate their improvised weapons, especially if it occurred to them to battle any unsuspecting underwater enemies. The last thing he wanted was some sort of lightsaber duel in the water. Their private hideaway did its job, enchanting the boys. It wasn't often that they played near anything that wasn't concrete or plastic. They had some relatives that owned a farm or something down in Jeffersonville, but they were their father's side of the family. Momma never quite fit in with the family.

The innocuous chattering of the boys strained Gavain's nerves, but only in a bemused-by-the-familiar sort of way. The boys beamed, amusing themselves, and that gave him time to read. He pulled a tattered copy of *Danny Dunn and the Smallifying Machine* from his back pocket, surprised by how much he enjoyed the ludicrous series. There was a quaintness to them that he liked.

Then something at the back of his mind nagged him, an unscratched itch. He searched for a word to describe the feeling. The water mesmerized him. Breathing in the loamy smell of leaves, the stiffness of the breeze, he realized what the feeling was that he couldn't shake. The weight of eyes followed his every movement. Someone watched him, exactly the way the little Korean beauty salon owners watched him when he bought stuff for momma. Someone on a rock down the beach, barely within sight: a body, light as bleached bark, nearly white in the furtive sun and slight of build, a woman perhaps, watched them.

Making sure those children didn't cause any trouble, he thought. He'd been on alert for indignant park rangers, full of their authority, coming to scare them off. The possibility of a chase gave him a thrill to look forward to. Not that he expected anyone else to be here: it kind of ruined his illusion that only he knew about the place. The woman stole away into the trees.

"Hey, did you see her?" Gavain asked.

"See who?" The boys answered in unison. Sand somehow managed to dust both of their fresh faces though neither was even up to his knees in the water.

"The woman over by the trees. She was staring at us."

"Probably a park ranger." Gary turned from Rath as if the two of them had to caucus before deciding the proper response.

"Then why didn't she come chase us?" Gavain asked.

"Probably one of those sun bathers then."

"Was she naked?" Rath finally chimed in.

"Don't listen to him. There probably wasn't no woman. He just trying to scare us again." Gary's eyes widened in a tacit plea to not taunt them anymore.

"I wasn't, but that does remind me of a story." Gavain squatted over an overturned log, drawing in the sand with a twig, waiting for the boys to come over to him. They did, they always did. "You remember that nursery rhyme you were singing earlier, Gary? Do you know what it's about?"

"No." Gary searched for his own twig and began to draw in the sand.

"There was this old witch without a name but folks called the Lady of the Lake."

"I don't believe in witches," Gary said, not quite looking into Gavain's eyes.

"Do you want to hear this story or what? Anyway, you see there was a woman who lived by a lake much like this one. One day she goes out for a swim, but the water…" Gavain trailed off, making his voice sound haunted, for good effect, especially if he wanted to frighten the boys into caution around the water. "Water can be a powerful thing, scary, but they don't make movies about it. It's not something that puts on a mask and chases you through an old house. It's deep. Strong. Mysterious. And things live in it. Things that scientists don't know about or can't explain. Maybe the Lady of the Lake got caught by one of those things. Maybe she became one of them. Maybe she was the mother of all of those creatures. All folks say is that she drowned, but every seven years, she comes back to claim a life, a life that should've been hers. Sort of a guilt offering. She comes for those who wander too close to the water's edge, grabbing their ankles with those long arms of hers, and pulls them to her, draws them to her underwater kingdom. And you don't want to see her in the water. Her skin is slightly blue and puffy from being drowned and all. She has long hair, greenish like it's wrapped in seaweed or somethin'. And she greets them with a kiss, a kiss full of her long sharp teeth. She stares at you with those big dead eyes of hers. She couldn't help herself. It was in her nature. They're the last thing that you see before you take your last breath.

"BOO!" Gavain yelled and jumped suddenly.

The boys reared back and screamed before hitting each other and laughing.

"Bitch done wet hisself," Rath said.

"Boy, I ain't gonna tell you again." Gavain tossed his stick at him. "Watch your mouth."

The boys scrabbled off, unfazed, splashing into the water.

"You comin' in?" Gary turned and asked. Gary had a way of asking for things that sounded not only like a command, but as if his whole life depended on you giving into him.

"Yeah, in a minute," Gavain lied. "Hey, if you can't stand up and be above the water, you need to come back closer." He didn't want to have to get wet if he could help it. His brothers might have bought the idea of their clothes drying out on the walk home, but the idea of wet, bunched-up underwear rubbing against him for an hour didn't appeal nearly as much to him as it did them. Visions of having to swim after one of the knuckleheads caused his fear of deep water to rear itself again. He wanted to spend more time in the water, but the shore was as close to the water's edge as he dared go. He shielded his eyes with his hand to better study the deceptive calm of the flat surface. Gary jumped into the water. Not used to the acoustics of the woods, Gavain thought he heard a second splash a little further away. It might've just been an echo. He scanned the periphery anyway.

The water exercised a strange fascination over him. He lost track of time, idling his minutes away, not really reading his book but only holding it in front of him while he studied the water. The splashes of his brothers grew faint. The book fell from his limp grasp. The lolling waves lapped against the sheltering embankment. The swishing susurrus made it easy to ignore the rising uneasiness that washed over him. The sobering shimmer of light, the dispassionate gaze of the deep, the sibilant call of the waves, held him in a spell that reached to an ancient, yet familiar part of his soul. The seaweed, like trees helplessly caught in a strong wind, unfurled, forming a chain that pointed toward the deeper part of the lake. The brown murkiness of kicked-up lake bottom swooshed about, as if something stirred to life. The water. A war waged within the waves, breaking the smoothness of the water.

That was when he noticed that Gary was in trouble.

Gary slapped at the surface, his head cocked up at an odd angle, as he fought the water rather than swam in it, spitting out mistakenly inhaled gulps of water. Rath was nowhere to be seen. Gavain clambered down the embankment, each bob of Gary's head an eternity whenever it ducked under the waves. The drooping branches whipped at Gavain. He stumbled over an exposed tree root and fell face down into the wet sand. Lines of smallish footprints crisscrossed the dark sand. They could've been the boys' footprints, but there were so many. Gavain stumbled to his feet and waded frantically into the water. Not a strong swimmer; he swam well enough to get where he wanted to go, but had no technique beyond his floundering variation of the dog paddle. His lungs burned as he took in gulps of water. He splashed about in near panic and tried to reach Gary who seemed only a few yards away from him. Frustrated tears stung his eyes. The water flowed thick and heavy, the painful rush of it towed against him like bottled-up rage. He strained against the water, but made little progress. The tide, too strong, swept them further out into the lake. Gavain thought that he glimpsed someone. A woman.

"Help them! Help them! They're drowning!" he cried out.

Gavain swam across the sucking, parallel to the shore; it was all he knew to do, desperately fighting against the watery vacuum that threatened to yank him under. He scanned for any sign of his brothers. Gavain stretched out his arm, almost within reach of Gary's hand. Gary's face turned toward him, blanched and exhausted, like a boy who'd seen a ghost, but was too tired to run.

"Gary." Gavain dug his arms into the water, his measured strokes like swimming through quicksand. He reached out toward him, spotting Gary's terrified eyes, his body seized in some invisible, powerful grip. The water climbed higher along Gavain's chest. The tug gnawed at him. He shivered, suddenly aware of how cold the water was; too cold for such a day. The water seemed so dark, murky. A cloud covered the sun and created deeper pockets of shadows beneath the waves. No, this shadow was small, heading towards him just out of reach.

Rath. Eyes bulged out, his face frozen in a rictus of panic.

Something scraped against Gavain with the bite of coral, like the sharp, thick nails of a large hand. The splashing ceased. Gavain searched for any sign, any shade, that could've been Gary. Nothing. The waves, its anger spent, subsided. Gavain imagined how his brothers spent their last moments. Their arms outstretched, fighting for air, their minds wondering where he was. Where was their big brother? He was supposed to look after them, protect them from bad things. Bad people. That was when he knew.

She had come for them, with her yellowed sinews, black blood pulsing through her veins. The Lady of the Lake, her belly bloated with the rage of the sea; head lolling from side to side, caught in its own current. He remembered something like hands brush against him. Like hands, but not hands.

He never forgot the hands.

CHAPTER ONE

King James White had spent his entire life on the
west side of Indianapolis. Despite being funneled
through Child Protective Services, in and out of
homes – more out that in by his teenage years – he'd
attended schools 109, and 107 (transferred to be a
part of their advance placement curriculum because
his high intelligence was noted despite his efforts)
for his elementary years, 108 for Junior High School,
and then Northwest High School for the couple years
he could stand being in high school.

The rhythms of this side of town were as familiar
as the constellation of razor bumps along his neck.
Exiting on the 38th Street ramp from I-465 – the
highway loop that circled Indianapolis proper – he
expected the same rotating cast of panhandlers. The
homeless vets who couldn't quite pinpoint what war
they were veterans of. The folks who needed money
in order to get home, who turned down rides to said
home. They swapped time with a woman whose sign
told the tale of her being pregnant and homeless.

The weather-faded backpack and mottled teddy bear wrapped in a blanket were nice touches, but she'd been "pregnant" for over two years now. When off shift, she or the vet or the lost couple were picked up by a van. Begging was just another way of life in the hustle.

Turning east off the ramp took one to the corner of 38th and High School Road. Three of the corners of the intersection had gas stations on them. The fourth – the north-west corner – was a collection of store fronts. The Great Wok of China's kitchen caught on fire a few months back, the timing of which worked out well for the lingerie and marital aids store next door. The owner had been embezzling money and the new ownership was in place and was planning on relaunching the store with basically the same name with the letters jumbled, familiar yet different. The adjoining Karma record store would be down for a month or so. Folks would have to get their drug paraphernalia somewhere else for a time. The lot behind the store fronts was a deserted concrete slab built on a hill nicknamed Agned for reasons no one any longer remembered, enclosed by a Dairy Queen and a Shrimp Hut, thus free from casual prying eyes, especially so early on a Sunday morning.

Though it was still Saturday night as far as Caul was concerned.

In a North Carolina Tar Heels jacket, Caul stood a bulky seven foot five, towering over both King and his best friend, Lott Carey. Under a thicket of dirty hair, his eyes gleamed red in feral madness. A jagged keloid ran down his left cheek. His thick lips drew back to reveal teeth painted black within his wide mouth. Curiously, he had neatly trimmed fingers, except for the nail on his pinky which jutted out an inch and a half.

"It's over, Caul." King cold-eyed the giant. Tall, though still easily a half-foot shorter than Caul, King wasn't overly muscled like one of those swollen brothers just out of prison. The sides of King's head were shaved clean. The top of his head in short twists, almost reminiscent of a crown. King let the wind catch his leather coat, allowing the handle of his golden Caliburn to be seen. A portrait of Marcus Garvey peeked from his black T-shirt. Skin the complexion of burnt cocoa. His eyes burned with a stern glint, both decisive and sure. His lips pursed, locked in a mission, as he focused on the task at hand. He stepped defiant and sure, confident without issuing a challenge. Though prepared to meet one if need be.

"It ain't over, you Morpheus-looking motherfucker. You ain't po-po. You can't arrest nobody."

Lott had told King he thought the sunglasses were too much. The weather was getting too warm to justify the leather coat. Still, King liked the look. Lott lowered his head to conceal an "I told you so" smirk.

"I'm telling you to go." King put both his hands up, signing for everyone to just calm the hell down. He pitied the thugs he ran across more than anything else. Social outcasts masquerading as the definition of loner cool, no one would have them, not school, not family, not friends, not relationships. They didn't know how to connect, and in their loneliness they turned angry, little more than sullen children destroying what they couldn't have. In Caul's case, he terrorized the elderly during their grocery store runs, jacked people at ATMs, and harassed women going about their business. The final straw, he threatened King's girl, Lady G. King and Lott took a personal interest then.

"You telling me something now? Don't think I didn't notice that you brought your boy."

"Boy? I'll climb all over you like a spider monkey." Lott checked his watch to mark the time before his shift was due to start at FedEx. He hated to wear himself out before going to work, but when King asked, explaining the threats made to Lady G, his face went hot and he knew he'd call in sick if he had to.

"Don't think that I can't snap your back over my knee and fuck the stump of you right here," Caul snarled. The keloid arched upward as if waving at King.

"What is it with you people? Always talking about 'fucking' other dudes then say how they ain't gay," Lott said. "How player is that?"

"It ain't gay if your eyes are closed," Caul said.

"Is that how it works?"

"A hole's a hole."

"We don't want any more trouble. We just need you to move on–" King began.

"Or what? You think I'm scared of you? Or your little gun? I've had guns pointed at me before. Been shot more times than I can count."

"I'm thinking there's not too hard to get to," Lott said.

Caul's world turned red. The heavy-lidded gaze of the fiend snapped to full fury. He hated when people assumed he was stupid. That just because he was large, he was also slow. His teachers had always treated him like the large simpleton taking up precious classroom space until the jails caught up with him. At some point, he bought into their beliefs about him and it angered him. But he stuffed that anger back onto itself, allowing indo smoke to chill him out most days. Today he needed to wipe that "better than you" grin off the tan-skinned one's face. With his FedEx uniform – as if that made him someone. Caul snarled and charged Lott without further comment.

"It wasn't my fault," Caul said as he swung, to the ghosts only he knew.

Skin the color of burnt butter, and with the delicate features of a male model playing at being thug, Lott danced out of the way of Caul's lumbering charge. True to his word, Lott skittered up Caul's back, wrapping his legs around the brute's chest while attempting to subdue him with a choke-hold. Caul cantered backwards, slamming Lott into the wall of the Wok of China. The air escaped from Lott with a sudden gasp.

King's vision blurred the scene before him, shifting, merging with another scene as familiar as memory. Caul lumbered toward him, stumbling from the shadows of a massive cave. Past two great fires he strode toward King. The giant gnawed on the bone of a human clutched in one hairy hand. Blood smeared about his lips like barbecue sauce after a ribs repast. The dreamy déjà vu sensation annoyed King, like weed getting his head up at the most inopportune times. King shook his head to clear it, then jumped back, barely avoiding Caul's thrown punch.

King ducked under the clumsy attack, cursing himself for an ill-thought-out strategy with no end game in mind. The fact that he and Lott's blood got so roiled at the idea of someone menacing Lady G was all but dismissed by the pair. The threat of the Caliburn was just that: an empty threat. King was loath to draw the weapon if the situation didn't warrant it. Ever since the Glein River incident. The weapon called when it demanded to be used. On its terms; any time else was an abuse. King threw a couple of quick jabs into the man's kidneys which seemed to annoy him more than anything else. What did he hope to accomplish? His only plan was to beat this man's ass under the guise of asking him to move on.

The mistake most people made – it occurred to King as he stepped out of range of Caul's massive

swipes while leading him away from a shaken Lott –
was to use the same weapons against all enemies.
There was nothing to be hoped for going toe-to-toe
with Caul. That was fighting a superior foe on his
terms. No, the only weapon against strength and size
was smallness, stealth, and speed.

As if reading from the same battle manual, Lott
charged Caul, tackling him at the knees. The giant
collapsed to his knees, catching himself before his
head hit the concrete. Scrabbling for purchase, he
hoped to wrench Lott into his grasp.

King withdrew his Caliburn. The gold glistened in
the early morning light. Lott's eyes widened. Caul
turned, following Lott's gaze, his sight landing on the
gun. Shifting his grip, King swung the weapon in a
low arc, clocking Caul just above the temple.

"So what do we do now?" Lott asked.

"Call the police?" King examined the unconscious
giant.

"And say what? Where I come from, snitches get
stitches."

"Self-defense."

"Trouble just seems to keep finding you."

The morning had barely dawned.

A pair of New Balance tennis shoes – gray and mottled with mold – dangled from the overhead phone
line. A schoolyard prank gone awry to the casual
passer-by; an advertisement, or ominous warning
and cause for alarm, to those more in the know. King

sucked his teeth in disgust and wondered how long they had been there and if it were too late to stave off the attempted infection of his neighborhood. His philosophy was simple: if a community didn't take control of itself and one guy entered who could think, the community would have a problem. If people in the neighborhood took control, however, that guy knew he had opposition. Most times before he stood against opposition, he would leave for an unprepared, less-resistant neighborhood. Now, in LA or Gary, they might go toe-to-toe with opposition. Not here. Not in Indianapolis. Not yet.

"Back it up." King waved the Outreach Inc. van back a few more feet then held his palms up for it to stop. Armed with a broom, he jogged around to the front and hopped up along the hood to the roof in a limber movement.

"This is stupid," Wayne said. Brushing back a few of his long braids which had fallen into his face, he turned all the way around, revealing a scar on the back of his neck. A tight knit shirt stretched across him, showing off the stocky build of a football player, with the light gait of someone who knew how to use their size should the necessity warrant. A quick smile broke up what otherwise would have been a hard face. "You better not leave any shoe prints up there."

"A little work now prevents a huge, pain-in-the-behind worth of work down the road."

Breton Drive separated the assemblage of town-houses of Breton Court from Jonathan Jennings

Public School 109. The school was designated a zero-tolerance zone and once Night's drug crew had been dismantled, it was one in deed as well as word. King stared at the shoes as if they personally mocked him.

"It's a pair of shoes."

"It's a declaration," King said. "Says someone intends on dealing out of here soon. It's a set-up notice. Well, message received. Now we're sending one back."

"Yeah, throw up a pair of tennis shoes and see how many brothers it takes to take them down."

"Two. One to do the work and another to wear his ass out with complaining about it." King waved the broom handle about, a blind conductor directing an unseen orchestra. Eventually one of his haphazard swings connected with the shoes and they tumbled free. "There. Now they know. You try to set up shop in this neighborhood, there are folks around here who care enough to stop it."

"Uh huh. If you close your eyes, you can hear your applause."

"Come on." King gathered the shoes, holding them with two fingers well away from himself. "We going to be late."

Fumbling for change, Percy emptied out his pockets, carefully counting out each penny with great deliberation. Percy tipped nearly three bills. Droplets of sweat swelled, coalesced, and then ran as a trickle down the darker knot above his left eyebrow. In the shape of a crescent moon, the keloid etched his burnt mocha-complected skin. He huffed with anxiousness under the weight of the eyes of the man behind the cash register of the Hoosier Pete convenience mart. The line behind him now ran three customers deep, with the bell on the door jangling as more people entered the gas station convenience store. A stack of Giant Sweet Tarts piled in front of him, his nervousness increased as he glanced at the total on the cash register and then his quickly dwindling pile of change. The pennies eventually stopped. Twelve cents short. Percy stepped back dumbfounded as if a set of equations didn't equal out.

"Come on, man. You see him all the time. You know he good for it," an older man said, dressed in an off-white hat with matching shirt and slacks with a pair of sandals. Old-school casual. A toothpick protruded from his mouth, a cup of coffee and a newspaper filled his hands.

"Nah, it's all right. I'll put something back." Percy's downcast eyes rarely met anyone's gaze.

"No, it ain't all right. It's not the point," Old School said.

"He not have it, he put something back. It's only twelve cents." The Indian cashier had witnessed variations of this scene every day. In a few minutes, he'd be due to be cussed out. Maybe called a sand nigger, despite being born in an Indianapolis suburb. Or told that his mother should have aborted him; that was, when he wasn't being accused of having sexual congress with her. He knew it was coming and the reality of the scene playing out again frustrated him.

"That's my point. It's only twelve cents."

"Twelve cents is twelve cents," the cashier said. He pulled at his black-streaked white beard. Weary eyes drifted from Percy to the lengthening line. He knew it was pointless to reason with people once they built up a head of steam, but he went through the motions anyway. "He short twelve cents. I let that go. You short twelve cents. I let that go. By end of day, no more shop."

"Leave that boy alone. You see he simple," another voice cried from behind Old School.

Percy grabbed a pack of Giant Sweet Tarts, but was told to put it down. This was about principle now. The rising hostility in the shop rattled Percy. Each face a mirror of anger, distrust, and resentment. Everyone was just so... mad. He felt bad for the man behind the cashier and searched his pockets again hoping he missed a quarter.

"Your shop is in our neighborhood," Old School said. "No more customers means no more shop, too. You move in here, happy enough to take our money out of the neighborhood, but you can't be bothered to be a part of it."

The Indian man trembled with his own missing rage. Uncertain eyes, not wanting any trouble, also didn't want to be cheated. The constant accusations, the constant attempts of folks to get over on him; the constant vigilance exhausted him. They didn't see their machinations as attempts to take food out of his family's mouths. The ugly mood in the neighborhood had been building for weeks now. This was why he bought a gun.

"Look at you. Even now I bet you think we going to rob you. Typical." Old School sipped from the coffee he hadn't yet purchased.

"This is bullshit. We regulars, too," the agitated customer behind him amened. "Can't you be bothered to know us?"

"Fellas, fellas... it's all right. I got it." The name badge on the arm of the FedEx uniform read "Lott Carey" and featured a grill-revealing smile. A thick, navy-colored sweatshirt over matching pants, the uniform had the formality of one having donned armor in preparation to joust. Lott strolled toward the front of the line with his pimp-roll strut for all the eyes to see. Obviously pleased with his "swooping in like a superhero saving the day" entrance moment, his smile showed off the row of faux gold caps which grilled his teeth.

"Thanks, Lott." Percy shoveled his candy into his about-two-sizes-too-small jacket.

The Indian gentleman took the quarter with a sigh of relief and handed the change to Percy, who then pocketed it.

Lott watched his change go into Percy's pocket but didn't say anything. "Come on, we going to be late."

• • • •

Despite the elbows pummeling her side – and the mad screeching of what sounded like a cat being slowly lowered into a wood chipper – Big Momma was slow to wake. Her eyes fluttered, spot-checking the rising sun against the accusing red glow of the night stand clock's numbers. With the care of not wanting to crush a newborn, she rolled over. The boy wailed, locked in a nightmare, and thrashed about beside her. She pulled her night gown tighter around her, conscious of the possibility of her heavy bosom spilling out.

"Had! Had, boy, wake up. It's OK, it's OK. Momma's here. Momma's here." She shushed the boy awake, reassuring him while guiding him from whatever nocturnal terror lay in wait for him each night. The boy's eyes focused with a hint of recognition, though Big Momma was rarely certain about what actually flitted through the ten year-old's addled mind. Had's mother smoked crack while pregnant, increasing her habit as it went along as if medicating herself through the pregnancy. The effects of which played out like a sad movie across his sullen face. His somber brow furrowed, fine crease lines worried into his head.

With Pokémon characters splayed all along them, the pajamas seemed wholly too young for him, yet fit him both physically and mentally. The brightness of the clothes only made his dark skin appear that much darker. He popped his thumb into his mouth and began to suck.

"Help me, Lord. Lord Jesus help me." Big Momma drew up her sheet. Holes began to wear through the threadbare material. She made do, treating them gently and kept neat, because she wouldn't be buying new ones for a while. Poverty was no excuse to not carry her head high. She threw the sheets from her and sat up, checking the curlers in her head. Thankful he was awake but quiet, she left Had in the bed. Her bones grated with her first morning steps as she eased into her day with a resigned sigh. The floorboard creaked under her uneasy waddle. She poked her head in Lady G's room only to see clothes slung along the headboard of the bed, perhaps to dry. The piles littered the floor without any discernible pattern except maybe to be able to know where all of her earthly belongings were in case she had to scoop and run. But it had been months and Lady G had neither scooped nor run.

Each step brought a huff as she descended in a sideways canter. Black smudges trailed along the wall. Creating a mental to-do list for that weekend, she'd have to scrub them and tell the kids to use the banister like they were supposed to. She ambled along the plastic runner from the door through the living room. Faded family photos and Polaroids hung on the wall next to a painting of a very European and beatific Jesus. Plastic covered her couches. Folding chairs centered around a large television. Toys littered the floor. Crayons rested on a beat-up coffee table. Gospel music played from the kitchen, always

Mahalia Jackson. The kitchen still smelled of chicken and macaroni from the previous night's dinner. Cereal boxes, cookies, and bags of chips lined the top of the refrigerator.

Lady G wiped her hands on a towel then placed it back on the oven door. A pink bandana tied her hair back. She pulled the sleeves of her black hoodie back down her arms. Black jeans led to black-trimmed pink boots. The remaining dishes from the sink were now dried and stacked nicely on a rack on the wiped-down counter. A few acne bumps dotted her forehead, red and swollen against her toffee-colored skin. Before Big Momma could step fully into the kitchen, Lady G turned her back to shield the view of her hands.

"Had awake?" Lady G pulled her fingerless gloves over her burn-scarred hands.

"Boy's going to send me to an early grave." Big Momma paused out of respect. Folks had secrets and shames, stuff they either weren't ready to talk about or would never talk about. There was no point in pressuring them with crowding them or leaving them without the space to protect their dignity. She averted her eyes by pretending to fuss about her day's clothes. "You up awful early."

"I already ironed your good blouse," Lady G said. "Started coffee. Got breakfast ready."

"I know I got no right this morning." Big Momma didn't have much by way of too many rules, but she didn't want to be taken advantage of. Everyone had to pitch in somehow, if not rent or bill money, then helping out around the house. No one lived free because life was about handling your responsibilities. Big Momma picked up the blouse in faux inspection. She sniffed the shirt, enjoying its freshly starched smell. When she took Lady G in, she wanted no more than to give the girl someplace stable. She had a lot to give, seeds scattered and sometimes they fell in thorny places, like with Prez (oh, that boy broke her heart) and sometimes the soil was fertile and grew up quickly. Like with Lady G. "But can I ask one more thing?"

"You always got the right." Lady G was one of the rare ones. She wasn't as hard as she believed she was. Hard, yes, because a child shouldn't have to live the way she had had to or see the things she'd had. Still, she wasn't through-and-through hard, the kind of hard that used up all the good and innocent inside. No, Lady G still had an innocence she protected, a vulnerability she treasured.

"Can you get Had washed and dressed?"

"Sure thing, Big Momma."

Had was a new case. He slipped in behind Big Momma to a bowl Lady G filled with cereal. Tipping the bowl to his mouth, he lapped noisily from it, all smacking lips and deep-throated gurgles. The little boy was a set of wide, inquisitive eyes over the rim of the bowl. His head seemed two sizes too big for his body. He stopped mid-slurp, as if aware for the first time that others were in the room.

"He's always just made those noises ever since you took him in," Lady G said.

"The sound of leftover nightmares, girl." Big Momma checked the wall clock. "Look at the time. Go ahead and go on, girl. You going to be late."

"What about Had?"

"Never mind. I got him. You go."

The days of the week blurred into a dismal sameness, but Sundays broke them out of their lethargy. This day was one with a spell cast on it, all blue skies and cutting chill. The Outreach Inc. van pulled up in front of one of the row homes which led to Breton Court.

"Right here, man." King pointed to the side of the road.

"You sure about this?" Wayne slumped forward on the steering wheel.

"We stop the little things, the big things take care of themselves."

"Looks to me like you trying to tackle big things, little things, and everything in between." Wayne checked his watch and thought to himself: we settle more ghetto mess before 9am than most people do all day. He pushed against the driver's seat, which sighed as he exited.

King opened his door without glancing back, purposeful and focused, and walked with that determined saunter of his. Directly to the second door from the end. He rapped five times, loud, but not a po-po knock. A plumpish woman, short but unintimidated, cold-eyed him.

"Excuse me, ma'am. I need to see you and your husband."

"What is it?" She wrapped her shawl around her tighter, about to get her church on, as she sized him up. She fixed a hard but without attitude mask on her face, her mood preparing to be potentially fouled by this busybody, do-gooder type who was probably used to his looks getting doors opened for him.

"Your son, he was down paintballing the candy lady's house. He needs to get down there and clean it up."

"DeMarcus? Get over here, boy." Pipe-cleaner arms ducked behind his mother. Ten years old if a day, unsure of the stranger at the door and instinctively seeking shelter behind his formidable mother. "This man says you out shooting up a woman's house with that paint gun of yours."

"Wasn't me." The words sputtered out as reflex. He stared without shame at King.

"Don't lie to me, boy," his mother said, used to coaxing the truth or at least navigating the lies of boys.

"Before we get po-po out here. Clean it up or Five-O." King met the boy's eyes. Treating him like a man capable of accepting responsibility for his actions. He had to catch them while they were young. "Which one he want?"

"I'm sorry, Momma." The voice was barely audible.

"What you do that for?" The mother grabbed him by the shoulders, more embarrassed than anything else.

"That old lady was talking crazy to me," the boy whispered, cornered by truth.

"So you go down and tear up her house?" King pressed.

"Thanks, we got this." The mother's still-respectful tone didn't invite dispute.

"Got my eye on you. Be checking on that house tomorrow," King said as a parting reminder to De-Marcus.

"You too much, man," Wayne said as they turned up the corner heading toward their actual destination.

"What do you mean?"

"You too much. What a brother can't ease up for nothing?" Wayne nodded up the way to the figure approaching them. "Lookee here, lookee here."

Poured into her jeans, braless beneath her halter top, her sashay had men erect from half a block away, Rhianna Perkins sauntered up. Always down for a party, a party that needed to be paid for when it was over, her eyes glimmered with recognition. Her hair flared, interlocked locklets in need of re-twisting. Despite the swell of her belly, she carried herself with a fierce sexiness. Upon closer inspection, her worn, bruised skin added a hint of purple to her sepia complexion. Something about her easy crocodile smile made her appear much older than her sixteen years.

"When you gonna come see about me?" she asked.

"I do. I never forgot about you. You're still part of our neighborhood," King said. "We got to all pull together."

"You all harambee like a motherfucker now." She licked her lips as if appraising a freshly prepared plate of filet mignon. "I know, you gone all crusader now."

"Just a man on a mission."

"You never struck me as a missionary man. Lady G don't give it up easy, so it must get lonely. Maybe I can help."

Scenes like this normally amused Wayne. King was a visionary type. It wasn't as if he considered himself above other people, he just wasn't as much a man of the people as he liked to believe he was. He was so caught up in how things ought to be, the behavior of people often left him confused. So whenever he was confronted with a situation he couldn't talk or punch his way out of, he was left with an awkwardness with belied his level cool. However, the sight of Rhianna hurt both of their hearts. The daily reality they had to relearn was that not everyone could or wanted to be saved.

"Come on now, sister. You better than this."

"I'm just open about what I do. Those other girls do dirt, too, they just like to hide it."

King had a reputation for being largely indifferent to women. Most blamed his break-up with his baby's momma and his subsequent estrangement from his daughter, Nakia. Yet, despite his protestations and the various walls he'd built around himself, Lady G got under his skin and invaded his heart like a hostile takeover. She held his interest and attention in a way few women had. And part of him feared that in the sharing of this tiny part of himself, he had done something dangerous. Which he had, for her. Lady G. King was drawn to her and she to him. He decided to risk loving Lady G, then and always.

"Come on, man," Wayne said, "let's get inside."

The Church of the Brethren was a victim of a spate of local fires. Fire investigators suspected drug addicts illegally squatting. Without the necessary insurance to rebuild, the standalone building was left as little more than a warehouse lot. Burn marks scored the edges of the sallow, off-white façade. Sheets of plywood – with the date of its condemnation spray-painted across it – served as the door. The stain glass windows above the doors remained intact. Off-white and yellow painted wood mixed with brick which had been equally painted, marred by scorch marks.

"I heard what you did down at Badon Hill," Wayne said.

"What'd I do?" King pulled at the rear door, the nails of the board pulling free with ease.

"Brought down another gang trying to get a stranglehold in the neighborhood."

"Man, I haven't done half the stuff they say I've done," King said.

"That's how legends get born."

"That's how fools get dead."

"If that's the case, we in the right place."

The inside of the building had been gutted, the stripped, water-damaged walls and seared columns stood revealed like charred bones. The remains of a soot-covered choir loft split down the middle before toppled pews which couldn't be salvaged. Black rocks scattered across the floor, like fossilized cockroaches. A giant cable spool commanded the center of the room.

"No chairs?" Wayne asked.

"No coffee and donuts either. We ain't going to be here that long, so I figured we could stand. I just thought it was important that we met."

"A symbol, good and round. You think like a king." Merle scratched his thigh, abating the itch of whatever had crawled on him during the night. The old man had his back to them though he seemed to appear out of nowhere. Unlike King's leather jacket, Merle wore a long black raincoat whose lining had been removed. A tall man, but the coat hung loosely on him, like a scarecrow lost within a blanket. A cap made of aluminum foil crowned his head. He stroked tufts of his scraggily reddish beard as he searched about the room as if he had whispered something.

"Each of us has a role to play," King continued, unperturbed.

"What's his? Minister of Drunken Crazy Talk?" Wayne asked.

"Hand holder. Life guider. Purpose pointer. Gift shaper," Merle said.

"Ass painer."

"Hold up. Here come the others," King said.

King didn't need to even turn to know Lady G had come into the room. His heart knew and leapt at her presence. His mood, so fierce and dark before, lifted like a breeze blowing away storm clouds. A shock ran up his body, his breath shortened in shivering excitement. In the same way, when she left a room, his world grew a little bleak.

Percy ducked under the door entrance. King didn't know what to do with him. Everywhere they went, the big boy-man was there. Not quite underfoot, but always around. He meant well, knew the players, and had a heart to match his girth, but King wondered if that was enough.

Lott trailed in Percy's wake, his head bobbing as he walked. His face only betrayed his thoughts if you knew what you were looking at. He studied the structure with an eye toward its integrity, possible ways it could be attacked, and escape routes. A quiet, pensive man with a restless heart, and who often let moments pass when asked a question, unafraid to allow an intimidating silence to build. Connected, instant and deep, King and Lott shared a strange kind of intimacy, a wary bond of old friends. Their shadows clashed against the wall like black swords.

"What you listening to?" Lady G made room for Lott next to her. She thought him too much of a roughneck pretty boy, but she put fingers on his arm as he sat down, an innocent, friendly gesture. He hesitated, a slight hitch to his movement before he sat down. Part of her enjoyed the effect it had on him.

"Going old school. Something King turned me on to."

Lott pulled the earphones from his ears and plugged his iPod into a set of speakers he withdrew from his backpack. The gentle strains of the Impressions' "It's All Right" began.

"Oh yeah." Lady G closed her eyes and gyrated to the building groove.

"All right now." King joined them.

Wayne took a seat around the makeshift table, then patted the spot next to him for Percy to join him. Wayne was always partial to Percy, reminding him of one of his brothers. Wayne carried around a silence with him. They all had pain in common, each of them with that bit of them which remained closed off. It reared itself, a creeping shadow, whenever the topic of brothers or family came up. A set jaw, clenched teeth, a determined silence. Resolute. Final. A pain unspoken.

An awkward lumber into place, Percy glanced around with a huge grin – the joy of acceptance – on his face. He wished Rhianna were here to see this. He studied the others for a moment as if gathering the nerve to fall in with their swaying.

Merle stood on the outside allowing them to take their seats. It wasn't his role to sit among them.

Without comment or planning, everyone chimed in on the chorus. "It's all right to have a good time, cause it's all right." Looking around at each other, they burst into a fit of laughter. It was a perfect moment.

"We a band of misfits," Lady G said.

"Surely the flower of the ghetto," Merle said.

"So what we doing here, King?" Wayne sniffed, though he otherwise ignored Merle.

"It's kind of like a brain-storming session. Trying to figure out our next move." King rubbed the back of his head, letting the coarse stubble across his neck scrape his fingertips. The razor bumps read like Braille, but he was due to get his cut trimmed up. Lady G could handle the twists. "We need to go bigger."

"Why us?" Lott asked.

"Why not us? If everyone kept asking that question, nothing would ever get done. I want us to be about something. A mission. Be about granting mercy and stopping murders. Defending and honoring women rather than using and degrading them. I want to end the fighting. I want to quit letting our community poison itself."

"You want to take the ghetto out of black folk," Wayne said.

Everyone chuckled except King. He wore the pained expression of not being taken seriously. Maybe he did dream too large. The wasted lives of good people troubled him; even if that was the life they chose for themselves, he couldn't help but pity them. Good people. Drugs were here to stay. Like cigarettes and alcohol, it was only a matter of time before the government and laws made their peace with them. Until then, someone was going to service the demand. Which meant gangs were here to stay, too. These were times of crises and opportunity.

"It's absurd to build a tower atop of two combating dragons. Such was Vortigern's error," Merle said.

"We need to do more." If King heard the doomful note in Merle's prophecy, he ignored it. He wasn't quite in the mood to divine if Merle spat out gibberish or was obliquely providing one of his lessons. Either way, it was less trouble to simply move on. That was King's way.

"We?" Wayne asked. "We been tearing around all over town. Feels like we the only firemen in a city full of brush fires."

"Why do we do the work of the gendarmes?" Merle asked.

"Ain't that why we pay their salaries? What's my tax dollars getting me?" Wayne asked.

"Like you've ever paid taxes," Lott said.

"To Caesar, render unto Caesar. And to all a good night," Merle said.

"It's not enough." King raised his voice to cut through the burgeoning chaos. "I don't think we've made a bit of difference."

"What do you want us to do?" Wayne asked. "Keep in mind, I'm on full-time with Outreach Inc.

now. They got me going into schools, building relationships with kids, trying to get them on the right
track. Lott here just got promoted at FedEx. Finally
getting a decent shift. And Lady G is earning her
GED and preparing for college."

"I know. Damn it. It's just not enough."

"Come on, King." Lady G took his hand. With her
touch, he began to calm down. "Let's take a walk."

Locked in dark thought, King believed dreams to
be important. Merle more so. His dreams lingered
with him, coming unbidden between moments.
Snatches of images. Dragons took to the air against
smoke-filled skies. Razed buildings. Cars on fire.
Only the occasional person seen running. Like an
owl on a field mouse, a dragon swooped down and
gobbled them in a single swallow. Slick and coiled,
serpents writhed, their bodies filling the streets,
crushing everything in their path. Their sides bulged
with digesting bodies. The grass slick with blood,
men fought with futility, their hollowed faces tired
of grieving. The dragons and serpents crowded the
land and kept coming. Inexorable.

It was why King rarely slept and drove himself and
those around him so hard. Each day brought a new
task. A new crew to get information on. A new
open-air market to disturb with his presence. A new
head to bust if things got out of hand. Lott especially
warmed to the task, loving to fight. Given a just
cause, he perfectly rationalized his violence.

Wayne, however, wanted no part of that; and the

blind relish the two of them took to their operation, the more uncomfortable he became. They were an unchecked fire and inevitably, the wrong person would be caught up in it. King felt responsible, burdened, and now refused to hear advice. Not Wayne's. Not Merle's.

"King is kind of closed off." Wayne watched King and Lady G skulk off. "I've known him longer than anyone. The man is a living wall." They were on the verge of something, something potentially transformative. Wayne sensed it and wanted to be a part of it, but hated the hound-dog way King sometimes carried himself. There was a fine line between being real and being seen as weak. And this was an inauspicious start to whatever it was King had planned.

"Child of the morning, I have the same old wound," Merle said, "but I believe he is the right man."

"Something made him hard. He guards himself and won't let anyone in. I know that I'm his boy and all, just like I know King is ride or die," Wayne absently brushed dirt from the table, not wanting to meet anyone's eyes. "Not to go all female or anything, but I have no emotional sense that King even cares about us."

"It's not good for brothers to fight one another."

The moody silence allowed King a retreat to his grim thoughts as he locked himself away in darkness. He grew sickened by his own rage. The hallway led from what was once the church foyer to what was once the nursery. Charted memory verses littered the wall. A pictogram of a white Noah on a huge boat, animals popping out from all over, sailed merrily across a sea of blue. Forty days and forty nights, God sent the waters to flood the earth to cleanse it of all unrighteousness. That was probably the only time the land knew peace. The kids sang a story about Noah collecting animals two by two. All King pictured was all the dead bodies the storm left in its wake.

"What are you doing, King?" Lady G slipped her hand into his and rested her head on his shoulder.

"You know what I'm doing. I'm trying to make a difference."

"Right. All cause a raggedy homeless guy says you have a grand destiny. An important role to play."

"We all do."

"I know, baby. But…" Lady G took his delicate, knobbed hands and ran hers along them. "You all over the place. You run from this to that, no rhyme or reason, just always running. Just caught up in the idea of being important. You don't have a plan. You don't have an endgame. It's like as long as you keep moving, keep doing, that's enough for you. You don't see how lost you are."

King only half-listened to what she said. He took comfort more in the idea of her. The warmth of her hand. The realness of her proximity. King saw himself taking shape in her eyes. She made him braver, more sure. Everything simply made sense when she was around. The two understood each other if neither knew why. Years of solitude made them secretive, self-protected, with that closeted fear that the more they revealed about themselves, the more folks won't like them. Years of pain and scars haunted them. Maybe they simply recognized the reflections of their own haunted expressions in each other's eyes. All he knew was that she held his demons at bay. She was the light to his dark. When he gazed into her eyes, he saw the faithful and honorable man he wished to be. They worked. But he couldn't escape the feeling that they weren't real.

"What do you suggest?" King asked.

"When was the last time you spoke to Pastor Winburn?"

The name caught him off guard. He couldn't even remember mentioning him to her. In a lot of ways, King was raised by Pastor Ecktor Winburn, the father he thought he wanted.

"I ain't spoke to him in a minute," King said in halting measures.

"Don't you think it's about time?"

"Do you?" King asked.

"I only want one thing."

"What's that?"

"For you to be true to yourself and come home safe."

"Go on off to school." King squeezed her hand.

"Bye, love." She raised their entwined hands and kissed them.

"Bye, baby."

CHAPTER TWO

Detective Lee McCarrell scanned the periphery of the scene, not listening to anyone in particular: the chatter, the radio squawks, the idling engines, the occasional horn or siren blare dissolved into a susurrus of a crime scene symphony. Though he hadn't had a drop all shift, his mean, green eyes appeared liquor-heavy. His protruding jaw dominated his profile followed by his high forehead. His long, slack hair threatened to bloom into a full-blown mullet, a hairstyle choice which did not combine well with his thin mustache, which made him look like he stepped right off a porn set.

"You're up."

"I know." As much as his last partner, Octavia Burke, put him off, better her patient brand of ball-busting than the too-eager grind of his latest one. Of course, bumping Octavia up to captain left a "brother" slot available which they quickly filled with one Cantrell Williams. African-American. Average height. Shaved bald. Clean-cut. Cigarette smoker, Kools his brand of choice. Leather hat. Leather trenchcoat. Young, smart, and arrogant – worse, he was good enough natural police to back up his arrogance. He handled each case as if it might serve as an opportunity for a grade promotion. The only things he lacked were people skills and experience. His "aggressive assertiveness" – evaluation speak for pushy – earned him a rep as a glory hound, a rep he did little to dispel. He double-parked in front of the playground at the Phoenix Apartments, his face caught in the slightly haloed gleam in the emergency lights.

"You ready to handle this on your own?" Lee turned off the ignition and let the engine cool for a minute.

"Am I ready to go solo after being under your capable tutelage for a few cases? Yeah, I think I got this."

"All you had to say was 'you're up'. Fuck me for caring."

Moldy brown leaves puddled along the base of the black chain-link fence which ringed the outer boundaries of the apartments. Weeds and broken glass choked a sea of cracked pavement. Empty bottles of Colt 45 littered the dilapidated equipment that passed for a playground. Rust held the monkey bars together. The swings had been thrown over the top of the metal frame of the set, out of reach of any would-be user. The yellow school bus jungle gym had been tagged. RIP Alaina. RIP Conant. Nobody wanted to be here – not the police, not the media, not the paramedic, not the tenants – all equally prisoners in a cycle of well-meaning benevolence.

"I take this seriously," Cantrell intoned a little too earnestly. Try as he did to keep an open mind about his partner, he recognized the half-a-cracker scent of festering resentment. "We speak for the dead. That's the job."

"Screw this job. Screw the dead. Screw this neighborhood. You watch, no witnesses, nothing useful. We'll be lucky if we can even ID the vic. They don't care about these animals, even when they prey on them much less when they get killed."

"Animals?" Cantrell arched an eyebrow.

"You watch."

Before he got out of the car, Cantrell muttered a prayer for the victims, the survivors, and their families. And then his partner. Though it was half-full and lukewarm, he gripped a Starbucks cup, toting it with the consciousness of an affectation.

The city took on an entirely different pallor at night. Darkness had a way of enveloping any crime scene. No matter how many street lights, flashing lights of emergency services vehicles, the brightness of the moon, or lights from the surrounding buildings, shadows swam in deep pools around them. Where there was darkness, there was mystery. Lee studied the shadows, uncertain of the trick of the ambulance's lights on his eyes. Pairs of red dots glimmered at him. A half-dozen sets at least. Hate-tinged flecks glaring at him. He blinked. The dark remained a smooth velvet sea of ebony.

Like red boxes in white trim, every bit like bricks in the wall of the Phoenix Apartments, three ambulances remained in front, without sound, with only their lights' intermittent flash acknowledging their presence. Police tape had been strung from tree to fence. Lee only grew irritated by the welling quiet he knew would soon settle on the gathering lookyloos. Full of sideways glances and growing stillness, as if a cloud of innocence descended on them with a spiritual anointing of silence.

"I see angels. Snow angels." A homeless guy, in a tinfoil cap no less, waved his arms flapping in the snow only seen in his head.

"I bet you do," a uniformed cop said as Lee and Cantrell approached the scene. "That kind of crazy had to be steeped in whiskey."

The uniformed officer had that young cop look about him: thin, but muscular; dark sunglasses, and eager, with an arrogant bossiness to his manner. The rookie raised the tape to let them through. Cantrell ducked under. Shards of glass vials crunched underfoot. He paused to survey the remaining landscape.

"I ain't ruining my new shoes stepping in that shit," Cantrell said.

"You worried about this? Some of the shit you'll be walking through, you'll be begging for a scene this clean," Lee said.

"We got a live one here," the uniformed officer said.

"There was a survivor? He conscious?"

"Uh, no. I meant it was a lively scene."

"Look here, rook…" Lee rolled his eyes, the pre-amble tell to an apoplectic fit Cantrell usually found entertaining if not useful.

"Why don't you stick to telling us what we got?" Cantrell cut him off and slipped on a pair of latex gloves. The red light bounced from their faces. The first body slumped against a wall. At first glance, he looked like a panhandler waiting for change. But his clothes were too new, clean-cut, fresh look. High forehead, eyes sunken in regret, thick-faced, heavy lips. Blood flared against his yellow vest.

"Looks like multiple shooters. Don't know if these guys even got off a shot," Lee said.

"Where are their guns?"

"Exactly."

"So, no guns recovered," Cantrell said.

"Not even theirs?" Lee asked.

"Someone needed souvenirs."

"I doubt memories of spring break is what they have in mind." Annoyed by Cantrell's tight-assed fastidiousness, Lee strolled around the scene.

The second body leaned out of the car, his blood mixed with a puddle that drained into the sewer. Thin, bright-eyed, the red lights caught in them making him appear possessed. His white teeth spread in a harlequin sneer across his face.

Lee leaned over the body. At first he thought the dead boy was Juneteenth Walker, would-be assailant

of Green, the former muscle for the Night organization. He had the same semi-scowl, the same years of
hurt worn into his skin, worn like an ill-fitting jacket
off the rack from Good Will. The images hit him all
at once. The blood. The bodies. The death. Lee pictured Green lumbering toward him, holding a
severed head in his hand. Bullets flying. His thigh
ached, his body remembering its violation. Noting
the boy's ashy knuckles and a short bus necklace, he
was certain of only one thing: this mutt didn't de-
serve a cop standing over him.

"What's his name?" Lee asked.

"Don't know," the uniformed officer said.

"DOB?"

"Don't know."

"So he's not going to be missed by anyone." Lee
wanted to roll the body, but knew the coroner would
jump his shit for weeks if he touched a body before
he got there. "What else do we know?"

"We know he was a part of a drug crew. Used to
work for a dealer named Night," Cantrell said.

"But you know they were strapped?" the uniformed officer asked.

"Holy Virgin Mary's rotten pissflaps," Lee said.
"Yeah, they were strapped. These fools can't floss
without pulling out their nines like they were tugging on their junk."

The last body had been worked over pretty good.
An inelegant beating, his face punched in, jaw broken. Bruising around his chest from a close wound:

execution-style, but there was no stippling. The way
his body sprawled along the sidewalk, it was as if he
were snuggling into a bed of concrete with the tarp
serving as his only blanket.

Cantrell hitched his pants up slightly and tucked
his tie into his shirt. He imagined photos of the boys
pinned by magnets on their mothers' refrigerators or
framed on what passed for mantles or end tables. He
humanized them to see them in schoolboy pictures
full of hope and promise.

"If I had to guess, this here was one of Night's
stash houses, and from the look of things there was
a firefight. Near as I can figure, an enforcer," Lee
pointed to body number three then to number two,
"and wheel man making a delivery or a pickup.
Street soldier over there," Lee gestured to the first
body. "Ambushed."

"Tire treads?" Cantrell asked.

"Nothing," the uniformed officer said.

"Assailants on foot?"

"Maybe." Lee's stomach churned – a queasy sensation that for some reason had him rubbing along
his scar. To the casual observer, it appeared like he
rubbed the sweat of his palms along his pants.

"How they going to sneak up on an armed crew
on high alert, take them all out, and disappear?
That's why you detectives and I'm a lowly uniform.
Earn them big bucks," the uniformed officer said.

"Fuck you and your big bucks."

Lee kicked at the tire leaning against the side of

the building. "Stash's still here."

"Cash still on the bodies." Cantrell flipped a pants pocket inside out to withdraw a roll of bills.

"Rules out a robbery."

"Rook, come over here."

"What's up?" The uniformed officer saw the wad of bills. And that Cantrell saw that he saw.

"You first on scene?" Cantrell asked.

"Yeah."

"See anything?"

"What do you mean?"

"No one messing with the bodies?"

"Not a soul on the scene." The uniform officer shifted nervously, afraid he'd missed something. Cantrell put a reassuring hand on his shoulder by way of dismissing him.

"Bodies weren't picked clean," Lee said with mild surprise.

"Hard to believe they were part of the same crew."

"There was more than Night and Green holding that crew together. But you take them out…"

"…and there's a mad scramble to…"

"…hold the center." Caught up in the easy rhythm of Cantrell, a glimmer of hope once again flickered in Lee that he might actually be cut out to work with a partner.

"I was going to say 'keep their shit together,' but OK." Cantrell grinned. No slack given. "How'd you know?"

"These mooks make numbers three, four, and five

to get popped."

"Five?"

"They caught a couple on night shift."

"Shit," Cantrell said.

"So let's take stock again." Lee tamped out a Marlboro and offered it to Cantrell, who waved him off as he took out a pack of Kools. "A mid-level dealer. An enforcer. A street dealer."

"Someone sending a message."

"New player in town. Or players. No one's safe."

"Shit," Cantrell said. "So someone's cleaning house preparing to move in."

"Yeah."

"How are we doing with witnesses?"

"Why don't you canvass the Greek Chorus over there?" Lee asked.

Hard faces glared from the fence. Lee returned their beady stares. Half-assed thugs probably with more questions than answers. A panoply of mean-mugging, concern, fear, and curiosity. In other words, the neighborhood in a snapshot. Lee decided to let Cantrell do the canvass. He'd probably have better luck with that brother-brother shit they do. And besides, Lee wasn't in the mood to bust any heads. The joy wasn't there tonight. All he could think about was the huge waste of it all. All the boys without fathers. He thought of his own father.

Lee's old man didn't take any crap. He grew up dining on his father's stories, chewing them up and swallowing them until they became a part of him.

Stories were like that. His father often wove the hard-luck tapestry of standing as his own man though he never stood a chance. His every career opportunity blocked at every conceivable turn. Better accounts handed to someone less deserving. Skipped over for promotions. Pay frozen or benefits cut back at the worst time. So much pain, bad luck, and anger could only be tempered by getting his load on in a bar. One night, the alcohol haze left him confused and he made a delivery to the wrong address, a neighborhood much like this. Robbed and beaten, his dad lost an eye. He was still a man though and made the most of his life. No excuses. In fact, soon as he got back on his feet, he went back to that neighborhood with a pipe and a few of his boys and showed them what for.

On quiet nights, along with his thoughts, especially as he sifted through bullshit for a living, Lee was used to how people spun their particular angle on things and had learned to parse stories accordingly. Everyone was the hero in their own stories. Even his father. Lee imagined him begging for his wallet. On his knees pleading to not be hurt. For them to stop. He never lost that flicker of fear and doubt, that anxiousness when one of *them* neared. His father had been so larger than life, especially to Lee; to see him reduced to a helpless pile of bandages incapable of even wiping himself after soiling his bed sheets, the incident left an indelible mark of humiliation on him.

Lee got back in the car and slammed the door.

"Can't blame folks for not wanting to mark themselves as a witness," Cantrell said.

"Oh, that's where you're wrong. I can blame them. And I do. They have only themselves to blame for this mess not getting any better." Lee flexed an insincere smile.

"Not when they have crusading champions of justice like yourself for them to trust."

"It's the white thing."

"More the peckerwood thing." Cantrell didn't trip. He'd been handling racists all his life. At least he knew where he stood with this one. He set the coffee cup back in its holder, still half-full. "Similar to how I pretend every time you say 'they,' you ain't saying 'niggers.'"

"I haven't said that."

"Your lips say one thing, your heart says another."

"I bet you say that to all your dates."

Octavia Burke leaned back in her large leather chair. It sighed. She wore her brownish-black hair naturally. Freckles dotted her medium complexion on either side of her wide-ish nose. She shifted her broad shoulders along the seat, getting comfortable. Bridging her fingers on her chest, she enjoyed the earned authority of the seat. Captain Octavia. Her voice was fraught with an air of quiet thunder and brooked little nonsense, though most of her ire was aimed at Lee. The familiarity between them had morphed into something tense. No longer partnering with Lee meant not having to deal with his day-to-day nasty-ass attitude. Being a boss in his house meant that she still had to deal with his messes, though she was used to his brand of work ethic.

"You said this case was a no-brainer," Octavia said.

"Not that deep. One corner boy gets got by another corner boy. We're there to sift through the muck and paperwork until that corner boy gets got." Lee nodded at Cantrell for solidarity. Cantrell's gaze remained locked on the captain's desk.

"So we don't have anything?" she reiterated.

"Nope," Cantrell said.

"The witnesses give a description?"

"Vague. Average height. Average weight. Average age. Black. Male." Lee smirked after emphasizing the color. "You could've poked out my eye and fucked my socket after that revelation."

"This file isn't vague. The body in the morgue isn't vague. I'm tired of vague. Get me something concrete." Octavia slapped the report on her desk. "Any ballistic matches?"

"None." Lee leaned against the wall, his face a mix of smug and bitter. His hands fidgeted in his lap as if he didn't know where to place them to give off an air of command and control. He hated the way she squeezed into her office jacket whose buttons threatened to pop whenever she moved. He hated the way she flipped through paperwork rather than look at him. He hated the way that when she did look at him, she peered over her glasses. Stared down at him over the rims. Dismissed him with a glance.

"Different shooter for each vic?"

"Maybe. All the wounds were through and throughs. No shells or bullets recovered. And there were some questions about the wound tracks." Cantrell faced the captain, the desk between them a respectful gulf, his arms folded.

"What sort of questions?"

"They didn't specify. Said they'd get back to us." Cantrell hid his frustration with his partner's unnecessary button pushing of their boss. He'd heard they used to be partners. The smart play meant they had someone upstairs in their corner. Leave it to Lee to sour that relationship to curdled milk.

"One other thing, this isn't just street guys," Lee said. "We're talking lieutenants, wholesalers… the infrastructure of the organization."

"Professional and clean," Cantrell concurred.

"For now. Only a matter of time before a civilian catches a stray bullet."

"The problem with a street war is that someone always wins."

"And we're left to clean up the mess." Lee shrugged to mask his disgust. He hated the power vacuum left by Night's demise and Dred having faded so far into the background, so damn untouchable he was reduced to being strictly a rumor. It felt like unfinished business.

"What's your next step?" Octavia asked.

"Going to tap my informant."

"Reliable?"

"The best." Lee grinned. A boy's gleam at being trapped in a toy store, though it had a lascivious edge to it. Though Lee had a way of making even talking about cotton candy sound lascivious.

"Work your cases. Hard," she emphasized. "We need to see some movement sooner than later. Something to reassure the public."

"And the bosses."

"Them, too."

"We'll get right on it, ma'am," Cantrell said.

"'We'll get right on it, ma'am.' You ever get tired of bowing and scraping?" Lee asked.

The neon bloodshot eye logo of the Red Eye Café seared Cantrell Williams' already tired retinas. A 24-hour bar and breakfast joint, though the café couldn't serve alcohol on Sunday mornings because of Indiana's blue laws. Small burgundy lights blinked along the window ledges as he stewed at his faux wood table. The place was the province of the young and used-up, as the hookers and strippers of downtown Indianapolis often strolled in here after their shifts. Cantrell ignored him as he bit into his Red Eye Chili Omelette.

Life as a detective was mostly this: inaction as they waited for a body to fall, paperwork, and figuring out where to eat. The murders played on his mind though; despite his cynical bravado, there was a grain of truth to Lee's sentiment. Soon this would be yesterday's news. As it was, three teen males slain in a shooting in a neighborhood no one cared about only rated a page three mention. Though he had no feel for Captain Burke: in his experience, all bosses cared about was to keep things local. If feds came in, things had a way of getting stupid. A high enough profile murder or too many bodies dropping or someone gets it in their head that there was a nefarious ganger of some sort to make their bones on, all bets were off and stupidity reigned.

Until then, Cantrell would work things his way. Build relationships with the community. A Pastor Winburn had been steadily building a rep as a community activist. Some knucklehead named King was busy taking a more direct approach, staying just this side of being a vigilante. Or at least being charged as one. Maybe he could rap with some of the local gang leaders, lean on them to lower the temperature in the neighborhood. That was Cantrell's vision.

"… place is a toilet. Always has been."

"Not always." Cantrell didn't even have to make the pretense of catching up on the white noise his partner's chatter usually faded to. He always came back to his favorite topic: the Phoenix Apartments.

"Even when it was the Meadows, it was a cockroach-infested sewer filled with rats who thought of little else but eating, slinging drugs, and shitting all over the place."

"My moms didn't seem to have a problem raising

us here." Eyes at half-mast, his body knotted with frustration and anger. Cantrell planted his palm on the table and leaned toward Lee.

"Oh, what, so... we gonna have a thing now?"

"Ain't no thing to be had." Cantrell relaxed and let loose a long sigh.

Lee turned away in a paranoid sulk. He wasn't racist. He didn't care how many times he was called cracker or peckerwood, he knew what he was and how he worked. Citizens got a fair shake, but animals were treated as animals. Police – true po-lice – dealt with the worst each culture had to offer and it had a way of coloring a person's view on that culture. Including his own, though, more often than not, he was summoned to black neighborhoods, not his own. That wasn't his fault, just the cold, hard real of his life. No point in bullshitting it.

Like this one time, this black student – honor roll, track star, showed real promise – got killed by three white kids. Wrong place, wrong time, wrong side of them tweaking. Lee hunted those bastards down as if they'd killed his own kin. Didn't care how long it took, how many sessions in the box, how many times he had to pull them in, he was going to get them. And he did. He wasn't a racist.

"Unclench, motherfucker. Damn. You let this stress get to you and it'll kill just as surely as a bullet."

CHAPTER THREE

Rellik stared into the mirror as he buttoned up his shirt, a simple white collared thing left from his last court appearance. Yet he dressed with the solemnity and attention of a man of occasion preparing for an evening out. Freckles collected in clusters on each cheek, offset by his light skin. Reddish-brown braids draped to his shoulders. Perpetual and bloodshot, his black eyes fixed straight ahead while the prison guard waited impatiently at his cell door. Though the day was slow in coming, it wasn't as if Rellik served the entire amount of time he could've. Should've. Guilty of many crimes he wasn't tried – much less been convicted – for, he followed the simple belief that confession wasn't as good for the soul as people would have him believe. He'd confessed only to as much as the state could prove, and even then, only to shave a few years off his bid. He strode toward the guard, who stepped back and allowed him to lead the way.

Allisonville Correctional Facility, a Level Four prison. The A-V. The Ave. Prison. Projects. Projects. Prison. Either way, cram too many desperate motherfuckers into a place and things were bound to jump off. Rows of white metal bars formed a gauntlet, one he'd run every day for seven years. The voices of his fellow inmates fell silent as he walked by. Cunning, private, unhousebroken, he was just another animal in a cage and the only thing the cages were good for was to better train animals. Breed them for contempt. Of themselves. Of each other. Of authority. Of society. Then cut them loose with bus fare, severed freedoms, and dim hopes to make a real fresh start in life. Because no one forgot and no one lets you forget.

"Gavain Orkney," the face behind the bulletproof glass said through a microphone.

Rellik bristled. It had been more years than he could remember since anyone called him by his slave name. And not since elementary school since anyone emphasized the pronunciation of "vain" rather than correctly as "vin."

"One toothpick, unopened. A set of cuff links. One Movado wristwatch. Three rings. And one cross necklace."

After sliding on each item in a protracted manner designed to drag out his time there – his shiny Jesus piece the last for him to don – he opened the toothpick and slipped it into his mouth.

"We ready?" the guard asked.

"Let's do this."

The metal gate at the end of his cell block clanged open, a metal mouth of two rows of teeth which snapped shut behind him. Three sets of such jaws stood between him and what passed for freedom. Surviving prison was all about clinging to some semblance of faith. He had to believe in something to make a real go of things. What and whoever it took to get a brother through. God. Allah. A girl. A guy. The myth people called love. Those things carried some people through, but not him. No, Rellik had faith in his crew. The game. It never let him down. Like anyone who had reached a dark night of the soul, those times of profound doubt and questioning when his faith was at its lowest ebb, he was forced to make mental gymnastics in order to keep hold of his faith. In his case, it wasn't his crew that let him down, who abandoned him, who remained silent when he needed them most. He had let them down with his weakness.

Rows of lockers. Signs regarding contraband. Warnings about personal safety. The gray walls. The gray and white linoleum. Rellik would miss none of this place, though it was the world he knew best. Clouds, like torn fabric, churned with menace in the afternoon sky. Under the harsh glare of the sun, he dreamt of freedom. The sky stretched, an infinite canopy of possibilities. In it, he cold lose himself and fly. He could forget that he was surrounded by concrete and that his feet remained locked to his earthen path. He took in a deep breath.

Rellik, a true OG, was coming home.

After a few hours on the bus, Rellik was ready to stretch his legs. It took a while to get his mind around the name The Phoenix Apartments. When he went inside, the projects were still called The Meadows. His mother moved him and his brother there to start over. As a kid, he ran the hallways, threw rocks at passing cars, rang doorbells and ran, and raced swings in the playground only to leap from them at the apogee to go sailing along the concrete slab. He played stinky finger with Gayle Harmon in an alcove. Lost his cherry in an Impala in the parking lot. Despite the name change and a fresh coat of paint, it was still the closest thing to home that he knew. Some things never changed and some people were fixtures.

"Look at this motherfucker right here," said an old man with a head too small for his body, from beneath the hood of a car. Revealing a teak complexion, and gray goatee, when he fully stepped from behind the car, he fumbled inside his shirt pocket for a pair of thick, black-framed glasses as if double-checking a vision.

Rellik returned a long, penetrating stare. "Geno."

The old man screwed up his face in mock disgust then raised his hand to give him a pound. Geno was one of the neighborhood home repair and handy-men, and was old when Rellik went in. An odd-jobber by trade and practice, he could fix refrigerators or televisions, bring in free electricity or gas, even install AC. The story of his life fell into two parts. In part one, during his real life, he held various blue-collar jobs. Then his story went the way of many stories and slipped into part two. He got laid off, lost the lease on his apartment, and became homeless. He squatted in any vacant apartment in the Meadows, now Phoenix, staying out of folks' way except to offer his services. Since he didn't "truck with no drugs" – and neither brought nor followed trouble – he was loved by the tenants.

"What's going on?" Rellik scanned the deserted lot. Eyes peeped him from the playground's lone bench attended by three boys. One took off after locking eyes with Rellik. Restless and frowning, still learning to wear the mask of street toughness.

"Same old, same old. You probably know the comings and goings round here better than most."

"They up there?"

"What's left of them." Geno wiped the oil dipstick with a rag then returned the rag to his back pocket.

"Same spot?"

"Yeah. Too lazy to change things up too much."

Careless and undisciplined. Too confident in their setup despite so much evidence to the contrary of it being a good one. Despite Five-O all but setting up shop here, coming and going as they pleased as if *they* owned the place. His boy from way back, Night had held things down, but with him out of the picture, operations were slipping.

It had been a while since he'd been to Night's "penthouse", two adjoining apartments on the sixth floor, the top floor of the tallest of the Meadows-now-Phoenix. The first laid out with a large screen plasma television. Four junior knuckleheads wrestled over the Wii controllers, shouting at each other, as they trash-talked their way through a game.

"I hope I'm not interrupting?" Rellik asked.

The crew froze in their spots, a garden of hoodlum statues along the couch and from the kitchen a steady beam of bewildered glares as they wondered how this fool got into their place without making a sound. The front door was reinforced, a bar locking it into place to slow down anyone using a ram to bust in. A man stood guard on it. And yet here this man stood, carefree and bold, unbothered by the host of men now drawing down on him. Rellik swished his toothpick from one side of his mouth to the other.

"Nigga, what's up?" A small-statured boy rose up, flexing manhood, but the smell of his mother's milk was still fresh on his breath. Small twists crowned his head, the beginnings of a thick mop of braids. Eyes the color of cooked honey studied him with practiced hardness. Despite how short he was, he had a bit of a hard body, gym locker room edge, probably the only class he didn't cut. The skunky odor of fresh bud clung to his clothes; he had the look of a marginal student who smoked marijuana to exclusion of everything else. No church, no friends, no sports, if he held a job he'd soon quit it as his grades careened towards failure. Lounging around smoking endo and playing Wii, obviously he didn't care what his life choices did to his folks. Yeah, Rellik broke him down in an instant. Because he used to be this kid.

"This is what's up," Rellik answered. "You ever point a gun at me again, I'll kill you. Now who am I talking to?"

"You talking to me." The boy held his hand up to put his men on pause.

"Am I talking to the right man?"

"You talking to me." The boy's voice gained an additional measure of stroke to it.

"You know who I am?"

"If I had to guess, I'd say you Rellik."

"A man shouldn't have to guess. He should know."

"I hear things. Heard you was getting out. Didn't think you'd jump back in as your first stop."

"A man's got to go to the folks who'd have his back." Rellik turned to all the guns. With a nod from the boy, the weapons lowered. "Who am I dealing with?"

"Garlan."

"Garlan." The name brought to mind his little brother Gary. Maybe this was what he might have looked like as a teen. "The crew good?"

"We got some niggas." Garlan hardened his face, except for the thin smile across his lips. It dared Rellik, let him know who had the power.

Rellik learned early on that he was good at fight-ing. The anger and the darkness were his only friends. Gave speed to his hands, gave strength to his legs, thickened his ability to take punishment. And not only could he take it, he could dispense it with-out conscience. The pain demanded regular sacrifice to assuage its hunger. Though many thought he was an idiot because of his girth and his lumbering stalk, he sought it out. But he was no bully. If the fight was fair – against another boy his size or bigger – it was on. "Good. You don't trust me. Caution's good. Till I prove myself, I don't need to know shit. He who controls information controls power."

"How you get in here?"

"I'm strictly old-school. I'll tell you this much: there are many doors if you know how to open them. Night's other place, next door, anyone been in it?"

"Can't get in."

"Good." The men still focused their wary intent on him. But they'd lowered their guard. Probably none had trained with Night. Assuming he was in a train-ing mood.

"You trying to take over?" Garlan asked.

"I ain't trying shit."

When Rellik was a kid, he began shoplifting; he rationalized his taking what he wanted because he was in need. A black hole of desire for comic books, action figures, clothes, electronics. He deserved it. He was hard and wanted to get high. And though he told the parole board about his plans for culinary school or maybe barber school, prison only hardened him further. And he sought power. Rellik gestured an all but Garlan collapsed. "We got a problem?"

"They all right?" Garlan asked though he didn't back down in his posture.

"Asleep."

"I got some folks I want you to meet. Strictly introductions. You don't like them, they off in any way to you, we move on."

"Yeah, I'm talking to the right man." Rellik took a seat on the couch. The other boys stirred to consciousness and cleared out for him. "I've been gone for a minute, so I'll need to go handle my business. We straight?"

"Yeah, we cool."

"Niggas will try to get at you all the time. Niggas take kindness for weakness. You have to be able to see the big picture, not just your next move. It's time to finesse this shit."

CHAPTER FOUR

Broyn DeForest drove with the care of a driver's education student under final review. The stretch of I-65 connecting Chicago and Indianapolis was the easiest part of the drive and was so familiar to him by now, he could make the run with his eyes closed. He set his nondescript white Toyota Corolla – sometimes a gray Honda Accord – on cruise control at exactly the speed limit and stayed in the right-hand lane for the entire trip. Once he was within a city, he grew more nervous. Being so conscious of using his turn signals and not weaving in and out of the constant stop and go of traffic went against his natural rhythm of impatient driving. No, today he was on the clock. Three kilos of raw product sat in the trunk. It might as well have been a beating heart under some floorboards the way it occupied his conscience.

It used to be that Broyn made this run barely once a quarter and that was usually only for a kilo. Colvin's operation worked in the shadow of Night and Dred, between the cracks of their respective territories. He'd carved out such a nice niche for himself, many feared that he would draw the attention of either of them and be swallowed up whole. Then two things happened. One, Night's operation fell apart seemingly overnight as news of his demise spread quickly along the street. At the same time Dred took a step back. The streets bubbled with rumors from Dred turning federal witness to Night getting capped, to the bizarre involving voodoo or some shit. Or maybe not so bizarre, considering the second thing. Colvin recruited some new... muscle.

Colvin had stepped up the game.

These days Broyn made the run twice a month and was told to be prepared to switch to weekly soon. Now, it wasn't simply a matter of pick up and drop off, but deliveries to be made. The first exchange was simple enough. Simple, if one didn't mind a trip to Gary, Indiana. Broyn would sooner deal direct with some of the dons in Chicago rather than have to stop in Gary. The city still competed to be the murder capital of the country. From downtown, he made his way to the usual spot Colvin had him do business from toward the main gate of the steel mill. Over on Broadway, north of Fourth, there was an abandoned train station on the right between two railroad overpasses. The sign on its front pillar read "No Parking. Cabs Only." though few cars ventured its way. A desolate, lonely place, an echo of ache within the city, the once-magnificent showpiece had been reduced to a home for pigeons and vagrants. The building was a mausoleum of silence and decay. Secluded enough for a simple transaction.

Broyn would leave a taped-down grocery bag filled with cash under his seat and the trunk of his car popped open. He'd step out and make small talk with his contact, Myron Smalls, who folks called "Stink." Broyn thought that – as fucked up as his own name was, with his mother trying to spell "Brian" some unique way – he couldn't go through life being called "Stink." They'd both watch for police. All Broyn had to do was get back in the car: the money would be gone and the product in the trunk. He didn't have to check. Then it was an uncomplicated drive back to Indianapolis. With Colvin positioning himself as a supplier now, Broyn made the reconnect, dropped off one kilo to another crew – though he hated dealing with the Treize – and then took the rest to a cutting house where it could be whacked and packaged and distributed. A smooth operation, all things considered.

His hair in twists, a scraggily beard jutted off his chin, a trail of razor bumps dotted down his face. Turning onto Lafayette Road heading toward Georgetown Road, already known as the drug corridor of the west side of Indianapolis, he hated that Colvin insisted on this route. It was as if Colvin dared the police, too. Carrying real weight, it was Broyn's ass on the hook for the years and was in no mood to taunt Five-O.

"What if they take me off?" Broyn had asked Colvin before he took off.

"They won't take you off. You travel under the protection of my name." Colvin had a dangerous sing-song to his voice.

"Yeah, but what if…"

Colvin's unwavering glare silenced him. All Broyn knew was that he was no Mulysa, Colvin's new right hand. No one even thought about fucking with Mulysa. Maybe that was Colvin's play: daring a motherfucker to mess with his shit. Broyn hated the idea of being the potential object lesson of some bold fool out to make a name for himself, but Colvin was not to be denied.

Rain-slick and deserted, especially this time of night, the bleed of wet asphalt wound past an apartment complex and gave way to an industrial park Georgetown Road got past 71st Street. The arms of the railroad crossing lowered, with Broyn not wanting to gun the engine to beat the train for fear of drawing unwanted attention.

Nervous enough already, his imagination called up images of bangers rolling up alongside him or car jackers creeping up on him. Checking his side mirrors with suspicious eyes for any lurching shadows, he adjusted his rearview mirror. The red lights blinked alternately, winking eyes taunting him. Bushes overgrew the view of the tracks. The rain fell at an intermittent spatter, not enough to justify turning the wipers on, but enough to obscure his windshield. Having to turn the wiper blades on then off only served to increase his anxiousness. The car idled with a mild thrum. He wished he had that internal steeliness Mulysa projected, much less Colvin. They never seemed to care, equally at ease watching television, being questioned by police, or staring down gun barrels.

Broyn threw the hood of his sweatshirt over his head and kicked the taped-down bag of money from his first delivery under the seat. Certain he saw a movement, he squinted as he peeked through the rain-blurred windshield, then flipped the wipers on again. The warning bells of an approaching train clanged.

The car roof buckled under the sudden weight of something landing on it. Broyn scrambled for the gun he kept in the glove compartment – stupid, he knew, but he hated to go completely unprotected with so much product and cash, and the idea of Colvin's name as a shield was cold comfort to him. Peering out each side window, nothing appeared, but he'd be damned before he got out and checked the car. First looking left and then right, Broyn double-checked to make sure no one approached. His right arm slung behind the passenger seat, gun in hand, he prepared to put the car in reverse and book the hell out. A tap came from his driver's side window.

The length of a sawed-off shot gun greeted him.

A nest of fine braids draped from the finely sculptured face of an ebony beauty with skin like heavily creamed coffee. Her almond eyes missed nothing;

she stood unperturbed by the rain. Broyn knew many black women who'd have thrown hell-to-pay fits being caught in the rain after having their hair done. She had a model's bearing, the nose, the cheeks, like European royalty. Except for her pointed ears. A pair of handcuffs dangled from her belt loops. She toted the shotgun with the casual swing of a matching purse. Omarosa.

"You know what I want." Her voice had a sexy, if terrifying, thunder to it. More so in her whisper. "Slowly. We all professionals here."

Besides the exuberance in her eye, the thrill of the game or her part in it, something else swam in her eyes. Something dark. Something terrifying. Something monstrous which lurked beneath her beauty. A slack-jawed looseness to his face, he dropped his gun with a flourish to show her he was cooperating, his hands in plain sight. Leaning forward, he reached for the taped-down bag, while his other hand lowered the window. He dropped the bag outside.

"And the trunk."

Come on, Broyn's contorted face seemed to say. He hunched his shoulders.

"A girl's got to earn, too," she grunted with annoyance.

He forced himself to turn from the shotgun, taking it on faith that she was professional enough to not twitch and send his brains spraying onto the passenger-side window. Still, over and over, his mind imagined the clap of thunder before his world turned black. Suppressing a shiver, he reached under his seat for the trunk release. Too scared to know what to do with them, unable to move, possibly in shock, he held his hands out, his mind so disconnected from the action, it was as if they floated on their own. Probably more trying to wrap his head around what to tell Colvin. His eyes were drawn to the pulsing red lights. Almost hypnotic. Then she was gone.

Subtle wasn't in Lee McCarrell's vocabulary. The door exploded open with his first kick. Shock and awe were his calling cards, not because they worked especially well, but more because he enjoyed the rabbit responses his entrance brought. Them "uh-oh" eyes. The dazed lucidity of junkies caught mid-cop. The fear and panic of a dealer. The copper tang of adrenaline on his tongue.

"You raising up on me?" Lee roared to the half-dozen young bucks lounging around the room. He often sprinkled his words with a liberal dose of street affect, letting them know he understood them and spoke to them in a language they understood. Them. Not us. These were nameless pukes. Omarosa had fed him their names, little more than chum in the pool of sharks. The possibility of her growing bored of him distracted him. Not that it mattered. There was no warranty on relationships and this one had about run its course. He'd made a meal on the tips she'd given him over the months. And he never questioned how she knew so much, or so accurately, for fear of busting a cap in the ass of his fine golden goose. She assured him this would be a bust worth his while, even if these were low-level players.

"How's business?" Lee smirked. He gave the first boy a long, inventorying look. A good kid, long and lean with bright, intelligent eyes. Even lying on a couch, with the chaos of cops bursting in, he didn't panic and exuded a commanding presence. Skin like smoked meat, he had child-like dimples though he tried to suppress a charismatic smile. In other words, a waste.

"Good, I guess." The boy sat up slowly.

People became cops for only a handful of reasons. To carry a gun and tell people what to do (the deputized bully), money ("a job's a job"), freak (too drawn to the badge), or a white knight complex (the hero's calling). Sometimes it took a bully to get things done. There was still plenty of room for Cantrell to play hero.

"You hear what happened over at Phoenix?" Cantrell asked the second boy.

"Some folks got got," the second boy said. Young, white, red-headed, the boy had a heroin thinness to him. And he had the disposition of someone who would sell out his dying mother for his next fix to avoid prison. One of his eyes didn't track properly. That area of his face webbed with healed-over scars. The eye was probably glass, Cantrell realized.

"What's up?" Cantrell's flat voice rumbled without humor. He ran his hands up the boy's socks and then legs. "You know we own this piece now. You operate at our pleasure."

"What we got here?" Lee stood over the boy's desk. A scree of papers cascaded across it.

"Homework," the first boy offered.

"Oh, so you in school now." Upon closer inspection, Lee spied the childish scrawl on papers and the remedial reading text. Lee had the common decency to not comment on this. There was belittling and then there was cruelty which aimed at stripping away all attempts at manhood and dignity. The latter only led to more problems.

"Come on now," the second boy said. "You fucking up my time, Cantrell."

"Oh, so now you know my name? All right. Let's chat about that."

Cantrell led him out of the room with a firm hand to the small of his back. Always out to save someone. Half recruiting informants, half trying to save these boys from themselves.

"So you fine upstanding boys were merely pursuing your academic interests."

"Just do what you came to do. Might as well earn yours for that trick smoking your joint." The boy knew he crossed the line as all the play left Lee's eyes and he blistered under his stare. Word on the street suspected Omarosa of having the peckerwood on drug patrol in her pocket. Perhaps throwing it in his face wasn't his best play.

Lee flicked open a pocket knife and let the blade

catch the light and the boy's full attention. Eyes still locked on him, Lee stabbed toward the boy's head. The boy closed his eyes and flinched, muscles locked until he heard the knife bury into the wall next to him. When the boy chanced opening his eyes, Lee maintained his cold gaze, not bothering with the charade of a search. He let him know he knew exactly where to look and didn't bother to offer the courtesy pretense of surprise at what he found: bricks of saran-wrapped cash. More money than he'd see in his check in a year.

"Whose money is this? This yours?" Lee asked. The boy turned away as his response. Lee turned to the next boy, but the question of "Yours?" was met with shrugged shoulders.

"Guess it's my lucky day then."

Leaning over him like a boyfriend doing the obligatory chat before an end-of-date make-out session, Cantrell chatted in amiable low tones to the skinny, one-eyed crackhead. A snitch he'd refer to as Fathead. As Lee exited the house, Cantrell couldn't help but notice the shrink-wrapped bundles beneath each arm. With a nod, he dismissed the boy, who slunk away without a backwards glance.

"What's that?" Cantrell asked.

"Street tax."

"We're going to have a problem."

"'We' don't have shit." Lee tossed the packages in the back seat. He stood in the shielding confines of the open car door, the roof of the car a gulf between him and his partner.

"'We' better voucher whatever 'we' expect to sign off on."

"Chill out, brother." Lee pronounced "brother" with every bit of the "er" on the end and with every bit of tinny cracker in him. "They simply volunteering to be your benefactor. They had a sudden stirring of conscience and decided to do something positive in the community. Perhaps donate to a mentoring program. They want to be, how did they put it? Ghetto sponsors. Don't that sound good?"

"Uh-huh." Cantrell remained unconvinced. The temptation of rationalization rattled around in his head, a nagging voice which grew louder with each minute he spent with Lee. The bust would have been no good anyway. They had no warrant and no probable cause. They were simply trolling for information, based on intel provided by Lee's mysterious snitch. The way Lee went about his business made him nervous. It was why Cantrell worked so hard to develop his own network of information. The fresh-out-of-the-academy rules which had been hammered into him had long since been tossed out the window, but Cantrell certainly was not out to take anyone off.

"Good. Cause the kids will be grateful. Real grateful. And that's who we do it for. The children."

Colvin was a pretty-ass nigga. He had skin the complexion of heavily creamed coffee and almond eyes, with full eyelashes which had an almost feminine quality beneath threaded eyebrows and set above his high aquiline nose. His good hair didn't have to be straightened, his teeth were scrubbed to a brilliant pearl, his nails buffered to a neat acrylic sheen, his skin lightly oiled with a lavender scent he favored. The idea of self-hate amused him. Many perceived him as being closer to white with that diluted blood being the standard of beauty, the features that defined his African roots as obliterated as the Sphinx's nose. But he had no time for intra-racial contempt; their hate was too small just like their love was too small. He was fey. He was the standard of his own beauty. A drop of fey blood made him one hundred percent fey. He was The Principle Beauty. Favored by his mother, he viewed his sibling – all women and for that matter, all that he surveyed – as an extension of himself. If the woman who writhed underneath him had a name, he hadn't bothered to learn it nor did he care to. She was a series of orifices who bucked in all the right ways, a piece of meat who offered herself as a paean to himself. A flesh-and-blood sacrifice on the altar of his dick. Sex with him was an offering of worship. He admitted to himself what few did: that people formed relationships that were altars to themselves. People sought out those who they had a lot in common with, who were like them, or who simply liked them; an external validation of their need and worth of being loved. The vanity of humanity. There were truths he dared not face. Like how sex was a balm. That it took another to give him meaning, make him feel like a man.

Born with intelligence, luck, and the confidence of transcendent beauty, he didn't consider himself one of the light-skinned princesses who thrived on the attentions of others and then pretended that it annoyed them. Relationships were the comfort of another being only a hip turn away, a staunch of the open wound of loneliness they hoped to bandage. Colvin would never know the void of unfilled spaces within his heart because he trusted in the love of one who both knew and loved him intimately: himself. Turning to the camera hidden in the vase which sat on his mantle, he'd enjoy watching the playback of this session later. And pleasure himself to it.

"Colvin!" A deep, dry voice called from the other room. "Colvin, man, we got a problem. A serious problem."

"I'm busy, Mulysa. Can't it wait?" Colvin cried out in mid-stroke.

"Nah, nukka, it's that deep."

Colvin's was a long-lived people, and he'd spent so much time in the world of man, he'd learned their posture of adulthood, drank on their rage, and took on a man's role of conquest and bravado. He withdrew from the woman whose name he'd never know and wiped himself on her tossed-aside panties. She drew the sheets up about her in an "I'll be waiting for you" pose, but he'd already forgotten her as he dressed. Colvin put his gun into his pants. He never went anywhere without being strapped.

His wave cap tied in back, Mulysa's brown eyes contained amber flecks. A scar underlined his right eye, acquired in prison. He had a broad, flat nose, the nose his mother hated because it was his father's nose. His complexion was what his grandmother would have described as sooty and his breath was the dragon. He wore defeat in the thick of his neck and roll of his shoulders. His faded blue jeans hung from his thighs such that he had to spread his legs whenever he stood still. He stank of sweat and what his boys called "African funk" behind his back.

"What's up?" Colvin asked.

"Tell him, nukka." Mulysa was a genial rogue, a self-destructive fuck-up, but he had wit, charm, and most importantly, he produced. A lot was forgiven when you did the work.

Broyn, on the other hand, was like an accountant. Quiet, dependable, and not for the life. Still, he had his uses. Some situations called for a square motherfucker who wouldn't draw attention to himself. Harried and haggard, Broyn began to speak with the wariness of a child recounting how a vase got broken in front of a temper-prone parent. How smooth the run went, along with the first exchange. And how on his way to the second meet, he was jacked. No money, no product. At each salient point in the story, he paused ever so slightly to measure the temperature of Mulysa, of Colvin, and of his place in the room. The messenger rarely fared well in such situations.

"What did she look like?" Colvin asked.

"Like one of them high fashion models with tight braids. Light-skinned. And her eyes. Beautiful, but there was something scary behind them." Broyn stopped before he added, "like yours."

Colvin let out a scream of pure rage. "Omarosa!"

"Baby, what's the matter?" The woman, sheet half-drawn up around her naked body, stood in the doorway.

"You better close my door like you got some fuckin' sense."

"When–"

Colvin whirred, drawing his gun in the same movement, and let three bullets fly. Two dead center of her heart and one in her head. The body of the woman whose name he'd never know crumpled to the ground. A stain clouded Broyn's pants.

"Who?" Mulysa asked, unfazed, knowing this would be a mess he'd have to clean up later.

"Omarosa. Only she would dare such a brazen..."

"Who she?"

"A fucking two-bit street thief. And my sister." Colvin turned to Broyn. "The question remains, what do I do with you?"

Broyn's eyes couldn't move from the body of the dead woman. "Colvin, it wasn't my fault," he said more to the corpse than his employer.

"Shh." Colvin pressed a finger to his lips. "Mulysa, could you bring one of your bitches out to play?"

Mulysa squatted low, face to face with Broyn, the

full assault of his hot fetid breath on him. A walking amalgamation of self-loathing out to revenge himself on a world he blamed for his place in life and his own inadequacies, Mulysa's hands danced with the precision of a master loomer. He produced a long Japanese tanto knife and placed the flat of the blade beneath Broyn's chin to raise his chin to meet his eyes. "My bitch."

"What's her name?" Colvin said with the deliberation of a set-up man's cadence.

"You don't name a bitch." Mulysa licked the flat of the dagger, cleaning the salt of Broyn's nervous sweat from the blade.

"She looks like she could carve through a body."

"Like a hot roll from O'Charley's."

"Those are some good rolls. Think you could collect a head for me?'

Mulysa pressed the tip of the blade to Broyn's neck. The brief contact produced a teardrop of blood. "My bitches work for me. Here good?"

Broyn's breathing hitched. His face flushed with heat. He hated the weakness of having tears squeezed from his eyes.

"Not his," Colvin said after a moment of deliberation. "Hers. I still have use for Mr DeForest."

Mulysa flashed an expression of mild disappointment, a "maybe next time" grin, and turned his back on Broyn.

Broyn focused on Colvin as he desperately tried to ignore the wet sounds of rent flesh. The sticking of blade against bone. The terrible hacking rasp. Mulysa carried her by her hair with not so much as an after-thought. With blood trailing along the floor, tendrils of flesh dangled from her neck stump.

"We're missing something." Colvin pulled a cable from behind his television setup. "This'll have to do. Desperate times and all."

He fastened the head of the woman to Broyn. Her eyes had rolled upwards in their sockets, upturned to his.

"There we go. You head on home now," Colvin finished.

"Head." Mulysa chuckled and then wiped his nose with his sleeve, his blade still covered in gore.

"But…" Broyn protested.

"Before I change my mind about whose neck Mulysa's bitch should play with next."

Broyn scrambled out the room without further protest.

Colvin exhaled, the display of bravado somehow left him winded. Mulysa slumped in a chair next to him, already debating if it would be easier to just set the place on fire or clean up the mess they made.

"Damn her," Colvin said almost to himself.

"That was a lot of product."

"Don't you think I knew that? Things were tight on the streets as it were. This could create quite the drought."

"Judging from what the man said, Treize got theirs."

"Shit." Colvin thought about his dwindling customer base. There was no such thing as customer loyalty, so the fiends would go to whoever had the fresh product. Didn't matter if the dealing hands were black or Latino. And once word got out... Shit, shit, shit. "Omarosa has no use for product. Her only interest is money. Get word out that we're interested in relieving her of her ill-gotten gain."

"So she gets to earn off us twice?" Mulysa asked.

"No. I'll deal with my sister. Put some caps on her ass."

"Yeah, nukka." Mulysa carelessly licked his bitch again. "That's what I'm talking about."

CHAPTER FIVE

Dark and as stiflingly close as the inside of a coffin, Lady G's choking coughs woke her. Her eyes fluttered open, adjusting to the dark. Something thickened the air, unseen in the night-time shadows. The darkness seemed to move. Her heartbeat throbbed in her throat. Her still-waking mind slowly processed the smell. Smoke. Something was on fire.

Scrambling out of bed, her foot caught in the tangles of her blankets and spilled her onto the floor. She ran to her window and ripped open the blinds as if she'd never looked out her window before. Her grandmother's two-story home was old, kindling with a mortgage payment. She could shimmy out; the slanted roof's steep pitch was survivable. But what about her baby brother? Or her mother? One hand covered her mouth and nose, the other searched along the hardwood floor. The smoke burned her lungs. She tried to hold her breath, but when her air ran out, she only gulped down more of the acrid air. The sting of smoke brought tears to her eyes, further blurring her vision. She crawled toward the door. It was marginally easier to breathe down there. She opened the door cautiously. Events happened so fast, the surreal movement of time when the mind couldn't cope with all of the contradictory images.

Thick columns of smoke undulated with a knowing intent. They turned toward her, a predator catching a new scent. The flash fire roared through the house, hungry and desperate. Orange and yellow tongues licked at the curtains. Pictures charred in their frames, the faces, and background turning brown then black. Golden flames crawled along the thick carpet. She banged on the walls. So hot. She sucked in smoke, to the protest of her scalded lungs.

The house creaked as if assaulted by a gust of wind. The wall cracked and buckled, a filigree of ashy veins. Crickety things at the best of times, the stairs lurched in unsteady and tentative steps. Her head throbbed as if ready to explode, racing with wild speculation. Her grandma (*Grandma!*) sometimes burned a candle on a chair; maybe it had tipped over. Keeping her back to the wall, fearing the flames devouring the banister and her tumbling into the heart of the inferno, she sobbed, scared and anxious.

The door to Michah's room canted ajar. His crib used to be her cousin's and another cousin had already called dibs on it once Michah no longer needed it. Heedless of the fire, she swatted at the flames with her hands. Tendrils flared and bit into her with each swipe. His form tiny and still, his skin hot and bubbling. Lady G scooped up the bundle of flesh, the smell of burnt skin, both his and hers, seared her nostrils. She cooed at him in hushed re-assurances that everything would be OK.

"Is he dead?" a hoarse voice whispered from the shadowed corner. "I just need to make sure he was dead."

Her mother's dark skin steeped in a cloak of night. Wizened fingers tugged at the edge of her shirt, threatening to pull herself into it. Vacant eyes, un-fixed and filled with psychotic detachment, silently pled for understanding. From above, the ceiling cracked with the peal of thunder, then something hot fell onto her face.

Lady G snapped awake. Remembering the old hurts, she shivered in her bed and held herself. Not unlike when she woke from her two-month-long coma after the fire. *January 22nd, 2001*. The date burned into her mind. Pain reared up when least ex-pected and had a way of never quite going away, but rather burrowed itself deep within. Like a wound healed over a piece of shrapnel, mended enough to make her drop her guard, but pain flared afresh when something bumped against it. She no longer wanted to feel, but only desired the lure of a mor-phine drip. The dreamy haze where nothing hurt as bad as it could. She just kept packing down the pain, stuffing it deep inside and moving on. Each hurt a tiny brick, each brick stacked upon one another, with her mother the source of many, many bricks in that terrible wall.

"I live with it, Vere." Her mother's name for her. Lady G hated her name and only ever recalled it whenever she had to fill out government forms. Or thought about her mother. She could still picture her mother on the chair across from her bed. Her first sight after she had clawed herself out of the darkness of her coma, struck by how small her mother looked. So very, very small. The fire had been ruled an accident, but Lady G knew. They both knew. The pain, the memories, they were too much. Lady G peered at her, a tube down her throat, her hands in soft restraints, probably to keep her from pulling the piece of plastic out of her mouth.

"I was so young when I had you. Children change your life. You love them and they drive you insane. Bit by bit. And you love them some more. But Michah... Michah had his father's eyes."

"Momma, did you ever love us?" Lady G's mind called out, needed to know. As always, her mother didn't hear her and went on about her own concerns.

"I remember those eyes. How they'd follow me when I walked past him. How they lingered on my behind or down my chest any chance they got. How they sneered whenever I shut his game down. How angry they got. How quick they were to fill with hatred and something animal. And dangerous. I just couldn't help but keep wondering: would Michah's eyes glaze over, see me as less than human, as a piece of property or meat? Would I just be a pair of tits, a piece of ass, or a slick piece of pussy for him to decide to take? He had his father's eyes, Vere, and I couldn't take him looking at me, needing me, or depending on me anymore."

Her mother collapsed into hard tears, hard because she never quite broke the way truly sorry people did. Her tears were defiant, sure, and angry, but tears nonetheless. She laid her head on the hospital bed. Lady G stretched out her hands. Her burnt hands. Third-degree burns, incisions had to be made to release the heat. In her last act as "Vere", Lady G stroked her mother's hair in hard forgiveness. Hard because she didn't forgive, though part of her understood, and knew that she needed to release her mother. Her touch feigned love, but was concerned, scared, and angry. She resolved at that moment, "I don't want to make someone else." And she vowed not to get involved with them.

Men.

They were brutal and couldn't help but use others. Bottomless pits of selfish need they vented upon women and called it love. Or sex. Or fucking. It was a silly vow, young and foolish, like love. Her "no men" rant became almost its own persona, a routine she put on for her friends. Going on about how she didn't need a man, how she was a princess who saved herself. How she'd remain single and unsullied by these dogs, these boys who played men games.

She knew the image she projected, how people assumed that she was strong, capable, wise, and independent. Her life was her own. And she wanted to be the woman people guessed her to be. She presented that woman as if she had arrived. Yet she felt hollow.

A part of her believed she "doth protesteth too much" when it came to men, but another part of her was equally adamant. She really didn't want to make someone else. She had no interest in bringing another messed-up person into her messed-up world so she could mess them up and have them go off and mess up others. She simply opted out of that life plan.

Dreams and memories. Lady G seemed trapped by them, not knowing how to move past them, becoming entombed in a morass of emotional quicksand she couldn't escape. The need for love, to fill the ever-present hole inside her; she remembered desire, but she had forgotten how it worked. How to lower her guard, allow entry past her wall of bricks, and allow someone in to see the most precious parts of herself. She had forgotten what it was like to have someone touch her heart. She only knew the cold comfort of loneliness and had learned to grow comfortable with it. Her heart had numbed over.

Then King brought her back.

The months since finding him had been good. Made her whole and rekindled desire in her. She enjoyed the flattery of his attention. It drove her girl Rhianna insane with jealousy. And Lady G enjoyed being needed and seen as special. Things were cute early on, but they turned into something selfish. She didn't think she misrepresented her intentions. He wasn't enough. No, that wasn't quite it. He couldn't complete her the way she wanted to be completed. And she knew part of him resisted her. He wouldn't let her in, not all the way, not to his most precious part: he loved her the best he was able, she knew that, but it wasn't enough.

She wanted more.

Big Momma fidgeted uncomfortably in her seat. Every quarter she attended the condo association meetings. Every meeting played out the same way. Roger Stern, president of the board, sat front and center. Officious glasses rested on the tip of his nose to not only study the papers before him, but to be able to peer over them in his condescending manner at whoever was speaking. His wife Holly, a frumpy, pear-figured woman, dressed in floral patterns too bright for the season. Any season. She took the minutes as vice president and secretary. Lipstick smeared across her mouth with a clown's sneer, and blush applied by the brushstroke, she obviously got made up for her appearance as First Lady of Breton Court. On the other side of Mr Stern sat Neville Sims, the groundskeeper for Breton Court. The only black person at the table, but also the only one of the three who did any real work. His cap pulled low on his head, lifted whenever he wiped the sweat from his forehead. His matching blue coveralls had a thin film of grime on them. Leaning forward, hands clasped in front of him, he spoke with a hint of hesitation and appeared as uncomfortable as Big Momma.

A reporter from the community paper scribbled her notes. Perhaps the reporter's presence caused Mr Stern to go through the motions of paying more attention. Big Momma upticked the side of her mouth in mild derision, making a note to have her niece show up in a skirt, sensible shoes, and waving a notepad around during the next meeting.

The crowd went through the usual litany of concerns every meeting: the trash bins were ugly, unsightly and not emptied often enough; the street lamps along the parking lots needed to be fixed; the whole place required a face lift, something more cheery and inviting; the patios were in need of repair and uniform appearance because with half knocked over, the wood rotting through, others unpainted or with huge holes in them, they looked like a third-world nation.

Big Momma played the "remember whens" of the neighborhood. *Remember when he used to be clean? Remember when she used to be pretty? Remember when they did good in school? Remember when the neighborhood was calm, with none of this shooting? Remember when they played real music?* Ironically, none of those memories were as true as she believed. He was never that clean. She was never that pretty. They never did that well in school. The neighborhood was always jumping and the music played was complained about by their parents, too.

"What are we going to do about them boys?" A dapper-dressed older gentleman asked. Big Momma knew him as Old School, one of the barbers from up the way. She had no idea he lived around here. Gray salted his beard, but not in an unattractive way. But his eyes roved a little too much for her tastes. Even as he asked his question, he had time to check out the hem line of the reporter.

"What do you mean?" Mr Stern made what appeared to be a note on his sheet of paper, either noting the issue, checking it off his list, or doodling for the appearance of paying attention.

"They play their loud music at all hours of the day and night. They congregate on porches, on the sidewalk, in little packs."

"We can't punish people for being in a group."

"A gang is more like it."

"And we can't go around treating every group of boys like a gang." Mr Stern wasn't a liberal by any definition of the word. He didn't care about political correctness, civil rights, profiling, or anything like that. He was, however, lawsuit-averse.

"So you ain't gonna do nothing?"

Mr Stern met eyes with the reporter. Her pencil raised, poised for his next words. "We will talk with the police. Increase patrol runs. Maybe look into private security." He smiled at her.

"Talk, talk, talk. I'm tired of talking. We need to do

something." Old School turned to the audience for approval.

"Or get someone who can," someone echoed.

"Mmm-hmm," the rising chorus began.

The same song every meeting. Frustrations rose to a crescendo, peaking with the calls for elections. Mr Stern caressed the stack of papers in front of him. A political animal firmly in control of his little fiefdom, the elections were already locked up. For all of their talk about nominating and running someone else, the idea never occurred to anyone before a meeting. The actual occupants attended the meetings; the votes were cast by the homeowners. The paper stack in front of Mr Stern were the homeowners' proxies and allowed him to do whatever he wanted.

Big Momma rose. Her pudgy fingers folded the paper detailing the meeting's agenda. Slowly, but with intent, she made her way to the center aisle. Diabetes stiffened her movements, but she remained stout and formidable. Her eyes focused on Mr Stern.

"Folks around here call me Big Momma."

"We know who you are, Big Momma. You're a fixture around here," Mr Stern said with a grimace of indigestion.

"Exactly. So I know the neighborhood and its people." She nodded to the reporter as if checking to see if she spelled "Big Momma" correctly in her notes. "Don't pity us. Don't condescend to us. Don't hold us to a lower standard."

"I don't–" Her hand wave cut him off. She would

be heard. Mr Stern could just turn beet-red and glower over his glasses until she was through.

"We live in a community. We here every day. We see what's going on because we live here. Here in this community. Where do you live, Mr Stern?"

"I don't think that's—" Another hand wave. Another deepened glower.

"I've always lived in the community. We may not have much, but we have each other. We share what we have, we look out for each other as best we can, and we help each other as much as we can. That's the way folks around here brought me up. My parents had their problems. Abandoned me. But the adults in the neighborhood decided to raise me and hid me from CPS whenever a social worker came around, because they would just have sent me to foster care. The people here moved me from spot to spot so I could stay in the neighborhood and go to the neighborhood school. That's how I finished high school. So I know the value of education and I preach it to everyone I take in. I got married to a man from the neighborhood, God bless his soul. And when he passed, some five years ago, I stayed. In the community. I'm Breton Court through and through.

"You want to make us promises? Fine. You want to talk to folks? Talk. But in the end, we're a community. And we take care of our own."

The room burst into applause.

The reporter kept taking notes.

• • • •

Near the heart of downtown, on 16th Street just east of Pennsylvania Avenue, one of the major prostitution boulevards in the city, Herron High School provided a classical liberal arts education. With an emphasis on the arts, it steeped their students in great historical thought, the school aimed to prepare them for college. According to the brochures, the school's curriculum was structured around an art history timeline and emphasized the classic art and literature of many cultures.

The five minutes until homeroom bell clanged, sharp and grating. Isabel "Iz" Cornwall closed her locker after slipping her backpack into it. Sunken cheekbones bookended a face with a long nose with a stud, slightly notched where it had been broken in the past. Slim, short, hair dyed black, she had an unadorned face of simple beauty which would rise to gorgeous with the right make-up application. A tattoo of a dragon crawled along the base of her back. This was the third day this week she wore her blue jeans. Her nose was no longer sensitive to her own smell. She pulled a white cardigan over her pink T-shirt, covering her braless, small breasts. The T-shirt was worn yesterday, but she hoped no one would notice under the cardigan. She pressed her books to her chest, eyes downcast, slouching to be unnoticed.

"Damn girl, you wearing those clothes out." A black girl with a thick frame, large breasts, and thighs like oaks, her thick black hair had been processed into straight hair. Blue contact lenses didn't hide a wide nose and full lips which faced her in the mirror, and she took out her self-loathing on the world around her.

"Leave me alone, Andret."

"Just saying, you may want to give your outfit a rest. It's getting ripe enough, I bet them jeans could find their own way to school by now."

Iz lowered her head to push by. Andret hooked her arm in front of her.

"What? You too good to speak to me now?"

"She ain't got nothing to say to you. I might have a word or two though." Tristan Drust spoke with the timbre of command though she chewed a piece of gum with an open-mouthed flourish. Draped in a hoodie, her head crested with a thick nest of braids, most of which were dyed mauve. Big-boned and sturdy, without a trace of fat, anyone who knew anything about posture would have noticed how balanced her stance was. She knew more about fighting than most men. Her amber eyes with gold flecks counted off the girls with military precision. Andret was the mouth, the alpha of the group. Her wing girls could tussle, but if Andret was taken out quickly, they'd lose heart for a fight.

"Enter the dyke," Andret said.

"Now you've gone and hurt my feelings." Tristan squared up against Andret. Her eyes flashed challenge, a silent push. Andret inched forward, a tacit shove back.

In the end, much of life could be reduced to lessons learned on the playground. Random encounters, bullies and bullied, friends and foes, the workplace of life all gathered in the same place. There were those who were simply not meant to get along with one another. Spaces not meant to be inhabited by both parties without rage bristling off each other, ready to jump off. Without boiling up in them, a living fire that needed to lash out and scorch the earth about them just under the surface, a seething they didn't know what to do with; once the veneer was scratched it erupted.

Iz appealed to Tristan's better nature, preaching about finding better ways to respond to hostile situations rather than let them control her. "Blessed are the peacemakers" was a luxury Iz could indulge, but there was a reality she didn't understand: not everyone played by the rules of peace and some people just needed to be knocked on their ass. Folks who believed others infringed onto what was theirs and what the world owed them. Otherwise the world walked over you, the way so many had abused Iz. People like Iz needed people like Tristan.

Moving her weight to her back foot, Tristan knew how to throw a punch. She struck with her shoulder, not her arm. She pivoted her hip into her blow, punching through her target. The jab flew with an angry whisper, not wasting any more time with idle talk or the pantomime of threat. She wasn't one to waste a shot. Andret's neck snapped back, nose exploding on impact. At heart, Tristan was a fighter. The other thing about fighting was knowing how to take a punch. Tristan loved going up against people who sparred against heavy bags or practiced shadow boxing, because no matter how exquisite their technique, a fight was won or lost based on how well they handled having their bell rung. Andret fell into the arms of her compatriots, the group piling onto the floor. Students crowded around them as Tristan loomed over them. She read their eyes: they wanted no part of her.

"You OK?" Tristan asked Iz. Whenever they were together, the rest of the world retreated.

"I'm a full-time student, so I got to lay it off." As a kid, she wanted to study math. She had a head for numbers and loved their patterns and symmetry. Numbers measured the world. Unfortunately, the path of education was discouraged by her father. As far as he was concerned, she was an incubator on legs: he regularly informed her that her duty was to get married and have kids. As her brand of rebellion, she became studious and intense and developed a love of reading.

"You takin' notes?"

"Right here."

"All right then." Tristan took her in her arms and kissed her lightly on the forehead.

"What's going on here?" A teacher popped his head out of his classroom.

"Nothing," Tristan said.

"You know her?" He glanced at Andret, who cradled her face and slinked off with her friends.

"I don't know anyone."

"Go to the office, young lady."

"I don't even go to this school." Tristan flipped her hood over her head, turned on her heel, and flashed two fingers. "Deuces."

Before the teacher could summon security, Tristan was gone.

King couldn't afford to be sensitive. He lived in a hard world, a dangerous world. Pastor Winburn called it a fallen world. Fallen into what King was never sure. A state of disrepair, an invisible "unfinished business" sign lodged on someone's to-do list when they... He... got around to remembering the people left behind. Much like the church he used as a meeting place.

Out of habit, King grabbed a nearby broom and King swept the floor of the abandoned, burned-out husk of a church, keenly aware of the futile gesture. Vandals would one day break in and loot anything the owners missed. Crackheads would use it as a safe haven from the elements to get high. Prostitutes would throw discarded mattresses in the corners and use it as a flophouse for their johns. But King straightened up anyway because he had to do something, no matter how small or ultimately futile.

"You appear haggard and worn." Merle sat, legs

crossed over one another at the ankles. Black cracks veined the surface of the circular table, browned with rain rot.

"Not enough sleep."

"You wear your dreams."

"Something like that."

"Hmm." Merle ran his finger along the top of the makeshift table. He licked the soot from his fingertip. "I won't always be with you."

"You dying?" King stopped sweeping and focused on the man for the first time.

"We're all dying. I know my death will be shameful and ridiculous. If you find my remains and I'm in a closet with a belt tied around my neck, wrists, and my gentleman's gentleman… all I ask is that you cut me down at least."

"So you are dying?"

"My safety word is 'apples.'"

"What are you talking about?"

"You have to be prepared. Events are in motion, some courses set, but we are not Destiny's concubine. We have decisions to make. Choices."

King trusted few people. Yet from the beginning, he knew he could talk to Merle. Perhaps it was just that with his brand of lunacy, anything King said would be forgotten moments later. More in truth, King sensed there was something ancient about their bond. "Can I get your advice on something?"

"Most people don't want advice, only agreement."

"I want your honest opinion."

"I know nothing but half-truths and veiled interpretations, but I'll do my best."

"What do you think of Lady G?"

Merle tapped his lip with his sooty forefinger. "If I should tell you she was a poor choice, young, foolish, and empty-headed, would you believe me?"

"She's not even close to that." King's pulse quickened, as if his heart reared at a threat to be confronted. Something about Lady G stirred an overprotectiveness within him, as if he couldn't stand even the thought of anyone speaking ill of her. "That's not the woman I know."

"A grown man fixed by a girl." Merle etched his finger into the table, drawing pictures only his mind envisioned. "What if the girl was not a girl?"

"A monster? An enchantment?" King's mind raced with possibilities. Anything to explain the... hesitation he felt with her.

"No. A plug."

"What?"

"She stops up the hole in you." Merle adjusted the fit of his cap as if tuning in the proper signal. "Somewhere between birth and burial, people learned to twist the simple longings in their hearts – rest, belonging, affection, validation, peace – and tried to fill them with other things. Food. Drugs. Sex. Yet try as they might, the hole remained."

"Try again."

"I see that's too much for you to get your mind around, O Hesitant Spirit. Let's try this more practically then. What if I was to say she would betray you for another, perhaps one of your closest; would you believe me?"

"I'd say you were way off. She's not that type of girl, Merle."

Merle threw his head back and began to sing. "*When a man loves a woman…*"

"I haven't said anything about love."

"Here's the thing about love," Merle continued, ignoring him. "It goes against the laws governing the universe. Laws of probability. Laws of nature. Laws of common sense. None of them need apply. Love trumps all."

"It all comes down to the right girl."

"The future is like love: something we don't have the luxury to believe in," Merle sniffed. "I need to attend to the others."

Little more than a fallen museum, a curator preserving theologies no longer relevant to the community it served, a layer of dust settled upon the church like a burial shroud. Three chairs presided on a raised platform behind a toppled altar. Promises of health and wealth reverberated in the empty anteroom, echoing only along the cobwebs strung between the chairs. The choir loft cracked under its own weight, a broken bow on the ship of the church stage; an abandoned stage whose dwindling audience found better speakers, better empty promises, or greener pastures to lose themselves in.

His steps pronounced and precise, a boy entered with the solemnity of a wedding's ring-bearer. Except instead of a ring, he carried a white gun – with a pearl handle grip and white shaft – rested atop a purple pillow. With each footfall, flames erupted from candle stands. Two boys, both with the scrawny physique of angry twigs, trailed him, each holding candelabras with five candles.

Last in the processional was a young girl, short and curvy with engorged breasts. Her arms outstretched before her as she held a cup. Pure gold inlaid with precious stones, the cup produced its own luminescence. The hall filled with a suffuse light, dimming the lights produced by the candles. The girl turned and presented the cup to Percy.

"What do you think it means?" Percy asked, his voice held the slightest hitch of a restrained stammer.

"Means you dream of being a pimp," Merle said.

"Really?" Percy sat up, surprised at himself.

"Simple Percy, pure and true. Simple Percy, pure-hearted fool."

"I'm not stupid." Percy's eyes turned downward, stung by the words of someone he wanted to be his friend. Merle put his hand on the boy's beefy shoulder.

"No, no, you're not. Far from it. You're probably the best of us. Thus a pure fool. And still, here you are yearning for the infinitely desirable, yet unattainable."

"A woman?"

"Her love? See, you aren't so dim."

"Why won't King let me come along when they go out?"

"It's dangerous work." Merle turned from him.

"I ain't scared."

"No you're not. And you're more ready than they realize. Don't worry, your time draws near."

"How do you know?"

"Your dream says so."

A nearing *thwack-thwack-thwack* interrupted them as Rhianna Perkins padded along the carpet in a pair of flip-flops with an orange band. With good hair, though tender-headed, and fine-boned, she walked with a slight waddle, a stride developed because of the fullness of her pregnancy. Her breasts, swollen and tender, stretched out her black and white striped tank top over a lacy pink bra. Her belly protruded as if she attempted to hide a basketball under her shirt. She bent forward. Percy caught a glimpse of her panties rising above her jean line.

"Boys." She caught him peeking. His eyes retreated and he turned his head.

"Milady." Merle bowed. "I see your most sacred of ovens bears up nicely. May I?" He reached out his hands.

"Sure."

Merle placed his hands on either side of her belly. Then pressed his ear to it. "Oh my. Yes, you are. Be patient."

"What's he saying?" Percy asked.

"What happens in the womb stays in the womb."
Merle winked.

Life made her tough, not brave. Sex was a position
of surrender, a searching for sorrow, a space to fill
the loneliness. There was nothing special between
her legs or in her center, and she went to bed with
men – boys really – with easy aplomb. The idea of
rejection or abandonment or being used never entered her calculations. She was a tabula rasa of
femininity. One could write any story onto her and
she was happy to oblige for the semblance of a relationship; the presence of a man was all the illusion
of a relationship she required. She found it easier to
open her legs than her heart: a brash emotional lazi-
ness. Her mental efforts focused more on figuring
out how to stay alive from day to day.

"He active though." Rhianna grimaced, then
pressed her palms into her lower back. "Got no
sense. Just like his daddy."

"A hard road, raising a young one alone," Merle
said.

"She's not alone," Percy said.

"True." Merle, again, patted the young man.

"Anyway, I'm looking for a new man. King's
taken."

Rhianna toyed with the gangsta set. She believed
that she wanted a thug, just not too much of a thug.
Enough to be tough, because she definitely didn't
want a softie.

"What about Lott?" Merle asked. His voice had the timbre of urgency, a desperate urging.

"I don't do yellow men, but he's nice."

"Love. It never ceases to baffle me."

Sweating in the field, King's back ached, stretched by the day's labor. Little more than a boy stripped from his mother; man enough to do the work and live the life. A bit filled his mouth. With an angular face and tubercular frame, the white overseers had checked his legs and teeth on the auction block, little more than a work horse's inspection. They didn't take full measure of the wildness in his eyes when they put it in his mouth. Chains clanged with his every movement. The twinge of anger burned, a constant fever beneath his sweaty skin. Drawn up and yanked back, his lips parted. He tasted the iron in his mouth. Spit pooled in it but he couldn't swallow. He vomited, choking as it oozed back down his throat with nowhere to escape around the bit. His tongue brutalized, both by the bit and the bile. And the clenched hatred. His eyes untamed, savage and unbroken, yearned to be free. Not letting anything – not the pain, not the humiliation, not the self-hatred – into his personal world.

King snapped awake on the green checked futon in his living room, legs akimbo. The cuff of the chains still bit into his waking flesh, where he rubbed his wrists. Lady G sank between his spread legs and nestled her back into him. His arms wrapped around her and she felt a rare moment of being safe. He shifted slightly, but there was no hiding from the erection her very proximity caused. She didn't mind. She rather enjoyed the effect she had on him, if only because she knew he'd never make a move she wasn't comfortable with, no matter how much he burned. She liked that.

The living room of his Breton Court town house doubled as his bedroom. He might as well not have owned the second floor as he never ventured up there. He lived without roots. Sweatshirts, T-shirts, and jeans in their respective piles between where the futon stretched out into a bed and the wall. A large television was on another stand, a tray of burning incense beside it. A small stereo system and a stack of books were the only other furnishings in the room. A basket held folded socks and underwear (which he covered when Lady G was over). An end table held an array of colognes, an odd affectation, as if he were never pleased with his own scent and was constantly in search of his true one.

This was their time, their special time. Away from their friends, away from their family, away from their responsibilities, they carved out this space, this time for them, if only to sit and hold one another. They shared the little things, the secret things and the unspoken things.

"What is it, King?"

"I haven't wanted anything in a long time. Haven't felt…" He didn't know if he could find the words to express that, around her, the pain in his chest ebbed and died. It was dangerous to love anything too much. Better to love just a little bit. How he feared that he might be desperately in love with a woman, little more than a girl, whom he should not risk loving because he couldn't afford to lose her. How he had spent a lifetime shying away whenever he thought he found such a love, but she managed to slip under his radar, his wall, and sneak upon him. He leaned down and whispered. "I don't want to give you up."

"I have no intentions of letting you."

"You're a... I should know better." He couldn't stem the spread of weakness, love, when it came to her. His foolishness made him think fondly of himself. So feeling. So ordinary. So full of the helplessness of love. What was it about her that penetrated his defenses? Her woundedness, her strength, her light, her innocence? She had a bird-like defenselessness, fragile pieces of glass, which was his to protect. And he swelled at the idea of being her champion. In his arms, she came to feel unorphaned. He had grown addicted to their moments together and often bent his schedule to maximize their time together. To live for her, to die for her, to never want to let her go. She was his drug of choice and he planned to ride the high for as long as possible.

"You're a child molester!" She exclaimed in faux shock. He talked to her, really talked to her, not talking down to her. He not only listened to her, but expected intelligence and great things from her. She liked being seen and treated that way, though she wasn't always present with him. Not in any real way. Bereft of a part of her soul, she thought. Stingy with her affections, she guarded a virtue only present in her own mind.

"Don't joke." He touched her face. "You're not just eighteen. You talk and act much older."

"There are no children out here."

"I should have the sense and strength to send you off to find someone your own age. Some simple boy."

"You want to be with me. I want to be with you. Eyes wide open." She thought there was space for her in him. Not love, possession. The longing for her. When she looked at him, the thoughts behind the gaze were distant. He wanted to be pulled into her view. He wanted those eyes, that attention, that hungry intent for himself.

The fine bulges fascinated his fingers as he caressed her neck in body worship. She exposed more of herself to his touch. His breathing deepened. Trailing to her breastbone, without protest, he traced the swell of her breasts. He slipped his hand down her top. Her head nuzzled him. Cupping her full breasts and encircling her nipple with his thumb, he found the edges of her areola and circled it. Even a flick failed to elicit a response. No low moan, no sound of any sort. Only non-protest. It was as if she couldn't feel. She didn't feel the kiss he pressed on her. Her internal elusiveness, preserving part of herself as if by instinct.

He turned her head and kissed her. Hungry and probing, his tongue pushed past her lips. He ran his hands along her belly, pressing his hand along her shirt. He kissed the underside of her neck. Pulling at her jeans, he lowered them. To a tremble, a hint of resistance. He slowed. He turned her onto her belly and tugged at her shirt. Her hand gripped it. He knew her worry. The scars. He held firm to the shirt, determined, until she let go. Her back a filigree of scars, spider webs of raised welts and keloids. He followed each delicate bend with his finger. Then with his mouth. Tender, he kissed her back, each kiss an acceptance of her body, of who she was, of her sum of scars. He lowered his attentions, trailing further down her back.

And she offered no protest.

Two broken lovers poured out their sorrow on one another. Not making love as much as reaching for a life preserver before they drowned in a sea of their own pent-up pain. Theirs was the connection of tragedy, even if they never spoke a word of it.

King laid next to her, watched her the entire night, indifferent to his fatigue. He matched his breathing to hers as to not disturb her. To listen to her more clearly. Anything was better than the silence. Yet even her sleeping form threatened to overwhelm him, fill every part of him.

And he couldn't afford to lose her.

CHAPTER SIX

On the corner of New York Street and Rural Avenue, Outreach Inc. bustled with newfound life and excitement. Not that their old ministry home was a bad place: they had shared space with Neighborhood Fellowship Church, however, the penitentiary-styled refurbished school wasn't quite… "them." It didn't achieve the atmosphere they wanted, unlike the renovated double home they now inhabited. Home being the key word.

Brown furniture and wood shelves filled the olive-green walls of the great room. A television armed with Nintendo 64, which had been donated: the ministry always a generation or two behind the latest game system.

Wayne stood in the adjoining dining room which also ran the width of the house yet seemed so much brighter than the great room. Perhaps the sky-blue walls reflected light better. Five teens studied the blank pieces of paper in front of them, as if they contained alien script they struggled to decipher. Baskets of crayons, colored pencils, and markers filled their respective baskets in the center of the table. Wayne's Rottweiler, Kay, lay at their feet, his head on his paws. He lifted his head high enough to loll his tongue over Wayne's outstretched hand. Kay chewed up furniture at home, more out of boredom and loneliness rather than anything malicious, but Wayne didn't have the heart to crate him. Instead, he brought him to Outreach Inc.

"You are making this too hard. Just draw a picture of what you think it means, what it would look like for you, to 'Make It.'" Wayne clapped his hands on the back of Lamont "Rok" Walters.

Rok's mind danced with images of new cars, a Benz, with new rims. Jewelry, lots of fat rings. A house, maybe one for his granmoms, too. New clothes from which he could pull a roll of money from his pants. Huge speakers for his system. Resting poolside with some honeys pouring Cristal for him. Then he realized he was in an MTV video and that his imagination had run dry. The last time they did this exercise, Rok drew a close-up of a black arm with a swollen vein like a bulging blue python throbbing as if nearly sated. Dangling from the arm was a needle, the pink swirl of a load about to be plunged into the arm, a thin trickle of blood escaping the piercing point. All against a backdrop of dark clouds, bulbous and threatening. The assignment was to draw a perfect day.

Rhianna crayoned a page from a coloring book merrily to herself. It didn't matter her age, she was suddenly six again, her tongue stuck out in fierce concentration as she chose her colors and stayed within the lines. The purple, violet red, and mauve, for the wings of the smiling butterfly, its body black and its smiling face peach. Not brown, which Wayne found interesting. Not content to simply color the picture, she drew in the background, adding a lawn, a few flowers, and sun and clouds against a blue sky.

As Wayne prattled on about the possibility of any of them becoming doctors or lawyers, or having a spouse and kids, he might as well have been talking about discovering that they were really a Jedi or a superhero.

"This is bullshit." Rok pushed away from the table. All eyes fell on him and rather than face their curious scrutiny, he dashed up the stairs.

"Esther, you…" Wayne gestured for Esther Baron to watch to the rest of the kids. She nodded that she could handle supervising them. Wayne hadn't initially thought much of Esther. She was a nice enough volunteer, but volunteers came and went and he thought she had the whiff of a suburban girl slumming to make herself feel good, so he'd all but dismissed the possibility of her lasting. Still, she was there the night the Durham Brothers attacked Prez and Trevant, associates of some of his clients. And she returned without a mention of the evening.

The stairs creaked in alarm at Wayne's heavy-set frame in quick ascent. He understood the simmering frustration most of the kids – like Rok – experienced.

Like never having the right words to express the confluence of complex emotions swirling within him. How he had to break them down into simpler things he understood. Hurt. Anger. The call and response of the streets. Quietly, and he'd never admit this to anyone except a fellow staff member, Wayne was pleased with Rok's retreat. Not that he had run from the table, but the fact that Rok chose to run upstairs rather than out the door. Positive steps had to be measured and counted differently, Wayne had long ago learned. In this case, whether Rok realized it or not, he had fled to the prayer loft.

Rok huddled in the back corner of the room, arms around his pulled-up knees. A hint of the lost boy inside the fifteen year-old budding man struggling to burst free. Haloed by prayers other folks had scrawled upon the walls. *I give up. I'm so sick inside. Just give me a little hope, something to hold onto through the night. I want my baby back. I want my mommy back. I want my family back. I want to be whole.*

"You OK?" The words sounded terribly naïve to even Wayne's ears, but he had to start somewhere. Rok simply eyed him. Not cold or hard, but wary as if wanting to lower his guard if only once. Wayne was good at reading faces, to know when someone was struggling and needed prayer for them to hang in there, struggling alongside them as if willing hope upon them. Praying for God to use him like a mirror, for them to see themselves as he saw them: precious, beloved. And he knew he couldn't always wait for them to make the first move. Believing in the power of presence, Wayne scooted near, but without crowding him.

"Have you ever lost anything?" Rok asked the air.

"Yes." Wayne brushed some accumulated dirt from his Timberlands, careful not to meet Rok's eyes. It allowed the boy a measure of privacy, space to be vulnerable.

"Have you ever lost everything?"

"No."

"Well I have. About twelve times. Maybe I'm tired of losing everything."

The words hung in the air without the need for comment or the reflex of offering a contrived platitude. Wayne didn't pretend to have all the answers, and as much as his heart wanted to wave a magic wand and make all the hurt go away and make everything better, nothing lasting was ever built that way. So Wayne simply listened, reassuring Rok that he'd be there as much as he'd let him and help him develop a plan to get to where he wanted. By the time they walked downstairs, the other kids were leaving, papers in hand. Rok walked out without meeting either Wayne's or Esther's eye.

"That go OK?" Esther asked.

"Okay as can be expected. Even baby steps are steps forward." Wayne began to clear off the table, returning the crayons to their boxes and stacking the unused paper.

"That how it is?" Esther brushed a curl of hair back

behind her ear, then collected the scissors and bottles of glue.

"Yeah, you learn to re-evaluate how to measure success doing this work. Don't matter their situation, they're just like the rest of us: too often can't get out of the way of their own bad decision-making and instead take ten paces back."

"Oh."

"But you seem to be getting the hand of how things work around here." Wayne flashed her a reassuring smile. Some people weren't built for the continual heartbreak the job entailed. Pouring themselves into a person only to have them make bad decisions, or continue to hurt themselves or worse.

"I guess." Esther Baron believed in hope. She had been raised in a family who believed in hope, and strove to pass on that hope. She had been with Outreach Inc. for nearly a year now because she wanted to be a part of the hope. Quiet, though not shy; more thoughtful than anything else, maybe lacking the confidence to share her thoughts, she plunged into Outreach Inc. with both feet. To this day she couldn't describe what she did: mother, sister, friend, confidante, advisor. She was… there. If she had business cards, that's how they would read: *Esther Baron – There*.

"Don't sell yourself short. The longer you stick around, the more you'll see some stuff that will make you question the world you live in."

"Like…" Esther's eyes widened and she blushed as if wanting to swallow that last syllable and pretend it didn't happen. Yet there was the pleading of unasked questions yearning for answers behind the strained grin masking her face.

"You want to talk about it?" Wayne asked out of mercy, reading her need to finally talk about what happened that night. That was another thing he had learned about people: they talked when they were ready.

"It's just…"

"You don't know where to start?"

"Is that normal?" Esther eased into one of the dining room chairs.

"Ain't nothing normal out there. Actually, it may be better to redefine what you think of as normal." Wayne pulled a chair out across from her and straddled it backwards.

"People being killed."

"Too often."

"But…" Esther hesitated. "Ripped in half?"

"I…" Wayne started then thought better of his initial response. There was no immediate transition into a world of trolls, sorcerers, zombies, and dragons unless there were some ten-sided dice involved. Better to start in an easier place. "You see the kids we work with? They're invisible. No one sees them. They may have a sense about them, the same way you could be in a darkened room and know that you weren't alone. People know when to walk around them or speed out of the way of a bum begging for change. Their powers of invisibility are huge: if you stop to talk to a homeless person, you seem to disappear also. People turn their eyes from you as if you no longer exist. That can do something to a person's psyche."

"So you're saying I'm nuts?"

"Not at all. Your eyes have been opened. Most people have no idea what goes on in this city. At night. In other neighborhoods. In the shadows of downtown."

"The kids whispered about dragons over at the Phoenix." Esther let the words float out into the ether, not knowing if she hoped he would deny it or pray that he wouldn't. She sensed she was opening a door she wasn't sure she could close later.

"That would explain why we've had trouble catching a cab."

"I'm serious."

"There's a whole other side to the city. Probably every city. I'm not going to say you get used to it, but you learn to be open to the ideas of other lives and possibilities."

The moment of silence between them gestated. Then, suddenly aware of it, they glanced down. Maybe he meant to just be reassuring, but without realizing he did it, he had reached across the table and taken her hand.

Many of the boarded-up buildings surrounding the spot at 30th and Central looked like bombed-out brick shells. The sidewalk was chewed up, dented in and split as if something heavy had been dropped onto it at regular intervals. Rush-hour traffic sped along, the snap of car doors making sure they were locked whenever they were caught at a stoplight. The faded purple awning was an oasis, a reclaimed spot within the blight of the neighborhood left to decay. The name Unleavened Bread formed a cross around the "E"s. Amber lighting suffused the café. Two rows of long black tables – topped with glass bowls filled with artificial flowers and surrounded by uncomfortable, tall-backed, wooden chairs with wicker seats along them – led to a formica counter-top. Off to the left, a space had been carved out for community or church groups to meet. A mountain vista had been painted on a wall by a local street artist. Wood paneling ran halfway up the wall, the top half of the wall stenciled with gold and purple script of Bible verse references. *Revelation 21:1-3. Psalms 34:1. Romans 13:1* and *10:9. Deuteronomy 30:19.* And of course, *John 3:16.*

A woman everyone called Queen took in ex-addicts and ex-cons to employ, believing that everyone needed a chance to turn their life around. A jowly-faced woman, with short curly hair and dark blotches on her face and thick lines worn about her mouth, wandered from the kitchen to the counter complaining that her sugar was up. With a slow amble, stiff-jointed thick legs and swollen ankles, glasses dangled about her neck by a chain over her orange and black frock. Her heavy bosom rested on her belly.

"Name on the ticket?"

"Percy."

"Hello, Percy. I'm Sister Jackie, but folks round here call me Queen. What can I get for you?"

"I'll take a bowl of beef vegetable soup." Percy pointed to the daily special. He tended to order whatever was written on top. Or by picture. Queen also let folks who couldn't afford a hot meal stop in to fill their bellies without question or shame.

"Good choice. Everything in the soup is from our garden in Mulberry, Indiana."

"You have any toast?"

"We know how to improvise. It's how we do. Make the best of what you got." Queen smiled then ambled back into the kitchen.

Not wanting to flip through the copy of Our Daily Bread devotional tucked between the salt, pepper, and sugar, Percy found a discrete corner and plopped down to read until his food was ready. A comic book, Cullen Bunn's *The Damned*, caught his eye. The idea of demons and gangsters had a newfound appeal to him. Sister Jackie brought him out his soup, which he ate without thought or muster. So he never noticed the man sliding into the chair across from him.

"I knew your daddy." Born Robert Ither, Naptown Red smiled as he settled into the chair. Naptown because Indianapolis was always so far behind all the other big cities, always sleeping. Nothing going on. Red because of the slight reddish tint to the man's hair. Like soldiers, everyone had another name. His back to the wall, he surveyed the other customers and kept note of anyone entering the café. Black pants, slick purple shirt, and a crocodile smile under "cut-you-for-nothing" eyes, he didn't look like anyone Percy wanted to hang out with.

"Who are you?" Percy rolled up his comic book. Black moles circled each of the man's bloodshot, heavy eyes. Splotches checkered his face, parts of his skin closest to his hair line lighter than the others. His long feral auburn hair had been straightened but kept unkempt. Percy smelled the alcohol wafting off him. The man rubbed his belly, a sated chieftain, and tugged at his privates too often. Percy always looked into the details of everything.

"Folks call me Naptown Red. What you going to do with your life?"

"I don't know. School. Got to get through that."

"Thinking about the future. What part you want to play in this here game." Red fancied himself maneuvering to pick up where Night left off, gambling that it would be easier with the would-be heir in tow. To do right by the boy would give him added street credibility. But as he studied the overweight and all-too-soft boy, Red took Percy for weak. All knightly virtue seen as a weakness to this would-be next king of the streets: courtesy, patience, gentility, chivalry. All such things needing to be mocked or punished.

"Ain't thought none on it. Don't seem like it's for me."

Queen brought out his soup without comment. Red eased back until she left. Percy smiled and nodded his appreciation.

"I'm offering you an opportunity. I got a package coming in. Thought I might take care of you with it."

"Why?" Percy asked. The man bothered him. All of the talk of taking care of him, of looking out for him reminded Percy of his momma. All of her fiendish attempts at parental provision always had the taint of using you for her own ends.

"Like I said, I knew your daddy."

"Nah, I don't think so." Percy brought his spoon to his mouth, blew, winced at its heat and blew again before taking the bite.

Naptown Red cut his eyes. There was nothing hard about the boy. He had trouble believing he was any kin at all to Night. Night was one of the baddest motherfuckers he knew. He came up fierce. Hard. Feared.

"Are you finished?" Queen said without any trace of disdain in her voice despite her wary gaze cast at Red.

"Yes, ma'am." Percy cleared his arms as she took the bowl from him.

"You could be running the sweeper on them rugs out there," a voice yelled from the kitchen.

"Right after my cigarette break," Queen said. "Gonna take two pulls and call it a break."

"Look here, boy." Red leaned towards him once Queen was out of earshot. "You got to choose which side of the line you going to stand on."

"I think I have."

"You in church or something?" A man for bad plays, Red gave him another once-over as if he'd mis-read the menu. That thing ticked in his chest. Weed took the edge off his anger and he'd been angry for a long time. Pushed into the life, he fucked the world because he felt fucked, but the first and foremost victim was himself. The boy wasn't the one. He'd have to make other arrangements. "You sure ain't your daddy's son."

"No, I guess not." If Percy was insulted, he gave no indication. He simply opened up his comic book and kept reading.

Good Hope Missionary Baptist Church was dedicated in 1891. The church had a lot of history. A *lot* of history. There used to be a dirt road out front where folks would hook up their horses and buggies. The streets had changed, living in their own separate world, with the economics of poverty: extortion, prostitution, gambling, stolen property, drugs. All enforced by the violence of gangs and subsidized by welfare checks thus tacitly approved by government neglect. Police rarely patrolled for fear of their own safety.

"Lord have mercy, you'll see me on the TV." Big Momma scooted out of her chair with a dancer's grace heedless of her stiff hip, sore legs, and swollen arms when she saw King come through the front doors. She raised one hand, palm out, and hopped in place. Then she suddenly stomped five times. "That's how good it was. Do you hear me?"

"I hear you." King stopped in his tracks. A portrait of Redd Foxx cast his eyes to heaven from his shirt.

Big Momma was hyped up to a near-wail, stoked on a spiritual high, a one-woman amen corner. "Who did it?"

"God did it," voices from the hallway called back.

"I just can't keep it to myself. Do you hear me? I done cried and shouted and danced, OK? And I thank God for the rain. When you get the Lord in you, you can't just keep Him to yourself. You got to share Him. It just keeps getting better and better and better. I'll go on a mountaintop telling people what the Lord can do. He'll carry me through. He answers prayer. We been praying 'send some help' cause His people were struggling. Then you rose up."

"I didn't do anything special." King stepped back, uncertain if she was actually talking to, or even about, him.

"And He ain't through blessing us through you yet. You know how they say if you take one step, He'll take two? Who did it?"

"God did it!" the voices from the hallway called out.

"Is he in?" King asked.

Big Momma stepped in front of him with a conspiratorial whisper, as if requiring a code word for him to pass. "Who did it?"

King let out an exasperated sigh. "God did it."

"He in his office."

Pastor Ecktor Winburn felt his calling to evangelize the unsaved as well as the un- and under-churched. Hustlers, drunks, prostitutes, drug dealers, drug addicts, all the left-behind, fall-through-the-cracks folks. He was also in King's life, the man who showed him how to be and live as a man.

King's father, Luther White, ran the streets, hustled, and stole, and thus ended up dead before King had entered pre-school. His mother rarely spoke of the man, though when she did, it was like he was two different men: the would-be gangsta and the man she knew and believed in. When others talked about his father – uncles, friends – there was a near-reverent air. Luther was cool. Admired. Half of them wanted to be him.

All King knew was that he was dead and gone.

He missed having a father, that firmness that could put him in check. Then his mom got hooked on drugs. King could never remember having a one-on-one conversation with her after that. By the time Pastor Winburn came into his life, he'd already seen his share of trouble. Smoked a little weed, getting into fights, telling teachers what they could go do. Because he imagined himself in charge of his life. His life changed after he got caught and arrested for stealing. The court put him in contact with Outreach Inc., who helped get him back on track. It was his then case manager, Wayne, who put him in contact with Pastor Winburn. Once King started going to his church, Pastor Winburn became a bit of a father figure, affecting him whenever they chatted. He helped King learn how to rein in his temper. They went on spiritual patrols, walking through the neighborhood, praying for and talking to folks. Pastor Winburn taught him discipline, and how to be a man, but the life still called. And though many years had passed, King still had a lot of unanswered questions about God. And still struggled with his temper.

"Someone certainly got her praise on this morning," King said.

"That's what we do here. We praise God not only on a Sunday, but it could be a Wednesday. A Thursday. A Tuesday. If it ends in 'day' we ready to praise." Pastor Ecktor Winburn leaned back in his chair. A low-cut Afro with gray streaks drew back from his forehead lengthening the appearance of his face. A black suit hung from him as if he was a scarecrow funeral director, his tie too thin. He hunched his shoulders close and bridged his spider-like long fingers, his suspicious eyes taking the measure of him. "The lesson was on One Accord. If we can't come together down here, what we going to do in heaven? We should be a foretaste of heaven, but we pretty much taste-testing hell."

"It's bad out there."

"I don't need to hear tales of how bad it is on the streets. I know all about the rapes, drugs, murders, and violence. You think it's bad now? Fifteen years ago you couldn't slow your car down here without twenty folks running up to you to sell drugs." Pastor Winburn hesitated, choosing his words with care. King remembered a time when the man shared freely with him. "Only God has the remedy."

"God is not my friend. Not these days. Not while things are like this."

"You ought to come by some time. We a live wire here." Pastor Winburn lowered his voice.

"I remember."

"Look here, churches plant where they plant and deepen their roots by drawing on the community they dwell in. When we in the hood, I don't look for my members to come up over the mountain. We're made up of who we are, where we are." Pastor Winburn smiled and spread his arms in his all-are-welcome embrace. King had heard the sales pitch before. "This is our neighborhood. I know I taught you that. Not what you been doing."

"You mean this?" King pulled the Caliburn from his dip. He let the light reflect from it for a moment, then laid it like a sacrificial offering before Pastor Winburn.

"So what I been hearing is true? Is this what I taught you? Is this how you solve problems now, to return fist for fist and gun for gun?" The pastor rubbed the bridge of his nose, the gesture managing to convey disappointment. "What is this, King? You set up a private police force? Your own little army with you as the general? Are you making your own gang?"

"It's the best defense, because the police don't show. I'd like to do things your way, pastor. But it's hard when it seems no one cares or no one is around. Not the police. Not the church. Not God."

"Look at you." Pastor Winburn got up and circled King. "You always worried about doing something big. You as flashy as any of these other knuckle-heads. Forget that all you have to do is reach one, teach one. No, you might as well go ahead and get yourself a cape and put a big K on your chest."

The no-nonsense edge of him keened against King, as well as the sweetness of the man. "It's not like that."

"What's it like then? If you fight your enemies with what tools you have, you'll be defeated. Maybe killed. The system is part of the problem."

"Exactly." King finally jumped in. "That's what I been fighting against."

"I don't know why you so quick to amen some-body. Your wild ass is part of the problem, too. Look here, you can't give someone a block of cheese a day and then ask, why are you hungry? Cause, damn, I only got some cheese. But next day, where am I? Down waiting for my next piece of cheese. The system provides a chain, not a safety net, just enough to string us along, not enough to let us go free. On the other side, if all I'm doing is waiting for the next crumb from master's table, I ain't no better. And you just out there shooting up all the cheese you can find."

Pastor Winburn came up from Alabama, working everything from oil to iron, until he ended up in Indianapolis searching for new job opportunities. He'd made so much money in his little businesses, he thought it was time to give back to the community. So he decided to become a pastor. He leaned against his desk in a conversational pose, but he'd caught the fire of his rhythm.

"From the pulpit to the back door, we scared of these folks. Scared of our own. People who had leprosy had to stay so many feet from you because they were scared you were going to catch it. Here's the thing: a doctor can't examine you unless he touches you. And we have to lay hands on this neighborhood. People don't live here cause they want to. They didn't look all over the city and say 'I want this slum.' They live here cause they have to. There are two kinds of black folks: those scrambling to get out and those who give up and stay here. See, those scrambling to get out, they always looking to live where white folks live. I don't mean that in no hateful way, I mean they chase the same picket-fence dream white folks do. Always dreaming to get away from 'bad elements' and such. Not a bad dream, I guess. Other folks get a different story trapped in them. They don't think they can do any better, believe the world is against them, since they don't got any opportunities nor any point of dreaming, white folks' dreams or otherwise. So they spend they days trying to get by or get over. They do whatever they have to do to survive. That's a bad story. If not bad, then venomous. Defeated.

"Now, me? I'm a been there, done that type. I don't believe that a person who's never done anything can help anyone here. It takes a certain type of shepherd. We relate well. We can show that God did it for us. So I have a mission here. Built a third type of folks. Those who choose to stay here and commit to making a difference. And the mission has to get down on its knees to get results." Pastor Winburn fully slipped into the comfortable glove of his sermon rhythm, straightening and letting his arms go to add emphasis to his words. "The people have a desire to work, they just need to be coordinated. You remember the story of Nehemiah? Before he got there, no one was doing anything. But when he got there the whole city got together and started working. The people had a mind to work. Now there were those who were standing around in the first place not doing anything, and when he started doing something, they wanted to come up and talk. Come on down and let's plan what we're going to do. Well I'm on the wall and I don't have time to come down."

He'd come in hoping to catch a word, not be blasted by the fire-hose torrent of judgment. He didn't have time to formulate any response before Pastor Winburn continued.

"I guess that's my warning to you. Serving as your personal prophet. The role of a prophet is to bring the word of the Lord to bear on a specific situation, to shake up your spiritual life. You have to make a choice. What the future holds if you stay on your present course frightens me.

"On the other hand, God is a God of restoration. He's restoring hope in this neighborhood. He's restoring lives. He's restoring dignity. And you do it one person at a time. You need to be a part of His program, not Him getting on board with yours. A leader leads by example. You can say what you want from the pulpit, but you have to go where your people are. Model what it is you're teaching. Christ met needs then preached the gospel."

King shifted his weight under the appraisal. Part of him still sought the old man's approval. "I'm just one man."

"One man makes very little difference. I don't care who you are, King. But all of us together, we can do anything. Now choose." Pastor Winburn had always challenged him, pushed him to be a better man. He laid the facts out like a dinner spread on a table then said "now choose." Right or wrong, it was always his choice to make and Pastor Winburn would be there.

King stood up to leave. Pastor Winburn spread his arms in a way that reminded him of holding his hand out to a dog to let it catch his scent before petting him. The pastor put his arms around him in an embrace. King didn't exactly return the hug, but he didn't pull away either. He returned his Caliburn to his dip.

• • • •

Cool air cut through King, his T-shirt offering little protection against the elements. Sitting on the front stoop of the church, he needed a few moments to collect his thoughts, to sift through Pastor Winburn's words. The old man had a way of getting under his skin and pushing his buttons. The neighborhood smelled of car exhaust and backed-up sewers. Damp sidewalk and pooled water against the curb provided evidence of the rain burst. The cars sped along, too many in a need of muffler repair, their tires rumbling over the uneven strips in the road. The church faced a network of alleys, carving up the block and snaking between homes. Brown vines filigreed the fences. Pairs of sneakers hung from the lines overhead.

A shuffling from the alleyway caught his attention, putting King on high alert. A figure staggered out of the alley, and then collapsed. King darted across the street to the wail of screeching tires and blaring horns. King crouched over the crumpled form and rolled him over. It took him a moment to place the emaciated face.

"Prez?" King asked.

Somewhere between what should have been his sophomore or junior year of high school, the boy stank of nicotine, stale beer, and crack sweat, shaking like a pair of dice. Cuts on his face were half-healed, jelly-like wounds of having been raked with talon-like fingernails. His face bruised to blue, his lips swollen and split. His hair littered with flecks of fuzz and pebbles. A series of scrapes and scratches along his long, lanky arms.

"King?"

"It's me, Prez."

"They're out there. And they're coming for us."

CHAPTER SEVEN

Rellik was a jailhouse nigga through and through. He'd spent more time inside the system than out and found the rhythms of prison life more natural than the existence folks called freedom. By the age of fifteen he'd already entered the system and had to bury his mother from prison. Running the Merky Water set from inside; since his family couldn't afford it, he sent his gang to the funeral home to make the arrangements and pay for it. If he wanted the prison shut down, it got shut down that day. The guards and superintendent were impotent and apathetic: they were there to make sure no one escaped. Everything else was just paperwork. Even the chaplain was scared to talk to him about Christ. Heaven would be better off without him as far as clergy was concerned.

The streets ran little differently than The Ave. There were crews to be overseen. Po-po, be they Cos or Five-O, to deal with. Product to move. Rival factions to navigate. Power to be seized. No one operated in a vacuum and he knew no one could survive without allegiances and loyalty.

The lines of territory were ambiguous at the moment. Everyone respected the space Dred had carved out, too afraid to outright move into it for fear of his retaliation, despite his general absence. It was as if he haunted the streets, and his ghost terrified them. Back in the overly romanticized day, none of the crew were allowed to touch drugs, but they could strong-arm around it, make sure a dealer broke them off some. Eventually money, especially with so much of it to be had, drove things out of whack and dudes started selling it. It got so good that when the original kings got locked up, the dons never said anything against the drug-dealing. They allowed the selling to keep going. Back then, the gang was a unit. They talked of family. Old school.

New crews set up shop along the edges of Rellik's reclaimed territory, though none ventured into Breton Court. King blocked that. King. That young buck might prove to be a problem later, so Rellik made a note to keep an eye on him. Night's crew was in chaos, easily absorbed into Rellik's Merky Water. The Treize carved up the far west side, just south of Breton Court but inching ever northward. Which left ICU and other independent operators. That was always their mistake. The Nights and Dreds of the world viewed themselves as operators, the game little more than a means to an end. Business. New school.

His black Cadillac CTS-V, a new whip, was probably too flashy but he allowed himself the indulgence. The smell and feel of a new ride was the one thing he missed as much as pussy and no amount of closing his eyes pretending a hole was a hole would allow him to simulate the experience of driving. As he pulled up to the Meadows, now Phoenix, Apartments, young men stood at attention, the peewees taking note at the respect the older ones issued. Hip hop blared as smoke wafted about, nicotine cutting the marijuana smell. These boys were unfocused and undisciplined. The last of the package took forever to unload. More time spent tugging on their junk and showing out for the ladies rather than doing business. There was plenty of time for that nonsense off the clock, but on, business was business and they needed to be professionals. Low-ranking members ran errands for him. Affectless, young, with dead eyes. He didn't let them carry guns unless they were gearing up for war.

The apartments thrummed with life in the ordinary. Families reclined in lawn chairs on their porches absorbing the neighborhood sights like it was a beautiful sunset. Kids along the curb drew chalk rainbows on the sidewalk. A few teens held court beside some bushes, pestering each other in a courtship dance of showing and chasing ass. Reassured by the rightness of the scene, Rellik approached with the easy saunter of a cowboy entering a saloon. Hands extended to him, heads nodded as he walked by, the subtleties of recognition and welcome. He came, he saw, he got over.

He simply wanted a place to die, publicly if not privately, accepting the evaluation of his life. For the briefest of moments, he wondered what the hell he was doing. For all of his machinations, he had no real plan or direction. Only the reflex of same old, same old, wallowing in fresher, bigger piles of shit, biding time until he was killed or jailed... and calling it a life. Then he remembered this was the only life he knew, the only one he'd been shown, and he'd make the most of it.

"What's the good word, Rhianna?" *That girl got around*, he thought.

"Still hustling, baby." Rhianna paced the sidewalk wearing a half-jacket with nothing underneath, exposing her pierced belly and a tattoo on the small of her back, over blue jeans. A cigarette pursed between fingers, she held it out for him to take a pull. He waved it off. She blew smoke from the side of her mouth.

"We all hustlers. We all informants, too, if the right circumstances pop off." All hustles were respected as long as they didn't fuck up anyone else's hustle. Which made trading in information such a delicate balancing act. Secrets were power, much of their power residing in them being kept. It wasn't always healthy to see or hear too much. The wrong word to the wrong ears could result in a bloody smile opening up along one's throat.

"Hear what happened to The Pall?" Rhianna crossed her arms and took another drag. She always had an angle to play. Information was simply another commodity to be traded. Good ears collected information someone wanted and smart ears kept it to themselves, unless presented with a situation: like an ass-kicking or contempt charges, bruises or jail. Or worse. "Ain't that some shit. Pimping ain't easy."

"Pimping can get you dead if you ain't careful."

Pimping was a full-time job, not a good side business. Strictly speaking from a business point of view, the margins simply weren't too great, on either side. The problem was ignorance. From the ho side, they earned their little twenty dollars, then they spent their little twenty dollars. Rock, rings, whatever, it got spent. They couldn't earn enough because they spent it, or more, as soon as they got it. So every day they started off with nothing, or worse, in the hole which made them scramble and claw all the more. From the pimp side, between keeping a stable fed and clothed, needing to have bail money on hand, hospital visits, drug use, and them being prone to thieving, prostitutes required too much attention. Rellik settled for a flat fee to handle out-of-control johns and allowed both to operate in his territory.

"All right, what you want to know?"

"Where's Dred?" Rellik asked.

"That's the question of the day."

"Maybe you need to concentrate on finding an answer." All the charm drained from his eyes. Beneath

his stoic exterior, his flat lifeless eyes – the dark constellation of freckles around them squinched into
something ugly – and fixed grimace, he exuded the
promise of violence. A blind fury – the most knucklehead aspects of it held in check – once released
keened with the force of nature. The inevitable, non-
negotiable, firestorm. Rellik hated unknowns. He
needed to know where Dred was and what he was
up to, and if she didn't know she could certainly find
out.

"All right, Rellik." Rhianna butted out her cigarette against the bus stop sign, then ground it under
the flat of her pumps.

"You got something for me?"

"You know I do." An honest prostitute, or as close
to one if there were such a creature. She played
things as straight as could be expected, kind of like
the tide: regular, expected, the occasional terror, but
mostly scrolled in her relentless sort of way. Also, she
was a bit of a romantic, still clinging to the hope of
her prince. Such was the fairy tale she wrote for herself, but every story had a monster in it.

The Meadows, now Phoenix, Apartments held all
manner of hustlers: pimps, car thieves, shoe/shirt
sellers, prostitutes, squeegee men, food sellers, clothing makers, baby-sitting, candy sellers. People sold
license plates, Social Security cards and small appli-
ances out of their vans. They pirated gas, electricity,
or cable. Everyone had their own hustle, part of the
shadow economy of the streets. Rellik collected a tax

on all action occurring in his territory, even taxing pimps for use of stairwells, alleys, or empty apartments. He'd control the flow of things as long as they abided by his rules. They couldn't hustle out in the open. It drew police along with other unwanted scrutiny and he wasn't interested in any additional attention. Nor could they hustle during family events. Neither could the homeless nor strangers. BBQs, block parties, family reunions, after-church picnics. Nothing. They couldn't hustle by playgrounds. They had to respect the kids. And none of them could loiter there either.

"You know you need to move someplace else," Rellik said.

"Damn, nigga. You hard." Rhianna ran her hand along her locklets as if primping them into place, then turned on her heel.

"Relentless."

Everyone needed a place to put their head up. He could've stayed at the Phoenix Apartments, move into Night's old spot, but he left that to Garlan. No point in punking the boy out of his own place. Besides, he was a potential earner needing room to come into his own. Rellik respected that and in his own way, nurtured it. He chose to hold up in an abandoned home down on 24th and Pennsylvania, a bright lime-colored house from the Arts and Crafts era with brown doors and trim, clay-tiled roof and a wrap-around porch made of stones. Some fiends had

got to wilding there not too long ago and the property stood abandoned, even by fiends and other
squatters. Its windows were boarded up, sealed outside and fortified inside. The first-floor interior was
gutted out. At one point it had been carved up into
four apartments; now only the original walls were
in place, much of the lathing exposed, brittle ribs on
an emaciated retiree. Much of the recessed cabinets
and shelves had been pulled out. The basement door
nailed shut. Mildew rotted the stairs through, dis-
couraging anyone from mounting them.

Upstairs was little different. With much of the
plumbing exposed, a cracked toilet bled thick urine, its
base coated in a grimy yellow paste where urine had
dried. Two of the bedrooms were left bare, rotted mattresses piled in the corners. A locked door cordoned
off the master bedroom. A fresh coat of white paint on
the walls. A walk-in closet converted into a bathroom.
The wood floor had been refinished and polished.
Boards protected the windows, more to keep prying
eyes out; twin windows led to a deck outside above
the porch, an emergency exit should he need one. A
large flatscreen television hung on the wall adjacent
to the one which backed the long leather couch on
which a woman perched, reading a book.

"I heard you were out." She curled on the couch,
legs drawn under her, allowing her skirt to reveal
enough of her perfectly shaped legs to draw his
eyes along them. "I see you've done something to
the place."

"Morgana," he said, the feigned disinterest in his voice meant to disguise his hunger.

"How you doing, baby? Aren't you happy to see me?" she cooed, her voice thick like warm honey, which she intended to lick from his body.

Her face cold and composed, not betraying any emotion other than her cruel smile. A fierce intention rode her eyes. Morgana was an agenda within a scheme. Her presence signaled trouble at the very least. Still, she was one of the best lays he'd ever had. A woman who knew her trade – fleshcraft and necromancy – and he suspected that she was not above murder. And she knew how to please and use men. She patted the empty spot next to her, inviting him over.

"Dred know where you are?" Rellik asked.

"You care? Isn't having me with his full knowledge part of the thrill?" She trailed a lone finger along his arm. A high yella, stone-cold beauty whose large breasts pushed her shirt straight out, exposing her flat belly over her tight jeans. Her Asian eyes and long black hair framed an intoxicating face. Using men against men, teasing out vulnerabilities, to exploit their weaknesses, her flaw was that she discounted their strengths. Her own brand of enchantment left his will slacked, honor drugged, and canceled his conscience with lust. Hers was a deadly game; even knowing how she operated made her no less effective, or him any less prey to her advances.

"Same old Morgana. Still using the same tricks. You play a dangerous game."

"Most risky gambits can be successful, if under-taken boldly and without hesitation."

Rellik had his own agenda. And orders. The offi-cers, even the Ngbe who ran the bulk of the traffic in Indianapolis, served at the pleasure of the Board of Directors. The Hierarchy brought him in because things were in disarray. Not content for lieutenants and captains to report to him, Dred vied to get to the Board. And now he was nowhere to be found.

Rellik pulled her close to him. For his part, he used women like some people used drugs: to numb him-self from the pain of his world. She feigned protest until a mischievous smile snaked across her face. It was her nature. She couldn't help herself. She knew him and accepted him as he was and as much as she was capable. In her own twisted way, she loved him.

The idea of love, its sheer tenacity, scared the shit out of him. Love stayed right there with him during the ugly and dark times. All love did. Love clung right to the person he was meant to be and helped move him along toward becoming that. Love didn't let him off the hook, nor did it want him to define himself by his sin or failures. He couldn't outrun love. So he knew he'd one day have to kill her.

"Is there anything I can do for you?" She plunged her tongue deep into his mouth. His hands explored her back, before scooping her up and setting her on the edge of his couch. She fumbled at his shirt, their tongues never breaking from their mutual explo-rations, while he hiked up her skirt.

She really wasn't wearing any panties.

The depth of his entry caused her to break their kiss. In a well-practiced move, she winced through closed eyes, and threw her head back. Her arms locked around the back of his head, then she moaned long and deep. There was making love and there was a hot fucking that burned bright and brief, threatening to break them both in its intensity. He rode her in slow strokes. The sex was as true and vital as the first time he smashed her.

Morgana wasn't one for cuddling afterward. The night called and she had much to do before dawn. She left him to his empty room, his thoughts and his life. Unlike many of the squares who went to their cubicle worlds and went through the motions of life, pushing papers, accepting berating bosses, and underperforming and back-stabbing colleagues, he could say he put in a good day's work. True, he couldn't say "I built that." He couldn't say "I taught them." The devil whispered in his ear. That dark voice that came to him in the still times. When he stopped moving, stopped playing the game, when he didn't distract himself with the pretense that he wasn't alone and unloved. He wasn't fooling anyone. His dreams tormented him. Sometimes flashes of what life would have been like with his brothers, with anything approximating a real family. Other times, his nights were filled with water, dragged under, his breath fleeing in a desperate gasp. He paced the floor, an unsettled cat, then drew his

Taurus 92 from beneath his pillow. Plopping on the edge of his bed, he aimed his gun at his heart. It'd be easy to end the pain which haunted him, without name, without reservation, without relent. One day he'd find the strength to squeeze the trigger.

"I miss my brothers." The sound of his own voice startled him.

In the end he knew how empty his life was. All he knew was that life was accidental.

Only death was deliberate.

Behind the Phoenix Apartments, a grove of trees lined a path, its banks formed a natural green space that had become popular as a walkway. During early morning hours, many a citizen walked its path for exercise, each armed with a stick or bat in case of emergency. On occasion, people held dog fights back there. Cars crowded the rear of the Phoenix Apartments parking lot, sealing it off into its own little world. Folks knew they were entering designated Switzerland, a "no beefs allowed" zone. It was its own, lost world.

The sounds of cars traveling along 38th Street drifted in from the outside world. Cigarette butts and beer bottles littered the ground. Overgrown masonry protruded from the earth, large cement slabs which were the foundation from a previous building. The trees grew at odd angles in this fairly isolated thin trickle of a creek. The older ones half-uprooted as if a great upheaval had once taken place there.

This was where Omarosa agreed to meet Colvin. Not neutral territory, but they weren't here to parlay. She knew the lay of the land and it was enough into Rellik's tightening control for Colvin to have to step lightly. Omarosa moved swiftly and without sound. Her light footfalls slipping through the foliage without displacing a leaf. She was prepared to take out a guard, Mulysa, or at least a young buck which passed for security. But there was no one. Colvin stood alone and vulnerable in the center of the field.

A faint light illuminated his features. Despite his evident beauty, his heroic jaw, and his angular setting, his face contorted in pain and concentration.

"It's been a long time," Omarosa interrupted.

"I'm trying to decide if it's been too long or not long enough."

"Didn't expect to see you handle this personally."

"And trust this to Mulysa?" Colvin asked.

"He's your boy and all."

"Would he still be standing here if he had a bag full of money? Easy pickings."

"I let your courier scurry along home."

"To let me know you were responsible."

"Still, you, me. Out here. Alone. You getting bold in your old age. We gonna do this now or what?"

"You unarmed?"

"You alone?"

Twins shared a special knowing. There was no psychic connection, no special power given them. There was just a simple knowing. They understood their doppelganger because they shared a womb with them, knew them in the most intimate and close of settings. So both Colvin and Omarosa appreciated the little dance of cordiality they both endured and inflicted on one another. No need to voice their history of quiet resentments and litany of perceived slights. Her mother always favored Colvin. There was always something fragile about him, despite his bravado and narcissism. A palace built atop rotted timbers. Not that Omarosa consciously picked up on it. She tried to love him, but there was no room for her in his world. That was what she told herself.

Their estrangement had nothing to do with how many times she tried to kill him over the years.

"So we gonna do this?"

"Yeah, but let me ask you something," Colvin said.

"Go ahead."

"Do you keep up much with the old ways?"

"The old ways are not for us. Let King and his dog, Merle, truck in those parlor tricks. I got better things to do. Like finish this up, crash at my crib, and count my ends, you feel me?"

"Yeah, about that... I'm afraid there's been a change in plans. You see, I didn't come alone." A jade spark burned just above him. It trickled down like slow-moving lava, leaving a suspended trail in its wake.

Omarosa recognized the glamour of hidden doors. A half-dozen men tumbled from the nexus. They stood about to her waist, with bulbous bellies and faces like old men. Nude save for their spiked iron boots and caps faded to a deep carnation.

"Red Caps? Seriously?" Omarosa pulled out her sawed-off shotgun from the bag. "I didn't exactly come unarmed."

Their weapons sprung to their hands, slings firing shots like iron thorns. Omarosa fell backwards, dodging the first volley while getting off a shot. The first creature fell back, blood erupting from the wound of the shotgun blast. It slowly rose, the attack not lethal. Hardy bastards. She dove for cover behind one of the jutting concrete slabs. Her side burned as if lanced with a hot poker.

The men scattered, converged on her spot from a variety of angles, each serving as a distraction for the others. Their teeth ripped into her flesh as they swarmed at her, a host of maggots writhing on a still-twitching carcass. The full weight of one of their bodies slammed into her back from above. The iron spikes of its boots, like nails hammered into her back. It drove the breath from her lungs. Others wrestled her, attempting to subdue her. With a curse, she kicked free, then thrust her elbow into the groin of the one behind her. It slackened its grasp enough for her to twist loose. Her arm was wrenched from underneath her, nearly toppling her.

"Damn it," she muttered.

"Getting slow in your old age." Colvin tramped toward her dropped package. He was stunned: she really did bring the product. Though, he should have been: he had really brought the money. They were fey after all. Straddling the line between what they called honor and the necessity of betrayal were what they did best. He turned to leave, deciding whether to watch the rest of the show or go ahead and depart.

The Red Caps jabbered amongst themselves with titters and croaks not meant for human throats. Not even half-human ones. They drove her back by their sheer weight of numbers, all talons and teeth gnashing and swiping towards her: a pack of hyenas tearing into a wounded lioness. Strength ebbed from her limbs. She bled from innumerable scratches and tears. But she was fey. And you neither took a gift from her kind, nor made them angry.

A scarlet fugue state burned in Omarosa's emerald eyes as the fierceness of battle overtook her. The rage which so often fueled her when her back was pressed against the wall and the desperation of survival was all she had left. She rushed headlong through them to break their purchase. Lashing right and left, she struck with tepid punches more designed to throw them off than inflict any real damage to their tough hides. She swung her leg in a high arc and caught one in mid-air; the back blade of her boot heel slit its throat and it was dead before it hit the ground. Her spiked heel crunched down on a skull, a spike driven through it. Its opened throat spilled blood over her new boots. They'd never come clean again.

She barely dodged the taloned hand. Its nails would have opened up a scarlet trail along her chest. The better course of valor brought no shame to the fey. She would live to see the blood of her enemies spilled. Through the stark stretch of open ground, she bolted for the tree line with speed which easily outpaced her pursuers. The occasional elf arrow whizzed past her. She turned, nearly invisible in its shadows, to see Colvin salute her. A bag in either hand.

He was sloppy and brutal, no finesse or style to his game. But he was fey.

CHAPTER EIGHT

The sun rose a violet and orange backdrop to his lakeside perch. Lott slept soundly beneath an apple tree, bone-weary, with the gentle laps of the lake providing all the lullaby he needed. He'd always found comfort at lakes. The heavy footfalls of an approaching brigade stirred him from slumber. A staggered caravan of four figures on horseback coalesced into view. Though quite a distance away, it became readily apparent that the parade consisted solely of women. Each wore a red cap, a beret of sorts, and slowed as she neared as if beckoning him to follow her. Few women crossed him. Fewer still drew his attention.

The first had a familiar bearing as if she'd always been around the way, a presence in the neighborhood he'd taken for granted. She drew back her long black hair from her Asian-looking eyes. Her horse, black as death and hate. Eyes reflecting ambition and power. Glaring at him, she found him wanting. The horse snorted in disapproval, and she rode on.

A commanding dark-skinned beauty if one could see past the layers of clothes with which she wrapped herself, Lady G rode second. Her horse a wild-eyed, wildfire-red stallion, untamed and unfettered yet she rode him with a practiced, graceful aplomb. An inviting flutter of her eyelashes framed the sidelong glances of her slow-moving eyes. Her lips curled with understanding. Romantic and ridiculous, she took peace from him, her vicinity smashed right into his nature. His eyes couldn't help but to follow her. Despite other horses coming into view, he always went back to her.

The third horsewoman was Omarosa astride an ashen horse with a grey, mottled mane. She carried a great sword. Drawing up, she paused at the far side of the lake. She dismounted from her horse and let it drink while she crouched beside it to scoop water into her mouth. Her vanity held out for conquest.

Lott wondered where Lady G had ridden off to.

The fourth rider was unknown to him. Atop a white horse, a bow slung around her and a crown atop her head. She rode with the confidence of a conqueror. His heart leapt at her approach, yet he allowed her to pass by also, too preoccupied with tracking the movements of Lady G.

"The thing about women is that we don't share. It's not in our nature," Omarosa said, her voice as clear and close as though she stood next to him. Its waters clear and deep, she glided across the surface of the lake. "I've spent a lifetime listening to men who seek prostitutes. Some blamed their wives for making them choose to spend their money to be with another. Others wept with guilt and shame, though that didn't stop them from having a head bob in their laps in car seat trysts. Others, in fits of machismo to mask their childishness, spoke in grandiose terms about their lives, bragged about themselves, wanting to be praised. Or they even turned violent. All to satisfy the demands of an ego to show they didn't actually need to pay for it."

"I–"

"A fierce battle, a war, wages within you. Greatness must be earned and not just by leaping to rescue every queen that comes along your path. This queen rescues herself." Omarosa turned on her heel, reducing the lake to little more than her personal catwalk. "Be careful when you help the women. Not all of them are damsels in distress. Most will take advantage of a young handsome knight."

"What about you?"

"I'll devour you." Her skin, slightly blue and puffy as if she'd been drowned, and long greenish hair, damp and drawn like seaweed. "I'll drag you straight into my underwater palace where my most prized knights await. And you, above all knights, should lead them."

Lott sprang up from his pillow. Disoriented, it took him a few minutes to recognize the confines of his room. Then he fell back onto his pillow, knowing he wouldn't be drifting back to sleep. So began Lott's daily work of beating back the past, haunted by dreams. He'd managed to work out an arrangement with the manager of the Speedway Lodge, formerly a Howard Johnson's, where he stayed, offering on-site security now that he worked second shift at FedEx. This filled his nights and left the early hours of the morning for him to sleep. Or run around with King. All the better knowing what waited for him in his dreams.

The 1950s-era lampshades cast the room with an orange pallor. All of his belongings fit into his back-pack or a drawer so he could pick up to leave with no notice should life carry him elsewhere. His root-lessness matched his restless spirit. The dream stirred up something else. Or perhaps the fact that he slept in his brother's shirt stirred the dream.

Lott stripped off the shirt, letting it catch on his shoulders, not admitting to not wanting to let him go. His brother, Morris. The shirt was a connection, though it had long lost any scent of him. It wasn't as if he had grown up laying awake at night one day hoping to work for FedEx (though he knew he couldn't be a UPS man in their shit-colored uni-forms). In another life, Lott dreamt of being a rapper. Music filled his head and songs played in color. Rhythms and beats formed his skin, and spat lyrics formed his palette. Pouring out his soul in his music, it was easy to notice the laughter, if not the pain be-hind the song; easy to be caught up in the dance, behind the beat, with the anger which could be marketed. Exploited.

"Your brother, now he was the smart one," Lott's mother said, her voice as clear in his head now as it had ever been any of the times she tore into him. The pain of his mother's indifference lashed out in desperate ways; undealt with, it ripped into those closest to him before turning inward like a metastacized cancer. *"Such a beautiful child."*

"All the neighbors said so." Lott knew her soliloquy by heart and filled in the next bit, even matching the cadence of her voice.

Her eyes narrowed to slits, the only warning, before she sprang up and slapped him for the disrespect. If he knew what was good for him, he would allow her her time, her story, and her way of telling and he'd listen to every word of it at her pace. The imprint of her hand stung his cheek.

"He had potential. Those fools he ran with… not two nickels' worth of sense between the lot of them. But they were drawn to my baby. My baby boy."

Morris was fourteen months younger than him.

Lott touched his face where the memory of pain lingered. He braced himself for his mother's next words. *"You and your music are a complete waste of time, effort, energy, and resources. What good did it do your brother? You let him down. You let the whole family down. You had one simple job. One damn thing I wanted you to do: look out for you brother. Guard that spark. But… damn."*

Now was that precarious time. She either found her way into a bottle of something cheap to get her head up, or she'd lash out, grabbing whatever was handy – broom, bottle, one time the cast-iron frying pan – and slam it into Lott. It wasn't his fault. He tried, he'd once tried to defend himself.

That was the last time he attempted to mount a defense. The frying pan slammed into him with the force of a hurled brick. Though maybe she'd spend the worst of this attack in her slap, perhaps taking enough of the edge off so she wouldn't explode. Knowing how not to catch the predator's attention, Lott stirred from his seated position, on the love seat – the threadbare material allowed the sharp corners of the couch to scrape him – arms and legs untangling not too quickly to draw undue attention, but with furious intent.

Not that he could point this out to his mother, but Morris was always half a fool himself. Always running around playing gangsta. At the ripe age of eleven...

... talking shit about jacking fools up and giving paybacks. On one shoulder, a six-pointed star with the letters B, G, D, and N in four of the points; on the other, two crossed three-pronged pitchforks drawn in permanent marker. They strolled through the parking garage next to Market Square Arena. The lot mostly deserted, they trolled about for hood ornaments to take off. The parking lot wound about, serpentine concrete walls little more than waist high. They often spit on those coming up the lower levels when more people were around.

"I'm straight up Black Gangsta Disciple." The words echoed with a boom with the strange acoustics of the concrete structure. He didn't notice the hard-faced diesel brothers up the way behind him. Lott elbowed him in the side and ticked his chin toward them, warning him to be easy. But he would have none of it and didn't care that, too late, he had their full attention.

"*Da fuck? Say that shit again,*" a brickhouse of a brother said. Wide as he was tall, a poorly grown goatee outlined lips, his mouth as big as Lott's fist.

"*He didn't say nothing,*" Lott stepped between them and his brother.

"*Wha? Nah, for real, what did he say?*" the second one said in a measured tone meant to convey calm and complete reasonableness. Lott heard the echo of a snake's rattle in the timbre of his voice.

"*Nothing,*" Lott repeated.

"*I ain't scared,*" Morris said. "*My boys got my back. Black Gangsta Disciples.*"

"*Oh yeah? Spit your lit.*"

"*What?*" Morris asked.

"*A prayer better come off your lips real soon, boy.*" The first man crowded Morris, the other barring him from Lott.

"*I don't…*"

The two men caught each other's eyes and upended Morris over the side of the parking garage. They each held fast to a foot.

"*Say that shit again,*" the first man demanded.

"*Say it again and I will end you,*" the second man dared.

Morris thrashed about, the street loomed beneath him. Lott punched at the two men. "*Let him go!*"

"*Say that shit again. What set you claim?*" the first asked again, ignoring Lott's swats.

"*Black Gangsta Disciple.*"

Moments.

The surreal passage of time, life-changing instants occur with Lott frozen or with things moving so fast he couldn't *react. Lies clouded memories, all dark whispers unchecked as guilt and shame longed to take root. Perhaps he sensed his mother's favoritism and wished it extinguished. Perhaps the need to finally be seen was born from wanting to see his brother gone. Perhaps part of him resented his brother. Perhaps any of that held him to his spot.*

The two brutes released him then leaned over the concrete balcony further to better study the piece of street art they had just created. Morris's cry unfroze Lott. He tore ass down the main stairs. By the time he reached the ground level, a crowd had already gathered. Starlings bobbed around it like curious children, scattering at his approach. Morris's face was an agonal mask, lips drawn upward. A grotesque statue with his arms rested at unnatural angles to the body. His jaws hinged. The blood soaked his clothes black. Eyes open, fixed on…

… him, filled with rage and resentment. Nothing close to the love one would expect from their move. Accusing, blame-riddled.

Lott didn't know what or how to feel.

Sadly, it wasn't even the worst thing he'd seen in gangsta life. He studied the scars on his hands. Remembering how Lady G held his hand, ran her hands along them, he thought about how they matched. All their scars, they were a patchwork.

Prez sought out craziness. His dreams were all fat rolls of dollar bills, girls on each arm, and respect accorded from the neighborhood when he came through. The drugs gave him purpose and focus: get money, get high. Life was a simple equation. Yet nothing fixed that torn-up sense within him, nothing stitched together the fragments of himself he hadn't realized had been rent asunder. The abandonment of his father. The shunning by teachers. His mother's misplaced rage. The low value he placed on himself. Knowing the whys didn't help.

Reduced to a collection of emaciated bones shrink-wrapped with grayish skin, Prez writhed in silent panic on the couch, the sheets kicked off and around his ankles. Wide-eyed disorientation and mouth half-opened in an unvoiced scream, he looked absolutely lost. Like he didn't know who he was, where he was, or how he got there. His arms flailed in sudden panic, attack, or defense landing weak punches. Then he pissed himself. Lacking the strength to put his foot back under the sheets, he never imagined himself sinking to such a point. Bitter. Broken. Hurting, too bad to see who he was or how he could live.

No different than King, really, if King were truly honest with himself. Most of his days were like this, even if he gave no indication of it on the outside. This was his daily internal war.

Mouth twitching, eyes jumpy, hands shaking, Prez was a ghost of the boy King had moved into Big Momma's house so many months ago, barely recognizable. The boy's feet drew King's attention. Both were ashy, but one was ragged and raw as if it had been caught in a food processor. King felt compelled to wash them. Getting a towel from his bathroom, he wiped the excrement from Prez's feet. During the best of times, Prez slept a lot during his detox. King had brought him back to his place, explaining to Lady G that he owed it to Prez. He never quite found the words to explain how he blamed himself for failing Prez as a friend and as an example. As a leader. That perhaps he could find redemption for them both if he could see Prez through this dark time. Walk beside him through the worst of it, even if it meant wiping shit from the boy's feet.

His sheets soaked through, his pillow smelling of thick sweat and the bite of body odor, Prez's lucid dreams bubbled up, little more than memory fragments.

"How much you make on a package?" Prez asked, *slouched against the couch with warm butter coursing through his brain.*

"Why? You lookin'?" Naptown Red asked. *He had once waved a gun around in a misunderstanding with his live-in girlfriend not too long ago. By all rights, po-po should've shot him on the spot the way he was carrying on. Instead, the tale growing with each re-telling, he found a measure of a reputation as six officers wrestled him to the ground. He was out in less than a day.*

"Maybe."

"So you want to get into dealing this nasty shit?" The *two passed the pipe back and forth.* *"It's one thing to dabble in this shit on the side…"*

"Recreational use and shit," Prez repeated from previous schooling.

"Exactly. It's a whole other deal getting in on the business side of things. You sure about it?"

Prez took another hit from the pipe. "Yeah, money. Let's do this shit."

With Night out of the picture, the crew dissolved into chaotic disarray, patches of crews working independently and sometimes at odds with one another. Prez was only the mildly ambitious sort. While he branched out with his ill-fated ESG – Eggs, Sausage, and Grits – venture with Trevant, he didn't feel comfortable striking out on his own. Security rested in working under someone like Night and Green. Or Red.

Red wandered back in from the bedroom, closing his cell phone as he flopped back down. Prez offered him the pipe again, but Red waved him off.

"Folks'll be by in a few." He took a tone of sudden seriousness. "I give you my connect, it's my ass on the line. I have to vouch for you."

"I'm straight. No need to talk to me like I'm some fish."

"School's in session now, boy. If we gonna do this, you need to be able to handle your business. Never let the other guy get up on you. Never trust anyone. Never do your own product. Never do anything out of charity. Out here, in life, it's all about business."

"Are there any always?" Prez leaned forward to appear intent, but didn't know where to put his arms. He almost tottered over.

"Always be strapped." Red snapped open a baggy and

filled it about half an inch deep. "Typical customer, here's what you give them."

"The baggy looks kinda pale."

"The more on the hook they are, the smaller the baggies you give them."

"That's cold, man."

"That's business. It's all about that dollar, son."

The dream memories churned in fits and spurts. First steps, twelfth steps, whatever step it was that put Prez on the path to this couch, trembling like an errant leaf in a fall breeze. Maybe the step came earlier, with his hollowed-out self. The hunger was pure, elemental, and he knew how to sate it. This he could control; fix the outside and the insides would take care of themselves. Stumbling through back alleys, searching for ground scores hoping that food, maybe a burger, might be found discarded but still edible. He missed the days when McDonald's had their Beanie Babies and whole meals went to waste in bags as patrons bought Happy Meals just for the toy prize.

His head seemed too big for his gaunt frame, giving the illusion that his thin neck was unable to support its weight. His cheekbones stood out above washed-out and cracked lips. Splotches dotted his skin. How much time had passed? Hours? Days? Weak and still shivering in bed, sleep eluded him. He clawed at his skin as if wanting to scrape it off. Nothing eased the suffering. It seemed cruel, a punishment too harsh for his crime. He was guilty of only wanting to feel better, of wanting to feel complete. Happy. Wanting the hurt to stop. Ashamed and terrified, King was the only person he could trust.

"Let me out of here," Prez said to the shadowed form he glimpsed through tear-blurred, half-open eyes.

"I can't do it, Prez. And you don't want me to."

King daubed the perspiration sheen from the boy's forehead, a little too sternly, definitely lacking a mother's tender touch.

Breathing through his open mouth, Prez's thrashes grew weaker. The smell of him filled the room, his sweat soaked through his shirt and sheets, a mildewed stink. Prez told himself over and over that he was going to leave all this behind him, all the thugging and gangsta posing. Even before that last deal went so wrong.

"What the fuck?" Red put fire to the blunt, drew in its smoke, closed his eyes to let it do its work, and blew out a thick stream of smoke.

"What's up?" Prez turned from the television, a rerun of some cop show on TNT. Naptown Red hunched over a table, stacks of bills in front of him and a few scattered tester packets. More than a couple he had sampled himself.

"We short. Nearly a G." The patches of his face seemed to swirl, a Rorschach in varying shades of brown. He ran his hand through his dry, straightened hair.

"*What you mean?*"

"*You stupid, motherfucker? Fathead done shorted us. Trying to punk us out.*" Fathead Wallace was one of their new distributors. Red was uncertain about putting him on, but Prez vouched for him, saying they went back years, both having squat in the same places off and on.

"*Let's go talk to him. I bet we can straighten things out.*"

"*Talk? What did I tell you? 'Never let the other guy get up on you.' Anyone who tries, we got to fuck up or else we the ones who look weak.*"

"*But there might be a simple mistake.*"

"*You got a few hundred in your pockets you forgot to give me?*" Red slipped his Taurus into his dip.

"*No.*"

"*You got a few more ounces have gone unsold?*"

"*No.*" Yes. Actually, they got smoked up behind that old burned-out church. Violating Red's other rule, "never do your own product." But, as much as Fathead was his boy and all, he wasn't about to admit to stealing from Red. Might as well cut off his own hands.

"*You up for fucking someone up or are you one of them all-talk niggas?*"

Prez never wanted to be thought of as weak. Not that he wanted to be one of those hollow-eyed brothers, like Green or Junie, folks so ate up by the streets they had nothing left inside. He didn't need to be hard like that or have his name ring out like that. He was no gangsta by any means, but he was no punk neither. Played out as weak, he might as well not show his face around as everyone

*would be seeking to get over on him. So all the way over to
Fathead's place, Prez talked about how he was going to
fuck up Fathead. Punched his own hand in a pantomime
of a beat-down. Made the noises of someone taking a
punch then pleading for them to stop. Talking all kinds of
shit about "naw nigga, you shouldn't have played us. You
earned this. You better let everyone know not to cross us."*

*Naptown Red listened patiently. He'd sparked up before
they left, getting his head right before going off on a mission. Tooled up, his mind was definitely intent on getting
either his money, his product, or someone's ass.*

*"This the right place?" They stood in front of a white
shotgun house, which stood out on the block from the other
more Arts and Crafts era-inspired houses.*

"Yeah."

*Red tamped out a cigarette, lit it, and took a long pull.
Leaving the cigarette dangling from his lip, he stepped back
and kicked the door in.*

*Two brothers reclined on a couch, jumping to attention
at Red and Prez's entrance. A skinny white kid missing
one eye, struggled to find his sea legs. He knocked over an
opened pizza box with only a quarter of a pie left. A half-
dozen empty soldiers of Blatz toppled along the table,
which Prez remembered Fathead once calling "the Muska-
tel of beer."*

*"Which one of you motherfuckers is Fathead?" Red
asked, as if more than one of them was missing an eye. No
one spoke up. Red glanced back at Prez, then traced his eye
line to the skinny boy. Prez sheepishly turned away. Fathead curled up his slip at the sting of betrayal. "You got*

the rest of my money, bitch?"

"What money? We straight," Fathead said. Fine scars framed his fake eye. He'd seen a movie where some dude kept having different glass eyes, like one was a yellow smiley face. Fathead wanted to draw a skull and crossbones on his. That would be some tripped out shit.

"Naw, motherfucker, we far from straight. We about a grand from straight."

"You better take that up with your boy," Fathead said, hands raised and in plain sight. "Came over here, I told him the package looked a little light. His eyes all fucked up, I knew he'd been hitting it. I ain't tryin' to rip nobody off. I'm just out to earn. And I can't earn if I burn my connect straight out the gate."

Red calculated the P/F, profits to fiending, ratio. Fathead might have been up on pizza and cheap beer, maybe a blunt or two, but that was it. Prez itched his forearm, eyes swimming in his head. In a whirl, Red grabbed the neck of one of the bottles and smashed it against Prez's skull.

"Ho shit!" Fathead skittered up the back of his couch, not taking his eyes from the scene.

Prez clutched his head and called out to the Lord, apparently now on a first-name basis with him. Naptown Red snapped his knife to life, poised to carve out his missing money from Prez's narrow behind when the sound of a high grinding metal whine pierced the room.

A seam of light split the air. Red and Fathead pushed past him, tumbling out the door. The poor fool, Prez, turned back and received a claw across his face for his troubles. Blood. So much blood. A small creature pulled its lips

*back to reveal teeth like a shark's. It removed its cap to
daub the stain of blood left by Prez. That was the last
image he remembered – the row of sharpened teeth –
before King found him.*

Prez knew all about the twelve-step programs. He
tried them as a condition of getting food from
churches. He hated the fact that churches always
made him listen to their spiel before doing anything
for him. They couldn't just give him a free meal,
couldn't just take one look at him and see that he
was in need. He always got stuck on that third step
of the program. They always talked about a higher
power, but prayer struck him as rather desperate.
Crying out to an invisible friend who obviously
didn't give two shits about him because if He were
any kind of friend, He'd have never let him get as
low as He did.

The image of Fathead's "what the fuck?" grimace
as if betrayed flashed in his head.

"I don't know what to say. Even if I believe in
Him," Prez said.

"Then tell Him that. And what you want," King
said.

"God, I don't believe in you, but I need help. I
can't keep going like this. I need help." Broken,
wondering when he'd feel whole again, faith was the
only thread left to carry him through. And hopefully
not unravel the tapestry of his life. He didn't think
he'd have the strength to fight through the difficult

moments without the faith that things would get better.

King nodded for him to continue.

"Dad, please." And he didn't know if he were talking to God or his own father. "Please help me. Why won't you talk to me?"

CHAPTER NINE

The eastside of Indianapolis, a model of urban decay under the city's knowing eye, was left like a corpse, while people spoke of what a shame it was. With nothing for them to do, no jobs, where poor folks lived. Only a couple of places existed for kids to hang out. A Boys' Club down on 30th Street, but soon as a kid acted a fool, they kicked him out. No sit down, no nothing. Bam! If they had their way at school, soon as a kid bucked, they kicked him out. No sit down, no nothing. Gone! Kicked out of school. Kicked out of the Boys' Club. So with Momma at work and no daddy around, they were left to sit around and play video games all day, talk on the phone, get on the computer, or run out in the streets. Where Colvin could prey on them.

Colvin radiated a bloodless calm as he stepped with the carriage of authority. Deep, hollow eyes in constant assessment, creating a mental checklist of who was doing what or rather who wasn't. Melle had become one of his top earners, the little man due to be promoted. A young hothead in a wife beater and baggy blue jean shorts, with the scarecrow build of a krumper. He had shaved off his wild, unchecked Afro because Five-O could identify him from blocks away. Noles was a slack-jawed plate of hot mess who only sprang to work when he knew someone in charge of his wallet was around. One of Colvin's white boys, with hair in a Caesar cut, a razor-thin goatee and a random growth of a beard only over his Adam's apple. He dressed like a redneck business executive. Otherwise, he did as little as possible while talking a big game about his exploits, usually taking credit for other people's work.

The abandoned Camlann Apartment building on Oriental Avenue, three stories of what was once a showcase place. Many organizations had put in bids to rehab the building, but the owner refused to sell and refused to do anything with it except allow it to wither. So the city declared eminent domain and it was due to be razed. The lawsuits and counter lawsuits had delayed the process, allowing it to further fall into dangerous dilapidation. Left to politicians, it would stand for years, a testimony to pain and suffering and lost hope.

The informal gallery smelled of burnt crack, urine, vomit, sweat, and other noxious effluvia. With mattresses strewn about, the apartment served as both flop house and sexual bartering place. On the stairwell and landings, overseen by Noles, a group of young men stood about, guards at a check point, drinking and smoking while doing their duty. An endless sea of shadows in thick down jackets and work boots. The unventilated chamber concentrated the vile smell. Puddles of an unknown liquid pooled, stepped around by all passers-by.

"Tell him," a young red-headed woman said, her eyes aged and used up, her skin dusty. Her breasts hung low in her grungy gray T-shirt, once pink with the word "Hotness" now missing its "t", she remained plumpish despite her habit, loose flesh hanging with a collected slackness, cradling her three year-old.

"I'll suck your dick," the toddler said on cue.

The woman beamed with pride, her eyes alight with the intimation that the offer was no mere party trick. It wasn't the first time Colvin had such an offer. A few years back, a lady traded her nieces for $50 of crack. It was a rolling party for six months, molesting them at will until he got bored and passed them on to his crew. Eventually they were sold to The Pall as street earners. Colvin stepped past the woman, leaving her for Noles to deal with. His appointment was with Mulysa.

The bare bulb burned to life at the tug of the dangling string that scattered dust in its beam. Stripped down to his shirt, Mulysa sat cross-legged in the center of the room, his bottom bitch next to him in easy reach. Bowls of herbs and holy water were placed in a sort of unholy feng shui arrangement apparent only to him.

"We 'bout ready?" Colvin asked.

"Damn, nukka. This shit ain't easy." Mulysa opened his eyes, ending his prayer and meditation.

"Don't act like I'm one of them knuckleheads you got working outside. I'm from a bloodline of magic and not easily impressed with a summoner."

It was a quiet dig, fully intended as Mulysa heard it, as a slight meant to humble him and keep him in his place. Colvin didn't want him to think too much of his gifts or what he did. His service was expected. His obedience was expected. His talents brought to the table a given, or else why bring him in?

"A-ight then." Mulysa chafed nonetheless, not anxious to please or prove his worth, but to simply be respected. And he'd get that respect.

Lacking an original grimoire or anything, only what he could glean from the internet, he nevertheless took ritual magic very seriously. Especially since it served as an additional source of (undeclared and thus untaxed by Colvin) income for him. He didn't consider himself a major-league summoner, but he knew enough to be able to call up a spirit, any supernatural force, really, and subjugate it to his will. More or less. Enough to keep them from tearing him to shreds like so much used Kleenex. He fondled his bitch, studying the way the golden light of the brazier reflected from it. While visualizing flames, he dragged the blade against his floorboards, carving a magic circle with the knife as a barrier against the outside and to help him focus.

Incanting in an old tongue, he mimicked the words more than pronounced them. They almost seemed to form themselves and spring from his lips, as if all they needed was the attempt to stir them for them to finish the articulation. The words came easy to Mulysa.

"Come in the stillness,
Come in the night
Come soon and bring delight
Beckoning, beckoning, left hand and right
Come now, come tonight
Come malice, come; come malice, come.
Peter stands at the gate,
Waiting for your vengeful hate. Come malice, come!"

In his mind, he ran around a fairy ring on the first night of the new moon. Alone and thus without embarrassment. Nothing he could do around these nukkas without ridicule. Simple motherfuckers never cracked a book unless there was a dollar in it for them. They didn't understand power. Or the sacrifices of what it took to lead.

Music and laughter bubbled up from the ground. A trickle of green light began as a teardrop suspended in mid-air, pooling before trailing down. The pulse thickened, a seam cut by invisible scissors.

Colvin's heart leapt. The panorama resonated with an ancient part of his fey heritage. The sounds, the smells recalled a pageantry his life longed for, opened a door to memories, blood memories old and familiar. Then came the tramp of men marching, the sound near and distinct.

A troop of men, if men such creatures be called, emerged. Red Caps. None taller than three feet high, with wiry builds other than their bulbous bellies. Their iron boots ground into the wooden floorboards with an impatient scrape. Long and curved, claws sharp as steel carried slings which allowed them to throw stones from faraway positions. Long stockinged caps, faded to a dull pink, covered brushwire hair. Ragged, pointed teeth within drawn, gaunt faces gave them a sullen quality. Except for the poisonous glare of their red eyes. Every time Colvin laid eyes on them, he squashed the need to laugh at their absurd appearance. Much like the pygmy tribes of Africa, their diminutive appearance belied the fact that they were among the most feared warriors of any tribe. Red Caps made homes in crumbling castles and haunted places with a reputation for evil events. And nothing was more evil than the neglected poor.

"I have a job for them," Colvin said.

"Omarosa?" Mulysa asked, but got no reply. They were long overdue to get payback over the mess with Broyn.

"Want I should lead them?"

"I got it." The implication being that he didn't trust Mulysa with a task he deemed too delicate.

"I summoned them, I should lead them."

"Who have you ever led? Don't strain yourself, I got this. Your gifts are better served elsewhere. Make sure our other talent is ready to go."

"A-ight." Part of Mulysa seethed. He'd risen as far as he was able and wasn't about to be trusted with more. His bubbling anger needed to be vented. Someone had to hurt.

A squirrel bounded along the black, cracked pavement of the sidewalk at a house just a little south of the Phoenix Apartments. Rumor had it that this was once Dred's mother's home. Rumor had it that Dred's mother had a bit of a falling out of some sort with her son and hadn't been seen since. Rumor had it that the home was once one of his convenient banks. To the non-discerning eye, it was just another boarded-up two-story. The squirrel stopped, indifferent as it sniffed the air, then scampered up a pole and ran along an overhead wire. It hopped over the pair of tied sneakers dangling from it. Again, it paused, this time it chirped, a squawk reminiscent of a chicken, its tail raised like a cobra striking the air.

A tree hung low over the roof, its branches scraping the shingles and brushing the overhead lines. A group of three young men cloistered along the sidewalk. Today's topics steered towards trick, lesbian bitches, LeBron James, the latest product, exaggerated tales of Omarosa, whispers about Dred, Young Jeezy, and rims.

Sir Rupert dropped nuts on them.

"What the fuck?!?" They threw up their arms to shield themselves.

"Ah, Sir Rupert." Merle snuck past the distracted lookouts. "Ever the gentlemen's gentlemen."

It was said that when the angels fell, the ones who fell on land became faeries and the ones who fell into the sea became selkies. It was said that he was born the son of an incubus and a virtuous woman, though he doubted anyone had ever once considered the mad harridan Mab virtuous. A tale well spoke, however, once said that she met a priest and asked him if there were any way for her soul to be saved. "Of course," he said, "none are beyond saving. Why don't you say the Our Father with me. 'Our Father which art in heaven…'" After a hesitant tremble, she opened her mouth and began speaking. "Our father which wert in heaven…" She caught herself, midprayer to the fallen one. The priest, mouth agape, watched as she ran off in tears. Later it was whispered that upon his birth, Merle was entrusted to that priest at birth who hurried him to a baptismal fount.

Merle adjusted the fitting of his aluminum foil cap. The voices said a lot of things and it was harder and harder to sift through them all and divine the ones worth listening to. Merle delighted in mystery and causing wonder. Wise and subtle with the gift of prophecy, he knew the dark corners of the human heart and moved, like a dream. And dreams were what brought him here.

"I feel like I am walking backwards through my life, passing myself on the way down." Merle fingered the small stone in his pocket. He'd found it at the first scene where the bodies at the Phoenix Apartments had been discovered. "I see angels," he repeated to himself. After he heard snippets of Prez's story he choose to investigate that scene. He wished he'd been able to examine the bodies like he did in the old times. Searching for a hairless spot in its side or any lump beneath the skin, any sign that they had been trow-shot. The strange pellet slipped back into his pocket. According to the old ways, anyone who found an elf arrow was immune from their hurt if they kept it with them at all times. If it were given away, the generous soul was liable to be kidnapped away by the faeries. "Youth is primal. And wasted."

Though not along a ley line, a natural place of power, Merle was still drawn to this place. If he thought of magic as a lake that folks dipped from, leaving ripples in the wake of their use, he could track back the riptides created from massive use. Someone was pumping like a lift station from here. The familiar click of a switchblade springing to life froze Merle in his tracks. The blade then closed. Closer still, it snapped open again and clicked closed. Nearer still, it snapped open again. Merle turned. Baylon held his dagger like a sword pointed toward the ground.

"You're certainly the biggest fairy I have ever seen," Merle said. "I will scoff at you with a slight French accent."

Baylon smelled of the grave and atrophied muscles, the stench of bed sores, the mildewed tang of
body odor and spilled food. Grass stained his once-
white Fila jogging suit, as did dirt and the grime of
trash bins. He gestured with the weapon for Merle
to walk toward the rear door. Once a faithful lieutenant, he didn't know why he stayed with Dred.
They were boys from way back and there was a time
Baylon would have done anything for him. Back in
the early days after joining the Egbo Society. Him,
Griff, Dred, Night and Rellik. When they were one
huge family. When they had it all and thought it
would last forever. They were living the dream. Dred
brought him on board, with the lure of the two of
them starting and building their little slice of the
kingdom together. Baylon imagined the two of them
weathering any storm and fighting back enemies of
all stripes. Together. The two of them. Dred provided
the vision, Baylon made it happen; the head and the
facilitator. He supposed some of that was hero worship, with the way Dred swooped in and was there
for him after the death of King's cousin, Michelle. A
terrible misunderstanding which ended when her
life did and was the death knell of Baylon and King's
friendship. Dred was there, picked up the pieces of
his life, and gave him purpose and direction again.
Saving him from his darkness.

Then Dred stole it all from him.

It had to be Dred. One moment Dred was in a
wheelchair from a bullet wound Baylon blamed

himself for; the next he walked around as if the bullet had never plunged into his flesh, split muscle, vessels, and nerves; while Baylon became trapped between life and death like a zuvembie. He didn't know what Dred did, but the life, the vitality of his essence drained from him. Dred never denied responsibility, hell, he didn't deign to answer Baylon at all.

These days, Dred went his own way. Baylon seemed almost an inconvenience to him now, an uncomfortable reminder of what used to be. Yet he shuffled about, still followed him around, still connected to Dred. Still jumping to obey his orders. All from behind the scenes, like a secret Dred was ashamed to share with the rest of his crew. A faithful dog, though even the most faithful dog could only be kicked so many times before it didn't come home again.

Baylon ushered Merle up the stairs, recalling the days before the transformation, before the bullet changed everything. Though inside prison, Rellik had been promoted to general, overseeing all of Indiana. Neither Dred nor Night were connected to any gang, but came up under his colors. Night was reluctant to bring in Dred. Too unknown, but bowed because of the flex to his step and the power he represented. He learned the rituals, the prayers, and they never realized how much he knew.

Merle entered the chamber. Smoke slinked along the floor, thin wisps dissipating with each step. The clouds reverberated through his bones with a stony chill.

Dred mastered the dragon's breath, or what was left of the residual embers within the earth after the passing of the dragon. The age of magic had been pronounced dead many times; every time the rumors proved premature. The age of science was at its zenith, but it too now waned though many hadn't realized it. But Merle did. Just as he recognized the smoke ritual.

The Iboga was a small perennial shrub of the Apocynaceae family used by the Bwiti cult. Its roots contained a powerful hallucinogen that provided a mystical experience. The root tasted of copper, bitter to the tongue, which numbed the inner part of his mouth. With bloodshot eyes ringed by fatigue, Dred remained awake for the entire night, accompanied by a state of euphoria with hallucinations. The room blurred, as if lost in a fugue of heat waves, then slowly faded. Dred's heart slowed. He matched his breathing to theirs, those whose dreams he wished to intrude upon. Nudging a thread, not shaping the tapestry, he willed a dream into them. Then, as if sensing Merle's presence, his heart sped back up and his attention focused. He returned to the living presence, a leopard-swift predator with a new scent.

"We need to talk."

Any abandoned house was fair game for a squat. At Washington and Oriental Streets, the Camlann

Apartments weren't the worst Tristan and Iz ever stayed in. They shared their last place with two other couples, with one room lined with a tarp to collect feces.

Tristan passed a few fiends who staggered about, zombies to the pipe. A couch had been discarded by one of the nearby homes and now was in steady use on the front lawn. Squatters had a lifestyle of running: running from police, family, someone they owed money. A portly redhead, with a mischievous smile and bright blue eyes that never met her eyes, stumbled with her lumbering gait. She was shy, except for the occasional passing bon mot. With a snaggle-tooth smile, she wrapped a belt around her arm and prepared to launch.

The unimaginative brown eyes of her male companion tracked her movements with all the dullness of a cow chewing. Nearing a freshly pressed and over-starched white shirt with loud patterned tie, Khaki pants, and hair laid flat on his head in a Caesar style, he must've been going to or returning from an interview. Scratching his arms, he needed to shave the ridiculous patch of hair at his throat. A baby cried from down the alley. Tristan tried not to think about it though alleys always managed to trigger memories. They appeared different during the daytime, different but the same. She'd been on her knees in enough of them. A dick inside her mouth while two others waited their turn. Boys playing at manhood, passing the time it took their friend to finally

ejaculate in her mouth by calling her a litany of degrading names. Nausea welled at the dehumanizing
memory, more like a typhoon of emotion given a
physical thrust. She gave that part of herself to feed
their habit. Pussy was currency and it was better
than being a career baby momma. The things people
did in the service of love and need.

Love was every bit as potent as heroin. Not even
love, most of the time but all of the underlying feelings folks called being in love. The desire, the
jealousy, the possessiveness, the need – when you
broke down love, it was a junkie's craving. All-con-
suming, filled your very being and devoured your
mind to the point you couldn't think straight. And
was willing to do just about anything to please or
provide. The nearly chemical impulse some people
had on her heart, their absence could spiral her into
depression if she didn't hear from them. Her mind
occupied itself with the anxiousness of wondering
where they were, what they were doing, and who
they were doing it with, addicted to the motions of
romance. Perhaps just the idea. Still, she needed,
craved to hear Iz's voice.

Wrapped within a hoodie with a black pearl and a
heart, dagger through it, over a long tank top, down
to mid-thigh, with too tight, skinny jeans tucked into
boots, red accented Iz's hair, lip gloss, and eyelashes.
Her long legs were unhappy at rest. Tristan loved her
smooth white skin. Dropping the bag of McDonald's,
Tristan snuck up behind Iz and wrapped her arms

around her and held her close. Iz stopped what she was doing, closed her eyes, and snuggled into the embrace. And they danced.

"You didn't call me on your way home," Tristan said.

"What, you need me to check in with you?"

"No, just like to hear you is all. Like to keep you company while you walking. Know you OK."

"It can be a little smothering," Iz said.

"I just want to protect you."

"What were you going to do? Put on a cape and fly to wherever I was?" Iz turned to face her, not breaking the embrace.

"You are protecting me. Just you being around makes me feel safe. I just don't always need you so…"

"Close? Am I that bad?" Tristan asked with an un-characteristic ping of hurt in her voice. Like a child who worked so hard on a clay ashtray for her father, only to have him dismiss it as ugly and useless. And her filling in the unspoken rest "just like me."

"It's not bad. I enjoy spending time with you. I just need some space of my own. Room to make my own mistakes."

"I'm not going to apologize for being there for you."

"No one told you to. Just loosen up some." Iz swatted her arm.

"I can do that."

People like Iz needed people like Tristan. People to stop others from hurting and misusing them, no matter who, even if it were their own father. People to watch out for them when they ran away from home, changed their name, and carved out a new life at a new school. People who did whatever it took to provide money and shelter for them, or save money for community college (Ivy Tech or even IUPUI); even if it meant their own degradation. Until they were able to put their other learned skills to better use. Her blades weighed heavily in her jacket.

"That man came by here looking for you." Iz broke their embrace. She had her serious business face on.

"Who? Mulysa?"

"Yeah." Iz refused to let his name drip from her lips. "I don't like him coming around here."

"I told him not to. Especially when I'm not here."

"I don't like the way he looks at me."

"He looks at everyone that way," Tristan said.

"Not you."

"Only cause he wants to keep his eyes." Memories of the alley scraped her. "Anyway, he might have work for me."

"I don't want you working for him. I don't like what it does to you."

"Now who's being over-protective?"

"I'm not kidding, Tris."

"Knock, knock." Mulysa announced from the door. Though not physically all that large, he filled the entranceway, imposing himself in its space.

"Speak the devil's name." Iz also hated the way Mulysa thought he could come and go as he pleased.

Tristan had her blades in her hand as reflex. The blades twirled between her fingers with an easy grace, an implied threat. Mulysa cold-eyed her, not daring her to make a move, but letting her know with the deadness in his eyes that he didn't care either way.

"What you need, Mul?" Tristan tucked her blades back into her jacket.

"Got a job for you."

Iz sucked her teeth, grabbed the bag of McDonald's, and left the room.

Mulysa's gaze followed her out of the room, sizing up her assets like a top piece of sirloin. He mentally licked his lips. He wanted Izzy to himself and then in his budding stable. Jealous of Tristan getting to lay with her and run her tongue into that fine pussy. He pictured himself, ramming his tongue into Iz's ass, turning her out for real.

"Mul. Get your eyes off my girl."

"Your girl."

"My. Girl. Mine."

The emphasis of the words, the weight of violence in them, were the opening salvos in the battle of heart. Tristan stood there, waiting for him to move aside. Mulysa had no choice but to finish his business. To back down, to slink away, meant she'd won without a fight. Most battles were won through the power of presence, of intimidation, reducing life out here to a perpetual pissing match. No wonder every street and alley smelled of stale urine.

"Whatever, nukka," Mulysa said, turning aside. The thing about security heads was that they were always happiest in times of war. Despite Colvin's lack of people skills, he understood that. Friend or foe, war was war and he wouldn't mind a chance to go toe-to-toe with Tristan and her hard-bodied self neither. She was heavily muscled like a man, but he'd jailed before and believed his ten inches of pipe might turn her around on the whole pussy-munching thing.

Tristan led them to a room on the other side of the kitchen area, further away from Iz. The hallway went down two steps and wound around the corner past another door which the city had sealed with plywood. An alcove filled with pellets of feces she hoped belonged to a cat. Streams of empty donut packages, papers, wrappers, moldy magazines. Clothes and soiled towels from previous occupants. Shafts of light burrowed through the sides of the boarded-up window. The room was private enough from ears seen and unseen.

"What the job?" Tristan asked.

"Meet me up at that lot across from the fairgrounds. We can hook up there and I'll break it down. Tomorrow. Eleven."

"In the morning?"

"Shit, girl, I ain't trying to roll out before noon."

"I don't know."

"Pays two large." Actually three, but if she went for the two, he'd pocket the difference. "Two and a half."

"You don't even know the job."

"I know you," Tristan said.

"Done. Don't forget your gear. We gonna squad up for real, nukka."

"Good times."

Tristan watched Mulysa leave before joining Iz in their living room. Milk crates and old chairs, three backpacks in the corner. Tristan had two, one with her work gear in it. Iz ignored her entrance, chewinglanguidly on a French fry. She ate the small ones first, saving the long ones, her favorites, for last.

"I got a thing tomorrow night," Tristan said.

"I heard."

"You have to be careful about what you hear."

"Then don't do business in my house."

"Our."

"Our house." Iz offered her a now-cold French fry. Tristan ate it from her fingertips.

Love, especially the young, tempestuous variety, had a way of complicating life.

CHAPTER TEN

Stalking the periphery of the apartment on the floor below the penthouse some of his boys used as a party place, as a general Rellik sometimes felt reduced to middle-management duties. Shit, downright janitor's duties. Rellik had always been ridden hard, hard enough to be pushed into a bad place. That constant grind wore on a person, eroding like wind-scourged trees rather than smoothed by sandpaper. Glass, trash, used condoms, all the usual remains from an all-night party. He needed to send guys over to clean the place or Sister Jackie, the building community liaison, would be pissed. She could make things difficult, getting the tenants riled up, bringing in police attention, complaining to the superintendent or property owner. With her flat, broad nose and swollen lips, dark rings under her eyes, she had the face of a woman smacked with a 2X4. With the body of a mack truck, broad and immovable, she had a stroke a few years back which didn't seem to slow her down much. The burdens of management weighed on his shoulders as the managerial woes of a bored CEO weren't exactly what he imagined the life of a king being. He had to work around community leaders like Pastor Winburn, or deal with Sister Jackie who was like a one-woman labor union. It was simple business: don't piss off mommas and the neighborhood complains less. He wanted to be more than a criminal, so he'd work with politicos, community groups, churches looking to turn gang members' lives around, whoever. He made a mental note to assign some of the peewees to clean the building, such menial jobs being exactly in their job description. Their asses would jump if he said so. Funny how they could run his errands yet couldn't be bothered to work at McDonald's as being too good to earn minimum wage or be bossed around.

"They here?" Rellik asked.

"Most of them," Garlan said. They stood in the landing of the stairwell, overlooking the gathering. "Some of these fools wouldn't know a watch to save they life."

"They lack discipline."

"I got it handled." The implication clear that if Garlan couldn't handle his people, Rellik would find someone who would.

By his count, Rellik had nearly a hundred folks – peewees, soldiers, and wannabes – to coordinate. The way a man looks at a boy and sizes him up, he needed to pull together his whole crew to see what he was working with. Which meant he needed a space to hold meetings. When he ran his crew, he brought in a few of his boys he'd known since high school. These days, with so many doing jail, dead, or out the game entirely, his officer crew was pretty small since he trusted so few. Garlan was solid and was a liaison between him and his unfamiliar crew. He thought it would be a good idea to hold it in a church. Pastor Winburn was one of those do-good types always out for an opportunity to build up relationships with Rellik's type. With such a convergence of opportunity and need, he was practically obligated to have this meeting at Good News. As long as the Pastor minded his own when it was time to get down to business.

This summit meeting saved him the trouble of visiting all the crews separately. His security detail, led by Garlan, drove ahead to give them all clear from rival gangs. At his arrival, one member, Rok, collected all the drugs and cash and had them escorted from the scene so there was never a direct link to Rellik. When a dealer went to prison or was killed, the crew took care of his family. It lessened the worry about a coup, fostering loyalty to the crew.

Over the next few hours, with Garlan a step behind him high on the rush of power, Rellik grilled his crew. He asked about any loss of regulars, measuring the impact of encroachment by other crews. The Treize. ICU. He fielded any reports of product complaints or any of their regulars buying from someone else. Anyone watching. No one new popped up on that front besides Cantrell, partnered with that crooked-ass cracka, Lee. Pastor Winburn, Sister Jackie. He even put his ear to the ground about any new hustlers working the scene. He didn't care how low on the hustle pyramid they were. Geno. Rhianna. Omarosa. If they operated within his sphere of influence or were potential threats, he wanted to know about them. Like King. Lastly, he asked about any niggas. Naptown Red, fool nigga trying to play. Colvin, on the other hand, bore keeping an eye on.

Next they took sales reports, tallying the week's receipts, drugs lost or stolen, inventory lost. Members causing problems. Like settling the dispute between Rok and The Boars, each of whom ran a six-person crew.

"No disrespect, Boars..." Rok rose quickly through the thin ranks, promoted more due to the thin talent pool of who was available, like some ghetto affirmative action. A young buck, skin the color of weak tea, rail thin and with a softness about him. An uncomfortable fit, he was unsure about his position but he took to the job and enjoyed the level of respect it engendered. However, he didn't wear the mantle with ease and his men sensed it.

"The Boars." Black as seal skin, with a full beard shaved low and a bald head, Bo "The Boars" Little was a beefy boy in a man's body. He was the left tackle for Northwest High School because the nigga just loved to hit people. Needing some walk-around money, he got into the game. No, that wasn't the real reason. Already having the adulation of fans and peers, he found it wasn't enough. He craved the street rep.

"Ain't but one of you out here calling yourself Boars. We ain't confusing you with anyone." Rok had honest eyes, but there were no truth tellers out here and Rellik trusted the honest-looking ones least.

"The Boars. You mean no disrespect? Respect my name." The Boars gravitated to power, craved it like he was hitting a pipe. Greedy, ambitious, brutal, and simple, barely contained anger steeped in his mean little eyes.

"All I'm saying, The Boars, is that I've come up short."

"That's your problem."

"No, it's both of your problem," Rellik said. "Rok thinks he was underpaid. The Boars thinks someone was lying about how much product was moved. Someone's in the wrong. Give us a minute."

Rellik and Garlan stepped toward a corner, all eyes on them, a tide of steady murmurs.

"Who you believe?" Rellik asked.

"The Boars is an earner. Little man's too soft. Probably lost the product or had folks steady taking him off."

"Yeah. That's possible. My gut tells me The Boars is gearing up for his own operation, though. Skimming bits here and there to build up a war chest to buy in on a package. No one noticed until Rok caught him. No one."

Garlan chafed under this latest bit of schooling from Rellik. The OG dude might have seen himself as trying to raise up some young uns, but Garlan was a man. A man with pride who didn't need to be undercut every time he turned around. "So what we gonna do?"

"It's a light offense. A beat-down should do it."

"He a big boy. You up to it?"

"Heh." Rellik reached into his pocket and pulled out a ring. Old and worn, silver strands wove in an intricate pattern and black filled in the empty spaces. "This is for you."

"What is it?"

"Power. You earned it."

Garlan took the ring. He turned it in his hand several times, inspecting it, then slipped it on. The ring fit his finger like he was born to wear it. "Now what?"

"You turn it and no one can see you." Rellik leveled his gaze at him to assure him that he was serious. "You want to test it? Handle The Boars."

Garlan turned toward The Boars. The man had him by half a foot and over a hundred pounds easy. Not enough to make water pump through his veins, but enough to give him pause. Garlan looked back at Rellik, who pantomimed the turning of the ring. Garlan did.

The world turned silver and black, like staring at

film negatives. The effect dizzied Garlan, who stumbled with his first steps. He steadied himself, quickly becoming used to seeing the world in shades of gray. A few heads turned, those who had been watching Garlan and Rellik chat now craned about, searching for any trace of them. Garlan approached Rok and waved his hand in front of him. Then flipped him off. Rok gave no indication of seeing him, but grew uneasy, feeling crowded. Garlan stepped back and the boy seemed to relax a bit.

The Boars stank up close. One of those stale-sweat jungle funks some brothers couldn't scrub off no matter how many showers they took or how much cologne they put on. As he neared, The Boars tensed, suddenly on edge. Obviously a fighter, some ancient warrior sense within, alerted him; he assumed a defensive posture. His boys backed away from him, possibly simply fearing that he might swing at them.

Garlan circled the man, wary and testing his limits. The Boars' frame was even more massive up close. What some might have taken as fat was more muscle than not. From his stance, he knew how to use his weight and was much lighter on his feet than one might guess. Still, no matter the size, every Goliath could be taken down by a well-placed stone.

Garlan punched him in the throat. The Boars clutched at his neck, bending forward enough for Garlan to land a heavy punch which exploded his nose. It was strictly cosmetic damage, but he aimed for an effect of blood spurting everywhere rather than damage. Toying with him, Garlan jabbed at the man's kidneys, an ax taken to an old oak, bit by bit, wearing him down. The Boars swung wild, hitting only air. The scent of blood started to get Garlan's head up. He swept The Boars feet from under him and rained kicks into his side. The Boars curled up to protect himself as best he could, not knowing how many assailants he had to fend off.

"That's enough," Rellik said. During quiet moments, he wondered if he'd been away from the game too long. Perhaps prison was too far removed from the grind of the streets, made him out of touch with these boys. All doubts were pushed aside because the rules never changed. Public punishments acted as a deterrence. All ambitions ran through the head and he decided when you were ready to step up. And they ensured solidarity, because they were all on the same page now.

He dreamt of being like the Black Panthers of the '60s, agitating for real change and improvement in the neighborhoods. Oblivious to the irony of drug trade and violence eating away at community. Rellik knew the power he had. Wages, shifts, spikes in supply and demand, they were all part of the calculations of industry. The game took care of its players. He felt the obligation to take care of his people. His soldiers couldn't do drugs. The last thing he needed was one of them tweaking out or having their heads not in business. He demanded they stay in school or at least got their GED. He donated money to youth centers, bought sports equipment and computers. He was all about the trickle-down theory: drug money redistributed fiends' money back into the community, and he was a key player in that system. True, there were the Nights, Dreds, Colvins, and fools of the game who were little different from corporate execs who embezzled pension plans for their own gain. But Rellik was about the system. Then there was the police, always with their hands out deciding which businesses could launder cash or which crew could operate freely. Biggest crooks of them all. Never around when you need them, but Johnny on the spot after the fact.

"Rip currents, like a levee break, form channels which pull everything in them out to the reservoir," the sheriff, a fat white man who hid behind mirrored sunglasses and a broad hat, explained. *"Usually a wave hits the beach and flows back to the lake as gentle backwash. The way this little alcove here is set up, with the strong winds blowing towards the shore, water collects on the beach side of a sand bar. When the trapped water breaches the sand bar, it flows away real quick from the beach and forms a vortex beyond the surf."*

Gavain sat in the sheriff's car with a blanket wrapped loosely around him. He shivered under the blaring sun and toasty wind. His mother hollered then collapsed at the sight of men loading her sons, sheets pulled over their heads, into the ambulance. Gavain stared at the lake, thinking about the hands that pulled him to shore, sparing him.

He missed his brother.

"How'd that feel to you?" Rellik said to the air. "You need to turn the ring back."

Garlan appeared in front of him. "It felt good. Right."

"You get used to it pretty quickly. Sometime a nigga's just got to be beat-down." Rellik watched some of the young'uns help The Boars to his feet, help he shrugged off. "They have to fear you."

"They do."

"They do now. Before, you were one of them, you might have told them what to do, but to them you gave suggestions, not orders that demanded to be followed. Most of them followed because they were too lazy to come up with something else. The Boars was different. Just biding his time.

"I love these niggas. They my family. But I don't trust them. No one. Especially my friends. The higher up you go, the less you can afford to go soft." Rellik didn't mind though. As he worked toward his larger ambitions, his goal was to go mainstream, to get out the game and take his people legit.

"We got any more problems, we squash them now." Rellik prepared to wrap up the meeting. "You pay taxes, you get to call the police or your city councilman. You niggas ain't paid a cent in taxes. But you know we all know. Round here, we all pay. And we only have Merky Water to call on. This here's your job. A job's a job and when you're here, you on the clock. Your ass needs to be here on time and on point. You put in the work, you get paid. This ain't no minimum-wage gig so you better take pride in it."

With that, the group was dismissed.

"Any new business?" Rellik asked Garlan away from listening ears.

"Got a line on raw product sounds pretty good."

"From who?"

"From Dred."

"Oh, yeah?" Rellik asked. "He play too many games. Spike that shit with something. You never know."

"He a steady connect."

"Got to think of this like a business. Dude over here wants to sell to me at regular rate now, make sure I'm a steady connect then discount me twenty percent next year. Dude over there wants to discount me ten percent now if I sign up with him. Who would you go with?"

"In this world, there'll always be fiends. Think long-term and go with the deeper discount."

"You thinking. I like that, but naw. Thing you forget is that ain't nothing guaranteed. This time next year, you, me, either dude could be locked up, dead, or out of the game. Take your discount up-front."

"Go for the guaranteed money."

"That's my nigga," Rellik said. "And leave Dred alone. That nigga's never up to anything good."

• • • •

A mural of a Jamaican flag filled the left third of the wall. An Ethiopian flag was painted on the right third, the two framing a portrait of Haile Selassie. Dred perched beneath it, ensconced in a high-backed wicker chair. A thick plume of smoke issued from the side of his mouth. Short and stocky, he had a prison workout body despite the fact that Dred had never seen the inside of a cell. Wearing a Pelle Pelle red hooded jogging outfit, the word "DEATH" scrawled over crossbones. Dismissing Baylon with a nod – the half-dead man retreated to a far corner engulfed by shadows – his vaguely Asiatic eyes studied Merle.

Baylon thought he detected a trace of fear in Dred's eyes. From what he observed, Dred took several steps away from the streets licking his wounds and re-grouping, rethinking his strategy. Perhaps he over-reached with his first charge at power, his feint at King, underestimating the man.

"I know all your thoughts," Dred said. "Every move you're going to make."

"That makes one of us. Please excuse all of the gibberish going on in my head." His mouth caught in an exuberant grin, Merle reached into one of the deep pockets of his raincoat. His slate-gray eyes sparkled with amusement. He took off his aluminum cap, wiped a thick coat of sweat from its brow – squeezing his eyes at the onset of the voices – and returned it to his head. "Luckily, I usually say what I'm thinking."

"I don't need you to tell me what you are thinking. In fact, it's easier if you don't because most of what comes out of your mouth is lies anyway. Everyone has body language. Most folks don't think about the message they send out: a curled lip, a hunched shoulder, a twitch here or there. I do."

"It must be exhausting to be you."

"It is. It really is." Dred stepped to Merle, close, almost too close. Some might have taken it as a threat or challenge. Merle was unmoved. The artifice of the bum as crazy-ass cracka was obvious, almost on the verge of a glamour. In fact, it was a glamour of sorts: the glamour of the mundane. The lowest of the low was often ignored.

"Well, since you know all my thoughts and what comes out of my mouth is lies anyway, why are we talking?"

"It's part of the game."

"Games? I like games." Merle smacked loudly as if enjoying a piece of candy.

"It's like playing chess."

"I've never been real good at chess," Merle said. "But it sounds like you'd be great at it. Thinking so far ahead. An enemy you can read."

Dred ushered him into the anteroom. A chess board occupied the center of the room, exquisitely carved jade pieces all over it, a game already in progress. Dred took a seat. He gestured for Merle to sit across from him but the mage remained standing.

"In chess, you have pieces. Cold, porcelain pieces

are useless. I need to be able to read the guy behind
the pawns. I don't know if that makes sense. It does
to me and that's all that counts."

"You study the player, not his game."

"Try to get in his head. Fuck with him a little. Get
him talking about anything, then his language and
body movements will betray him. How quickly he
moves his piece. How tightly he grips it. How firmly
he places it. You watch his face and body. It all
telegraphs his thinking and strategy. His motiva-
tions."

"His tells."

"Every word, every phrase. It's all about nuance.
It's all about learning how to read people."

"So which am I? Pawn or guy behind the pawns?"
Merle asked.

"Both… I suspect." Which was as true as Dred
could guess. There was always someone between
Merle and the drama. No direct contact, always directing others. He hadn't quite decided if Merle
moved King or if both were subject to a greater
gamesman making them fulfill their roles. Either
way, his moves had to be accounted for. Dred moved
a knight to take out a pawn and place his opponent's
rook in jeopardy. He then spun the table to play as
his opponent.

"You have your mother's eyes."

"Do you know where she is, world mage?"

"She's nearby. Closer than either of us care to
admit."

"I need to see her. She has one last lesson for me."

"She'll be the death of both of us," Merle said, taking greater interest in the game.

"I don't think so. I think her time draws to an end."

"But that's not what you summoned me here for."

"No. I need to know if King is the man you think he is."

"The sapling mage is at a crossroads? Neither this way nor that?"

"Something like that. I hear things. Rumors about what King hopes to do and achieve. And I want to believe in it. In him."

"He's just a man. A dream."

"I believe that, though I don't know if you do." Even as Dred rethought the game, his strategy, and his position, he never revealed his entire hand. Through the last of the dragon's breath, he had poked and prodded, testing his opponents and teasing out their weakness. He could already tell that they were on edge, not as sharp. Exhausted and harried... and thus vulnerable.

"You also have doubts."

"I just need to know what's this nigga's story."

"You know it as well as anybody."

"I mean, what's he about?"

"He's the story."

"He's a story. The echo of a story. Young, charismatic, do-gooder types. Social organizer, community activist type. Troubled youth made good, with a rise to prominence backed by a religious leader."

"You make that sound like a bad thing."

"You know your Bible?"

"We haven't always seen eye-to-eye."

"Revelation 17:11 – 'And the beast that was, and is not, even he is the eighth, and is of the seven, and goeth into perdition.' Daniel 8:23 – 'And in the latter time of their kingdom, when the transgressors are come to the full, a king of fierce countenance, and understanding dark sentences, shall stand up.' Daniel 11:36 – 'And the king shall do according to his will; and he shall exalt himself, and magnify himself above every god, and shall speak marvelous things against the God of gods, and shall prosper till the indignation be accomplished: for that that is determined shall be done.'"

"What are you trying to say?"

"I'm not trying to say anything. It's already been said. Even foretold."

"If you think King is some sort of… Antichrist, then this would be one of those non eye-to-eye moments."

"I think King is an echo of the past that points to the future. He may mean well, but he doesn't see how his actions can hurt people.

"Says the drug lord."

"I'm a simple businessman. No further ambition than to make money. What I do, hundreds of others do. But King, he's special isn't he?"

Merle remained silent.

"King has potential," Dred said. "He draws people in, sweeps them along despite themselves, like a tidal vortex. It's what he does. Unites people, forges a kingdom, accrues power. Until…"

"Until what?"

"Until it all falls apart. Tell me, is he the real deal? Is he a man worth following?"

"You are your mother's son."

Dred toppled the jade king. "Tell King I want to meet with him."

"A parlay?"

"If anyone can pull together a parlay, I'm sure it's him."

The summit meeting was the business portion of what was Rellik's homecoming party. Off to college, off to life in the military, out from prison, such rites of passage were met with community celebration. Rellik was a west side nigga at heart, but he was equally at home at the Meadows, now the Phoenix, Apartments. This wasn't some alien landscape meant to be avoided or sped through with locked car doors. This was home. Under electric-blue skies with the hint of chill in the air, but still warm enough to have a party.

Sparing no expense, a row of three tables held a snow cone maker, a popcorn maker, as well as room for hot dog and nachos stations (which proved especially convenient for those wanting chili and cheese on their dogs instead of chips). Another table held coolers filled with juice drinks and pop. For anything harder, they needed to go to their car trunks and make their own drinks. On the far side of the church lot were three inflatable gyms. One for basketball, a jumpy slide which tottered precariously in the breeze though none of the kids cared, and a boxing ring with inflatable gloves the size of a toddler. Boys ran up on one another at full tilt with faux menace, amped up to pummel one another with the gloves which proved heavier than they anticipated.

The DJ had to be snatched by Big Momma as the mic had to be protected from the errant freestylers. As it was, the music spun featured lyrics quickly running out of superheroes to do things with their hos. Pastor Winburn bobbed his head. "The neck knows," he said to Big Momma's mildly disapproving gaze and the giggle of some of the pre-teens.

Three BBQ grills kept the meat coming. Geno wiped thick smears of sweat from his forehead with his apron. He manned the racks of ribs personally, not trusting anyone else's eye. He had a burger man and a chicken man, each flipping stacks of meat like a well-rehearsed orchestra.

An area of tables had been cordoned off, the tablecloths flapping in the wind, but held down by duct tape. Chairs allowed the grown folks to eat in peace, hold court, or play cards and dominoes. Having run out of those, some of the kids had to make do with milk cartons. Seven year-old boys flashed gang signs when out of the eyeline of any other adults.

On the other side of the church, The Boars and other young men crouched in the shadows hunched over their piles of cash. He shook a set of dice, eyes heavy on him, all still conscious of the beat-down he took, but now it was business as usual and none dared speak of it. They gave him room to lick the wounds to his pride and they feared his eruption to reclaim it if provoked. Money spread on the concrete. The Boars rolled the bones and snapped his fingers. The dice came up sixes. Money changed hands amidst grumbles about the boxcar roll.

"Y'all want in?" The Boars asked.

"I'm in," Rok said, throwing a few ends onto the pile. They were still a crew and not only didn't he throw and punch, he was equally unnerved by the invisible assault. It also helped that he lost the last roll to The Boars.

"Who's up? Who's up? Who's up?" The Boars continued.

"If I ain't steppin' on something..."

"Yeah?" The tentative way Rok approached getting into The Boars' business, almost deferential, appealed to him.

"It true?"

"What?"

"I heard you got them boys."

"Who?"

"Dred's crew."

"Walked straight up on a buster and capped him in the head," another echoed.

"Served him up. One in the face," a third chimed in.

Rumors swirled about the bodies dropping all over town. Some with a simple bullet to the head. Some scenes described as straight out of a horror film, with bodies tore up, raked through, and blood everywhere. The Boars didn't mind some of that name recognition landing on him. Though he didn't want to directly claim it either. It was a dangerous business taking another person's credit.

"Same blood, not the same heart."

"You ice cold, man. There's no forgiveness to you."

"I hear that. A lot." The Boars snapped his fingers at the dice roll.

"It's all that Cobra you be drinking."

"I don't drink that watered-down piss. The KKK runs that shit."

"Shut up, fool. You think the KKK runs everything," Rok said.

"It's why he don't wear no Sean Jean gear," another voiced added.

"But that's P Diddy's line," Rok said. "Sound like maybe his competitors started a rumor."

"Klan. I'm telling you," The Boars said.

"I never did trust that too-pretty nigga no way," a peewee said. They all turned to see who had snuck into their circle.

"Why do so many niggas have to be such sugar drops?" The Boars lightly shoved Rok. "You too, nigga. You have to come strong. We need to get you on a workout bench. Get you pumped up."

Still rattling the dice in his hand like dead men's bones, he paused when he noticed the duo approaching.

Mulysa wanted his name to ring out, the sole ambition of his eyes jacked up by drugs. A stain dirtying everything he touched, he was a melanoma on the skin of his family. One they attempted to scrape off. For as long as he could remember, he learned to take the beatings, the abuse. And learned to smile – that dangerous half-smirk ready to jump off – because in the back of his mind he thought "one day." One day he'd be big enough. Like a pit bull bred to fight, he responded to what he'd been taught. He dined on pain and suffering every day and internalized it. It got in him, built his muscles, wired his thinking, flowed through his veins. The pain, the anger, the hate. He closed the space between them, meaning to crowd them. His hands shook when his blood got to racing. His arm twitched, the flinch that signaled he was about to go hard.

A tightness clutched his stomach as he remembered the child he had been. Sneaking a cup of sugar and a packet of Kool Aid in a sandwich bag for him and his friends. They'd all lick their fingers and swipe at the pile of powder until there was nothing left but a gooey pile. Every break between what few high school classes he attended spent smoking blunts. Weed affected him in ways different from his friends. More deeply. Something he couldn't identify drove him and he couldn't stop. He smirked at the idea of his friends. He couldn't recall any of their names now, and even their faces were vaguely recalled silhouettes.

Mulysa took a corner, sold dime bags of marijuana for his cousin who had a supplier out of the eastside. Then came juvenile, which completed his education. Confined with gunmen and killers, it kept him low and it killed anything good in him. Something he planned on passing along to Tristan.

"What's up?" Tristan asked.

"I'm drunk. That's what's up."

"Recognize." She knew that fire dancing in his eyes. That rush which at any moment might spring at her. "What's with these fools?"

"Let me milk this cow. Y'all just hold the tail," Mulysa said.

"I ain't trying to do no jail."

"See this here? This is a pack of dogs. Each one scrappin' for their piece. Times are a little lean and they a little wild so it's easy for them to scrap too hard over a little piece of meat. Some try to go off by themselves, some try to set them up as the big dog."

"And you here cause you the Alpha dog?" Tristan asked.

"Naw. Colvin's the Alpha dog. I'm the stick he uses to train them. You, too."

"Train them for what?"

"Shit. You beat a dog when he a young pup, he thinks twice about rising up on you later on."

At the sight of Mulysa, thickly muscled, an upright pit bull, and Tristan, rangy yet sturdy, no play in her eyes and scattered. The boys with the appointment knew it was pointless to run. They eye-fucked the locals to scare the need to witness out of them.

Mulysa menaced a smile.

Tristan lagged behind without having to be told. A sign of intelligence, Mulysa thought. She knew her business. The first time Tristan hooked up with Mulysa, she and Iz were completely ass-out. She dozed during the day under a bridge while Iz went to school and stayed up to guard them at night. One time while she slept, some fool jacked all her stuff; just grabbed her backpack and took off. She never cried when she told Iz, only took her hand and leaned her head onto her shoulder. A rare moment of lowering her guard.

They'd have left then but Indianapolis was all Tristan knew. Then Mulysa showed up. Said he recognized talent when he saw it. The bullshit didn't matter, the money did. Though she felt no obligation to him, in a way, he was there for them when no one else was. He was a predator of the first order and she was every bit on guard around him as when she was on the streets. The money was straight though.

Rok opted not to move as Tristan attempted to brush by – a tacit challenge she understood but had little patience for.

"What we got here? A little game among gentlemen?" Mulysa dropped to his knees and hovered over the money. "Civility is the name of the game."

"What you here for?" The Boars asked.

"You do the speeding, you get a ticket."

"Whose street are we speeding on?"

"Colvin's," Mulysa said.

"Colvin? Shee-it. I thought you were talking about someone serious. Not that high yella, wannabe peckerwood." The Boars assessed his six-to-two advantage and confidence crept into his posture. "He's another one. Got a little sugar in his tank."

"You sure that's the tone you want to take with me, nukka?"

"You might want to look around you, dog. You and the missus… you a little out-gunned up in this piece." The Boars challenged with his eyes, though a skim of sweat trickled along his hairline.

Born on Christmas Day, Mulysa was taken in by CPS at two. A dealer friend called CPS, having been given the boy to pay off a debt. He was five years old when he was first raped and beaten in a foster home. With no place else to go, he went back into the system.

"What led to arson?" Arson followed battery as juvenile followed boys' school. All sort of docs tried to crawl into his head. He suffered headaches. Adderall, Wellbutrin, a prescribed menagerie to address his anger problems, they often found it safer to sedate him with drugs. None helped. His mom and dad came into money, a settlement from an accident from when a security guard wrenched his mother's arm in a store (the fact that she was there to shoplift notwithstanding) and they got him back. Even sent him to a private school. His thoughts drifted to jail and the ordered life there, the peace of the streets. So one day he left. Most times he lived in an abandoned bank. Some times he dropped by the Camlann Apartments complex. The streets were his home, his headache his sole companion. No matter where he went, no one saw him. He knew he was just a joke to them. A nigger joke.

Mulysa withdrew a knife and twirled it in his hands, the six-inch blade stopped, handle in his palm. The Boars' mouth went dry.

"As big as your dick. Bigger."

"It ain't the size, it's how you use it," Tristan said, her handcrafted blades curled around her fists. They were overkill, she thought, and put them away. She attacked with sudden ferocity, catching The Boars off guard. Speed and guile on her part made up for the mismatch of his bulk versus hers. Most of the shorties scattered, probably racing back to sound an alarm. Her movements were smooth and elegant. The edge of her hand chopped at his throat followed by a punch to his solar plexus. Without passion, it was nothing personal. She directed a blow to a nerve cluster in his arm, painful, and would leave him in a mood to not continue a fight. In another finesse move, she leg-swept the approaching boy, toppling him, then kicked him in the side until he curled up in surrender. They were perfunctory blows. Other than The Boars, these were boys, not hardened soldiers. Water pumped in their veins.

Mulysa took greater relish in his attack. The crunch of bone beneath his pummeling fist only drove him to greater heights of bloodlust. His nostrils widened as if snorting the blood scent. His lips pulled back in a mad rictus. His name would ring out for sure. To march into the heart of Rellik's territory, to put a beat-down on some of his troops in the middle of his own party. Shit. He grew heady on waves of his soon-to-be-swelling rep. He drew his dagger – damn near a machete, his bottom bitch – and turned to go at Rok. Tristan stepped between them.

"Enough. I think they got the point."

"Let's bounce before these bitches find their heart."

"And gats." Tristan glanced back at Rok with a nod. "Deuces."

CHAPTER ELEVEN

Hot Trimz had only been open a few months. Some of the barbers from Stylez across the street didn't like the booth rent arrangement and launched their own shop, taking up the space next to the Hoosier Pete convenience mart. They constantly handed out postcards to the Hoosier Pete regulars and had an ongoing special of a ten dollar haircut to any customer before 1 pm. An Obama '08 plackard hung alongside other signs: "Walk-ins welcome." "Multicultural." "Stylists Wanted." Several outdated issues of XXL, Vibe, and Scoop, the newspaper for the local night scene for black folks, lay scattered along the benches. The Commodores' "Lady" played in the background.

A white linoleum-tiled floor lined the thin strip of a shop, black mats beneath each station. The unsturdy benches were flush against the wall, hard on the ass and back. Three barbershop hairstyle guides were on display on the walls. From the beauty salon on the other half of the shop, female stylists talked crazy to the barbers over the dividing wall.

"Bunny!" Davion "D" Perkins, an earpiece always on his ear, said.

"I told you not to call me that," a female voice cried from the other side of the dividing wall.

"Grow up, D," Old School said in a tone of mock chivalry.

"Ain't that the pot calling the kettle negro?" she said.

"Old School, handle that," D said. "You ain't got your girl in check."

D had fast eyes and missed nothing. In a black vest over a white T-shirt, a casual display of his former athletic build, he swept the hair from around his station.

"Look at Old School. He like a little kid, hiding his hair under his chair."

"Look here, when you got it going on like me, you forget little details like a little hair."

"Yeah, you know all about a little hair." D went ahead and swept under Old School's chair.

"Why they call you 'Bunny'?" Old School asked.

"Uh oh, hurry up, here she comes," D said.

Before she could come around the corner, a cowbell clanged against the front door as it opened. A dark-skinned woman, her skin made darker against her sunflower-yellow dress, walked in. Her swollen breasts and plunging cleavage made Old School lower his glasses. No more than twenty years old, she towed a wailing four year-old.

"Boy, sit down and be still." She plopped him down in D's chair. "Up here looking crazy."

"We all big boys in here," D said, draping a drop cloth around the boy's chest. Then he clicked on a set of clippers and waved them about to let the boy get used to the noise. The child continued to bellow, inconsolable. His attention shifting from D to Old School, back to his mother. The boy's tiny hands rose and made grasping motions toward her.

"He just cutting you up." The woman crossed her arms in a practiced pose of defiance, daring someone to cross her.

"Get your hair fresh to match your outfit," Old School said.

"Want to check out these keys?" D pulled a jangling mass out of his pocket. The boy paused mid-bellow, an uncertain air as he studied the keys. "You got them boys. Go to that escalade out there."

"Let him push buttons," Old School said.

The child burst into a renewed fit of tears, squirming out of the raised perch as the clippers neared his curly, light brown locks.

"Put some muscle in it. He'll be all right." His mother sucked her teeth in impatience.

"You got this, D." Old School tip-toed away from her to ease back into his chair. He flipped open the latest issue of Scoop and pretended to read.

"I know he ain't stronger than you. Just rip him."

"He keeps moving around and I don't want to nick him," D said.

"Hold him down. Who's the adult?"

"I ain't trying to lay hands on someone else's kids."

The show went on for a few more minutes, D angling clippers at the boy's head, each time as if considering the best attack approach. His mother clucked, sucked her teeth, checked her watch, and muttered loud enough for all to hear about how real men could handle a crying boy. The cowbell clanked again – D made a note to get a real chime – as King strode in. Prez followed behind him scratching his arm, in a skittish manner as if ready to break out in a full sprint at the next low sound. The boy stopped crying.

In his late forties, not a speck of gray on his head or in his beard, and wearing a black lab half-coat, Old School slapped the seat of his chair. Prez wandered into his chair, first checking to see if anyone else stirred for it, and chewed on his lower lip as he eyed the line of King's hair. Old School wrapped the paper neck cuff around Prez, then his huge arms draped the cloth around him in a flourish. Turning up his nose after catching a whiff of Prez's funk, he leaned the young man's head back over the sink and began washing his hair first. "What we need today?"

Prez's eyes caught King's, almost seeking permission to answer – if he were sure at all.

"Let's just bald him up. Go clean all the way around and start fresh," King said.

"Change the hair, change the image," Old School said.

It had already been a long day. King and Prez had played basketball for a few hours. It had been a while since King had been on a court. Too long. His legs lacked the grace and coordination which made the game come alive for him so long ago, like he had to learn to run all over again. Not that it mattered as Prez huffed and puffed before the score reached 2-2, having no wind and nothing close to stamina in his rubbery legs. Their game was complete slop, spending more time chasing down errant rebounds than playing. Despite his wheezing and slow gait, Prez continued to ball, jogging around the half-court, amiably hounding King and calling it defense. No one joined in their game, sensing that the game wasn't the point. There was the sense of intruding on something personal.

Though his muscles ached and his sweat reeked of toxins seeking release and his stomach roiled with sickness, Prez knew he'd be fighting against his own body for a while. Callused, scarred, and stiff, his hand felt foreign. His breath came in hard rasps, the threat of erupting into a fit of coughs with each struggling wheeze. The game slowly came back to him through a thick fog of muscle memory, as if he played on someone else's legs.

"How does it feel?" King asked as they collapsed against the pole. His eyes closed as he let fatigue wash over him, his sweat trickled down him, and his muscles throbbed with deep ache. Not painful, but more in a good-to-be-alive sort of way. For all of his running around, King was never truly with anyone. Never invested himself into anyone. Never gave or sacrificed much of himself. It was safer that way, he didn't have to risk much of himself. Sure, he opened himself up to a core few – Wayne, Lott, Lady G – but after that, everyone was kept at a distance. Even Pastor Winburn. After a few moments, he realized Prez hadn't said anything and he opened his eyes. Prez wept to himself.

"I forgot about this," Prez said.

"About what?"

"I don't know. All of this. Life. I took it all for granted."

"So what do you want to do next?"

"Live. But…" Prez trailed off.

"But what?" King knew the answer but he waited for Prez to find the words.

"I don't know where to start."

"Make a list of what you want out of life. Nothing ridiculous."

To be healthy again. Car. Relationship. Family. Friends. Forgiveness. King made him write them down, something tangible that he could come back to when he needed reminding. King suggested he might want to begin with finding a job. He helped Prez make a résumé. The next step was for him to polish his look and present himself as professionally as possible. They both hoped for a break, just an opportunity, for a second chance.

"Either I'm getting slower or you getting faster,"

Old School said as D brushed his face with a pow-der-laced brush. Rubbed "botanical oils and razor relief lotion" on his head.

"You slow." D collected ten dollars from the mother.

"You don't miss nothing."

"You make me scared to get old."

"Have a good day, you hear?" Old School called after the girl. She glanced at King and smiled, not that he noticed.

For his part, King battled against a sense of per-sonal failure. Not that he'd been entrusted with Prez or that he really knew the boy, but he felt like he'd let him down. The community bulletin board enrap-tured his attention. In God's Hands child care. Lawn Service. Insurance. House cleaners. The community reached out and helped its own. He had been so con-cerned about the big battles he forgot about the everyday ones; the people around and closest to him. King had failed Prez once and he wouldn't fail him again.

King handed Old School a twenty and didn't wait for change. Prez got up and offered Old School a fist to bump.

"I don't have time for all that snapping and slap-ping," Old School said. "Just shake my hand."

The bell clanged again. Detective Cantrell Williams held the door open for the young woman and son to exit. He'd have probably tipped his hat to them if he wore one. Even if he wasn't known, the room would have made him as a cop. Stiff, straight-backed walk. His stare imposed, a challenge to any who saw him. He locked onto King immediately, who nodded toward D's office. D returned an approving nod. The two closed the door behind them, King planted himself behind D's desk.

"Your boy's late," Cantrell started.

"Yeah, Lott runs that way."

"Well I ain't got all day."

"You heard my pitch or you wouldn't be here. If I'm going to have the major players come to the table for a sit down, I'm going to need police support. Or non-involvement, as the case may be."

King understood his burgeoning rep. His name rang out on the streets in ways his father's never did. However, he also understood the ways of power. Cops had real power. They controlled where and how open the gangs operated. They could put anyone in jail at any time. Yet they rarely arrested the leaders. Perhaps it was a matter of better the devils they knew as opposed to an unstable and unpredictable leader or, worse, a power vacuum.

"You make some folks… nervous." Cantrell leaned in. The close feel of the room gave the conversation the feel of an interrogation.

"So?" King said, unintimidated. He had been brought down for questioning enough times. Suspicion of battery. Questioned about assaults. Rumors of him brandishing a weapon in public. But there were never any complaining witnesses. Only his name coming up, in vague, and soon forgotten, accounts.

"You ain't hearing me. Some in the department think you trying to do their job. Some think you trying to get dirt on them. Either way, you making enemies you don't have to make."

"That's why I reached out to you."

"Me, huh?"

"Yeah, you seem like a brotha I could trust. Could work with."

"You mean a brotha you could work." Cantrell eased back in his seat.

The two squared off, neither quite understanding how they came to this point. Distrust was part of the game, the latent defensive hostility that comes with folks always being out to get each other. They sparked each other, hackles bristling, despite wanting the same thing. King decided on a measured step backwards.

"You see that boy in there?" King nodded towards Prez.

"The raggedy dope fiend? Looks kinda rough."

"Looked rougher a few days ago when he was dry-heaving all over my living room."

"What about him?"

"I brought him around a few months back. He was supposed to stay with a friend of mine and his feet barely hit the sidewalk when he fell in with Green and Night all caught up in the rippin' and runnin' of the street."

"Seems like the life caught up with him."

"It catches up to all of us. Chewed him up, got involved with that glass dick, next thing you know, I'm scraping him up out an alley."

"So?"

"So? So I failed that boy."

"You ain't responsible for decisions he made," Cantrell said.

"True. But we all in this together. He do his thing, but we don't have to let there be a 'thing' for him to get into. We have to look out for one another."

"What you want from me?"

"A light, and I mean light, police presence. You at the table, strictly as a representative."

"By light you mean out of sight but nearby."

"Parlay or not, stuff could still jump off with the wrong spark or if a knucklehead gets carried away."

"You dream big, King. I'll give you that."

"Someone's got to keep dreaming."

Cocooned in a scarlet sweater, Esther Baron stood on the front steps of her apartment building. Her thin-running blood left her easily chilled. She used to live up in the suburban wasteland of Fishers, too north of Indianapolis with its cookie-cutter strip malls, chain restaurants, and monolithic culture. She thought it too far removed from the heart of the city, convicted that in her heart, she, too, was fleeing from "darker elements" as her father euphemistically put it. Irvington was much closer to her liking and personality. Ten minutes from Outreach Inc., near downtown, and one of the city's art districts, the neighborhood had history and personality.

Wayne pulled up in one of the Outreach Inc. vans. Kay poked his head out the window, tongue wagging as he took in the day in healthy gulps.

"Good morning, Sir Kay." Esther petted him through the window. Grabbing each side of his scruffy face, she let him lick her. When she opened the door, he hopped into the back and laid down in the back seat.

"Sir? He won't know what to do with such treatment," Wayne said.

"He seems like a sir. See the way he gave up his seat for a lady?"

"Chivalry isn't dead."

"I know. Just like I noticed you didn't question me calling myself a lady."

"I'm a gentleman and a scholar."

"Outreach OK with you having him in the car?"

"They got no problem whatsoever... once I promised to detail it afterward. Plus, we're on an errand of mercy."

"Where are we heading?" Esther noticed them going the opposite way on Rural from the Outreach Inc. house.

"Breton Court."

"Breton? I hear that area's pretty rough."

"It can be, but mostly things get exaggerated." Wayne made sure to keep his eyes on the road and not meet hers.

"You have any clients over there?"

"Hmm. I think I got nearly a dozen fellas fresh out of juvenile wandering around over there."

"So it might not be so exaggerated." Esther let a thin smile cross her lips. She didn't need him trying to manage her fears.

"You got a point." Wayne noticed that he sat a little taller in his seat around her. None of his slouch-behind-the-wheel-in-a-gangsta-lean stuff. The way he spoke, formalized wasn't quite the right word. Nor would he say "whitened." But being around her made him very aware of how he spoke and behaved.

"And Kay is joining us?"

"I'm dropping him off."

"Dog sitter?"

"Sort of. King was talking to me about the latest kid Big Momma done took in." There, he made a point of sounding more like him. He spared a glance to see if she noticed. Or took offense. Then he silently cursed at himself for not being able to relax around her. "Anyway, little boy they call Mad Had."

"What a horrible nickname."

"Out here isn't exactly built as a self-esteem booster."

"I see."

"Mad Had was a crack baby. Doesn't speak a lot. King got to thinking that maybe a dog might open him up some."

"Animal therapy. I've read about that.

Of course you have, Wayne thought.

They rode for a while in silence as Wayne hopped on I-65 N to take him to the west side. He fumbled at the radio tuning it into the Tom Joyner Morning Show before thinking that maybe Esther was more of a Bob and Tom Show girl. He flipped the stations, getting a curious glance from her.

"It's OK, you can listen to what you want."

"Passenger's prerogative. 'What thing is it which women most desire?'"

"That from a poem?"

"I don't know. I think I read it somewhere."

"Their will," Esther said with a calm resolve. Her eyes were bright and large and had a way of unsettling him whenever they fixed themselves fully on him.

"What?"

"Their will. Women want what they want."

Wayne didn't expect any answer, much less this one. He took a tentative step out on a limb to feel out her thoughts more. "Makes women sound kinda... vain." He tried to sound sensitive. Who the hell was he turning into?

"A lot are."

"So you didn't roll out the feminist side of the bed this morning."

"I certainly slept under those covers. I'm just saying when it gets down to it, women want their way. Sounds very feminist to me. Don't act like men are so deep. As long as she's young, pretty, and high-class, you'll chase her to the ends of the earth and let her have her way."

"Ah, see there, you wrong. With age comes discretion and wisdom. 'With those whose beauty is inside comes security and character.'"

"And those of... 'low degree'?" Esther wondered where those words came from. She became all too aware of their easy banter, as if reciting lines from a familiar script.

"Humility and gentility."

"You one of those 'beauty is on the inside' guys?"

"I guess I just know beauty when I see it. Even when many miss it when it's obvious."

"I see." Esther Baron smiled more fully, then self-conscious of it, turned away when it didn't leave her face.

The west side saddened Wayne as they exited on 38th Street and passed the Lafayette Square Mall and a series of increasingly vacant strip malls. More businesses had "For Lease" signs on them than not. A Texas Steakhouse had closed; a sign promising that a new Mexican restaurant was "Coming Soon" draped like a sash across it. The Krispy Kreme was boarded up. As was the O'Charley's. Red Lobster was still packing them in though.

Esther couldn't remember the last time she was on the west side. Maybe to go to the Indianapolis 500. Or picnic at Eagle Creek Park. She mentioned that to Wayne, but he grew uncomfortable at the mention of the park and changed the topic back to Breton Court.

"Not so bad," Esther said as they slowed over the speed bumps.

"Like every other apartment complex. Townhouses, technically. There's Mad Had now."

Mad Had curled up on the step outside of Big Momma's condo. Ensconced in a lawn chair, she took in the business of the neighborhood. She grinned at Wayne's approach, him with that cute little white girl at his side. The girl was short, not overweight, but thick. Had an awkward walk about her that brought to mind the image of a shuffling mushroom. But Wayne had his chest all puffed out, that dog of his on a leash like they were a couple out for a late morning stroll.

"How you doing, Big Momma?"

"I'm doing fine, baby." She pronounced "baby" as if she was talking to her grandson. "And how are you this morning, miss lady?"

"I'm doing OK." Esther stifled the need to curtsey.

Mad Had sucked his thumb in silence, his dead eyes tracking their movements.

"What brings you out this way? King's not around. Some hush-hush foolishness he's up to."

"I'm not here to see King. Got someone who wanted to say 'hi' to Had." Wayne tugged at the leash to draw Kay's attention to the boy. The dog trotted up to him gave him a sniff, then licked him like he was the last bit of gravy on a plate. Mad Had raised up, grasping the rott around his neck as if holding a life preserver.

And laughed.

"Lord, look at them," Big Momma said. "Ain't they a sight."

Mad Had stretched his legs along the ground. Kay rested his head on the boy's thigh as he was petted.

"I thought it might be a good idea to let Kay stay here for a while. Between Outreach and King, I don't get to spend as much time at home as I'd like."

"I don't have time to take care of no dog," Big Momma said.

"He's a good dog," Esther answered. "Knows how to treat a lady."

"Maybe me and Had can take care of him. Would you like that, Had?" Wayne asked. "I can check in on them. Visit my boys."

"It's your responsibility." Big Momma tried to sound firm, but her heart wasn't in it. It was the first time she'd seen Had light up with any spark of real life.

Tenth and Rural was the place hookers went when they were too old, too strung out, had the bug, or otherwise were unable to compete with the ladies working downtown. With no structure or support, they forged a life for themselves among the discarded and forgotten. The place had a way of weighing down on a body. It seeped into your bones and gnawed at your soul. Plenty of homeless folk milled around, especially after the government shut down Central State in the 1980s. Flowers, stuffed animals, and candles formed an altar of remembrance, circling a tree in front of the house of Conant Walker, six year-old murder victim.

In a white tank top which went over one shoulder and stretched over a blue halter top over a cut-off blue jean skirt, Rhianna stood on the corner smoking a square as if waiting on the bus.

"What's up, Rhianna?" Lott sidled next to her.

"I'm standing here going over my list of reasons I shouldn't kill myself and can only come up with three reasons and one of them involves a stuffed French toast breakfast I'd promised myself for later in the week. Which only means that next week I'll still have to re-evaluate."

"Still hustling then."

"We all hustle. But not full-time though. Just to feed the kids when my man don't help out. I got regulars who I go with."

"Rellik's your pimp?"

"Nah, I just have to play by his rules." She blew smoke out the side of her mouth, away from Lott. "I ain't like the hos in it to feed a habit. I don't mess with no drugs. Don't mess with no pimps. I just clear things with Rellik's crew."

"Listen, I need you to get word to someone."

"What I look like, a messenger service?"

"Girl, you know and I know ain't fewer people tighter on the vine than you." Some folks went places others couldn't go and heard things most people couldn't. Or shouldn't. Murder, gossip, or drug news. Even more so than the ghetto telegraph of stoop to barbershop.

"Service ain't free. A girl's gotta earn."

"I didn't ask for a freebie." Lott pulled out his wallet, careful not to let Rhianna see how much remained in it. She was still one of his people, but he knew his people. Money had a way of making even friends a mark to run game on.

"Options always open. For you."

"Yeah." Lott shifted an awkward pause. "I'm putting word on the wire for a meeting. Done got a hold of Rellik. Need to get up with this dude Colvin."

"Look at you... carrying King's water an' all. Getting all the players to the table is he?"

"Something like that."

"What about Dred?"

The name shot through him like a bullet through the spine. Caught him short, an anxious skip of unfinished business to his heart. "If he around, he knows."

"Ears everywhere. So no insult not to invite him direct. Others though might not be more sensitive."

"Who?"

"Naptown Red." Rhianna tapped off the ash of her cigarette.

"Who?"

"Bit player."

"So why invite him?"

"Just saying. Niggas like to get their ego stroked."

"Rellik. Dred. Colvin. Respect due the real players." Lott handed her a fifty dollar bill. "This do?"

"They'll know before your head hits the pillow."
Rhianna blew out another stream. "Or Lady G's."

Broad Ripple nestled toward the near north-east part
of Indianapolis. The White River wound along its
north side; the ever-crowded thoroughfare of Keystone Avenue pulsed along its east; Kessler
Boulevard meandered along its south; and the officious Meridian Street stood rigid guard at the west.
Originally founded to be a separate village from Indianapolis proper, Broad Ripple was the result of a
merger between two rival communities: Broad Ripple and Wellington, each vying for expansion.
Indianapolis residents built their summer homes in
Broad Ripple to retreat from the inner city. It even
had its own amusement park built to rival Coney Is-
land's, though it burned to the ground two years
after its construction. A park resided there now. The
quaint little homestead now sported specialty stores,
nightclubs, ducks along the river, and the Monon
Trail walkway.

Merle loved the old houses in Broad Ripple. If
Lockerbie Square was the neo-conservative hippie
of the arts community, Broad Ripple was its
patchouli-smelling cousin. Over-priced old neighborhoods existed in their own pocket universe, and as
the times changed, so did the street names. Bell-
fontaine no longer existed: above Kessler Boulevard
it was Cornell; below it was Guilford. So 5424 Bell-
fontaine was practically a rumor. A house with no

street. A dwelling in the shadow of a dead street. An obvious place for her to live.

A two-story Tudor-style house, its high-pitched roof held a lone arched window, an unblinking Cyclopean eye blinded by the pulled curtains. In fact, the vine-covered windows all had their blinds drawn so that the windows appeared tinted black. Far away from the road, it was the discreet kind of house that one drove by a hundred times without ever truly noticing.

Merle rang the doorbell.

A well-preserved forty-something year-old answered the door. All sultry-eyed and smoldering saunter, she held a glass of red wine in her right hand as she held the door open with her back. Morgana.

"Look what the cat pissed on and left on my yard," she said.

"Fountains. I love the fountains," Merle said.

"You never cease to amuse," Morgana noted. They all had familiar, if not quite familial, roles. Morgana was an instigator, though between her digging comments, she drank her wine under a smile. Pure malice danced in her eyes. At the best of times, she was prone to bouts of darkness, but she seemed withdrawn, either by nature or by choice. "I see you found me."

"Just had to know which bell to ring."

"On a street that doesn't exist."

"Maybe you should try a different glamour spell,"

Merle said. "Or maybe you simply tired of playing at goddess-hood."

"One does not turn one's back on what one is," Morgana said.

"Only you, princess, still consider us even close to gods. We never were. We were ideas. When people cease believing in gods, the gods die. When they cease to believe in ideas…" Merle said.

"They cease to dream."

"They cease to exist."

"And we're still here." She set her chalice down on a table he couldn't spy within the foyer. She guarded her home and her secrets and wasn't going to let him nose around any more than she had to.

"Your son seeks you."

"Our dance is almost over."

"He says you have one last lesson to teach him."

"Does he now? An ambitious little scrapling. I have more than a few tricks left in me."

"He thinks it's almost time."

"What do you think, mad mage?"

"I think…" Merle adjusted the fit of his aluminum cap. "You are harder to get rid of than most things. The hardiest of cockroaches."

"Sadly, I know you mean that as a compliment." Morgana's eyes never left Merle. Secrets within agendas within schemes. The woman was maddening and fascinating. And had a way of stirring up old feelings.

"It's not in my best interest to be rude."

"Ruthless, but not rude. You don't have me fooled, mage. I did learn one lesson while under your... tutelage."

"What was that?"

"Never teach your student all of your tricks."

"And you do have many... students."

"Is that a hint of jealousy I hear? Don't worry, mad one, you will always have a special place in my heart."

"And I shiver at the thought of what a cold, dark place that is. What about Dred?"

"Leave my son to me. You've done your duty. Consider me warned."

"The least I could do. For old times' sake."

Now that Mountain Jack's had closed down, Rick's Boatyard was King's favorite restaurant. Tucked away on the west side, it overlooked Eagle Creek Reservoir itself, on the other side of I-465, a man-made boundary that separated Breton Court and the apartments and neighborhoods surrounding it from the neighborhoods that bled into the suburbs. A chalkboard proclaimed the day's special: the chef's soup of seafood and andouille gumbo, a main course of South African lobster tails, with Mojitos as the featured drink. The clink of silverware and the thick murmur of pleasant conversation speaking above the easy-listening jazz coming from the speakers filled the air as a live band warmed up, playing some luke-warm Kenny G impersonation.

The ceiling recalled the inside of a lighthouse. Fish and flatscreen televisions, each like prize catches, were mounted on the walls alongside New Orleans jazz scene paintings and hanging ferns. Sails created canopies for the booth. The evening proved too cool to sit out on the deck but they could still see the waves of the reservoir. Ominous and calm, deep and mysterious. The perfect place for a romantic dinner. Just King and Lady G.

And Prez.

A blue dress, a silky number with a plunging neckline, stopped high on Lady G's thigh. She had borrowed a pair of evening gloves from Big Momma that ran to her elbow, which she decided finished her elegant look. King wanted to take her someplace special, he said, and she wanted to dress the part. Though he lived on his accrued Social Security benefits from his mother's passing, he wanted to be the man, the knight, she deserved. She wanted to play the sophisticate yet she felt so young and inexperienced around him. She rummaged through Big Momma's closet forever, eventually finding herself in the low-ceilinged attic which housed artifacts from her aunties. Outfits dating back decades. She searched through every box until she found the perfect dress. No relationships happened by accident. She couldn't shake the nagging feeling that there was something degrading about the whole thing. That sense that she was little more than arm candy. So very devastated, an emotional cripple in many ways, she scrambled to be good enough for him, to please him. And part of her struggled with the notion that she wasn't with him, but rather with the idea of him.

She sighed, too loud, drawing the attention of both King and Prez. She decided that her mood was probably put off because King decided to bring his newest puppy along with them.

Not quite hidden behind a menu with the words "Fresh Jazz, Live Seafood" splayed across its front, Prez stared at the array of silverware before him. The letters in gold script on his black hoodie read Light Fingered Brigade. He wondered why he got followed in stores.

"Start from the outside in," King said.

"What?"

"As they bring you out dishes, salad and appetizers and stuff, use the forks starting on the outside."

"Can't just use one fork through the whole meal? Seems awful wasteful," Prez said.

"White folks got too much time and too much kitchen help to worry about that," Lady G said.

"Just a different way of doing things is all." He resented the unspoken implication that he was trying to turn the two of them white.

Though pissed that King had brought his latest special project along with them, Lady G couldn't stay mad at him. He was so good with Prez, almost like a father. Probably doing what Pastor Winburn did with him years ago. She always gave into King's wants and requests. Partly because she wanted to please him, partly because everything he did seemed so... important. King was large, not just physically imposing, but his life seemed lived on such a grand stage. His every action and decision seemed to carry such weight. It was intimidating. Timid and hard-headed, yet boisterous and fierce-sounding, she was still the shy little girl whose time was better spent in a book. And she resented the flash of sentiment that perhaps she was every bit the special project to King that Prez was.

"You sure I'm not intruding?" Prez asked.

Yes, Lady G thought. "Naw. King too scared to be alone with me."

"It's cool." Though pleased that Lady G acquiesced to letting him bring Prez along, King knew he might have been pushing things a bit. A hard, impenetrable man who would die for those he loved, inside he was still the frightened boy fearing the monsters that came for him in the night. "I just wanted to take two people I care about out for a nice evening. It's all about possibilities, you know."

"Yeah." Prez's eyes glazed over, not knowing what King went on about. The food felt good in his belly though.

The dinner passed uneventfully. King and Prez talked of the Pacers' penchant for big white farmboy acquisitions, and the holes of the Colts' defensive line. They talked about the best places to eat ribs. They talked about school and passed knowing glances at women, King's arched eyebrow asking to Prez's shake of disapproval as waitresses walked by. Nothing too deep, though the conversation about school was cut short by Prez as it veered too close to thinking about the future and making plans. No, tonight was about being: being still, being present, and being with each other.

Back at Breton Court, Prez ducked immediately into King's place. King walked Lady G over to Big Momma's place.

"Sorry about that. Just thought with him having no place to go, it would be a bad idea to leave him by himself," King said.

"I don't care that he came along, it's just..." Lady G hated to sound pathetic and needy. Like a girl. "I just thought it was going to be only us."

"I thought I could do both: be with you and help him along."

"I'm not some item you can just multi-task to check off your 'to do' list."

No competition, no domination, they held on to each other, rushed into each other. What one had to give the other was pleased to take, like sweet-tasting fruit. But too much of even the best fruit spoiled one's diet.

"It's just... there's so much work to be done. Not enough time to do it all. Not enough workers. Not enough people care. And as much as I want you beside me, it's also dangerous. So I want to keep you as far from it as possible."

"There you go again. Trying to determine folks' business. Who elected you our Black Messiah?"

"What?" King thought he'd opened up and poured out his romantic soul. He didn't expect the sharp sting of words.

"You don't get to decide that for me. It's my decision to make. I'm tired of the men in my life trying to tell me what's best for me."

"Is that what's bothering you?"

"I said it, didn't I?" She held a steady gaze behind a deceptive mien. He made her see old things with new eyes. He gave her confidence, shared her secrets and felt loved. He helped her define herself. King was the one person who accepted her. Who knew her. Who had been real with her. She couldn't hide from him.

"You just seemed off is all. A little preoccupied," King said finally.

"Just a lot going on. Life with you is hectic. Still getting used to it is all."

"All right then." He read her face like emotional tea leaves. Whatever he saw there he decided not to press the matter.

She kissed him, which lately she did more often, when he asked too many questions, camouflaging her discomfort in an expression of love.

CHAPTER TWELVE

A sculpture of Robert Indiana's agape-inspired painting "LOVE" and the huge series of fountains were the first things people noticed when they entered the grounds of the Indianapolis Museum of Art. Three main areas made up the IMA: the museum proper, with its Oval Entry Pavilion, a three-story, glass-enclosed jewel box of a building, the Gallery Pavilion, and the Garden Pavilion; the Virginia B Fairbanks Art and Nature Park; and Oldfields, Lilly House and Gardens.

The twenty-six-acre Oldfields estate was named for the former farmland on which it was sited. A French chateau-styled mansion, Oldfields overlooked the White River valley. The twenty-two room mansion was built for Hugh McKennan Landon and his family between 1912 and 1914. In the early 1920s the Landons built the Ravine Garden, a design masterpiece of bulbs, perennials, wildflowers, ferns, and flowering trees and shrubs that featured a bubbling brook that descended the fifty-foot hillside and fed three rock-rimmed pools. In the 1930s, Josiah K. Lilly Jr. acquired Oldfields. For all of the IMA's picturesque beauty, no one ever asked why it was closed on Mondays.

"Where are all the ladies in bikinis?" Prez asked.

"This ain't a rap video, fool." Lott shoved him playfully in the back of the head. Wayne, Lott, and Prez took up positions as escorts, feeling every bit as ridiculous as Wal-Mart greeters, but King wanted the arrivals to be respected and welcomed.

"They're going to be late," King reassured them. His leather coat swirled around him like a low-lying cloud, perfectly framing the image of Dr Martin Luther King Jr on his black T-shirt. His Caliburn was safely tucked away, but not on his person, per the rules of parlay.

"Had to prove who's the biggest man. Make the others wait," Wayne agreed.

"So we could be here all night just waiting for them to show." Detective Cantrell stood arms folded over one another, his face a sculpture of solemn, bemused, skepticism. His posture the incarnation of the words "I told you so."

"Someone has to be first," King said.

In the face of the event possibly flopping on its face, Pastor Winburn beamed in silence toward King with something akin to pride.

The cleaning staff came through Oldfields every other evening with great care, erasing any traces of that day's traffic. Eight historically refurbished rooms reflected their 1930s appearance. Pristine furniture of a bygone era, preserved, restored, dusted, polished dead dreams. Visitors typically started at the Entrance Hall, with its circular staircase and then moved into the Great Hall, the grand artery of the house that accessed most of the other rooms. It was the main room for entertaining.

However, the players weren't gathering to entertain.

Lined up within the long drive of Oldfields, the various crew leaders pulled up with their respective security entourages. Sports cars, SUVs, long green Continentals, all freshly washed, with immaculate rims: a funeral procession, built on the backs of a poisoned community. The first out of the vehicle was always bodyguard. Foot soldiers guarded the cars. No one worried about any beefs because all parlays were respected and any issues squashed.

"I think that's Rellik's ride pulling up," Prez said.

Garlan stepped out of the Cadillac CTS-V first, followed by The Boars and Rok, checking the place out with a quick scan before giving a nod to Rellik. He shook out his shirt in one final act of preening, then walked toward Oldfields. Lott and Prez moved to greet him, but Wayne put his arm up to hold them back.

"I got this," he said in a flat tone devoid of any humor or joy, a tone so unfamiliar to either of them it froze them in their tracks. Wayne walked toward Rellik. He didn't have any words prepared. He hadn't rehearsed this moment in his head. Once his brother left the family, his name was hardly brought up. A ghost who ran the streets, he might as well have been as dead as his other brothers. He had heard Gavain was out and given the worlds they ran in, knew the possibility of them running into one another was constant. But not necessarily inevitable. When King detailed his scheme, the idea of seeing his brother still didn't seem real to Wayne. Yet here they were.

"Wayne." For his part, Rellik didn't know how to play the situation either, besides cool. It had been too long and without any vibe of brotherly affection, wasn't no point in going too far out the way to be... brotherly.

"Gavain." Wayne moved in. The scar of the back of his neck itched. Garlan took note, ready to move, but relaxed as the two embraced. More cordial than any true warmth. It was a start.

"Don't no one call me that no more." He cut his eyes toward Garlan. "It's Rellik."

"I heard that's who you were now. Which is it, killer or relic?"

"Which do you hope it is?" Rellik let the question hang in the air. "You look good, money. Played a little ball, I heard."

"For a minute. Blew out my wheel though."

"Now you out here saving kids."

"They save themselves. I'm just here to help them stay out they own way."

"Keeping them from drowning." He wondered if Wayne had any love in his heart for him. Gary. Rath. Their deaths weren't his fault but they were under his care. They were his charges, his responsibility, and he fucked it up. He fucked everything up. His actions blew up the family as they were never the same afterward. Just walking into the house made him sad. His mother's eyes betrayed the sense of blame and judgment she never gave voice to. Not that their eyes ever met. She spoke to him when she had to, always pleasant enough. But that was all it ever was. Brief. Courteous. Affectionless.

"Come on. Folks'll be lining up soon. Let's get you situated." Lott sensed the apprehension of the moment ushered them along.

"King," Wayne introduced. "This is Rellik of the Merky Water crew. My brother."

Rellik was the old brother and he shamed Wayne. He was the hope of the family, the one they all admired, and yet he proved himself every bit the fuck-up his father was. And his father before him. Wayne was the good one, the heart of the family. If pressed, the most Wayne might have confessed to was... annoyance at Gavain. His presence, the idea of him, to be caught up around him and his nonsense would have been too much for Wayne and what he wanted to do and how he approached the world. Better for Gavain to become Rellik, the villain he believed the family and the community viewed him as anyway.

King raised an eyebrow. Wayne rarely talked about his family and King hadn't pressed. Still, this might have been a bit of information he might've mentioned.

"What's up?" The pair clasped hands and bumped shoulders. "You can go on inside. Wayne will take care of you. Your people are free to hang out in the front room."

Rellik and Wayne departed, followed by his entourage. Within the door, Cantrell waved a metal detector wand as a security check. No weapons allowed past that point. The steps had barely been cleared when the next set of cars arrived. Mulysa and Tristan were the first out of the car. Broyn exited next. Colvin cut through the center of them, flanked by Mulysa and Tristan.

"Colvin," Merle whispered. "He stinks of fey."

"He favors Omarosa," King said.

"He should. He's her twin."

"Keep an eye on your wallet then."

"Colvin of the ICU set," Prez announced.

"King, well met." Colvin ignored all except King. The two squared off, not with any tension, but in a moment of sizing one another up. Colvin a man of languid grace, King much larger, but with a fluidity of his own. They clasped hands and bumped shoulders, then King dismissed Prez to escort Colvin to the inner chamber. They led the entourage to the great room where Pastor Winburn began the dance of getting to know the kids. Flat-faced and downcast gazes,

not a smile among the lot, they were a bored classroom with a substitute teacher. Lott remained next
to King, not wishing to leave him alone as the last of
their little gathering showed up. He knew the toll
this must take on him and didn't want to leave his
friend hurting any more than he had to.

"King." Dred's voice ran like ice water along his
back. Dred's scraggily goatee never grew in right,
adding to the natural boyish look of his face. His nest
of hair coiled out in serpentine aggression. Eyes the
color of cold onyx, though bloodshot and rheumy,
fixed on him.

"Dred."

"Parlay's a beautiful thing. A time for old friends
to reacquaint themselves and chat freely."

"Wouldn't have asked you here otherwise." A
shuffle along the shadows drew King's attention.
Baylon stepped into view. King remembered his
once-flexing gait. Not quite the full pimping stroll,
but enough to convey the fluid movement of his
prison-built bulk. Eyes half-closed in onsetting
ennui, as if bored with all he surveyed. The man before him was shriveled, not in size, but in the way
he carried himself. Like a drained old man with a
stiff-jointed shuffle. His jogging suit had seen better
days, but not damn sight of a washer. "Damn, son.
You look rough."

"Such are the winds of fortune," Dred said.

"Come on. Let's go inside."

• • • •

Naptown Red scurried up the steps just as Detective Cantrell Williams was set to close the door. He wanted to arrive last, making the others wait on him. He parked his whip over in the lot of the museum proper and walked over, not wanting anyone to see his rusted-out '88 Oldsmobile. The car was pimping in its day, a classic, to Red's mind, but might have gotten him laughed out this here player's ball.

"Damn, you trying to rush a nigga?" Red asked.

"Who are you?" Cantrell studied him.

"Naptown Red." Black moles formed a constellation around each of his bloodshot, heavy eyes. The color of his skin was uneven, giving his face the appearance of a mask which didn't fit correctly around his hairline. His dry feral auburn hair had been straightened and pulled back. And he bathed in a cologne which smelled a lot like Crown Royal. He tugged at his junk in anticipation of entry.

"Who?"

"Red. I believe I'm expected."

"All those on the list are already here."

"Yeah, you cute. Ain't no one having a meeting of players in this here town without me."

"No disrespect. But I ain't heard of you." Cantrell ticked through his mental Rolodex of perps and junkies.

"My name'll ring out soon enough."

"Till it does…" Cantrell opened the door. "We talking to the lieutenants in here. Trying to get a big-picture view on things."

"I ain't no damned lieutenant."

"No disrespect." Mindful of King's edict to keep the peace, Cantrell opted to massage this no-account fool's ego. "I was hoping you'd be able to give some insight these other brothers can't provide."

"Kind of like a consultant."

Red liked the way this officer deferred to him with that "no disrespect" stuff. "Yeah, now that's what I'm talking about, son."

The walnut-paneled, Georgia-styled library was on the south end of the mansion, both remote and private (Mr Lilly collected rare books meant to showcase). They also passed the Game Room with its floor-to-ceiling bookcases and marble fireplace. A rather apropos meeting place considering their gathering, but, no, they met where such occasions warranted, the Drawing Room. An overly formal, pretentious room with its hand-painted Chinese wallpaper and stuffy-looking furniture, fit for a royal tea party. A reproducing piano, not that anyone actually entertained with player pianos anymore, hid in the corner.

Rellik seated himself next to his brother, neither one comfortable, but both quietly needing the time to adjust to the other. Flanked by Wayne and Lott, Colvin eyed the scene, the newest player to the table and the one out to prove himself the most. On the other side of Lott was Dred, King between him and Rellik. Merle stood behind King's seat.

King arranged the room to be for the players only. Not strictly those who were powers in the game – that was only one qualification to earn a spot at the round table. The other was knowing the shadow side of their world. The magic. Merle promised that he'd arrange for the food and the attendants and that those gathered would neither be offended nor unnerved by them.

"I thought that before we got down to business, we could share a meal together," King said.

"Just like old times?" Dred asked.

"Just like," Rellik offered.

King upticked his chin toward Merle to get the food started. The meal was a calculation on his part. He didn't know the history and tensions in the room. Cantrell and Merle briefed him as best they could: Dred and Rellik going way back as boys. Colvin a rising power. But there was still much he didn't know. Food had a way of calming treacherous waters. A delegation of faeries wheeled in a series of carts. Each faerie stood proud and erect, bedecked in a tuxedo, replete with white gloves. The carts interlocked in such a way as to form a single table. Seamless, such woodcraft hadn't been seen since the days of Daedalus. Sprites flurried about, like winged balls of light, fussing about the guests, laying down napkins, plates, bowls, and placing silverware. An elf, in a green suit and with the bearing of a humble cup-bearer, poured quail egg and dandelion soup into the bowls, setting down baskets of bread before disappearing. The faeries returned, each carrying sil-ver-domed trays. They lined up and, with a flourish, pulled off the silver domes simultaneously. Poached pheasant, venison roast, grilled boar, and potatoes. All in all, quite the production. Merle was pleased.

"All my favorite meat groups are represented," Wayne broke the silence. The room seemed to ex-hale then. Once the faeries retreated to a respectful distance, all that could be heard was the occasional clink of silverware against plates, the sipping of water, and Wayne chewing his food with relish.

"It's so sad to see the fey folk reduced to mere ser-vants," Colvin said.

"Their time is past. They know it and don't try to cling to past glories," Merle said.

"Is this what you think we do?" Colvin asked.

"We live in this age, we should act like it. Instead, too many hold on to the old ways." Merle searched the room for allies, but even Dred averted his eyes. King furrowed his brow as if nursing a brewing headache. "Just making small talk."

"King, you called this meeting," Dred said. "I'm surprised you had the juice to gather us at a table."

Before King called for the summit, he met with high-ranking gang generals. The dons had come to Indianapolis during Black Expo and met in a hotel room. Bedivere. Howell. Craddock. The Board of Di-rectors. Worn couches and carpets stretched between large televisions and stereo systems. They paused their poker game with thirty to forty K on the table.

A table surrounded by pot-bellied men, tattooed and bedecked with gold and silver jewelry, their huge guts testaments to their capacity for self- or over-indulgence. Their guards left the room, but they were still armed with their Tec-9s. King had his Caliburn. The Steel Cutter. "If anything funny goes on, all of us are dying up in here. Ain't none of us walking out."

When men were so disposed, they would take as many out with them as possible. It was a bold gambit. The men had seen hundreds of deaths between them, had known its shadow as intimately as any lover. They wore death and it showed in their eyes. Its threat didn't move them. His brazenness, however, did.

"Look." King held his gun at the ready. "I'm about one thing: calling a halt to the slaughter. God changed my life. God told me to clean up what I messed up."

"We don't truck with no God," Howell said in a measured tone meant to convey calm and complete reasonableness. King heard the echo of a snake's rattle in the timbre of his voice. "And we don't truck with no jail or anyone who wants to put us there. We're… risk-averse."

"I'm not going to put you down, but I'm going to let kids know they got a choice. I ain't going to give anyone your names. Word is bond."

As it was, the dons thought bigger. As part of their greater vision, they had been calling themselves

"Growth and Development" sounding more like a mutual fund than a gang, and had gone legit on the surface. Their long-term strategy was to take over a neighborhood from the top down. Community redevelopment was in their best interests. They even provided scholarships for young people.

So word came down from the dons. "That's what we want him to do."

That was what gave King the additional juice to summon them.

"What is it you wanted to discuss?" Dred asked.

"It's been a long time since many of us have gathered in one spot. Some might say it's been too long. Still others might say not long enough. Some are new to us." King nodded to Colvin, who returned a cold-eyed glare. "Either way, here we are. You all represent different crews and control most of what goes on in this city. In our community. As a family. Rellik controls most of the drug trade these days. Merky Water took over Night's operation. Colvin, you are all muscle. ICU is probably the strongest outfit at the table. And no magic gets done without Dred knowing about it or doing it."

Colvin's mind began its own paranoid calculations, making a note to discuss with Mulysa the cast of his summoning.

"So what? You call us together, fill our bellies, and pat us on the back. Get on with it, nigga," Rellik said. "What you want?"

"I want the violence to stop." King waited for the

chorus of murmurs, "aw shit"s, and sucked teeth to subside. "It's simple business. When bodies drop, po-po comes around. The police have even been by to ask about business."

"Is that why Cantrell is here?" Dred asked.

"I trust that you didn't disclose any business." Colvin's measured tone was more threat than actual question.

"Cantrell is here as a neutral party because I asked him. The only thing I've ever told Five-O was that we've had our problems in the past, but they were just that... in the past. I have to live in this neighborhood, too." Deliberate and forceful, King let the words settle in, not allowing the insinuation to stand, but not allowing the accusation to escalate into any unnecessary posturing. "Yes, we've all had tragedies visited upon us. Some more than others. But any community, given enough time, builds its share of issues. We have the luxury of letting time heal those wounds, if we allow it."

Rellik met Wayne's eyes. Dred's did not meet King's.

"Five-O ain't ever off the clock. When you know a cop to not be a cop?" Colvin asked.

"He's here because I can work with him."

"You saying you trust him?" Rellik pointed a half-chewed leg bone at King.

"I didn't say all that." King stopped short of vouching for him. That was a weight he didn't need. "He's still police. And they crawl all up in your Kool Aid whenever there's a body. How does business go then?"

"So what are you proposing? A co-op? You want to get your hands dirty now?" Dred asked.

"No. I'm here strictly to represent the community. Me, Pastor Winburn, Cantrell, we the community."

It all came down to power. Rellik had power. Dred had power. Colvin had power. They gripped people's hearts and imagination. And they held the boogeyman fright, the monster in the closet or under the bed. Their stranglehold over the neighborhood propelled him.

"And what? We the parasites you trying to get rid of?" Dred continued.

Yes. King wiped his mouth with his napkin. "You aren't going anywhere. So we need to find a way to coexist."

"Or what? You come at us with your golden gat?" Colvin asked. "Yeah, I've heard about you, too."

"No. We mediate. Me, Pastor Winburn, and Cantrell. An impartial board to hear disputes."

"So all power runs through you?" Dred asked.

"You all have the power. Life and death in your hands. Every day you grind brings life and death into the community. I want us to dream bigger. To take better care of our community. And I think this is the first step."

Mulysa stretched his short, stocky body out of the uncomfortable Victorian-era chair. There were plenty of snacks and pop to be had, but nothing approaching the smells emanating from the other room. The pastor and that gay-ass detective talked their talk about community and trying to "connect" with them. That might work on some of the young uns. The Boars and Rok actually listened with something close to attention. Tristan stood off to the side, acting like she wasn't paying attention, but she took it all in. That was her way. He noticed that played-out fool Naptown Red sidled towards him as if he was slick.

"You Mulysa. Colvin's boy," Red said. There was an ugliness to his face, his dry skin accentuating the splotches along his face. His brittle-straight hair was in desperate need of a wash.

"Yeah, nukka," Mulysa said. "But I ain't no one's boy."

"I didn't say you his bitch… though he do treat you like one."

"You need to get out of my face or parlay or no parlay…"

Red put his hands up in an "OK, OK" gesture of backing off. "I'm just saying, I know talent when I see it. And know how to appreciate it."

Mulysa didn't say anything, but didn't turn and leave either.

"You know what you are to Colvin, don't you? Him and his half-white self. The blood of our oppression's thick in his veins. You know what you are to him?"

"I'm his nukka."

"You need to say I right. Nigger." Red's blood shot gaze held Mulysa's thickly vesseled eyes. His words carried an intensity, a truth, like the japes of a court jester. A weight Mulysa couldn't ignore.

"Nigga."

"Nig. Ger. Say it like it means something. Like it has the sting of history behind it."

"Nigger."

"Louder."

"Nigger!"

Tristan turned to him, her hand at the ready, a reflex itchy to wield her blades though she had left them in the car. Pastor Winburn and Cantrell raised up to see if there was any trouble. Red waved them off.

"Yeah, motherfucker. You just another nigger up in this piece. Ain't no American dream for you. Ain't no two point five kids, a car, a house, or a dog called Muffy. You a niggcr."

"A nigger." Mulysa knew. He always knew.

"A nigger who can't find no straight work. Who can't pay his bills. Who didn't finish school. No-account, no-hope-having nigger. Don't you forget that shit. When you ready to be appreciated, you come look me up."

"So what do you want from us?" Rellik pushed his plate from him, unable to eat another bite. They all had their part to play and Rellik couldn't help but think that his part was about up. This was King's game now.

"I just want you to think on it. Get up with me later."

"The way I see it, this here arrangement don't benefit me no how." Colvin said without defiance or bravado, but with a matter-of-fact plainness. "You said it yourself: ICU the strongest. We got our own connect. We got our own muscle. We don't need y'all. No disrespect. I don't want to step on your business, but we just going to go ahead and do our own thing."

Colvin pushed away from the table. King also rose, out of respect, not threat. Merle opened the door for him.

"Mulysa, come on. We out," Colvin barked.

"Sit, Mulysa, sit. Good dog," Naptown Red stage-whispered.

Tristan and Mulysa attended him, trailed by Broyn. Mulysa caught Red's eye one last time. Tristan slipped one of Pastor Winburn's cards into her pocket.

"Anyone else?" King hid his disappointment.

"I'm not committing to nothing, but Colvin raises a point. What's in it for us?" Rellik asked.

"Peace."

"So what, we carve up the city like we Churchill, Truman, and Stalin?" Dred asked. The implication was dirtier than King wanted to imagine. He was giving assent to their trade. Conceding the war for the sake of security. Dred's eyes seemed to dare him to cross a line.

"You already have your territories, Dred. You work that out in the spirit of cooperation. We will mediate disputes and hold the line."

"And if one of us goes rogue?" Rellik stared at Colvin's vacated seat.

"If they cross the line, we go after them," King said.

"So the crown rests on you after all," Dred said.

"All I want is peace."

"King's peace."

Merle summoned the fey folk to clear the dishes and bring the desserts. The room fell to silence, creating an intimacy no one wanted, and worse, most feared. Nothing broke the stilled conversation except for the sound of Wayne eating.

"So what is this? Warning or wake?" Merle whispered.

"Both," King said. "If we play things right, we may manage to get enough time to clean up this mess."

CHAPTER THIRTEEN

The triple homicide hadn't grown cold, but Lee and Cantrell were out of active leads and had worked other cases in the meantime. They'd put down a body dump at Eagle Creek, originally ruled a suicide until a contact of Lee's steered them toward a boyfriend who was screwing around with his gun and accidentally shot his girlfriend. They put down a case of a Hispanic male shot at the Eagle Terrace apartments. Turned out he was beefing with another dude over the attentions of a prostitute. A tip from Lee's confidential informant put them on the hunt for one Rondell Cheldric, aka Mulysa. *Cute*, Cantrell thought, "Asylum" spelled backwards. They were obviously dealing with a clever knucklehead.

Cantrell and Lee weren't friends. They weren't even partners, not in any real sense. They simply shared a vehicle. Lee was like the person Cantrell got stuck with on a long flight, the chatty kind who asked too many questions, didn't especially care about his answers, mostly loving the sound of their own voice. Ironically, it was Lee who preferred to ride alone, whereas Cantrell reveled in the idea of a partner. He longed for the company and conversation… just not with Lee.

"I just get tired of it is all." Lee continued the thread of conversation from his usual quilt of gripes. He'd roll his list of slights around in his head until they built up enough steam to sputter out his mouth like a leaky bowel. It was never too difficult to follow him.

"What? Black folks not showing your peckerwood ass enough love?" Cantrell studied the passing scenery. He avoided looking at Lee whenever possible. Lee's kind of ugly from the inside out, hurt him like staring into the sun.

"Ain't no love coming from–"

"Watch yourself now."

"… the hood. It's respect I want."

"What every man wants." Cantrell knew he'd regret asking the question which threatened to pass his lips, but the sheer weight of the misery Lee carried with him today had him slumped over, his thin face twisted into an expression passing for pensive. "What's the matter?"

"Just thinking about my girl."

"Please don't tell me about the two of you having sex. I don't even want the tangential possibility of the hint of the image of you naked."

"I think we're breaking up." The gentle green from the dashboard lights and the monitor of their computer cast a melancholy pallor on Lee's face.

Cantrell remained silent in commiseration. Though he had little interest in hearing a peckerwood go all emo on him, he turned his head back to the street to give Lee the space to continue.

"Yeah. Think she's bored with me. She been distracted lately."

"What she do?" A tentative halt hitched Cantrell's voice. He still feared the conversational thought was going to go straight into their sex life.

"Don't know."

"How could you not know?" Cantrell turned to him. His instinct stirred within him, suddenly making him very aware of his partner. "It's our job to know."

"You know women. One great mystery after another. And if you're lucky, you get a memo letting you in. So, it's not come up yet."

"How could…?" Again, the willfulness of Lee's ignorance troubled him. Still, the answer to that question probably involved them and positions Lee would take too much delight in detailing. "Sounds like your relationships may have other significant problems if you don't even know what she does."

"I know. But I been afraid to know."

"Why?"

"I think she might be a pross. Or worse."

Cantrell's mouth started to form a question, but it collapsed on his lips. Every scenario he imagined suddenly involved Lee handing him a flaming bag of shit for him to clean up. "Dating" a suspected prostitute was bad enough. The "or worse" part had him especially concerned. Either way, Cantrell was at ground zero, too much at risk of being collateral damage. When the shit exploded, if he didn't know more about what was going on, there'd be no way to determine the blast radius. The idea of a partner became less and less appealing. "What do you mean by 'or worse'?"

"She tells me things."

Intuition was a police detective's Holy Spirit. It guided and formed them. Helped them make leaps of faith. And warned them as long as their conscience was not too seared to hear its gentle whisper. And right now, its soft voice spoke to him with a disconcerting clarity. "Please don't tell me she's your CI."

"Not registered," Lee said.

"Oh fuck." Cantrell pictured a bag being lit and left on his porch.

"I run all her info through another CI and put his name on the warrants."

"Why. The Fuck. Are you telling me this?" Cantrell wanted to smack the shit out of Lee. This cracka-ass fuck-up held his career in his peckerwood palms and he better not be enjoying the jackpot he was putting him in.

"I just got a feeling is all."

"About what? No point in holding back on me now."

"I don't know. I just think she's more of a player in all of this shit than she let on."

"This bust a set-up?" Intuition. It spoke to all police. A gift, even to the worst of them.

And while Cantrell believed himself to be in tune to the whispers of intuition, he far from trusted the voices whispering in his erstwhile partner's head. Lee struck him as the type who spent hours practicing looking hard in the mirror.

"I don't think so. But I've had the feeling for a long time that she was pulling my strings for her own agenda. And the sex…"

Here we go.

"…was the price of my services." Lee let the words hang in the air to settle in, smug about his services rendered. Oblivious to the overriding fact that he may have been played.

"But the intel has been good."

"Spot on. Perfect."

"Too perfect?" Cantrell's eyebrows arched in suspicion.

Lee studied his hands and mumbled. "Yeah. Maybe."

"So 'or worse'… she some sort of player? Dealer?"

"Don't know."

"Thief?"

"Don't know."

"Hitter."

"Don't know."

"What do you know?"

"She's a wild ride. Enough to make a man turn a blind eye to whatever else she's doing."

Lee's face caught the strobe of the cruiser lights as they stepped out of the car. With great restraint, he managed to not make a wisecrack. It was time to put his game face on. He affected a pose of authority without a worry in the world.

Naptown Red put it on the vine that he wanted to get up with Garlan, Rellik's number two. The man proved more difficult to connect with than antici-pated. He had a way of just showing up, his crews suddenly much more productive as they never knew when he'd show up or how long he'd been among them. Listening. Invisible. He was a ghost.

Not that Red was much better.

He roamed the streets, each night finding a new spot to lay his head. By his metric, his life was his own. He lived as he wanted, where he wanted, an-swerable to no one and no schedule except his own. He was the god of his own world.

And he needed to go to the library.

The Indianapolis Public Library reminded him of a southside hilljack who decided to build onto his house. The original structure was a simple brick mason box matching many of the buildings and me-morials built downtown at the time. A couple dozen steps led up to its entrance. In the last couple years, a metallic and glass state-of-the-art structure was added, five shiny stories of computers, cafés, and es-calators. The bank of computers smelled of body funk and light smoke. The air circulation always

turned up to high as many homeless folks killed af-
ternoons there. Some days there was a four-hour
wait to get on a computer. Most days Red went up
there to check his e-mail and cruise the internet. The
security guards eyed him as he passed by. As they did
Garlan.

"What up, G?" Naptown Red asked.

"I don't like folks coming up on me." Garlan didn't
glance up from the computer screen.

"I bet not. You got my message?"

"I'm here ain't I?"

Their conversation drew the eyes of the library
workers. Some of the neighboring computer stations
peeked up at them like prairie dogs on a savannah.

"Come on, let's go somewhere we can talk in private."

Garlan unfurled from his seat, a slow and languid
movement, a sail for a ghost ship. Naptown Red led
the way to one of the empty meeting rooms.

"What you want, man?" Garlan took the seat
nearest the window. Three stories up, he had a grand
view of the comings and goings of the building. And
of whoever passed back and forth in front of the
meeting room.

"Can't a nigga be friendly?" Red scooted his seat
to an angle, not wanting his back to the door.

"I got enough friends. When folks come around
showing too many teeth, they have a way of reaching into your pocket."

"I got a proposition."

"What?"

"How are things with you and Rellik?" Red asked.

"What, you a headhunter now? Scouting talent for other crews?"

"Nah, setting up my own shop."

"Shit. You must be crazy. In this economy?"

"Dealing, hell, fiends are recession-proof."

"But Dred and Rellik ain't and I'm straight with Rellik."

"A-ight, a-ight. I ain't trying to split you from your girlfriend."

Garlan rose up. There was no heat in it, no posturing. Just boredom. He didn't have time for the penny-ante games of this fool. Having watched him at the parlay, Garlan thought he was worth hearing out. But if all he had were insinuations and weak insults, his time was better spent checking up on his crew.

"Chill, nigga. I'm kidding. How are you for jobs on the side?" Red asked.

"What you mean?"

"I'm asking if you exclusive to Rellik or if you can be your own man."

"I can do my thing," Garlan said.

"Good, that's what I want to hear."

"What you got in mind?"

"I need someone disappeared."

"Got?"

"Nah, just gone. For a time." Red's mouth quivered as if hungry for a cigarette.

"Kidnapped?"

"Something like that. Just out the way for a spell."

"Who?"

"King's girl."

"You crazy. His daughter?"

"King got a daughter?" Red perked up, whatever craving he had forgotten. Information and opportunity had a way of satiating quiet grumblings.

"A little girl. Nakia. Stay around the way with his baby momma," Garlan said.

"How you know?"

"Man like me... hears things."

"I'll be damned. Guess Mr Ghetto Saint is as pure as pissed-on snow."

"I don't think that even count as dirt round here," Garlan said.

"Anyways, I was talking about Lady G."

"Shit, that's just as crazy."

"I give you two large."

Garlan thought he'd have to haggle up for one grand. "I was gonna ask that for a nobody. She a special risk. So I need a... a..."

"Risk allowance."

"Yeah."

"Four."

"Five." Garlan sensed there was money behind this play. If Naptown Red was tossing about money freely, if he was good for it – cause any fool could toss out numbers – then he might not be a bad friend to have after all.

"Done." By Naptown Red's machinations, he just needed King out of play. Distracted, if nothing else.

Garlan waited.

"Damn, nigga. Now?"

"Money up front."

"Half now. Half when the job is done."

"Yeah."

"Don't fuck me," Red said with no play in his voice.

"I collect my ends. Word is bond."

"Word is bond."

The boundary of Breton Court was a tale of two strip malls, small-scale redevelopments, bringing a slice of suburban culture. The neighborhood changed by degrees before Baylon's very eyes. Just yesterday, it seemed, the strip mall running along the southern border of Breton Court – the two separated by a creek – was filled with a Target, an Osco Drug, a Comic Carnival, the Mattress Factory. Today, the Target had moved west to the other side of I-465, towards the suburbs; the Osco moved south, away from the squeeze of the Walgreens and CVS which had sprung up like pernicious weeds every few blocks; and the Mattress Factory was an empty space with a For Lease sign. Today the strip held a Peddler's Mall, a space for a fireworks store which set up shop two months a year, the Los Compadres Food Mart and the Marisco's Costa Brava restaurant.

A strip mall also girded the west side of Breton

Court, the two separated by a wooden fence and a
gravel lot. From the concrete-topped hill above the
court, one could easily see over the wooden fence.
A collection of landscaped, curtly cut bushes, deco-
rated the entranceway. Palmirana Bakery, Piezanos
Pizza, Carniceria Campos and Novedades Sandy (a
goblet formed from "Y") reparacion y mantemiento
de computadores; the wind carried the wonderful
smells of stewed meats and warm breads from the
restaurant. To the rear of this strip were stacked black
plastic crates, trash bins swarmed by flies, and abandoned shopping carts filled with flattened cardboard
boxes. Billboards proudly alerted the neighborhood
to the presence of Geico Insurance and Bud Light,
the frame of which having been tagged by "JUAN"
and "DRK." Additionally, they had spray-painted not
just the billboard base, but the side of the strip mall
and had been painted over on the side of one of the
Breton Court condos.

The creek which ran between the two malls was
overgrown with foliage and buzzed by dragonflies.
Kids sometimes trolled for crawdads or minnows in
the silt-filled streams. Budding maple and tulip trees
grew so thick no one could see to the southern strip
mall from Breton Court. The little bridge which
crossed the creek along High School Road was practically sealed off by plants. A trained eye could spot
the worn path through the weeds leading down the
side of the bridge through the overgrowth and to the
sheltering tunnel formed by the overpass. This was

where Baylon lived, in the shadow of his former home.

Early morning fog rose from along the creek bed, wispy ghosts along a whispering creek. A plank of plywood formed a makeshift lean-to, shielding a body from easy sight should the curious venture beneath the bridge. Used condoms were scattered on his bedroom floor, drifting in from the trickling current of the creek. Baylon searched among the cardboard and plastic and blankets piled beneath it for clothing, retrieving a pair of frozen socks. The creek was a natural ley line, and the bridge, though not his place of power, resonated like an echo chamber. It might prove to be sufficient. Dred sat on a milk crate, his eyes shut as he concentrated on his spell. His patience wore thin and he had better things to do than traipse through the underbush.

"I hear you were looking for me." Morgana appeared behind him. The sudden sound of her voice caused Baylon to drop the socks and he whirled around. She had a way of making things inconvenient for everyone. She could be like that.

"Mother." Dred rose.

"This better be worth it." Morgana studied the two of them. "The chicken comes home to roost. And you brought a friend."

"I have no friends."

"You are your mother's son."

"And my father's." Dred let his leather half-jacket fall open to reveal the handle of the Caliburn.

"I see that. You've grown into a handsome young man, your eyes filled with that same youthful ambition." Morgan stepped to her side, beginning a wary circling of Dred and not wanting to lose track of his faithful dog.

"I want what's mine."

"What do you think is owed you?"

"Power. It should all be mine. The wealth. The women. The reputation. I should have them. I want to be the king now."

"It's not your time. Not yet."

"Why not?" His voice shot to too high a register, too much of the hint of a whine in its undertone. He waited for an answer. Her silence spoke for her. "King?"

"You know what I mean." She strolled around him, her hand tracing a circle along his chest, around his back, and to his chest again. She placed the flats of both hands on his chest and stepped closer to him. "You should seize what you want."

"I can't."

"A real man wouldn't wait." Her breath ran hot into his ear. "What's stopping you?"

"I need more. One last bit of magic. Then I could step to him proper."

"One last… lesson?"

"For one of us." Dred grabbed her by the back of her head and kissed her. Thrust his tongue deep into her mouth, her tongue finding his in their macabre dance. He reached into his pant waist, brushing away her hands. And withdrew his Caliburn. He pressed the barrel into her side, aimed towards her heart, and squeezed the trigger.

At the report, Morgana's eyes flared open, a cruel smile crossed her lips. They both began to speak in a tongue older than man. As each heard the other, they spoke faster, racing to the end of whatever mystical sentence they had memorized.

To Baylon it seemed like a duel of incantations, each of them racing to see who could complete theirs first. Baylon heard the screams in his head. The scene of enjoined mother and son faded from view as other images filled his mind. Flames leapt up. Babies burned in a fire. A face melted away. The skin of a cat flayed off. A father's belt slapped bare buttocks. A mother ripped her unborn from her belly. Lovers cut each other with blades as the excitement of their love-making increased, each thrust exciting them to deeper wounds. A dagger sliced through his lung. His breath escaped him. He dropped to his knees. Darkness embraced him. And he opened his eyes. Dred stood alone. His mother's clothes still in his hands.

"It is finished," he said. "Now I can begin."

CHAPTER FOURTEEN

Rhianna took the number three Indy Metro bus to the corner of New York and Rural on the bus pass she'd received from Outreach Inc. Her butt switched as she walked. She had an appointment with Esther to discuss her GED and pick up a few baby things. Her swollen belly peeked from beneath her white shirt. Due any day, she rubbed it as if that might coax the baby to come sooner. She didn't care if it was a boy or a girl. She already had a girl who stayed with her auntie most of the time. It wasn't like she had room for her at her place at the Phoenix Apartments where she stayed most of the time. Percy objected to her staying there after the mess with Night, but the Phoenix was all she knew. Shit could jump off wherever she laid her head. There was no shortage of drama out here.

She remembered when she first came by Outreach Inc. With Lady G, their fingers clasped like long-lost lovers, her arm around her waist, head on her shoulder, a prom date of needles and glass dicks. A lifetime ago. Before the magic. Before the madness. Before King.

A contraction pain rippled through her. Stubborn-ass baby. Had to be a boy, acting like he didn't want to be born. Probably knew what awaited him. She planned to name him something wonderful. And strong. She just wanted someone to love her unconditionally, who she could love, who would stay with her.

Percy baffled her though.

The big fool followed her around worse than a faithful puppy nipping at her heels. Never wanting anything, never pushing up on her, never demanding anything, just… there. Around. Taking care of her.

Lott waited on the porch of Outreach Inc., craving a cigarette so badly his hands itched with the muscle memory. He watched her approach, his eyes full of anticipation without recognition, as if hoping she were someone else. Upon realizing who she was, his mouth curled into disappointment before catching itself and twisting into a warm grimace.

"What's up, baby girl?" Lott asked, putting his arm around her in a side embrace.

"You. Up here acting cute. What you here for?"

"Nothing. Drop before work. Maybe catch me some dinner."

"You come all the way out here for dinner?"

"Thought I could get up with Wayne."

"Wayne, huh. I see how you look at her. That can't be healthy." She plopped her backpack on the porch next to him. She decided to stay out of the direct line of sight of the house across the street and stepped behind one of the porch pillars. "The others don't see it, but I do."

"Ain't nothing to see."

"Keep telling yourself that. You might even believe it. But your eyes don't lie. That girl can't sneeze without drawing your full attention. Your heart practically stops till you see her start breathing again. Like I said, that can't be healthy."

"We're just friends." He was probably a little too sensitive where Lady G was concerned.

"See? I didn't even need to say who I was talking about, but you still want to sing that tired old song." Her words more combative, on the brink of a dare.

"In. Sta. Gator."

"Don't be mad cause I'm up here telling truth." Rhianna sighed. She'd said her piece and that was all she could do. She slowly gathered her things as if excused. Or dismissed. Either way, she knew her presence was no longer welcome, a fifth wheel. Bitterness in her smile, without warmth, only the legacy of resentment at never getting anything to call her own. "Fine. It just better stay nice and just friendly."

Rhianna rang the doorbell. Esther answered the door to let her in and held it open for Lott. He waved her off and she closed the door behind Rhianna. There were squeals of being happy to see each other, checking out how big Rhianna's belly was before she was whisked back to get something to eat. Lott didn't care about any of Rhianna's trifling musings. He knew what Lady G would say about her assumptions. That she was coming from a place of jealousy, wanting Lott's attentions for herself. Just like he knew there was no room for another in his heart. Unrequited love was the stuff of poets, the tortured soul which resonated with truth. It was safer to love one you could not have, his heart protected, locked away. His unrequited love was the purest sort of love. To love from afar without expectation was selfless. He loved her as if she was carved in ice. He lived to serve her, to be there for her, knowing her virtue and beauty and honor. To never sigh, yearn, desire, to touch her, his love was disciplined. But still, he burned for her. Oh, he burned all right. Like a man in fever, he kept her image burning in his brain.

He was a damned fool.

Another Indy Metro bus pulled up along Rural Avenue. Lady G stepped off, smoothed out her clothes, and trundled along the block. Lott straightened, suddenly aware of his slouch, but he couldn't seem to find the proper posture of cool. He really wanted a cigarette now.

"What's the matter with you? Face all sour like someone done took the last of your favorite Kool Aid." Lady G hugged him, a full-frontal embrace that neither seemed quick to break.

"Rhianna was just out here talking crazy about us."

"What about us?"

"Saying that we don't look like we just friends."

"What we look like?"

"I don't know. More, I guess. You know how she is."

"Always meddling."

"Yeah."

"I mean, you cute and all..." Her hand rested on his. Not flirty, but knowing. She enjoyed the effect she had on him. She played the silly games girls play, confusing him one moment, making him jealous the next. The petty cruelties of love. Craving his affections and attentions, she knew that she kept him for herself, held his heart by a dog leash.

The sound of her voice felt too near. "But you with King."

"I know."

What he said about King was true, but she felt like the bride of a war husband, a man divided between mission and family. Living such a split life, carving up bits of himself doled out to everyone who needed him or even just asked, King was his own worst enemy. And no one saw it, no one looked out for him. They simply kept lining up to take from him. And she also respected the image they represented in front of the group and she wanted to be seen as warm, loving, nice, and loyal.

Lott fit her. She loved Lott for his bravery, courtesy, boldness, and lack of guile, but it was more than that. Lott allowed her to be her. Young and silly, not always serious and driven. She didn't have to live up to how he saw her but could just… be. Lott was a simple man with a simple code and who would risk his life, but not his brothers'. He didn't have King's moodiness, darkness, and pent-up secrets. King was a frustrating, closed book while Lott was an open, simple one. At times she wanted to just hold him, stroke his hair. The idea of her and Lott was too costly so she blocked the idea out of her mind. But whenever he was around, whenever it was her and him, it was as if her thoughts and actions shifted into automatic pilot.

"You OK?" Lott asked. "You drifted off."

"But I was going to say that you're, I don't know, my best friend."

"Yeah." Lott rose, his body too aware of her presence. That was his way: rather than be tempted or mentally toy with things he shouldn't, he'd leave. "Anyway, I gotta bounce. Gonna meet King."

"Be careful."

"I will. Uh, could I borrow your scarf?" the chill of the air didn't bother him, he simply wanted to have something of hers close to his heart.

"Yeah." She handed her knight errant her slight blue veil.

Their shadows held hands.

There were wars and there were wars, and Naptown Red was a soldier to the bone. The idea of a war on drugs amused him. Wasn't no president launched troops into the hood searching for crack pipes of mass destruction. Nor were any planes deployed to bomb coca fields. No, there were police sent in to lock niggas up for trying to earn, the government mad too little of these dollars were lining its pockets. The money was out there, steady flowing, and where money went, so went power and interest.

All the wars did was turn police into frontline troops on the opposing side of the community. No one talked to the police. Police no longer talked to the community, trained to eye them with suspicion and dread, fomenting a spirit of distrust and uncooperation. They turned innocent bystanders, hard-working citizens not in the game, into enemy non-combatants. And Red into a freelance mercenary, because in times of war, soldiers were at a premium. He couldn't think of anyone he knew that didn't have someone who'd been locked up, was locked up, or was on paper.

The midnight air cool and crisp, he felt no pain beneath the sodium glare of the street lights. A bottle of Crown Royal wrapped in a paper bag, he held court at the Rural Inn on the corner of Rural and Michigan Street. He took a healthy sip and it bit into him real nice. Close to drunk, the low warm got his head up in a nice way. Roger's "I Want to be Your Man" was stuck in his head so he hummed along.

"What's up, nukka?" Mulysa's hands remained in his pockets.

"You come see about me?" Red offered him a taste. They danced the dance of street cordiality, through tightened jaws and forced smiles.

"You still looking?"

"I was just thinking that soldiers are at a premium out here."

"Who you down with?"

"I got no set," Red said.

"Everyone works for someone."

"I got my man, but he lets me be. Sets me up, lets me do my thing. I break him off." Mulysa stared down the block. "Like you want to do for me."

"Exactly." Red pointed with the bag-wrapped bottle and winked a bloodshot yellow eye.

"What I got to do?"

"See? A well-trained dog ain't used to being off leash. What you want to do? I could set you up on a package. You could run girls."

"Yeah. All of that."

"You a Renaissance nigga. I like that. Why don't you round up a girl or two and get started. Got someone in mind?" Red asked through the haze of a knowing leer.

"Yeah."

"Good. The sooner you get on that, the sooner you on your path to complete independence."

Hot Trimz closed at 6pm most days. Wasn't open at all on Sundays. However, they kept special hours for "appointments." Some clients kept discreet hours or otherwise demanded special treatment. If the price was right, the entire staff stayed over.

Omarosa leaned back in the chair as Bunny threaded one of her eyebrows. A short, stout woman, with red and purple hair crowning her head – the lone white woman on staff – Bunny's glasses pushed low on her nose. Her eyes held to grim slits giving her face a pinched expression as she concentrated. The cow bell at the front door clanged. Omarosa drew her sawed-off shotgun into her lap.

"Relax," Bunny assured her. "The boys got this."

Omarosa listened with lethal intent.

"How many you got?" Broyn asked.

"My book's full up," Old School said.

"Yeah. I can see that." Broyn eyed the row of empty benches. "How about later?"

"Tomorrow." Old School pulled out his appointment book.

"Name a time."

"7.30, 8pm. After-shop hours."

"A-ight."

D watched him until he slow-dipped out of sight. Omarosa relaxed her grip on her weapon, but didn't lower it back to her side.

"Let's have a Halloween party then go streaking out in the Quads," Bunny yelled over the top of the partition.

"How bout I just get buck nekkid right here," Old School said.

"Aw naw. Not buck nekkid."

"You'll have to take that out back," D said from his office as he tallied the day's receipts.

"I could do it up in the front window," Old School said.

"Not in the front window!" Bunny yelled.

"Some of them cougars might come in here to see what's poppin'."

"A cougar ain't looking for another cougar."

"Dag, Bunny, I thought you and me was cool."

"We cool. Just don't call me Bunny."

The cowbell clanged again. D made a note to get a real door chime. Again. King strode in.

"She in?" King stuck his head into D's office.

"Don't you have an office?" D asked.

"Yeah, yours." The pair bumped fists.

"She round back."

An optometrist shop was two buildings north of the barber shop. Along its back wall, a six-pointed star bookended by the letters G and D along with two three-pronged pitchforks were spray painted. No such tagging occurred on the shop. D prided himself on Hot Trimz being sacred ground. Everyone needed their haircut. D had enough juice left over from his bid in jail and his time on the streets. He knew the game, respected the game, but was out of the game. Still, God didn't create a fool: dealing with the Omarosas of the world required special gloves and special dispensations. And he was willing to bend accordingly to keep the peace. For a fee.

"What you no good, Omarosa?"

"I been a good girl, King. Don't need you and your gang after me. A girl could get all to quaking in her boots."

"I hear you still sticking up Colvin's people."

"You hear an awful lot."

"Broyn was just in here sniffing around. Probably waiting outside to follow you."

"He welcome to try." Omarosa eased her finger off the sawed-off and allowed it to rest across her lap. "So what brings you my way, King?"

"I wanted to check in on you." He spoke with a purposeful affection. In ways he didn't understand, he felt some sort of fealty to her. Not that she was his charge, or him hers, but there was the charge of responsibility between them.

"I look like a girl that needs checked in on?"

"You out here without anyone. No support. No one to watch your back. No one to—"

"Love me? You worried about me, my liege." Omarosa let the last words drip with venomed honey before she sat up. Without a glance her way, Bunny knew she'd been dismissed. "The more sophisticated the mind, the more slippery the slope into self-deception."

"What do you mean?"

"That's what you came to talk to me about isn't it?"

To her mind, King had two great loves in his life: Lady G and the streets. Love was his weakness. Omarosa had once broached the topic of he and Lady

G, her with her young eyes and need of a strong male in her life. And her lack of judgment. King wouldn't entertain any thought of Lady G's misplaced loyalty. It was like he couldn't hear of it.

"I know the life I'm living and I know the woman I'm with," he had told her.

"All due respect, you love the ground she pee on," Omarosa said then. *His loves would be the ruin of him. The old story.*

Nevertheless, even now, she pressed her point with renewed vigor. "I mean you've taken on the mantle and you wear the crown well... if lightly. Sometimes I think too lightly, but who am I to judge? The streets have been calmer though the mayor and police are quick to claim credit. You've even made it harder for a girl to earn."

"You look like a woman who has trouble taking care of herself," he smirked.

"You've done it, King. Taken hold of the streets, reached out to the young uns. Trying to train them up. You look around and see all the hurting still going on despite all you've done, and you look to do more. The problem with a man who wants to save the world is that he sometimes forgets about his family."

King feared the opposite with Lady G. Some days he considered all the work he did, the endless meetings and relationship-building to be his distraction from thinking of her. Or worse, his efforts to impress her. He knew her, understood her. Stared into the core of her, he became obsessed with her, wanted to be with her constantly. Part of him believed he could be her savior, so protective of her that he wanted to take her away from all of the hurts; desiring nothing more than to commit himself to her. Like a marriage.

And he told Lady G as much. "What we got goes deeper than a piece of paper. I'm not going to leave you. I'll be here for you as long as you let me."

King only thought about her, talked to her, wanted to be with her and was fueled by her. Lady G filled him with bliss, became his whole world. When they pressed close together and held each other, it was a tender and fierce snuggle, a desperate clutching after one another. Never wanting to let go because it was the only time he knew peace. And she felt safe. He was going to protect her forever; she would shield him as best she could. He belonged to her and her to him. They shared their essence, poured themselves out upon each other, needing the other to validate them. He wanted so badly to be loved by her. She wanted to be there for him. It all sounded so very romantic. It was a black hole of need. Things would be so much easier if he didn't give a fuck.

"Just try to have fun." Omarosa drew him back in to the moment. "It's allowed, even for you. Just don't get too attached."

"You know that's not how I roll."

"I know. You one of them 'fall in love with the pussy' niggas. But the game is deep. Any of us can get caught up if we forget that and lower our guard."

Iz sometimes missed when it was just her and Tristan. The apartment squat was nice during the rain or cold of winter, but there was something special about their summer squat. A tract of woods under the bridge across from the Indianapolis Zoo. On the banks of the White River, sealed off by a rusted trellis and a concrete overpass, it was their corner of the world. Few predators roamed the area, especially the two-legged variety. A couple of vets stayed down the way in a neighboring stretch of woods. Another homeless man who rode a yellow ten speed with duct-taped handle bars slept beneath the neighboring bridge. But this spot was theirs. A blue tarp stretched between trees; layered with plastic and insulated with blankets, it had the appearance of a tattered biodome. Yellow drums collected rain water. Tristan maintained a fire pit. Their world was them. She felt safe.

Three sets of candles, each on an overturned milk crate lit the room to a delicate amber. Too dim to read by, but enough to stave off the darkness whenever Tristan wasn't around. Sometimes Iz texted, checking her Facebook and e-mail from her cell phone. Most times she sketched in her notepad to pass the time between school and whenever Tristan returned from her business with Mulysa. Pencil etchings of black and white hands clasped together, a larger – though still clearly feminine – one engulfing another. Tristan's face. The way she captured the perpetual hurt in her eyes. The tiny scars on her neck which she never spoke about. The steel of her set jaw when she was about to hit someone. Tristan in profile peeking out the window. Tristan watched over her as she slept; Tristan not knowing that she knew she did it most nights.

"Knock, knock," Mulysa said from the doorway.

Iz froze. "Tristan's not here. I thought she was with you."

"She was, but I sent her on an errand. I'm here to see you." His eyes filled with hungry intent.

"I ain't interested." It wasn't as if she were in a see-through teddy. A white hooded sweatshirt over another shirt and faded blue jeans. But she still felt the probe of his eyes. She always wore her running shoes. Even to bed. Even when Tristan watched over her. Iz pulled her blanket up around her, not wanting him to see anymore of her than he absolutely had to.

"I ain't asked nothing."

"Whatever you selling, whatever you proposing, I ain't interested."

"You're a rude-ass host, nukka. Least you could do is offer me a drink."

A row of bottled water stood along the window sill like an Army troop at attention. Two sleeping berths had been scooted next to each other. Clothes piled between the bedrolls and the wall, a barrier against the cold. Two backpacks leaned against the wall. One had her journal and some personal belongings. The other was one of Tristan's, mostly filled with clothes. She kept her "work" backpack with her. Iz never asked what was in it.

"You want a water?" Iz asked.

"Don't mind if I do." Mulysa pulled up one of the upended milk crates. "I did have something I wanted to discuss with you."

"My answer ain't changed."

"Hear me out now, damn. Look here, I ain't tellin' you nothin' you don't know, but you one fine piece of ass."

Iz shifted uncomfortably. Her right hand crossed her body as if shielding herself from his lecherous view. She clicked a button on her cell phone to check the time.

"Hope you weren't trying to call Tristan. You know when she's on a job her shit gets turned off. Besides, I didn't want our conversation interrupted."

"You know she's going to kick your ass for coming in here talking shit to me."

"We ain't doing nothing but talking and having some water. I ain't done anything… untoward. In fact, I just wanted some company while I finished my business."

Mulysa rolled out his kit with the delicate precision of a watchmaker. Searching around the room, he found a jar that would satisfy his purposes and filled it with a thin layer of water. Removing a Q-Tip from a wad fastened by a rubber band, he ripped the cotton from one end. Iz's eyes widened in anticipation. He revealed a baggie of crystal and began to crush it up with a Bic lighter.

"As I was saying, you a fine piece of ass. I've noticed you for a long time. Done jacked myself off to the thought of you bouncing on the end of my dick on many an occasion. But what I was thinking was more along the lines of a business proposition."

Iz wanted to get up and run right there. The voice in her begged her to leave. The familiar itch, like worms inching along the flesh of her arm, and her mouth salivated, literally watered, at the familiar ritual. Her body remembered the dance of preparation and the anticipation of the high to come. It was never as good as the first time she slammed a load home, but she damn sure kept trying to find a blast to ride to recreate a close approximation.

"Damn you," she whispered.

"You say something?" Mulysa poured a bunch of the crystal into the jar and swirled the concoction. "Anyway, what I was thinking was maybe you'd want to get back into the trade. Maybe you talk to Tristan. I heard she used to run wild for some dick back in the day. But you? You'd be my special girl. Premium rates only. Like a ghetto escort, I'm telling you."

The worst symptom of her disease was the amnesia. The way it made her forget. She forgot her sunken-in eyes, her scaly skin, and her ancient track marks. She didn't remember the bruises, the lack of definition to her muscles, or how her skin hung slack and uneven. How some times she hunted for a vein for over ten minutes despite her diminutive frame.

Mulysa held the flame to the base of the jar until the liquid began to smoke and bubble.

Near her lowest point, she developed an abscess in her arm; the infection ran down to the bone. A mixture of white, yellow, and bloody pus seeped from the wound constantly, a cloud of stench dogged her every step. Eventually she ended up in the hospital. After they were done treating her, it left a gaping hole in her arm. They shot antibiotics into her ass and packed the wound using a long Q-Tip to stuff bandages into it. Much like the ones Mulysa had.

He dropped in the cotton then drew it up into a syringe. Pulled out and pushed, spraying the wall. Iz didn't budge at his approach. Her veins jumped up like an obedient dog called home. She watched the needle puncture her skin. There was something nearly erotic about having someone shoot you up. Blood coagulation at the head of the needles. The blood and drug mixture slammed home. Waves of pulsing warmth suffused with surreal calm. An utter vacantness to her eyes. No joy, no excitement, only need. She couldn't focus. The pattern of the floor boards dizzied her. She never hated herself as much as she did right then.

And part of her didn't care.

Didn't care about a thing.

Life was going to work out.

That certainly was the best part of the high.

Mulysa reached to unfasten her jeans. "There's more where that came from."

Water from the previous night's rain filled the dip in Big Momma's courtyard between the rows of condos. Garbage clogged the drain and filled the parking lot up to the ankles. Back from the service at Good Hope – Had in tow – high on the words of Pastor Winburn, she was all about joining in God's mission to be a blessing to the world. The drain distracted her. She hiked up her dress, wading through the water in her bare feet. Cleaning away the trash, unblocking the drain, she hummed Mahalia Jackson's version of "Precious Lord, Take My Hand" and waved at Neville Sims as he rode his maintenance wagon. Had splashed about in the water while she worked.

She watched the waters recede for a few moments then turned towards her condo. Had's hand in one of her hands, her still dry shoes in the other. Her door was ajar. One of her meaty arms slammed into Had's chest harder than she intended. There had been a series of break-ins throughout the neighborhood. Mr Stern talked about more security, but still hadn't hired anyone or put up any cameras.

Her living room remained unransacked but the house had the air of violation about it. She checked out the lower level of the condo, but nothing seemed out of place. The weight of her foot on the first step as she craned up the stairwell caused the planks to squeak. She took each step slowly, gesturing for Had to stay where he was, her back to the wall as she tried to peer around corners and over ledges. Her room was fine. Last was Lady G's. Her room only slightly more disheveled than usual. But her bed was a mess. Crayons and paper scattered atop pulled-up sheets. The light stand knocked over. Her piles of clothes tumbled over. She never had any boys up in there, but it looked like she'd been dragged out. Big Momma pulled out her cell phone, punching in numbers while still surveying the scene. Straight to voicemail. She dialed a second set.

"She's gone," Big Momma yelled into the phone.

"Who?"

"Lady G."

"What do you mean?"

"I didn't know who else to call," Big Momma said, not allowing her fears to overwhelm her voice. "I didn't want to... I couldn't get a hold of King."

"It's OK. It's OK. I'm on it."

Lott disconnected the call.

CHAPTER FIFTEEN

Tristan and Iz had avoided corners where action jumped off. Quietly, Tristan always feared for Iz. It wasn't too long ago she was out on the streets on her own and the urge to hustle not long buried. Tristan remembered the days at correction after Iz had become a kleptomaniac. Tristan learned to make food last. Once outside again, Iz seemed happy to not have a toilet in her bedroom and to be away from her warden's manner of discipline and control, and upright rigidity. The one thing she longed more than anything else after being released was a bath. The simple pleasures of soaking in a tub. The desire, the hunger, the insatiable need fed temporarily by drugs bubbled beneath the surface. The last couple of days, Iz had been different. Secretive. Closed off. Evasive even about the little things. Even if she didn't give them voice, Tristan knew the signs. It reminded her of the last time she had to confront Iz's need. Tristan stopped at the corner store to get smokes, gone for only an hour, only to come home to Iz.

No lament was sung alone. For every fiend there was a brother or sister, mother or father, friend or colleague who sang along with them. From money stolen from purses to stuff missing around the house to lies upon denials upon disappointments heaped up as a raucous chorus.

Tristan knew the bottom was about to fall out. She ran the gauntlet of fiends milling about the place. How they avoided her eyes. How they shuffled off without a word, cockroaches scattering in her presence only to regroup once she was gone. They knew.

When Tristan pulled back the loosely placed piece of plywood and stepped into the alcove, it was as if the spirit of their place had been violated. Part of her knew Iz had been using again. The fiend was not the only one to sound the notes of denial in the junkie's lament. A little weed she could excuse. Maybe a one-time slip-up, because they were only human and that heroin was the devil.

She noticed the smell first. Her blades found their way into her hands without a thought. Tristan booted open the door. Half-dressed, Iz passed the pipe to her john. The room lit to the shade of burnt honey, Tristan made sure the light glinted from her blades that he could clearly see the feral warning in her eyes. The john dropped his pipe and ran past her without so much as a backwards glance at Iz. Her arms embraced her raised knees as Iz cowered in the corner of the room. A long T-shirt barely covered her, leaving her bare buttocks visible from underneath it. Her skin a frieze of sweat trails and dirt. Sucking on a Coke can used for a pipe. Feeling more empty than high.

"Why?" Tristan's voice cracked with a hollow ache.

"Don't know. Guess I'll never be whole."

Tristan huddled on the floor with Iz and kissed her hands. "It will be all right," she promised. "I'll make sure it will be all right."

Colvin had nothing to prove.

Unarmed, unescorted, and without a security entourage, he wasn't one of the neighborhood boys out in the streets getting into fights in order to find out things about himself or test himself or others to see what they were made of. He wasn't out to learn what he could carry with him for the rest of his life. And he wasn't out to gain the respect of the street, wanting neither its fear nor love. Colvin was of the fey and such things were beneath him.

Colvin wanted power.

He stood in front of the Phoenix Apartments. Lookouts between each of the buildings and hidden in stairwells had already alerted one another to his presence. He waited until he knew all eyes were on him. They would whisper that he lost his God-damned mind. That this high yella, half a cracka, Mr Spock-looking fool was going to come up into Rel-lik's home base all on his own. He half-expected someone to take a shot at him from the shadows simply to put him out of his misery.

Maybe he *was* crazy. His plan was simple: he was going to walk into Rellik's chief stash house and abscond with any product and cash. It would hurt if not cripple Rellik, the shame alone might cause the dons to remove him, increase Colvin's own bottom line, and send all the message he needed to King. If in his pursuit of power, he earned respect, fear, and love – with his name whispered among the people – he could live with that.

Colvin closed his fists and opened them. The street lamps buzzed as if on the verge of shorting out. At their best, the lights didn't fully illuminate the court and parking lot but rather created ominous pockets of shadows. Colvin marched toward the main entrance. The red glow of a cigarette tip flared and then sailed through the air. Its owner went out to meet Colvin, grinding out the cigarette in a burst of sparks as he walked over it.

The Boars didn't tower over Colvin, but he clearly had a few inches on him and nearly a hundred pounds.

"You lost?" The Boars knew all eyes and ears were on him. The thing about being his size was that he rarely felt the obligatory need to constantly flex. His physical presence alone squashed most drama.

"I heard you had a surplus of money and product and needed help moving it."

"You heard that, did you?"

"Probably conjecture on my part. Either way, it seemed like a situation I could ill afford to pass up."

"You need to rise up outta here."

"I appreciate the courtesy of the warnings. So much so, I'll give you a moment for you and your crew to vacate. Or, if it's easier," Colvin shouted up to those listening from the windows, "you could just drop the money and product out the window."

"Get this fool out of my sight."

Bodies approached from the stairwell, some reaching into their waistbands, others toting bats.

Colvin began a low chant in a tongue unfamiliar to The Boars. As far as The Boars was concerned, it was some Satanic shit he wanted no part of, so he stepped to Colvin. Without breaking the rhythm of his incantations, Colvin ducked under The Boars' wide punch and kneed him by his kidneys. He jabbed his elbow into the back of The Boars' neck, sending him lights out before he hit the ground. Before the approaching boys could draw their weapons, he arced his arms down, green light trailing the downward strokes.

Though Colvin wasn't an accomplished summoner like Mulysa, he did know how to open and close doors. Other than his glamour, it was his specialty. The blue trails split the air, giving the men pause. The unzipped fabric of space parted, revealing a deeper darkness than the midnight shadows they were in. Twin red dots flicked on a couple dozen floating in the air. The men trained their weapons on the penumbra apertures and opened fire.

A hiss echoed from the opening and a small figure

leapt out onto the nearest gunman. Its spiked boots
landed square on his face, the momentum of its
jump toppled them both, while it remained perched
on top of him. Their fall drove his metal spikes deep-
est into his face. The bone of his jaw snapped with a
loud crack. His eye socket fractured. The spikes
pulled his eye free, attached to one of the nails, the
connecting muscle drawn out like a forkful of
spaghetti. The boys' screams erupted. Still looming
over the body like a predatory gargoyle, the creature
turned its attention to the next gunman.

Suddenly the entire court lit up with gunfire and
screams.

More creatures poured from the openings. Short
hairy bodies, stalking keloids of fibrous muscle with
grizzled beards. With the wizened faces of old men
contemplating a meal of oatmeal. The gleam of their
red eyes. A taloned hand raked though the meat of
an arm, stripping ribbons of flesh. Filed teeth coming
together like a living bear trap snapped on a man's
neck. Blood throbbed from the wound in time to the
pulse. The creature paused over him. Removing its
pink cap, it daubed the spurting wound until it
turned a foul crimson.

A half-dozen more tumbled out of the hole, taking
positions behind bushes. They whirred their slings,
releasing a volley of shots. Men tumbled from the
shadows. Rellik's men kept firing.

Colvin stood among the ensuing chaos. The
screams, the rent flesh, and gunfire combined into a

symphony of violence. A shot grazed him. It would take him hours to notice. The battle, however, was over in minutes.

"Don't make me come up there," Colvin cried up to the windows.

A bag tumbled from the window.

"And the product?"

Another bag followed.

Colvin carried one in each hand and walked down the sidewalk without a backwards glance. The Red Caps jumped back into their home between spaces before the wound in the air sealed itself.

Esther Baron loved volunteering for night drop at Outreach Inc. She always had the feeling that she wasn't doing enough. Standing behind the dining room table, she'd join hands like everyone else to pray for the food and evening. She doled out the food to the kids, not to keep them from being hogs – because there was plenty of food to go around – but to let the kids be served. It was a subtle message, to let them know they were home, could relax, and allow someone to do for them. Accompanying salad and broccoli – she encouraged them to eat their vegetables and oddly enough, despite them being teens, they usually requested seconds on the veggie of the day – was a spaghetti casserole repast.

Rok squirted some hand sanitizer on his hands then passed her an empty plate. This was when she appreciated Wayne the most. He warned her that folks typically came in with the idea of making a huge impact and turning kids' lives around… on one meeting. It didn't work that way. The only "doing" was the ability to open oneself up and love another. For one evening, she arrived with the spirit to serve, to be a blank tableau for the kids without judgment, to show them grace. Provide a space of stability that could help them take the next step toward their goals.

"How you doing, Rok?" she asked.

"Doing good, Miss Esther. You looking good with your fine-ass self."

"Rok," Esther chided, but in a mild tone, enough to let him know she wasn't playing. "You think that's an appropriate way to talk to a woman? I know I'd appreciate a compliment without the disrespect."

"You look good tonight, Miss Esther," he said without his usual bluster, awkward and sheepish. The way he glanced about to make sure no one noticed was almost cute. Wayne didn't hold the kids to some preconceived model of how they should be or act. He did believe in boundaries and letting them know what was appropriate between men and women.

Already at the table in the common room, Wayne chatted amiably with the kids as they came in. He asked about their day, teased them about their fashion choices, listened to them, and helped them through some of the decisions they made. The way he explained it, the time was about connecting. With them, finding out about one another and letting the impact of being in their lives speak to them. Success, even progress, had to be measured differently. But there was a look that would light up their eyes. Sometimes faint, sometimes bright, moments when they realized someone cared about them; cared without expectation or demand. He wanted everything for the kids, imagined them, saw potential in them in ways they couldn't for themselves. The job required a kind of fearlessness. A willingness to go deep with people, people who would likely disappoint. People who would likely make bad decisions. People who often couldn't get out of their own way. Not only was Wayne passionate for them, his passion was contagious.

"How're things going out there, Rok?" Wayne asked.

"Steady."

"No recession worries?" Wayne joked with him, conscious of not sounding approving of him, but not wanting to be yet another lecturing voice in his life to be tuned out.

"What?"

Wayne also didn't want to make Rok feel stupid or condescended to. He got enough of that at home. And school, when he bothered to attend. "You thinking about what we talked about before?"

"That GED thing? Man, you trippin' with that noise."

"I'm trippin', huh. Pass me a roll."

"They got more rolls up there," Rok said.

"Yeah, but then I'd have to get up. And you got three on your plate."

"You stupid." Rok handed him a roll.

"Why I gotta be all that?" Wayne bit into the roll. Not especially hungry, he simply liked to eat with the kids. Eat what they ate, not wanting any sense of "we're just here to feed the poor darkies." And he kept the conversation light, harassed them like family would at the dinner table, but still pushed in on their lives. "You got a head on you. You good with numbers. A little training, you could set up your own business."

"You think?"

There it was. That light. Rok entertained a new possibility for himself. That was all Wayne could ask for. But he'd stay on him, fanning that tiny spark until it grew into something. Wayne clung to the little hopes of progress.

The doorbell rang. The door was kept locked during drop, no one coming in without a staff member letting them in. Tonight was a closed drop which meant regular clients only. Frantic fists pounded on the door frame. Wayne bolted to the door, preferring to open it because he never knew what might jump off on the other side, and he wanted to be the first line of defense for the volunteers. Especially Esther.

Tristan held Iz up.

"Help us," Tristan said.

"What happened?" Wayne asked. Esther ran over

to help catch Iz and ushered her to the couch. Esther soaked a wash cloth and gave it to Tristan, who daubed her forehead. She balanced on the edge of the couch, giving Iz as much room as possible.

Wayne preached boundaries but didn't always practice them. Unless he was on call, he discouraged clients from calling him off hours (except for emergencies) and rarely answered his cellphone (preferring to check his voicemail). He maintained regular office hours and when drop night was done, he led the charge to hustle everyone out. But he didn't follow his own guidelines with strict rigidity. In the language of the best trained seminarians, "Shit happened."

Iz sprawled out on the couch, under the tender ministrations of Tristan. Wayne thought about calling 911 and still debated it, but Iz seemed to be just coming down from a high. Iz and Tristan took turns crying. Somehow the act seemed more tender, more anguished, coming from Tristan, the way anything tender broke from those who were used to being strong.

Rok lingered around after drop, under the guise of wanting to talk with Wayne later. He recognized Tristan from the summit meeting. Thought she was fine then, but seeing her with Iz, he knew she was not playing the same game he was.

"What it look like? She got fucked up."

"What do you want us to do?" Wayne asked.

Tristan wanted to say "make it better" or "fix her"

but the words sounded too needy. Too unachievable. "Look after her. She's been clean for over a year."

"And she got back on tonight?"

"Someone did this to her," Tristan said.

"We all make choices we have to live with," Wayne began, sympathetic but with honesty.

"I wasn't speaking metaphorically, nigga. Someone sabotaged her recovery."

"A… friend of yours?" Esther asked.

"Mulysa doesn't know what a friend is."

Rok perked up at Mulysa's name. And noted the hate with which Tristan spat his name.

"Mulysa?" Wayne remembered him from King's summit meeting. As he recalled, he and Tristan didn't seem cozy, more like work colleagues who tried to remain civil to one another. "He did this?"

"Yeah, but I'm gonna straighten his shit out."

"What does that…?"

Tristan hefted her backpack. "I'm trusting her with you. Do right by her."

"You can't…"

With that, Tristan slipped out the front door with two fingers raised. "Deuces."

Wayne punched a number into his cellphone. His call went directly to voicemail. He cussed to himself before deciding to send Rok to find him and/or Rellik. He left a message anyway on the off-chance he would check it.

"King, we have a problem…"

CHAPTER SIXTEEN

The eastside of Indianapolis suffered a slow, debilitating death. An early casualty, some say a reason, was the Camlann Housing Project. The project hadn't changed much: poverty reservations in practice. The police called it three-story run-ups, since no one was fool enough to walk if they could help it. Project was the right word for it: it was always a project in progress. There was always talk about the city giving it a face lift, much like they did the now-trendier art district of the downtown streets. Talk, anyway. Everyone also knew that the talk would never amount to much. At best, the complex would get a new coat of paint, something far short of a true refurbishing, but enough for people to forget and move along, abandoning its residents.

Mulysa rolled a tight one and sparked it up, a party of one. Breaking Iz off capped his night. Her over-muscled dyke friend would need handling, but if he were any judge of people, for the right price, she'd come around. Enough Benjamins brought the light of reason. Not that it mattered. When he got his head up like this, his thoughts drifted to dark places. Maybe it was time to put that bitch in her place. Use one bitch to check another. He brushed the hilt of his dagger. The image of him stabbing her in her breast and drinking blood from her nipple hardened him. Some real gangsta shit that would have people whispering his name in sheer terror. Yeah, he liked how that played.

He could smash a box of cookies about then.

Break-ins were the equivalent of nightly sport, robberies an experiment in ghetto math – taking nothing from nothing. Fights broke out regularly over the most trivial matters, mostly just to remind each other that they were still alive, usually an affront to one's pride since reputation was all that one truly owned here. Rowdy teens tried to be heard over the familiar hip hop drone of beats and attitude that passed for music; their cars and motorcycles peeling through the parking lots as they showed out for their friends. Many a night Mulysa fantasized about running piano wire across the street… about neck high. It wasn't the cracked dry wall or the fallen-off fixtures that he remembered most. It was having to shake out his sheets before he went to bed to clear them of cockroaches. He hated their midnight scurrying.

They scurried like over-muscled dykes sneaking up on him in the night. Tristan slipped in soundlessly, a wraith fully intent to flense Mulysa where he reclined. But to attack from behind without him knowing or prepared, that wasn't enough. That wasn't honorable. It was something he would do.

"I know you there." Mulysa didn't turn around. "It took you long enough to get here."

"We got some business to discuss."

Tristan's blades curved around each fist. Her grip tightened and loosened in steady rhythm, almost matching her heartbeat. She slackened her grip as if resolved to a new course of action, twirled them about her fingers in a gunslinger's flourish, and sheathed them.

Mulysa, for his part, didn't lower his bottom bitch. The time to discuss business was passed. Maybe it was time to test this overly muscled bitch after all. Put her in her place to make her see reason. Save him the Benjamins.

"This about your girlfriend?"

Goaded by the memory of Iz curled up on the floor, eyes slung back, with barely a trace of recognition in her eyes, the woman she loved buried underneath skeins of her high, her fallenness, her desires, and her crushed hope, Tristan charged after him. Mulysa leapt from the couch and lunged at her. She deflected the blow and snuck him in the kidneys. The two of them toppled over the couch.

Mulysa couldn't get leverage, kept off-balance by Tristan's shifting attack. He attempted a broad slash which she easily dodged and pinned his blade hand, smashing it against the floorboards, fingers dug into his wrist, until he released it. He raised his knee into her side, a glancing blow, but it knocked her enough to allow him to scrabble from under her. She fell heavily onto her back.

Scrambling to his feet, they circled each other in the dim light. The room was cramped and its shadows pressed in close from the odd outcroppings of the layout. Mulysa feinted with his knife, now ready, hoping to draw her into another impulsive mistake. Tristan smirked, thinking him a man hiding behind his penis, one which was smaller than he realized. The crunch of trash underfoot broke the tense silence. Mulysa might have had the superior muscle, but his was built by lifting weights and punching bags which couldn't hit back. Tristan's muscle had been formed strictly by hard living, a life of constant battle for each breath she took. If Mulysa had realized that, he was certain that with his bitch in hand, he was more than her superior.

They continued to revolve around each other in their delicate dance when Tristan slipped on a plastic bag. She flailed her arms to recover her balance, but Mulysa seized the opportunity to pounce on her with a killing stroke. She parried the blow as best she could, twisting her body out of the blade's trajectory, but the tip of the blade still pierced her side. Mulysa moved faster than she expected. He turned around with a high elbow to her jaw. They tussled through the room, with only the sounds of the grunts of absorbed punches heard. Bodies still entwined, neither getting an upper hand on the other, they slammed into the wall.

Still in close quarters, blood seeping from her wound, Tristan grappled for his blade hand once more. Her teeth ground against each other in a mad smile as she exerted the last of her strength into squeezing his wrist. Something popped in her grasp and the blade fell. Mulysa stifled a cry. Tristan head-butted him, which sent him to the floor. She bounded on top of him, grabbing for anything within reach. Handfuls of donut wrappers and moldy paper, and crammed them into Mulysa's mouth. She pressed a wadded up back of McDonald's into his face, blindly lashing out at him.

Heavy thuds at the door halted them.

"Police!" a voice cried.

Mulysa let go first only enough to check Tristan's reaction. If she flexed, they'd be right back fighting. But Tristan didn't move and allowed Mulysa to back away a few steps. He smoothed out his clothes, lip bleeding, fumed, trying to catch his breath.

"Don't make me go all P Diddy on you, nukka. Send you to Haughville and have you fetch me some breast milk from a Korean woman to wash down some donuts from Long's."

"This shit ain't over." Tristan turned toward the window. "Deuces."

The Martindale-Brightwood neighborhood had been designated a sensitive area. Riots broke out a few years back, over what no one quite remembered. However, the Black Panthers were active here, as was the Nation of Islam, and various church leaders. Each with good intentions, to help those forgotten by the system, give voice to those whose cries went unheard. To draw attention to the plight of their brothers and sisters. Each out to save their community... and in the process, either make names for themselves or prove their continuing relevance. King, Dred, and Rellik gathered at Good Hope. News of Colvin's effrontery traveled the vine quickly. A crisis was inevitable. Though neither Dred nor Rellik signed on with King, they were curious to see how he'd manage to lead them. It was his test. They knew they couldn't send in their usual troops. Street-level soldiers were fine if Colvin was a street knucklehead encroaching on territory or this was a case of some other day-in-the-life bullshit. Once things got... supernatural, only a few were qualified. Or experienced enough. Judging from Rok's reaction to what was going on, his face a mix of skepticism and trepidation, they'd be lost out there on their own. Merle ushered Dred and Rellik inside, but Baylon lingered back, catching Dred's attention.

King studied the poor wretch. He remembered his confident, flexing gait, built like a human Rottweiler with half-closed eyes as if bored. Not this thinned, ashy creature whose eyes were cratered within wrinkles.

"What happened to you, man?" King asked.

"After Michelle, you left me. Cut me out of your life." Baylon still felt things. He always had. His momma always said that was his problem: he felt things too deeply. It was why she believed he wasn't cut out for this here game. Every time he saw King, he wanted to apologize, to beg for forgiveness for fucking everything up. Nothing was the same: not the crew, not the block, not the family, not him. Everything got so disconnected. Everyone had to go their own way if only to not be reminded of what had been. Or what could have been. "It was too much."

"We were like brothers."

"That's why it hurt me so deep."

"You should've said that."

"I was a different man then."

"Look at you now. Out to save the whole hood. Everyone's redeemable, right?"

"Right."

"Even me?"

"Even… you. But you can't just say 'I'm sorry' as if that's all there is to it. You've got to change your ways. Prove that you've changed. Make up for some of the hurts you've caused. You may not make things right, but it's a start."

"What about us?"

"I done told you, too much time's passed. What we were…"

"Aces."

"We won't be again. Different time. Different place. Different man."

"But, if I could show I've changed…"

"We'll see. One step at a time." King didn't want to extinguish all hope, especially when his tenor reeked of wanting things… the way they used to be.

Ambition was the headiest of drugs. In its name, Dred was ready to sacrifice them – Baylon, Griff, Night, and Rellik – to get their power and reign supreme in the Egbo Society. Had no problem leaving Baylon to take the fall for it all. From there, with the power and mantle of authority, he would demand a place among the dons. Craddock. Bedivere. Howell. Fat old men whose time had passed. The dons collected tribute far removed from the street. He would be the young blood, the vision, necessary to take them to the next level.

Rellik studied Dred and thought about Wayne. In them he saw his future and alternate present. In Dred, he knew all the life would offer him. His days would be no more than chasing dollars, fending off takeovers, living life on a razor edge which threatened to slit his throat if he fell wrong. The life of the gun: putting down enemies only to have new ones rise up. It never ended and the thought exhausted him.

On the other hand, Wayne's was a life he couldn't imagine having. One equally fraught with peril, but buoyed by friendship. Loyalty. Trust. Life. Concepts all too alien to his reality. Rellik wanted to die. More like he was ready for it. He all but said goodbye to Wayne the last time they talked.

"You tippin' out?" Wayne asked. The summit conversation still heavy on his mind.

"I'm done, Wayne," Rellik said. "Ain't got the heart for it no more."

"Words like that could get you killed out here."

"I got it handled."

"Where you going to go?" Wayne grabbed his arm lightly. "I got a couch."

"Looking out for your big brother? I got a place in mind. It's OK." He hugged Wayne then broke free.

Tired of the killing, tired of the death, tired of the senselessness, Rellik knew he'd never be free of this life because he was in it too deep. No one would just let him out. Those under him would take him out to replace him. Those above him couldn't just let him out as a free agent. He knew too much, knew where too many bodies were buried. Ride or die or not, Rellik wouldn't be trusted. He didn't want to die crying for his mama like most men did in the end. He just wanted to go home.

"Colvin done lost his Goddamned mind," Rellik shouted.

"So it's begun," Merle said.

"What do we know about him?" King asked.

"He one of them Baltimore niggas," Dred said.

"He East Coast?" King asked.

"Naw, Baltimore Avenue. East side. Three-O Baltimore, forty-second and Post, tenth Street Dime Life. You know how they run."

"Just as soon split your wig as say please," Rellik said.

"Happy trappin' and gun slappin'," Merle said.

"Can't you do something about him?" Rellik asked.

His irritation at Merle reminded King of Wayne. Only then did he realize that he was about to mount a campaign and none of his most trusted people were with him. Wayne was tied up with Outreach Inc. who knew where Lott and Lady G were. Even Percy was nowhere to be found. Only Merle stood by him. The empty seats at the table mocked him. King bridged his fingers in front of him as Dred and Rellik spoke. He'd been so tired lately, so off his game, his mind harried and soft. He didn't know Rellik and certainly didn't trust Dred. However, matters of mutual self-interest bound them to him.

"He's right. Colvin's doing what he loves. There's no talking to him," Dred pushed. King felt like he was leading him. There was always the trap of the precipice with his words.

"What you fittin' to do? Make a citizen's arrest?" Rellik asked.

"We stop him." King didn't know what he meant, what all he was willing to do. He had to walk lightly between being a snitch and needing police involvement. But Merle was right, Colvin was above their pay grade. It was the same reason they would have to face Colvin themselves, not send in their soldiers.

Dred pounced on the opening. "King's right. We

aren't peaceable people. We fight for it. We take it. It's over."

"You hood as fuck, man," Rellik said. "That's your answer to everything."

"What say you, O Prince of Nap?" Dred said with a hint of contempt.

"Careful now," Merle said, though to King or to Dred no one was sure.

"Heavy be the head," Dred said, a serpent whispering into King's ear. "Don't grasp after power if you aren't prepared to wield it."

Rising from his seat, King released the magazine of his Caliburn. Pressing against the spring, he thumbed the top shell then palmed the magazine back into the grip. He tucked it into the waistband of his jeans, the grip turned rightward. Easily grasped by his right hand, it felt as natural in his dip as a sword in its scabbard. "Let's go."

"That's my young dude." Dred glanced back to King. "Time to tool up, son."

Smoke damaged the brick of the building façade from a fire over a decade ago. The cramped alcove, dark from the broken lights, but not black like the steep stairwells of the Phoenix Apartments, smelled of piss and neglect.

On the tip of Omarosa, they had run Rondell Cheldric, aka "Mulysa", through the Bureau of Criminal Identification. His sheet ran longer than anything he had presumably read, a litany of assaults, robberies, suspected in three rape cases – he even did a bid on a manslaughter – Mulysa was a keg of dynamite searching for an excuse to blow.

Huddled in the entranceway, the overhang was large enough to hold Lee and Cantrell and the first of the SWAT officers who held the breaching ram. Lee pressed his ear against the door, listening for any sound. Nothing. Cantrell flanked him. His case, his suspect, his bust, Lee would take the door, he told them plainly, not a man to be trifled with when it came to taking doors. Playtime stopped and everyone became strict professionals because taking doors was ten seconds of life or death. Octavia arrived on scene to supervise the take-down.

"Police!" he shouted and his fists thudded against the door. Lee took a deep breath. With his gun aimed at the floor in his right hand, Lee raised his left to count things down. Backing away from the door, they all gave head nods to signal that they were ready.

Three.

Two.

One.

The SWAT officer swung the ram. The door jambs splintered as his momentum carried him through. The men fanned in, eyes darting about. "Police!"

Taking one step into the foyer, Lee tried to determine if anyone was in the house. Flashlight beams cut through the darkness, criss-crossing like sabers. Omarosa said this Mulysa character stayed here. At times there were other squatters, but Mulysa was all about playing well with others and thus was probably alone by now. He had a way of creating messes that came back on him. The commotion continued as the word "Police" was shouted in the back rooms followed by the response "Clear!" They trudged through a carpet of fast-food wrappers and animal droppings. Lee grew disgusted that anyone lived here at all. Lee thought he heard something from somewhere in back. A furtive movement by a back window. They cleared the closets leaving only the bathroom at the end of the hall. The door was locked.

"You in there?" Lee demanded.

"Yes."

"Rondell Cheldric?"

"Yes." The voice sounded calm to the point of sounding rather annoyed.

"Come out. We want to talk to you."

"Can it wait?"

"No." Lee glanced at Cantrell with a perturbed, yet "is this guy for real" expression. Lee kicked in the door, fearing evidence being flushed. Mulysa stood at the sink, unflinching as his door crashed in, standing in front of a cracked mirror daubing a knot under his eye. His dingy clothes gave him the appearance of a postal carrier who did double duty as a trash collector. From the stench, the only evidence flushed needed to be.

"Hands where we can see them," Lee said.

Mulysa finished wiping his face. Either he was as cool as they came, or just plain stupid. He underestimated how close he came to getting his ticket punched with each uncooperative second.

"Can I help you?" Mulysa asked.

"We got a few questions for you," Lee said.

"No need for the drama. I would've let you in, but as you can see, I was, um, indisposed."

"You're coming with us."

"Sure." Mulysa had about reached his point. His blood was up after his tussle with Tristan and his head a little murky as he came down from his high. The cloak of civility strained him to breaking.

"We doing this hard or easy?" Lee stepped near to him, protecting himself through intimidation so that he didn't have to use force. Of course, the suspect had to be bright enough to perceive the threat.

"Nothing but easy. I didn't do nothin', so I got nothin' to hide."

Cantrell knew poor. Since he grew up poor, his heart went out to them even if he stopped short of respecting them. His mother made the best home that she could amid their own squalor. What little they had she took care of: swept her porch, kept pictures on the fridge, ironed their threadbare clothes. Another type of poor deserved their mess. If the corners of the room smelled of piss, the way a shooting gallery would or if food piled up and molded along the counters or floors. Mulysa had been reduced to living like an animal, and didn't seem to much mind.

Cantrell rifled through a pile of clothes and over-turned couch cushions. A bag jangled as soon as he jostled it.

"Look what I found," Cantrell chirped, toting a gym bag filled with an assortment of exotic knives. Lee took the machete in his gloved hand, inspecting it.

"Look here, you Uncle Tomming motherfucker," Mulysa reared with a litany of insults and eyefucks Cantrell had come to expect. "Them's my bitches."

"You like big knives?" Lee asked.

"Put her down."

"Give it a rest, Lee," Octavia started.

"What's the matter, Rondell?" Lee continued being a shit. Sometimes he couldn't help being such a cop. He ran his hand along the blade, deliberate and slow.

"Don't you touch her." A strain found its way into Mulysa's voice.

Cantrell rested a meaty hand on Mulysa's shoul-der, while he reached for a set of bracelets.

"Oh that's the way it is. You like that, huh?" Lee turned the blade over in his hands, an awkward fondling, antagonizing the twitch in Mulysa's eyes.

"No one touches her but me," Mulysa said.

"Maybe she doesn't mind stepping out on you."

"Dirty bitch."

With a wiry strength that they'd all underesti-mated, Mulysa easily slipped from Cantrell's grasp. The detective grabbed after him immediately, but the way Mulysa fought, Cantrell suspected he was up on something. Lee grabbed two handfuls of the man's shirt and shoved him into a wall. Despite the awkward angle and purchase, Mulysa lifted him from his feet. Cantrell punched him in his kidneys. Mulysa twisted and put his shoulder into the landing, taking the air out of Lee. By the time they were on him, Mulysa had Lee on the ground, punching him in the face. In the ensuing scuffle, Octavia caught a stray elbow in her eye. Even with Cantrell on one arm and Octavia on the other, Mulysa threw his body at Lee. He pushed off several detectives until the three of them pinned him down. Octavia was on the radio, calling for patrolmen. She put her knee into Mulysa's back as Cantrell fitted the cuffs onto his wrists. Lee staggered to his feet, only managed a half-hearted stomp on the thug before Cantrell pulled him up.

The door was ajar when they arrived at Rhianna's place. Many times Percy had begged her to move. He offered for her to stay with him where he could protect her. But Rhianna had her situation set up. Between being an emancipated teen, with Section 8 housing, and food stamps, she got by with a little hooking on the side. Percy had already checked in with his brothers and made sure they'd eaten and done their homework before walking Rhianna home. As much as he wanted to be with King, his first duty was to his family. So when the door wasn't completely shut, he put up his beefy arm barring Rhianna from passing. He pushed the door open and flicked on the light.

The place had been tossed. Quickly and not thorough, the thieves snatched anything of easy reach and quick resale value. He walked slowly through the house though he knew they were long gone. It was a terrible thing when your own home no longer felt safe. Stopping at each doorway, he prayed for God's protection on the house – for the reality of His presence to be made real for him. For a moment, guilt flashed in him. It wasn't but a few months ago he himself had broken into this apartment in search of anything of value in the name of his crack-fiend mother. He had taken a ring, but returned it later.

"It's gone," Rhianna said.

"What?"

"There was a cup. It had been in my family for years. I kept all sorts of valuables in it."

A ring. Percy knew, because that was where he returned it.

"This lady I used to stay with. Queen. She took me in and was sweet to me. She wanted me to have it. Told me I was its guardian."

"I'll make it right," Percy said. "I'll call the police. And I'll find the cup." *And the ring.*

"Oh." Rhianna held her belly.

"What is it?"

"I think my water just broke."

Rhianna retreated to her room. The pains grew worse now as she rubbed the swell of her belly. Her T-shirt wouldn't stay pulled down. Her blue jeans now two sizes too small, her belly bulged over her white belt. She waddled to the window. Kids played on the dilapidated equipment, too young to know that the swings shouldn't be so ragged or the monkey bars so rusted. The graffiti was a part of their world. All they knew was the color of childhood, and innocence was preserved even here for a time. Rhianna fell onto the edge of the bed. She set the radio to Hot 96.3 for some hip hop and turned it up. She didn't get that boy, but if she was going to cry, she didn't want Percy to hear her.

He honored her request to leave her alone. *Your honor's more important than my comfort,* Percy thought. But he called for an ambulance.

The fear came in waves. Not fear of the birth pains, those she'd handled before. The fear was the renewed fear of bringing another child into the world. The fear didn't come the first time. All she focused on then was her baby. It never seemed real and even now she felt like she played at parenthood. Visiting her baby when the mood hit her. This time around, she was really scared. Scared because things seemed more real this time. Part of her had really attached herself to the child, had committed to doing it right this time. Maybe it was the shame of having a baby to love her and then abandoning it when things got inconvenient. Maybe when confronted with the depth of her selfishness, she wanted to do things differently. Maybe she was just growing up.

She would have to find a way to provide for her child. Food. Clothes. Make a real home for it. Courage sprouted up like a tenacious weed, and she dared to dream. Maybe Outreach Inc. could help her get some food stamps and maybe get her first child back. Perhaps she could get her own place, a real place away from the robbing, drugging and killing. Some place safe. Some place where they could be a real family.

Another wave of contractions caused her to close her eyes. A low moan escaped her lips. She prayed that God would water her courage, allow it to take root and grow. Give her the strength to cling to the hope of a better life.

"Percy, get in here!"

Percy trundled through the door. "The ambulance is on the way."

"Just hold my hand."

With walls the color of coughed-up phlegm, the interrogation room – affectionately known as The Box by the detectives – was smaller a room than one might imagine. Manacled to the table because of his carrying on during his arrest, Mulysa rested his head on the metal table. Cantrell flipped open the case file one more time. The bodies at the Phoenix Apartments had been dropped by shots though the medical examiner was at a loss to give him a caliber

or make of gun. For all he knew, someone threw
rocks at them really hard. Knifings were almost always personal and rarely involved business, though
some crews employed knifemen. Yet Mulysa's de-
meanor betrayed no feelings, nothing could reach
his heart. In the young homicide detective's experience, it signaled that Mulysa was guilty as fuck. Now
it was a matter of figuring out of what.

"He been Mirandized?" Octavia double-checked as
she stared at Rondell Cheldric through the observa-
tion window that opened into the interrogation
room. Mulysa nuzzled his head along his arm, sleeping the sleep of the just.

"Yeah, declined representation," Cantrell said,
nose still buried in the file.

"As many times as he been through the system?
He should know better."

"He knows. And he knows we know," Lee nearly
spat with contempt. "He thinks that really proves
that he hasn't done anything."

"How do you want to go at him?" Cantrell turned
to his partner.

Lee smiled.

The impassive-faced detectives entered the room
and Cantrell took a seat across from him. Between
him and the door, not needing to voice aloud the reality that the only way Mulysa was to see the other
side of the door was through him. Mulysa was no
virgin to the system. The man rubbed sleep from his
eyes, not acknowledging Cantrell's presence.

Typically, Cantrell's approach in the box was to be ebullient and respectful, eventually garnering their confidence. Cantrell grew up in the neighborhood, always went with the "I can relate" approach despite the fact he was now po-po, the enemy, as relatable as a two-headed alien. But he ran the same streets, he shoplifted from the same shops, ate fried catfish from the same joints, and haunted the same clubs, like Pick-A-Disease as they called Picadilly's back in the day. None of the social niceties would be met with courtesy or appreciated, so a small-talk approach was wasted on Mulysa.

"What does it say about a people when none of the social pleasantries are observed?" Cantrell asked.

"What?" Mulysa grunted.

"Nothing. A rhetorical question."

"What?"

Cantrell leaned toward this would-be hardass, this brute, this self-proclaimed menace to society, who didn't retreat from the invasion of space. Quite the opposite, as he was comfortable in the close quarters, even matching the detective's advance. Mulysa's rank breath, decayed bits of pork trapped between teeth, sprayed his face.

"It is hot in here," Mulysa complained. "Why's the white boy got to be behind me?"

White boy. Lee's face grew hot at the epithet since it was more insult than accurate description. It wasn't like being called "nigger", which would have been automatic go time were the roles reversed. But the sting of derision was there, enough for his jaw to tighten. Lee took more than the occasional hard elbow on the basketball courts over at Northwest High School coming up. He understood the testing behind the comment and the court jostling. He was expected to take it and considering the white to non-white ratio of the streets and the school, he did. But he didn't like it.

"He make you uncomfortable?" Cantrell asked.

"Just don't like people behind me is all," Mulysa said.

"Remind you of when you got sent up?"

"Men behind you." Lee placed a hand on his shoulder. "Got plenty of them days ahead of you."

"Rondell Cheldric," Cantrell read while pacing back and forth before closing the file folder he cradled.

"You know my name?"

"Folks call you Mulysa. 'Asylum' spelled backwards."

"You got that, huh?"

"I'm a clever Uncle Tom."

"Yeah." He stopped short of an apology but flashed an "it's all in the game" slow nod. "We all out here: you, me, fiends. Like the circle of life. Doing our thing. But in the end, we all get got. Dirt piled on us like we was shit folks trying to hide. That's why it so important to leave a strong name behind."

"A fierce rep," Cantrell agreed.

"True dat."

"You in big trouble, Rondell." Cantrell had a way of using a person's own name as a club, repeating it in a way that forced the person to deal with him.

"Why? I didn't do nothin'."

"You hit a cop. That's something."

"He was touching my–"

"'Bitches.' Yeah, we'll get to that later," Cantrell said. "Assaulting an officer, in front of other officers."

"You going down for that, Rondell," Lee clubbed.

"You got to pay."

"That's how it works."

"You do. You pay."

This was the part of the dance that Cantrell loved, the stage on which they performed. When they fell into a rhythm, knew each other's plays, and today they were in the zone. Rondell didn't stand a chance as they took turns whittling the big man down to a more manageable, a malleable size.

"Do you know who we are, Rondell?" Cantrell eased away from the table, giving Mulysa room to breathe and settle down. Pull back on the throttle, let him take in the scenery and fully appreciate the jackpot he was in. They actually didn't have much of anything on him. It would have been a fairly friendly conversation – albeit with all the requisite chest thumping – had Mulysa not chosen to act all foolish. All they had was his name and knew that he was mixed up in the situation somehow. Anything he and his bitches had been up to hadn't been reported to the police. Still, he didn't know what they knew. Maybe his bitches would give him up. Blood was hard to clean up.

"You murder police." Mulysa came out of his stupor from watching the pair of detectives sidle back and forth.

"You know what that means?"

"Someone's been murdered."

"Exacta-mundo." Cantrell pointed the folder at him with the beaming smile of a proud parent, then set it on the table. Mulysa turned to face him. A scar underlined his right eye and he was thick like a tree stump, though his blue jeans still hung from him like drapes. Cantrell resisted the urge to snatch the boy's wave cap from his head.

"What do you do for a living?"

"Freelance entrepreneur."

"You hear this shit?"

"Drug-dealing scum. You got that on a business card?"

"I'm into a little bit of this, little bit of that," Mulysa said, not acknowledging Lee. He understood the dance. The disorienting effect of their back and forth, meant to unnerve him. Rattle him to the point where he gave something up. But they had nothing on him. Hadn't even told him what he was being charged with. So he relaxed and allowed himself to get caught up in their little banter game.

"How long have you been a 'freelance entrepreneur'?" Cantrell asked.

"Goin' on three years."

"You like it?"

"It a-ight."

"You like women, Rondell?" Cantrell sat down on the corner of the table closest to Mulysa, drawing his attention.

"Yeah." His breath reeked on top of the wafts of his body odor, a mix of garbage, funk, and unwashed ass.

"I mean, it's all right if you don't."

"I do."

"He look gay to you?" Cantrell asked.

"He could be half a fag," Lee offered. "Maybe he just prison gay."

"I ain't no fag."

"That's a double negative," Cantrell said.

"Means you are," Lee echoed.

"I ain't."

"That's what they call a Freudian slip," Cantrell said. "Part of you may think that you are."

"I... it... I ain't." The questions and innuendo flew furiously at Mulysa. He wasn't having time to think through the questions, much less his answers. Hated the way they twisted things, damned cops. Not to mention his head ping-ponging back and forth. Cantrell sat entirely too close. Lee pressed in on him with his imposing stance, glaring at him with clenched fists burrowing into the table.

"It's all right if you are," Cantrell said.

"These days you can screw fish if it's your orientation," Lee said. "Don't take the blame. Blame God."

"He made you that way," Cantrell said.

"He didn't," Mulysa said.

"You got a moms?" Cantrell raised up from the table.

"Yeah," Mulysa said, the sudden veer in the conversation left a slight tremor to his voice. He didn't know where this was going either. A spirit of unease crept into his posture. Though he had a practiced relaxed slouch, his thick frame sprawled out in the chair; he was suddenly conscious of it. Uncomfortable. But didn't know how to shift or straighten up without appearing weak. Or guilty.

"You got a sister?"

"Two."

"They bitches?"

"What the hell?"

"No offense, man, but you seem to like the word," Cantrell said. "Just rolls off your tongue with ease."

"Bitches." Lee emphasized the word as if savoring a fine filet.

"They your bitches." Cantrell quoted Mulysa.

"No. I'd never disrespect my moms."

"Bitches." Cantrell shook his head disapprovingly. "You like to hit women, Rondell?"

"Naw."

"Not according to your sheet. Looks to me like you don't like women at all." Cantrell pointed dramatically to Mulysa's sheet. "What's that say?"

Lee studied the sheet carefully. "Battery. Dispute with your girlfriend. Ended with a bloody nose."

"Those charges were dropped," Mulysa protested.

"They about the only ones," Cantrell said.

"I keep getting pinched."

"You been a bad boy, Rondell." Cantrell shifted his weight to edge closer to him.

"Bad boy, indeed," Lee echoed from too close behind him.

"She got off easy though, didn't she?" Cantrell pulled up another file, this time not letting him see the pages. Anyone could be broken down given enough time and the right circumstances. The need to confess, to get one's story out before it was written for them was a powerful compulsion. They were far afield of their original intent, but the vibe of the room dictated their conversation. And it felt like they were onto some dirt of his. Something with a woman. They needed to tread lightly.

"She never became acquainted with your bitches."

"Or is that your *other* bitches?"

"I never cut her," Mulysa said.

"Looks to me like you got all sorts of issues with women," Cantrell said. "Stems from issues with his mother."

"That's what they say," Lee said.

"What you got me in here for?" Obviously agitated, Mulysa's stone-cool facade faded into a distant memory. He straightened in his chair, stiff-limbed and uncertain. Cantrell smiled. Now they could really go to work.

"Where were you, September 3rd?" Cantrell asked.

"Man, how am I supposed to remember," Mulysa said. A high pitch slipped into his tone. "Where were you?"

"The man raises a good point," Lee said. "September was a long time ago."

"Maybe if something happened that day," Cantrell looked up toward Lee.

"Something that might jog his memory."

"Let's try something easier. What happened earlier tonight? Noticed one of your bitches…"

"Your bottom bitch?" Lee mused.

"… had a little blood. What are the odds that it will be a match to someone in the system?"

"I don't know, detective," Lee casually ambled toward Cantrell as if to whisper conspiratorially with him. Though for Mulysa's benefit. "Fine upstanding citizen like Mr Cheldric here, surely only associates with like-minded innocents."

"Some fine young thing."

"Maybe you were feelin' your Wheaties tonight." Lee turned, fully entering Mulysa's orbit, filling his field of vision.

"On top of the world." Cantrell matched his stance, fully hammering at Mulysa now.

"So much so that you think that you can talk to just anybody."

"And why not? Handsome man like yourself."

"And who is she? Just some dumb girl."

"Bitch." Cantrell spat the word curtly, like a gunshot. Mulysa couldn't answer, only turn from

Cantrell to Lee, not quite keeping up with their rapidfire performance.

"Probably looked at you like you were beneath her." Lee emphasized the words as if empathizing with his experiences.

"So you think to yourself…"

"No, he probably says it," Lee interrupted on cue. "'You think you better than me?'"

"Who is she?" Cantrell asked.

"Bitch," Lee said.

"She had it coming. Deserved what she got." By this point, they had leaned in so close, they nearly pressed their faces on either side of his. Cantrell continued, "This snooty…"

"Pretty…"

"Smart…"

"White…"

"Bitch," Cantrell ended. The word bounced against the tiles of the wall.

"I didn't… hurt her," Mulysa said without conviction.

"This is how folks get a bad reputation. You piss them off, they introduce you to their bottom bitch," Lee said.

"You like knives, Rondell?" Cantrell asked.

"Yeah."

"Big knives. Small knives."

"Yeah."

"Special knives."

"He's a connoisseur," Lee opined.

"Just like knives is all," Mulysa said.

"We know. We got 'em. All. You *really* like knives," Cantrell said. "We check all of your knives, we gonna find any blood? DNA don't wash off easy."

"Speaking of which…" Lee nodded to the reports.

"Yeah, I almost forgot." Cantrell thumbed through the reports. Mulysa had been up to something. Probably completely unrelated to the murders over at the Phoenix Apartments. But whatever nagged at him, whatever he was on the verge of talking about, could be leveraged for cooperation later. He perused the coroner's report from the active case as if it had something to do with Mulysa. "You believe in safe sex?"

"Li'l Jimmy wearin' a hat?" Lee included an insulting level of what he thought sounded like street affectation.

"Don't bother. We know you don't." Cantrell gambled at this point. The anguish on Mulysa's face told him everything he needed to know. He flashed a glance at Lee.

"Left semen all in her." Lee gambled with the bluff. Cantrell didn't cut him even the slightest of glances, backing his play.

"We're going to get a sample from you. Make no mistake about it."

"Court order's already on the way."

"Is it gonna match what we find in her?"

They both stood now, staring down at a hapless Mulysa. The silence grew cold as they waited.

"She's a junkie and a whore. It's her word against mine."

"Right, right. A junkie and a whore against the word of a fine, upstanding citizen like yourself. Tell us about what happened. Get you on record first and make it easier on yourself."

CHAPTER SEVENTEEN

Naptown Red was quite specific in his task for Garlan. He needed to disappear Lady G, King's woman, but not harm her. Leave her in a place where she could be easily found. Not one of those megalomaniac types, those control freaks who believed in only telling folks as much as they needed to know, Red had a different philosophy. The way he believed, the better you understood why you did things, the less you questioned them. Or him. He was on their side, after all. The object was to distract King, knock him off his game. Let him know that he or his people could be got at any time. Naptown Red wanted that knowledge playing in King's mind. Like a game of chess, it was about misdirection and getting in people's heads.

Garlan pulled into Breton Court in his Impala, a mint-green whip more boat than car. He sank into its driver's seat in a lean so fierce his eyes were barely visible above the dashboard. Early Sunday morning was the most peaceful time in any neighborhood. All the fiends, gangstas, hood rats, playas, and freaks had done called it a night. All the church-going folk popped their heads out, like rabbits on a savannah plain, unburrowing themselves to venture out. He waited for the large woman to leave the crib, a black-faced little boy in tow. Everyone knew where King stayed. Like it was his throne in a court, guarded by the power of his name. Just like folks knew Lady G stayed across the way. She deserved what she got, playing hooky from church and all.

Garlan twisted his ring. When he peered into the rearview mirror, nothing reflected back from the seat where he should have been. His sense of self was completely annihilated and no one noticed. Complete eradication, gone with no one caring about his absence. He was capable of doing anything and going anywhere. Some days he went places and just listened. His duties slipped, though he wondered if anyone knew. Of course he went to the high school gym to hang out in the girls' locker. Grabbing some tit and pinching some ass. Whacked off more than a few times. Loath as he was to admit it, pussy became boring. Surrounded by it, but no one knew he was there. He didn't exist to them. He didn't matter. They'd never hold him. Laugh at his jokes. Spend time with him. Do his hair. Make him a sandwich. Suck his dick. Nothing. He didn't matter to any of them. He didn't exist. He was a ghost intruding on their lives. Not even an intrusion, just a ghost. One time he twisted his ring to appear among them. They scattered in squeals, a hail of "get out" and "what the fuck?" Running out, he didn't care. He just wanted to matter. To be seen.

Other days he listened to his men. How they talked about him. Their ambitions. The ruminations on the minutiae of their lives. Pussy. Cars. Pussy. Sports teams. Pussy. Music. Pussy. Money. Pussy. Speakers. Pussy. That was all of life to them. And he'd appear, make sure they were on point, but his mind was no longer on his work. He had disappointed. A blank spot where a person should be. A lifetime of learned shames reducing him to what he already believed himself to be. Nothing. And nothing could do anything.

Creeping out the car, he made his way to the back patio. The rear wall was no obstacle. It wasn't too many years ago he used to run along the patio walls just like these, chasing his friends and playing tag. Running and jumping from them for the sheer exhilaration of being alive. Part of the thrill was watching those drawn to their upstairs windows by the nearby racket and seeing knucklehead children dash past at nearly eye level. Right now, anyone peeking out their window would only see their patio. Nothing special or out of the ordinary. Nobody important.

All of the condos had the same set-up, either a back window which led into a kitchen or a sliding back patio door. This place had the sliding door. Thing was, few of them latched properly. A few years of use and kids slamming them too hard either knocked them off their tracks or knocked the latch too far in to catch properly. Most owners of such doors had a security bar which acted as a lock. Those security bars cost money, about a week's worth of groceries, and the needs of an empty belly were always more pressing than the possibility of a bogeyman breaking in. Most made do with a stretch of fitted broom handle popped into place. No cost, same function. Thing was, there was a little-known workaround to the broom-handle lock: a swift, strong kick could usually displace it.

As was the case here.

Garlan slipped in. Though no more than a couch, a love seat, and a couple of chairs around a coffee table, all centered around a television, the room had a warmth to it. The furniture was well worn but not ratty. Care was taken in their arrangement, in the placement of knick-knacks and photos. The room had been cleaned, things put away, except for some scattered toys in the corner, but even those added a sense of life to the space. The room exuded family.

A telltale squeak gave him away as he stepped on the first step of the stairs. Frozen, he waited to see if anyone stirred from bed. He pressed himself to the wall and spider-slinked up the stairs.

Feigning sickness, Lady G had stayed home. Solitude, a chance to think and sort things out in peace was what she required. Propped up by pillows, she colored, as Rhianna had convinced her would help clear her mind. Not quite ready to get out of bed, Lady G drew a picture of a church in her book. She scorched its doorway with streaks of brown and black, traced a crack down its windows, and canted the cross hanging above its archway until the building resembled the abandoned church where they first convened their little circle. When it was just them, the core, before things got so big and drifted from what she thought they would do and be. To her, it would always be their special place. The place where the magic happened. When they believed nothing could get in their way.

The crayon ceased its scribbling in mid-scratch. Some primitive part of her brain alerted her with a prey's warning. Nothing she could point to, not unlike sensing the footfalls of a cat padding across carpet. Merely the nearness of another. Considering the racket made when she came home filled with the Holy Ghost, Big Momma and Had were still at church.

"Who's there?" Lady G asked the air. Suddenly too conscious of how her braless breasts hung through the thin material of her T-shirt, she drew up the bed sheets. The familiar click of a gun being cocked paralyzed her. Cold metal pressed against her temple.

The idea of being known, of being revealed while so carefully hidden intrigued Garlan. "How'd you know I was here?"

"I just knew is all. Just have to pay attention to what's going on around you." Lady G closed her eyes and took a deliberate breath. She wondered what her death would feel like. A sharp pain as the bullet exploded from its chamber and slammed into her skull. If she'd hear the splintering of bone and the shattering of her skull. If she'd feel the bullet tunnel through the soft, great pulp of her brain. What the sensations of life being extinguished would be. If she'd see a bright light or fade into the darkness of eternal sleep. She prayed the end would be quick.

"You scared right now?" Garlan withdrew the pistol from her skin.

"Make you feel good knowing I was?" The bravado of her words couldn't hide the shake in her voice. It wasn't the first time a gun had been pointed at her, but it wasn't an experience she longed to repeat.

"Heh. Come on, we need to go somewhere."

"I ain't going nowhere with you."

Garlan jabbed the gun at her head again. "See, you thought that was a request."

"Can I get dressed?"

"Go head."

Lady G backed across the other side of the bed. Piles of jeans stacked at her feet. "You looking?"

"You want me to lie to you?"

Lady G turned her back to the direction of the voice. She pulled the top pair of jeans up quickly, doing a bit of a bounce to get her full behind into them. She thought about how best to maneuver into a bra. A hand brushed the side of her breast. Not caring about his gun, not being able to see it anyway, Lady G lashed out, shoving at the area the intrusion came from.

"Hands off the temple."

Garlan slapped her with an open hand which she could neither see nor defend herself against and sent her sprawling into the standalone lamp. The bulb flashed with a lightning burst and went out.

"Girl, have you lost your Goddamned mind?"

"You gonna kill me, do it now. But you don't get to just touch me any which way."

"Come on. Let's go."

Lady G grabbed a sweater and a jacket. "Where we going?"

Where were they going? Garlan hadn't thought that far ahead. Lady G's colored page caught his eye. "I know a place."

The sky charged with a dull luminescence. Threatening clouds like glaring corner boys. Assuring them that he knew how to find Colvin, Merle led the group to the bus stop in front of the church. An Indy Metro idled at the stop. Though it was five o'clock in the morning, the bus was still driverless. What few passengers that waited at the stop behaved as if they didn't notice it. Or them. The six of them boarded the bus. None of the bus stop throng gave them a first glance, much less a second.

"There are people all around us," King whispered. "What's up?"

"Relax and act natural," Merle said.

"I don't get it," Rok said, "there ain't nobody fixin' to drive this mug."

"They won't have to. No one living travels these lines," Dred said.

"Do what?"

"These rides ain't for the living," Dred repeated. "Didn't you notice the people? They seemed more concerned about their own affairs than anything we were up to."

"So?"

"These are the dead lines. The ghost lines of the Metro Buses. Those in the know can simply board them and travel along the unlit paths. You sure you know what you doing, old man?"

"I got this," Merle said.

"The toll's yours to pay, then."

"Where are we going?" King asked Merle.

"When the bus stops, we've arrived."

The city landscape passed in gray and brown blurs. Through the bus windows, the city took on an alien aspect. The buildings canted at odd angles, the geometry of the city bent by shadows. Though they passed though areas of the city they knew intimately, the landscape was as unfamiliar as the moon's surface. For nearly an hour they rumbled along 38th Street, occasionally stopping to take on and drop off passengers while the night held its grip.

The door of the bus sighed shut. Still with no driver, the bus slowly shifted into gear. Rellik never considered himself a pessimistic individual. Life was darkness, so his history had taught him. All pain, loss, and death. And he had walked so long in its darkness, the light had to appeal to him, if he could believe in it at all.

King hated quiet moments, to be trapped with his thoughts. Unasked, they drifted to Lady G and his feelings for her; to Prez and how he failed him and looked for redemption for them both; to his vision for his mission and how things seemed to drift. Instead, he focused on the task ahead: how best to deploy the men, guessing what Colvin might do, how to turn the situation to his advantage. His life had been reduced to the next problem, the next mission, the next tussle. With dawning realization, he smiled, a rueful grin. He wasn't living, he was distracted. Adventure, busyness, was his drug of choice. Better the problems of his neighborhood than to wrestle with the issues in his own life. How long had it been since he'd seen his little girl, Nakia? Just thinking her name, he couldn't help but think that he was his father's son. Running the streets rather than being there for his child. His friendships with Lott and Wayne. He loved them, but they hadn't hung out, just hung out, in ages. He wondered if they saw his leadership as him treating them as equals or as servants to be ordered about. And he felt strange going off into a battle without them.

And then there was Lady G.

Theirs was a complicated mess of a relationship.

But when *didn't* he have a complicated mess of a relationship? If he'd ever had a normal one, he couldn't recall it. Things had to be sorted out. And her him. But was it enough? Was it healthy? Was it the best for each of them? This was why he hated quiet moments.

"Something on your mind?" Dred asked him. "You look… distracted."

"Just thinking about Colvin."

"And what you're prepared to do in case he don't see the light of your wise ways?"

The bus turned up High School Road, passing what they knew to be Breton Court, though none dared glance at what they called home through the tainted glass of death. High School Road stopped at 56th Street, the bus swung left then slowed to a halt in front of the entrance of Eagle Creek Park. With a nod, Merle led them from the bus. Its gears groaned and the bus sighed as it pulled away, scurrying away before the light of the rising sun.

An early morning mist settled along the woods, creeping along the forest floor with a cold dampness that seeped into the bones, ached joints, and sapped strength. The woods took on a life of their own. Tree limbs like gnarled hands raised in praise against the night sky. Light pollution drained the velvety pallor from the blanket of night, leaving it a tepid gray-blue curtain. The moon baked to a warm orange glow. Again King wished Wayne was by his side as he was at his best at this time. Although he relished the adventure of the situation, King's face remained solemn as duty and his shoulders weighted by obligation. They marched in an insolent stroll.

The sounds of crickets and tree frogs and other things moved in the night. Countless creatures populated the woods. Deer. Badgers. Foxes. Owls. Coyote. Snakes. All manner of predators and prey. The Eagle Creek Reservoir had suffered a series of algae blooms during the summer. They'd gotten so bad, it had affected the drinking water. The chemicals that the Department of Environmental Management dumped in to treat the problem did nothing to kill the taste. To Rellik, it tasted of seaweed. And reminded him of hair greenish with algae. Rellik hadn't visited Eagle Creek Park in well over 20 years, but even then he'd had to relearn the paths each trip. The trees had a way of shifting.

"What's the plan?" Dred asked.

He measured each man with his steady gaze. Merle shifted with an antsy energy as if searching for a missing friend. Rellik had his brother's beefy mien, ready to rumble into whatever. Rok was the least prepared, a squire among wolves. Dred challenged and dared with each word. He followed only so long as King's interests matched his own. Baylon worried him. He certainly didn't want to depend on him. All of them looked to him as if that were the natural order. "We go in. We take him down."

"That ain't much of a plan." Dred always pushed him, always questioned and cut him no slack.

"I want to try to talk to him first. Give him a chance to back down."

"Out to save him?" Dred asked.

"Give him an opportunity," King said. "Merle and Dred hang back a bit in case some weirdness goes down. Rellik, you and Rok with me. Baylon, keep out of sight in case we have any surprises."

"Sounds better."

"Didn't know you wanted the details."

King's smirk collapsed into a scowl as he spied the flashes of green light. The pale glimmer from a small hill unsettled him. It turned his stomach, an offense to the surrounding nature. The woods took on an alien quality in the luminescence, a ruin of forest circling the clearing. The trees gnarled, burnished gray like aged stone with an unpleasant quality. Their outlines grotesque, limbs bent at odd angles. Sweat cooled on his forehead. His heart thundered in a measured pace. As if the anticipation of combat calmed him. Tendrils pushed in at the edge of his mind, threatened to worm their way into his thoughts.

All sound ceased except for the sound of their own footsteps as they crunched along the dead leaves piled along the ground, a thick carpet of brown that crunched under heavy footfalls.

"Come on in." Colvin barely took notice as he met them, their faces grim and alert.

The excitement in his eyes wouldn't hesitate to squeeze a trigger and spray his brains along the tree line. They stepped into the clearing. "Something you want to say to me?" The muscles of Colvin's wiry frame nearly danced as he moved. His tan-brown skin, like calf's hide, made King's appear darker in contrast.

"This is madness. Come on now. You out here on your own. When was the last time you saw folks united? We poised to make a real difference." More of a gauntlet thrown rather than a statement. They glared at one another in established enmity. King's heart saddened that things had to come to this. But it was what it was. King was still somewhat self-conscious of the broadness of his nose and the deepness of his cheekbones. The twists of his hair jutted skyward in defiance, the sides and back of his head freshly shaven. His physique boasted a brawn now tested with regularity in the streets. He got real serious behind shit like that.

"That the thing: the only difference I aim to make is to my wallet."

Something about the set-up wasn't right. Rok couldn't remember if he'd ever been surrounded by so much green. He lived in a concrete world. The trees loomed taller and thickened, engorged on the foul emanations. They crowded against them. The muscles along Rok's stomach tightened and cramped. His mouth went dry. His palms slickened with sweat. Men like him, the kind of men he imagined himself to be, never carried fear like this. Their veins pumped ice. Their hearts didn't pound so hard their throats ached. He couldn't remember the last time he had a drink or took a leak, but needed to rectify both scenarios soon.

"King?" Merle was the first to sense it.

Dred sniffed the air as if catching a scent which disturbed him. He backed a few steps away from the circle, wary and on edge. Picking up on the tenseness coming from them, Rellik and Rok flanked King. They scanned the trees, not certain what they were watching for.

Colvin gestured with his fingers. Furtive movements somewhere between flashing gang signals and issuing sign language. His lips moved though King heard no words.

A green crackle of energy flared to life, a single flame suspended in the air above Colvin. The woods glowed as a few more flickered to life, emerald sparks which danced in an unfelt breeze. The flames mesmerized them, their breath half-held knowing they signaled only the beginning. The flames lengthened, trailing down, four strands of flame in the clearing. The light intensified, a flood of light bathed them. King visored his hand above his eyes, too late realizing that he couldn't see beyond the periphery of the light.

"King!" Merle yelled.

Shadows moved between the trees, advancing on them. Their sizes varied slightly, no more than a head's difference among the lot of them. Nearly a dozen of those they could see. A score of red eyes dotted the night and closed in on them.

• • • •

Lott's mind raced with dark possibilities. Life had a
way of jumping off in a variety of ways. There were
so many ways for pain to intrude upon them. Robberies. Beatings. Rape. Death. Try as he might to
focus on the task at hand, the possibilities for brutality
drove him to distraction. Big Momma let him in and
got out of his way as he bounded up the stairs. He
surveyed Lady G's room. They already knew the police wouldn't have done anything. Not even Cantrell.
To their minds, a teen – a homeless teen at that –
threw a fit and ran off. They'd be lucky if a pen even
found its way to a report. Yet Lott's next instinct was
to call King, but he hesitated and wasn't sure why.
Maybe he was too proud to ask for help. Maybe he
wanted to be the hero. Lady G's hero. Shaking himself, he made the call anyway. A small part of him
was relieved when the call again went to voicemail.
Again he left a message. It was now firmly on record
that he tried. The mind had a way of shaping circumstances it wanted to happen, as if he could will his
desires onto life. Still, he was no detective and had
few resources to speak of. He prayed that whatever
Providence guided him would lead him to her. Ex-
amining the bed – no struggle, no scent of anything
beyond hers... and he lingered at her smell – he spied
the drawing. It was a hunch, a wild hope more than
anything else, but he had nothing else to go on.

Lott hated walking up High School Road. A couple
years back, he was minding his own business on a
Saturday night when a group of teenage boys slowed

down and hit him with a cup full of Mountain Dew from Taco Bell. Random white punks out doing random hateful shit, though it was dark enough out that they might not have known he was black. Every time he took to the sidewalk, the same edgy anticipation swept over him.

He hadn't eaten at Taco Bell since, either.

The church didn't appear disturbed. The boards remained intact. Cracks filigreed the near yellow walls. Scorch marks seared the outlines of doors and windows. A few more gang tags marked it: a spray-painted cross with a six-pointed star on it and two swords crossed behind it; a heart with devil's horns coming out of its lobes; a pair of dice, one with a two facing, the other with a six. Around back, planks of wood, water-damaged furniture, and bits of ruined dry wall filled a dumpster. A stretch of plywood had been pulled from the rear door. Steeped in shadows, the narthex devoured the wan light let in by the loosed board. Upon it falling back into place, the darkness reigned unabated. The room took on a sinister cast, as if befouled by an unwanted presence. Lott crept forward, his feet almost sliding along the granite floor layered in ash. A fine-ground debris. He turned into the main sanctuary. Slits of light filtered through some of the uncovered stain glass windows hear the top of the room. He marveled that no one had hurled rocks to shatter them. The thin light cast the room in gray murk. A couple of columns, more decorative than load-bearing, had fallen on one another.

Lady G stood next to one of the untoppled columns. Just standing there, not tied up, but with the awkward stance of someone under duress.

"That's far enough," a voice yelled from nowhere.

Colvin wasn't plugged into a network, his ego obscuring the reality of his situation. His ambitions drove him to become a player, but he was too independent with no one watching his back. He'd always been that way. It was one of the reasons Omarosa chose to hit him. No trap car, traveling in thin traffic, Broyn was easy pickings. Colvin's entire operation was sloppy, amateurish. It was beneath who they were and he needed to be taken down a peg.

From her tree-perch vantage point, she watched the final act play out. She had been following Colvin since his rash raid on Rellik. Of all the feelings she could have had, after all he'd done, she still managed to feel sorry for him. He was her brother after all. She knew him, his ways, his weaknesses. Most times she couldn't be around him, not when he raged like this. Simple, brutal, and haphazard, he didn't think, only lashed out in his pain and anger. There were times when he had to bear the consequences of his actions, and she pulled away from him.

But he was still her brother.

A few of the tiny creatures stepped into view. Necklace of teeth. Painted bellies. Iron boots. Bracelets of sharpened edges of iron left burn marks where they rubbed against their wrist. Their caps varying shades of red. And they looked hungry.

To Rok's eyes they were half-naked midgets, more ridiculous than terrifying, and he choked back a snicker. Raising their legs like baseball pitchers, the tiny bulbous bodies tilted back as they sent another volley of elf arrows at them. Something whirred past his ear. Rok jerked his head to the side. It impacted against the tree like buckshot. Rellik and Rok opened fire immediately, not certain what their targets were. King took point, his Caliburn drawn but not firing. Dred began to chant to himself, his fingers locking, adjusting their configurations, then locking again. Baylon circled the periphery just outside the light of the hillside clearing. King, Rok, and Rellik took cover behind trees. They returned fire as best they could, pinned down by the advancing horde. Distracted.

"What the fuck are these ninja dwarfs?" Rok cried out.

"Red Caps. Feared among the fey folks." Merle squat lower against a tree. He leaned over to shout, but elf arrows ricocheted passed his exposed face and he withdrew. "Think of them as less personable pit bulls. With opposable thumbs."

Rok's tree wasn't wide enough to provide much cover. He took careful aim at the nearest Red Caps shooting at him. Swallowing hard, he fired a few rounds. He was pretty sure he hit one, but the creature seemed to shrug off the wound. He concentrated on shooting back at them, he didn't notice the earth rippling toward him.

The ground surged at their feet. All around them, the thin layer of leaves erupted. Hands clutched at them, like a horde of vengeful demons upon them. Soil sprayed in all directions, a cloud of earthen shrapnel. Bodies pressed against his, dragging them to the ground. Red Caps burst out of the ground.

Rellik remained quiet. The fey assassins rose up, a rising tide of hands he let wash over him before he began firing. His bullets wouldn't be as effective far away against their tough hide, he knew, but up close, it wasn't as if they were invulnerable. Fending off gnashing maws, he trained his gun on their skulls and squeezed the trigger. A tiny head exploded, spraying the remains of its face across that of its brother faeries. Claws scraped against his back as he scrabbled out of their grasp and fired.

"Why are you doing this?" King pressed his back to the tree, but leaned around to shout at Colvin.

"Fortune favors the bold."

King expected something along the lines of Colvin wanting to draw out his enemies, maybe testing the resolve of the fragile and tentative coalition. A young un bucking to prove himself. Little of that seemed to be in play. Colvin simply did because he had to. Because he didn't know any better. He dreamed big but didn't have the patience and didn't want to put in the work required. He wanted what he wanted. Now. Damn the consequences. Without thought,

King's hand reached for his Caliburn. The action felt right and natural, the situation just and warranted.

Colvin chanted to himself and the air shimmered. A green seam appeared, a surgical scar opening up as another half-dozen Red Caps poured out.

"Can you do something about that?" King shouted.

"We're on it." Merle turned and tripped over a branch. Remembering that he hated the woods, especially his fear of snakes, he scrambled out the way of charging Red Caps.

His gaze flicked from side to side.

"Cut off the head and the body dies." Dred questioned the strength of King's resolve.

Panic rose in Rok and settled on him, freezing his legs as he fired wildly. The arms grappled about him. Tiny hands fastened about his ankles. Rok fired at the ground. An explosion of pain ripped across him as an elf arrow glanced against his ribcage. At the searing pain, he dropped his gun to clutch his ribs. More hands appeared, tugging at him like a furious riptide of flesh. As he toppled to the ground, a Red Cap leapt on his back. A feral gleam in its eye, it revealed its shark-like teeth and tore into Rok's neck. The creature bore down in a grim trajectory through muscle and ricocheted off bone, through his carotid artery, channeling through his neck, a cloud of arterial spray spurted.

"Mama!" the boy cried out, then fell still.

• • • •

Scarlet streaks splattered across Rellik's face. Pain drummed behind his eyes in tune with his ragged heartbeat. A talon grazed his temple as pain arced across his skull. Staggering back a few steps, a Red Cap leapt upon him. Teeth tore eagerly into the soft meat of his upper arm. The creature chewed with relish, then bellowed as bullets from the Caliburn ripped through it. Ignoring the pain in his arm, a murderous glint of rage in his eyes, Rellik's balled fist pummeled the sneer from another creature's face. He pivoted to strike another, the bones of its neck snapped in his grasp. Three more pounced on him. Razor-sharp claws drove down toward his snarling face. Drops of spit flew from his mouth as he struggled against the creature.

Surveying the scene, Colvin grinned with a smile devoid of mirth.

There was a time when Lott didn't particularly care for Lady G. They had found themselves at Outreach Inc. at about the same time. Outreach was beginning its flirtation with the idea of using arts to have the kids express themselves. Lott entered the room, baggy pair of blue jeans whose cuffs dragged along the ground, white T-shirt, a set of gold grillz, and a light blue hoodie thrown up to cover the earphones plugged in. His head bobbed ever so slightly, his fingers tapped out percussive notes in the air as he let words come to him. Lady G and Rhianna couldn't content themselves with their drawing or inane chatter, nor could they pass up a boy at peace. They threw wadded-up paper at him, driving him to such distraction, he ended up jumping out of his seat, cussing at them then storming off. The girls giggled in delight. Luckily, Wayne was there to smooth things over. It was one of the first times Wayne had really spoken to him. Eventually, he had the three of them sit down and do a poetry exercise. Lady G read a piece about fires and mothers which caused Lott to soften towards her, though he did make fun of her word skills. All it took was seeing her in a new light.

"You OK?" Lott asked Lady G.

"I'm fine. Lott, he got a gun."

"Who does?"

"Me," the voice said from the air.

It was near enough for Lott to whir about. He stared in the direction of the sound. "What you want?"

"Where's King?" The voice had the slightest of southern drawls. Probably from Kentucky originally.

"He ain't here."

"I thought he'd be the one to come. She not important enough for him?"

"She..." Lott preferred to not think about her and King. Compartmentalizing his thoughts and feelings no matter the circumstance had become reflex. "No one can get through to him. You got me instead."

"That ain't the way this was supposed to go down."

"So what you want?" Lott backed up a few steps, beginning to circle around, triangulating on the sound of the boy's voice.

"Let me think." Garlan hoped his voice didn't sound weak. He hadn't been told what to do in the event King didn't show. Maybe this was distraction enough to see the other half of his money. He needed to make sure a clear message had been sent.

"Lott!" Lady G cried out.

Her scream pierced his heart. His attention immediately went to her, all of his fighting instincts focused on protecting her. A board broke over his back. Its force drove him to his knees. Lott wasn't one for chess-like maneuverings. For him, the best path was the straight line. Even if that meant going through someone. Lott stretched out his arms in a sweeping tackle, not knowing when or if he'd hit his target. He smacked into someone after only a few steps into his charge.

"What the–?"

Lott wrapped his arms low around Garlan, digging his fingers into his back as if a more secure purchase made him real. Garlan threw a flurry of punches. Lott stepped in closer. Covered up as best he could, his head ducked from side to side. He took the punches with no more than a grimace. Flexing his jaw, a fresh wave of pain jammed needles into his brain. The pain was there, but the boy had no steel behind them. He didn't know how to throw punches well though he could land them with abandon. The volley of blows caused Lott to release his grip on him. He raised his fists, prepared for another assault. Holding his ground proved difficult. The fine layer of dust and ash mixed on the floor left little traction to be found.

The ash smeared in a spot. The impression of a shoe. As if the weight had shifted to another foot. An impression formed and then another in rapid succession. Garlan circled him, preparing to launch another attack from a different vantage point. Lott gave no indication that he knew from which direction Garlan chose to come at him, his gaze firmly affixed on the dirt of the floor.

Lott charged him again, receiving a few blows thrown while off balance which bounced off his shoulders and back. The punches to the side were more swats than anything with power. Lott jabbed into the boy's gut. Garlan growled and launched himself at him then snapped his head up to catch the underside of Lott's jaw with his skull. He slammed through Lott's defensive stance. His eyes watered, Garlan staggered back and knocked over the round spindle the group of friends had once used as a table. Breathing hard, he could taste blood on the inside of his lip.

The tension left his body.

"We done?" Lott asked.

"We done."

"You mind telling me what this was all about?"

"Just a job. Nothing personal."

"Who hired you?"

Silence was his only answer followed by the sounds of retreating footfalls scooting across the floor in rapid succession.

"This was weird," Lady G said. "It was like watching you wrestle with yourself. Like you was wrestling your imaginary friend."

"Who you tellin'? Let's get you home." Lott allowed himself a moment just to take her all in. Without make-up, without a brush run through her hair, without clothes carefully coordinated, she was still the most beautiful person he'd ever known.

"Not just yet. Can we just… go somewhere?"

"Need to walk it off? Come down from the adrenaline rush."

He took her hand and she rested her weary head on him.

"Let's end this," King yelled. His Caliburn in hand, he ran toward Colvin. With each squeeze of his trigger, a Red Cap exploded, hit dead center or in the head. The gun was an extension of him; he didn't have to think or aim, he wielded it with the skill born of years of use. He cut a swath heading directly to Colvin. A tide of people lunged at him. Hurling Red Caps leapt like surprised children, their lashing claws swiped at the air.

The mad half-fey gestured furiously, his hand danced about. The occasional green gleam sparked, but dissipated as if shorted out. King strode toward him with furious intent. Colvin locked eyes on him, so focused he did not hear the click of a blade springing to life behind him.

Baylon fought for his throat, but Colvin twisted out of the way at the last instant. Not to be denied his opportunity, Baylon arced the blade again and buried the knife up to its hilt into the fey's belly. He turned the blade then drove it up, spilling his insides. Eyes splayed open in shock, his mouth agape as if pain was an entirely new sensation which caught him short, Colvin dropped to his knees.

"No!" King said.

Merle stumbled toward them, his coat wrapped around him. Bloodied and battered, Rellik approached but remained off to the side. Dred sidled alongside him. King knelt next to Colvin. A trickle of blood curled on his lips.

"It didn't have to be this way," King said.

The rays of the rising sun spread like a bloodstain of a crime scene photo across the sky. The melody came to her heart like an ancient memory. A mournful dirge of the fallen, the loss of family, the breaking of the circle, the song rooted almost all of them to their spot. At her approach, Baylon slinked off. He didn't escape her notice, but her anger could wait. It would have been one thing to die at the hands of the Pendragon, but at the hands of an ignoble knight? It was an insult to the memory of the fey. The men parted as she neared. Dred moved toward her, but Rellik put out an arm to stop him. She joined King, kneeling alongside him before cradling the body of her brother. She stroked his beautiful face, lifted him with ease, and stalked off into the morning.

It was said that when the angels fell, the ones who fell on land became faeries and the ones who fell into the sea became selkies. She returned to the lake.

Rellik surveyed the damage. Rok's still form rent to shreds, barely recognizable as human. The bodies of the Red Caps turned to ash without Colvin's vitality to sustain them, leaving no evidence of their time on this plane.

"I'm not going back, King," Rellik said.

"What do you mean?"

"I'm out. I'm done."

King returned his Caliburn to his waistband. "What does that mean?"

"The game done changed. This here's for you young bloods. I'm tired. I just want to go home."

"To Wayne?"

"To family, yeah. Tell Wayne…" The words didn't come off his lips.

King nodded. Rellik wandered off in the general direction of Omarosa. All that remained of their group were Merle, Dred, and King. King remained kneeling, not sure if he mourned the loss of life or the death of the dream he once had.

"You must be beloved among men," Dred whispered. "All these people rush to protect you. Speak to your defense. Put their lives at risk for you. Lay down their lives for you."

"I never–" King began, but words failed him also. They rang false to his ear before he finished. Who but he could have issued the call? Who but he would they have answered for? For what? More violence. More blood. More death.

"And now what? They all gone. Went down protecting you. Loving you. All the people who love you? Gone. They all fucked and you fucked them. It's just you now. All alone."

"This ain't over," King said.

"I know. We've got plenty of story left to write, you and me." Dred turned his back and walked away.

"It's not true, you know," Merle said, but in the end this battle was between him and Dred. The last temptation of the Pendragon.

"What's not?"

"About you being alone. You'll always have me. Well, sorta."

King scarched about. "Where is he?"

"I, too, have wondered about Sir Rupert. Always underfoot when not wanted. Not a brown hair to be found once bullets start flying."

"Baylon." King's voice was without patience, joy, or strength.

"He's gone. I fear he thinks he has disappointed the crown he sought to serve. He stays under the bridge by the Mexican joints by your house. But… perhaps it'd be best to let things lic. To let some truths, some realities, go unknown."

A quizzical stare etched on King's face. He hated the moments when it felt as if Merle read from a script only he was privy to. A script he could only hint at rather than say anything directly about. King made a circle with his finger and Merle nodded that he'd clean up the mess. An anonymous call to the authorities, from a homeless man who had stumbled across a body in the woods. He'd be held for questioning, no doubt. But it meant a free meal. Maybe two.

Better than the days ahead for King.

EPILOGUE

Every few years some politician or preacher would whip the City-County Council or the media into a frenzy, usually set off by some act of violence against a child or some other innocent – and there'd be talk about tearing down the Phoenix Apartments. There'd be discussions about the failure of projects, the entrenchedness and intractability of poverty and the need for radical new approaches to the problem. Remarkably, most of the "holistic approaches" involved razing the lot and building an upscale town-house development, with a few hundred units of public housing.

All of the talk would crash against the inertia of reality: the projects were forever. The islands of poverty weren't going to be demolished, no one was going to relocate thousands of black folks. Well-intentioned neighbors (read: scared white folks) would block construction of housing for black folks in their neighborhoods. Any sprucing-up of the existing projects failed to grapple with the reality of what it meant to be poor: they had little resources to maintain buildings and property. So now the previous hope for urban renewal was ready for demolition again. Such was the way of all such buildings.

On the penthouse floor of the Phoenix Apartments, a group of men gathered. Dred poured Cristal into a series of tall stemmed glasses eager to bear the mantle of king of the streets. He would christen his own knights.

"What King has joined together, let no man tear asunder," Dred toasted. "Where do we stand?"

Naptown Red chimed in, first raising his glass in salute. "Shit done fell off. Word is Rellik is out the game entirely, leaves open all of Night's operations."

"He packaged it up nicely for us. Got it running efficiently. You and the young un ready to step up?"

Garlan nodded. He played with the ring, sliding it up and down his finger though it no longer slipped past his first joint. The Cristal stung his lips, too dry for his tastes, but didn't wince or complain. It was time to step up his game.

"Colvin's out the way now, too," Broyn said. "And Mulysa's in lock-up."

"Then it's done. This here piece is ours," Dred said.

"What about King?" Naptown Red asked.

"He's out of play. The bigger worry is Merle. He's the loose cog in our machine. If we can take out that crazy-ass motherfucker…"

A knock pounded at the door. Not quite a cop knock, but one which demanded attention. Dred nodded toward Broyn.

"It's for you," he said from the foyer. A woman trailed behind him.

Her winter coat slimmed at the waist and drew attention to her too-tight jeans. Fur-lined white boots ended with a stiletto heel. Her skin the color of scorched oak, her handsome face both passionate and cruel. A comely form steeped in ambition. And eyes the same as Morgana's. "I hear you have a problem I might be able to help you with. Where can a girl go to get put on?"

"What's your name?" Dred asked.

"Nine," she said. "Think of me as an answer to prayer."

The circle is now complete, Dred thought. *It's just you now, King. You are all alone and I'm out here, waiting for you.*

Lott gave Lady G his hand to help her down the embankment. A scree of pebbles shifted underfoot as she slid down. The path had been worn down to the tan ground, but plenty of growth covered the entrance to the bridge squat. She slipped into the shade of the overpass with unequaled elegance. Piles of discarded fast-food bags and bottles of soda lay around the site, a couple bottles filled with a murky yellow liquid.

"Someone stay here?" Lott asked.

"Yeah. Rotates though. You know how it go. No one here now. I come here to think sometimes. It's kinda nice back here around summer time. Everything grown up and stuff. Like a jungle." She leaned against the embankment, her arms folded behind her back. "You lucky."

"What you mean?"

"You get to go out, run the streets. Do your do. Make your secret plans. You boys and your big plans."

"Wonder what they're up to?"

"Something more important than us." Her high-toned voice curdled into mild scorn. She pierced him with her midnight eyes.

They both knew the weight of loneliness, its ache and the wounds it left behind. Her hard look softened around the edges, as did the coldness in her voice. Frightened and bold at the same time, while she boasted of having no interest in boys, her sole encounter having been violent. Yet she had a way of drawing them to her and making them protect her.

There was a lot to admire about Lott. Things others didn't always appreciate. His bravery, he had heart for days. His lack of cleverness, because he didn't play games. He wasn't always stuck in his own head, lost in his thoughts. And she wanted him to think only of her.

"He loves you," Lott admitted.

"He doesn't love me. He thinks he loves me." The words stopped in her throat. "I don't know if he can love. Not really. I don't know if he even feels."

"And you?"

"I love him. But not the way I…"

"Don't…" His yearning for her paralyzed him, like the Biblical Lot's wife, a pillar of salted lust. She stood close beside him. Her face kept him guarded and stirred up.

Suddenly hot and shy, his was more than a brotherly affection and flirtation. A charged moment. As long as his eyes were fixed on the running water of the slow-flowing creek, on the sounds of traffic rumbling overhead, he was safe. If he trembled, if he turned around to see the reality of his potential mistake, he was undone. The desire to want to hold her, to feel the press of her lips, or her breasts against him as they embraced, he would certainly be drawn. His legs quavered as if unable to support his weight, the thought of his friendship with King pushed deep within. The thought of his personal integrity ignored. He could no longer hear the spirit of his own conscience. Lady G filled his soul and he was lost. Her scent filled him. His immobile face ever ready to smile for her.

With the face of an alert doll, Lady G took his hand and caressed it. She moved closer. They hugged again. The press of her far-too-womanly breasts intoxicated him. Her heat blinded him.

Their bodies locked together, their lips soon met. He searched out her form, probed with his tongue as he returned her light kisses. Lady G wanted to hear him call her name. Breathy. They threatened to devour one another, their hearts pounded to shatter ribs to find one another. They weren't fully aware of

their hands clambering over one another, pulling at
pants, and he had plunged himself into her.

He thrust wildly, his legs with quickly fading
strength, threatening to give out beneath him. He
convulsed violently, years of pent-up lust finding release suddenly. It was over before it began, their
clothes were still half-on. Their eyes awash with
apology, half resenting one another. With no words
left between them.

Neither realized that they had been observed until
a nearby thud drew their attention. Something
heavy landed nearby. Lott pulled up his pants, holding up an arm to shield her as he investigated.

"Oh no," he said.

"What?" A reedy thinness entered her voice. Her
heart feared what her soul already knew. "What is
it?"

Lott held a mud-covered object in his hands. He
wiped the hunk of metal.

King's Caliburn.

King slumped against his condo door, leaned back
and, very quietly, allowed himself to let go.

Mulysa waited in his cell, in the old wing of Marion
County lock-up. What it lacked in electronic ameni-
ties it made up for with cold bricks and solid bars.
Not like the transparent cubes that housed the other
inmates like valued collectibles in the newer wing of
the lock-up. His cell hadn't even been washed down

from its previous tenant, who experimented with finger-painting with his own feces. Mulysa cupped his head in his hands, a big man not quite weeping. His public defender, not worth the stains along his cell walls, probably wouldn't be able to get him a bail hearing. The first words out of his mouth advised him to be quiet and consider a deal. Distracted, Mulysa did not hear the footfalls of approaching visitors. The unlatching of his door drew his attention.

"Remember me, Rondell?" Lee said merrily. "We got some unfinished business."

"Who?"

"Don't remember me? That hurts. Not as much as my jaw. Maybe I should let your fellow inmates know that you're into kids."

"Hey, slow your roll. I ain't got no short eyes."

"You broke the big one: never hit a cop. You can run. You can lie. We expect that. That's part of the game. But you hit one of us – or worse, throw shots – well, things change. Messages have to be sent. We can't have you and your boys thinking that it's open season on cops."

"Guard!"

"Who you calling for? Another cop? You think they gonna help you? I'd say you got more than you can handle right now. A fellow inmate?" Lee raised his voice. "Hell, I want them to hear what happens to someone who hits a cop."

The spill of light hid the back-handed slap that caught Mulysa off guard, still sick from his abrupt, stuck-in-jail detox. He tumbled onto the floor and Lee pounced on him. A spray of blood dashed against the walls. Wet sounds and grunts filled the cell, followed by a sickening crunch of teeth on metal and then a tinkle of pebbles. Plumes of silence echoed, interrupted only by Lee's heavy breathing. And the low moans.

"On the gate." Wide accusative eyes averted their gaze as Lee walked by.

The abandoned Camlann Apartment building on Oriental Avenue, three stories of what was once a showcase place. Many organizations had put in bids to rehab the building, but the owner refused to sell and refused to do anything with it except allow it to wither. So the city declared eminent domain and it was due to be razed. The lawsuits and counter-lawsuits had delayed the process, allowing it to further fall into dangerous dilapidation. Left to politicians, it would stand for years, a testimony to pain and suffering and lost hope.

Tristan struck a match. "Deuces, motherfuckers."

The only thing Gavain, no longer Rellik, had left was his memories. The road slowly snaked its way through the thick glade of trees. The roads, like growing capillaries, branched in new directions. Gavain found it hard to believe that he was still in the city. That was one of the reasons why Gavain loved Indianapolis: it was a city that knew its place with nature and rarely resisted its intrusions.

His turbulent thoughts were a drunken whirlpool of half-images. Unable to attend his mother's funeral because he'd been locked up, he could only imagine it from the reports of the members of his crew he'd sent to organize and pay for it. The poster-sized photo of his mother's face was his idea, but it seemed so tacky in the light of sobriety. The funeral parlor smelled of mothballs and roses. A broken old woman, not embittered, who'd grown distant due to the ache of loss. She had wanted a large family, so had his father, but after that summer, his father had decided he could have a large family with someone else. Sometimes she'd even managed to peer at Gavain without any trace of blame in her eyes. When she did, he knew it still lurked beneath the surface. The cold place of haunted memories – things long left unsaid – festered in the hollow graves of their lives. His long face had grown tired, overgrown with stubble and unkempt hair, pummeled by time. A prophet wandering into the wilderness. A lost preacher. Gavain stopped at an intersection that branched into six directions. He studied the signs and searched for any familiar name.

Boat launch.

The road crept down a long hill and sneaked around the defensive posture of the trees before ending near a ranger's station. The maudlin yellow building reminiscent more of a pre-fab home than anything rustic. His heart fluttered for a moment until he remembered how disused this part of the park was; the park posted ranger stations every few miles, but most rangers patrolled the picnic areas and beach, not unused boat launches. The new link fence at the end of the path barred further progress. The fence grinned like new braces over yellowed teeth, protecting the dark maw of the walkway. "No Swimming." The sign hung from its links.

A grassed-over gravel pathway led through the secluded grove. Trees crowded in, guardians of the one thousand five hundred-acre reservoir. It was a warm day with cool air; warm only in direct sunlight, the cool air chilled his nostrils. He kicked a stone and listened to the crunch of dead leaves when it skittered into the brush of the forest.

"You sure it's all right to be here?" someone said, a long time ago.

"'For You had cast me into the deep, Into the heart of the seas, And the Current engulfed me. All Your breakers and billows passed over me.'" The passage sprang to mind as clearly as the day he first memorized it.

The water stank of dead fish. He couldn't see any, but the entire alcove reeked of it. Praying to see those hands, he continued to wade into the waves' slow embrace, pulled along by the gravity of guilt. He longed to be a kid again. To crawl into…

ACKNOWLEDGMENTS

There are so many folks to thank who have helped me on the journey of this book. My family for their love, support, and patience as I squirreled myself away in my office for long hours. My church family, the Crossing, for teaching me so much about what it means to walk with people. The Indiana Horror Writers for their continued support.

My first readers, Trista Robichaud and Sara Larson.

Jerry Gordon, Gerald McCarrell, and Jason Sizemore. They know what they did… and we've sworn to never speak of it again. •

And my writing family who have kicked me in the butt along the way to make sure this got done. Brian Keene. Wrath James White. Gary Braunbeck. Lucy Snyder. Rober Fleck. Debbie Kuhn. Steve and Becky Gilberts. A better family one couldn't have.

And Chesya Burke. Where would I be without her? Writing is such a solitary endeavor, so it helps to have a dear friend who calls you regularly to, if not encourage you, then demand that you tell them how great they are (because that in turn should inspire you... I guess).

Thank you, Angry Robot, for the opportunity, and Steve Stone for another kick-ass cover.

ABOUT THE AUTHOR

Maurice Broaddus is a notorious egotist whose sole goal is to be a big enough name to be able to snub people at conventions. In anticipation of such a successful writing career, he is practicing speaking of himself in the third person. The "House of M" includes the lovely Sally Jo ("Mommy") and two boys: Maurice Gerald Broaddus II (thus, he gets to retroactively declare himself "Maurice the Great") and Malcolm Xavier Broaddus. Visit his site so he can bore you with details of all things him and most importantly, read his blog. He loves that. A lot.

Maurice holds a Bachelor of Science degree from Purdue University in Biology. Scientist, writer, and hack theologian, he's about the pursuit of Truth because all truth is God's truth. His dark fiction can be found in numerous magazine, anthologies and novellas.

www.MauriceBroaddus.com

Here's an extra short story to tide you over until
King's War – the soon-come conclusion to the *Knights
of Breton Court* saga.

Collateral Casualties

No dream lasted forever and few people ever saw the
bottom rushing towards them.

Big Pez was a merry captive of the rhythms of his
simple existence. Born Marlon Wainwright to Brody
(who drank himself into an early grave) and Mar-
jorie (who bore her bruises in silence) Wainwright,
he knew he was destined for better things. Still
weary from the night before, Big Pez wore the same
shirt under the same soiled Army jacket for the last
three days. The "N" from his high top Nikes had
peeled off his right shoe, so he scraped the left one
off to match. He was the height of haute couture for
the business of obliterating oneself. His ashy lips and
sunken eye sockets gave evidence to the inescapable
horror that he may need to ease up in his drug use.

Beckley wasn't a town renowned for plentiful opportunity, however, an enterprising dope fiend could pursue his hunt for the perfect blast with minimum encumbrance.

J-Clev sat next to him, sucking on a glass pipe. Born Jesse Cleveland to Sherry Cleveland and one of a series of one-night stands she had to make rent. A red and black flannel shirt drooped over his oversized jeans that rode low on his hips. Long hair trailed from the back of his camo ball cap which had been pulled low to shadow his heavy-lidded eyes with their wide pupils. His unkempt beard, the hairs of which turned at peculiar angles long untouched by any form of a comb, couldn't disguise his gaunt face and sallow complexion. Sores, shaped like the bloody lips of an infant, opened along his neck.

The headlights of a turning car illuminated the truck bed briefly, the sudden light causing them to wince with its interruption. The remaining shard of the broken window handle jabbed Big Pez in his side when he shifted. He jolted upwards, stirring the landfill of papers (mostly bills and collection notices), sausage McMuffin wrappers, and coffee cups filled with ground cigarette butts. The truck's blue vinyl interior, cracked and brittle, scraped his clothes. Big Pez closed his eyes and once again tilted at windmills, chasing the same, elusive high from his first blast. Tonight was different. Tonight he simply wanted a jump start so that he could go about his business. The plan was to break into Beckley Junior

High School and steal lab supplies for their own lab. They had dreams of big time gangsta life down in Balmer, though part of them knew full well that they were going to pawn anything they could get their hands on to chase their next high. A couple of city goats trying to pretend that they weren't more than a couple of meth heads.

Nudging J-Clev, Big Pez slowly opened his door and stretched slowly, his gangly form unfurling from the Chevy pick-up (originally blue, but now almost red with the rust which ate away at it like a pernicious lung cancer). Two students out for a campus stroll before their midnight classes. Definitely not two dropouts shipwrecked in life, their hopes dashed against the reefs of ignorance and hopelessness.

The school developed a terrible aspect at night, its architectural design reminiscent more of a penal institution than a learning one. The steps alone were a series of foreboding shadows leading to the recessed darkness of the entryway. Big Pez searched the retreating lot for any unwanted eyes, then squeezed between the chained doors.

With eyes downcast, Big Pez walked past the office, part of him afraid the principal would charge out to have him wait in her office. School was something he endured as long as he could, with only the cold glare of his mother's disapproval awaiting him at home.

"What about the guards?" J-Clev asked, sucking in his imagined gut as he slid through the mild gap between the chained doors. "Alarms?"

"Ain't no security to speak of. You see how old this place is? Ain't no one pouring money into this joint for on-site security. Or fancy alarms. Way they see it, not much here worth stealing no ways. I guess they depend on the scary stories to keep folks away."

"What scary stories?"

"Beckley Junior High used to be a hospital during the Civil War," Big Pez said.

"Thought that was Beckley-Stratton Junior High?"

"Over on Grey Flats? Naw, it was built a few years back and there was never a hospital there. The building that had the hospital had long been demolished, but it was all right here."

"What's so scary about that?" J-Clev stroked the scraggily wisps of his mustache, a gesture he always did when calculating the risks of a potential score.

"The way I hear it, there was a young woman named Hannah who worked as a nurse treating the wounded soldiers." At some point in the story, as best Big Pez could remember, some slaves got locked up in a room, but that part always confused him so he picked up the story at the part he remembered best. "Hannah was killed and her moans and footsteps could be heard up and down the halls."

The hallways stretched before them, spider web strands in wait. A few lights remained on, creating pools of shadow down each corridor. The artificial confidence provided by his meth had Big Pez sufficiently decisive, striding the hall with the giddy excitement of a kid embracing being locked in a toy store. His thoughts grew abrupt and fragmented. His hands balled into tight fists, hoping his instincts would navigate the labyrinthine halls to the science wing. Or a computer lab. Or the media room.

The few fluorescent lights remaining on hummed then sputtered to lifelessness and the shadows slithered from their lairs. With each step, the darkness pulsed with a life of its own. The surrounding blackness created an envelope seal of obscurity. Big Pez moved as if in a separate world from J-Clev, his hands a blur in the abyssal night. Time stretched to disorienting flatness, each heartbeat a measured thud in his throat lasting a minute.

"Did you hear that?" J-Clev stopped short, the wizened teeth of his fingers clamped onto Big Pez's arm. Drawing near, J-Clev wore the expression of irrational terror, his eyes widened, fueled by the unpredictable passions of his high.

"Nah, I didn't hear nothing." Big Pez extricated himself from the grip. "You know this shit'll make some folks paranoid."

The corridors branched in every direction, every sound coming at them from all sides with a gallows echo chamber. Staccato clicks, with the gasp of someone choking on coins, reverberated. Voices rushed with the ethereal hush of approaching whispers through a cornfield. The shadows shifted again, the corridors multiplying, a web of choices taking them further and further from where they wanted to be.

Big Pez took off running, without warning to J-Clev (who dutifully followed suit). With no destination in mind, he followed his instincts down the nearest hallway. The ceiling lit up under the occasional eruption of light coming from the failed emergency lighting. Above him, pipes – corroded veins originally for gas lighting – jutted from the ceiling. He thought he spied a door. Big Pez shuddered as he neared it.

The strong, dank smell of moist rot emanated from the door. Opening the door, he brushed through cobwebs and cemetery shadows. The dark smelled of spoiled potatoes, wood rot, and termite shit. The looming shadows coalesced into an image, an ancient movie projector focusing to life under the dreary pallor of light and the pall of mortality. Lanterns hung around the room revealing a procession of beds, crowded with moans. With forlorn and defeated faces, men hobbled about on crutches. The stench of gangrene clung to the air, smothering men buried beneath thick woolen blankets as if posed for their caskets. Emaciated and spiritless, locked in a fevered sleep, staring up at ceiling longingly with the steady gaze from bloodshot eyes, a death mask fixed on their faces.

A woman, shapely as the black dress draped around her would reveal, got up from rolling bandages. Her white apron betrayed the severity of its scarlet stains as she drew closer. Strands of her hair frayed from the bun she had it tied into. The wounds of another patient needed tending as maggots crawled in his sloughing flesh. She scooped wine mixed with water and sugar, from a bucket.

"Hannah!" A surgeon had his sleeves rolled up to the elbows, his bare arms and linen aprons smeared with blood. As he called for her, men lifted a wounded man onto the table, his shrieks of pain adding to the nightmare din. The surgeon quickly examined his wounds, knives clutched between his teeth. He snatched a knife, wiped it twice on bloody apron, and began cutting. Big Pez covered his ears to smother the sounds of the grating of the murderous knife.

Hannah fixed a pillow beneath the man's head and stroked his sweat-soaked hair. She gently daubed water on his face and neck. The surgeon tossed the freed limb to the corner. Pools of blood radiated from the pile of discarded amputated arms and legs.

"Next!" the surgeon yelled. Hysterical tears trailed down his face. His gaze locked on Big Pez and J-Clev.

Hannah grasped J-Clev's arm, her fingers digging into it like shards of broken glass.

Big Pez staggered out the door, almost stumbling as he turned to run. The door closed behind him, not quite muffling J-Clev's fading screams. He ran blindly until he found himself by the front office again. Hoping to hear J-Clev following him, he cocked his ears to the silence. The sure tapping of footfalls emanated from the trailing darkness.

"J?" he called out, little above a stage whisper.

A chorus of whispers rose in response. The cries of the damned. "Doctor?" "Help." "God!"

Big Pez's heart pounded, his hands trembling as he fumbled at the chained doors. He shook, almost too violently to squeeze back through door, but the icy brush of fingers scraping at him panicked him through.

That night, huddled in a fetal ball of fear and drugs, he dreamt of shadows and blood.

And if you really, really can't wait, here's the opening of *King's War*.

PROLOGUE
The Glein/River Incident

All stories ended in death.

Lost in the white noise of the engine, that was the first thing that popped into King James White's mind as he idled down 16th Street. Sitting tall and straight in the car seat, he shifted uncomfortably, visibly muscled, but not with the dieseled appearance of prison weight. A head full of regal twists fit for a crown, he had the complexion of burnt cocoa and fresh crop of razor bumps ran along his neck. The thin trace of a goatee framed his mouth. He scanned the streets with a heavy gaze, both decisive and sure. He hated driving and doing so put him in a foul mood. Not a gearhead by any measure, he neither had oil in his blood nor an overwhelming need to be under a hood. For that matter, he didn't have any love for huge rides, trues and vogues, ostentatious rims, booming systems, or any of the other nonsense which seemed to accompany a love of cars. A ride was just a ride. He much preferred walking, to have the earth solidly under his feet.

His ace, Lott, who rode silently beside him, simply believed him to be cheap, not wanting to pay the nearly $3 per gallon unless he absolutely had to. Lott always seemed a week past getting his low cut fade tightened up. His large brown eyes took in the passing scenery. His FedEx uniform – a thick sweatshirt over blue slacks; his name badge, "Lott Carey" with a picture featuring his grill-revealing smile, wrapped around his arm – girded him like a suit of armor. Lott drummed casually to himself, caught up in the melodies in his head.

Scrunching down in his seat again to check the skyline – as if maybe the creature might fly by in the open sky line by day – King turned at the sound of a beat being pounded out on the dashboard.

"What?" Lott paused mid-stroke under the weight of King's eyes on him.

"What you doing?"

"Nothing." Lott grinned his sheepish, "been caught" smile, both beguiling and devilish. A row of faux gold caps grilled his teeth.

"We supposed to be looking for this thing."

"We don't even know what this thing is."

"What kind of man would I be if I ignored that?" King asked.

"A man. An ordinary man." Lott began drumming again. "Ain't nothing wrong with that."

For days King trailed a beast strictly on the say so of a mother's plea. Not even a year ago, he'd have dismissed the tale as another barber shop story told to pass the time, little more than a campfire story in the hood. The only monsters who prowled about in the dark were strictly of the two-legged variety. That was before he found himself caught up in a new story. One filled with magic, trolls, elementals, and dragons. The shadow world, an invisible world, once seen couldn't be unseen. Now the world of demons and creatures was far too real. All he knew, all he had sworn, was that nothing would prey upon the weak and defenseless in his neighborhood.

Descriptions of the creature changed with the teller of the tale. Sometimes it had wings. Sometimes the body of a lion. Sometimes it had the body of a snake. Sometimes claws. King feared he might be dealing with more than one creature, which was equally as bad an alternative to facing one creature with all of those characteristics. Even in a concrete jungle, life belonged to the swift, the strong, the smartest. King stalked among it, the latest generation of street princes. And heavy was the head that wore the crown.

"We heading over to Glein?" Lott asked in his lazy drawl, obviously pleased with himself. He loved accompanying King on his little missions.

"That where the Harding Street bridge folk ended up?"

"As long as the problem is swept under someone else's rug, the mess is considered clean."

"I think so. Been hearing reports about it. Been wanting to check out this 'tent city.'" For his part,

King was energized by Lott. It was like there was nothing he couldn't accomplish with Lott by his side. King the pressure piled on more these days. Everyone seemed to turn to him for answers. To solve their problems. The streets were becoming his even moreso than they were his father, except he hated the sheer… responsibility of it all.

Lott rolled with it all. The FedEx gig was working out. The company would be promoting him soon and he'd get a better shift. His story, too, had changed much in only a few in an abandoned house. He had a job with a future. And, for the first time he could remember, he had a friend who'd walk through fire for him, one for whom he'd do the same. Lott wasn't one to swear oaths to allegiances to anyone, but once he called someone friend, he was loyal to the end. And King was his boy.

King wasn't the type to make friends easily. Investing in people wasn't worth the effort: in the end, they all abandoned him. A melancholy cloud had settled on King over the last few months, but it wasn't anything either felt the need to talk about. Not every little feeling had to be talked through. Sometimes it was better to just let folks be.

They continued west on 16th Street passing Martin Luther King Jr Boulevard, Methodist Hospital, and the Indiana State Forensics Laboratory. On Aqueduct Street, they pulled into a gravel lot. Signs pointed toward the Water Company, but they were more interested in the park across the street. Calm and resolute, King stood motionless, taking in the tranquility. His tall and regal bearing swathed in a trenchcoat, matching his black jeans and black Chuck Taylors. The wind caught his open coat ever so slightly, the brief flutter the only movement, revealing the portrait of Medgar Evers on his T-shirt. And the butt of his Caliburn tucked into his waist. And he never looked more lonely.

Only a few nights ago, they cleared a corner. It was one of those little runs King didn't tell Wayne Orkney – the other member of their triumvirate, who was also on staff at a homeless teen ministry called Outreach Inc – nor his mentor, Pastor Ector Winburn, about. The grumbles of their disapproval of his off the book runs would echo in his ears for weeks.

But Lott would be all in.

For all of his bravado and certainty whenever he went about his business, King needed someone to watch his back. To Lott, he wasn't Robin to King's Batman, but rather Batman to King's Superman. He rather reveled in that image.

Dred, though eastside hadn't been heard from; Night, once king of the west side, had been dropped by King (so the story went). The Eagle Terrace apartments bordered, but was a respectful distance from, Breton Court, King's undisputed dominion. A couple of non-descript fools, in baggy t-shirts and baggier pants who couldn't have been more than fourteen years old, not even a hard fourteen. Lott could practically smell their mother's milk on their breath. The first one leaned toward tall, a little bulk about the shoulders but with thin legs, like a basketball player growing into his body. A threat from the waist up, it was a dead giveaway that he'd found a set of weights and concentrated on his arms and never worked his legs. The other was short, stocky, with brown eyes too big for his head. Too quick to show his teeth, he cracked endless jokes about doing the other's girls heedless of the fact that he was on the clock. And that two brothers who meant business stepped to them from the shadows.

"You gonna have to move on," King said with no play in his voice.

"This is our spot. Who gonna move us?" the tall one said. His head had been filled with how good he was, the tone of entitlement in his voice.

"I am."

"I know you?"

"Name's King. Don't make me tell you again."

He'd said it and he meant it. King wasn't much older than either of them, but he had the hard and tested body of a man. As it was, it wasn't a fair fight. Lott hung back, mostly to enjoy the show and guard for the unexpected. But these two boys? King had this.

The lanky one turned as if to walk a way, but King read the positioning of his feet and the shifting of his weight to know that the fool planned to swing on him. When the boy pivoted to throw his punch in "surprise," King jabbed him in the kidneys, grabbed him by the throat, and slammed him onto the hood of a parked car. King had a way of blazing in and dropping fools before they knew what hit them.

A grin had broken and then froze on the face of the other boy. He reached under his shirt tail. King drew his Caliburn and trained it on the boy. Whenever he pulled out the Caliburn, folks knew what was up.

"You got something you want to show me?"

"No," the boy slowly dropped his hand to his side.

"Good, cause I'm only saying this once. This here was a friendly warning. Our neighborhood is tired of this mess. So why don't you give it a rest. We cool?"

"We cool."

Lott reached into the boy's waist band and removed the Colt. He emptied it of its bullets and tossed the weapon into the bushes. "I didn't want any surprises should he scrap together some courage as we walked away."

King and Lott walked down the alley of the apartments nodding but not smiling to the folks they recognized. The respect left Lott so swoll, more so than any workout; respect born out of the work, of doing right by the neighborhood.

"You a good man."

King trained himself to keep full reign on his emotions. Prided himself on his ability to compartmentalize, remain objective, and disciplined. Some mistook it for aloof or indifferent, as if he didn't care, but Lott knew he cared too much.

With the Caliburn tucked into his dip, King adjusted his stride. He rolled his shoulders slightly, like a boxer entering a ring. Though it fit in his hand with a natural ease, as if he was always meant to wield it, he was still getting used to it.

"You need that?" King asked as Lott retrieved a bat from the back seat.

"Ain't all of us got weapons tucked in their shorts."

"Don't be jealous. It's not the size."

"When that thing busts a cap all premature, don't come limping to me."

A hill rolled down from the street leading into an impenetrable tract of trees, a scenic backdrop to the park. Lott put on his pimp roll strut for all eyes to see as he moved toward the bridge. His was a puffed up exaggerated gait accompanied by a cool blank stare, his face locked into a grimace of put on hostility purposefully designed to make old ladies clutch their purses and white suburbanites cross the street if they were in his path. He always saw himself as a wrong time/wrong place sort, always getting caught up in situations he didn't start but felt compelled to finish. In his experience, only jail or the grave were the typical finish lines that awaited him.

Despite his carefully contrived appearance, there was no way to ease down the hill and maintain any sense of street cool. They could take only a few awkward steps at a time, down the steep incline, as rocks littered the grass and made it difficult to maintain their balance and sure-footing. Down, down, down they went and it was as if they left one world and entered another. It didn't take long for the sounds of traffic overhead to fade against the steady thrum of the rushing White River. The currents roiled, the water climbed high up its banks due to the melted snow and recent heavy rains. The greenish water appeared brackish with up tilled silt, not that the White River was the healthiest of waterways to begin with.

Scattered among the thin brown weeds passed for grass was rebar and smashed concrete. A red and white umbrella canted against a tree. A bed of large white stones formed a channel leading from a pipe to the river. The bridge loomed above them, dwarfing them. It never seemed this large whenever they drove over it. The slate gray arches gleamed, only a few years old since the city remembered this side of town. The arches created an echo chamber as the water rushed under it.

"Some nice work." Lott nodded toward the groups of tags along the base of the bridge. The spray-painted figure of a life-sized, 1950s-era wind-up robot with a head of a kangaroo. Two sets of names in so stylized a script, the letters were indistinguishable. The final figure was of a Latino boy with his cap turned to one side with an expression reminiscent of Edvard Munch's "The Scream".

"Too bad you can't tell what they're saying." King squatted in front of the formation of rocks on the opposite side. Half-rotted textbooks, newspapers, and Mountain Dew bottles littered the ground in between. Sweatshirts, pants, the occasional blanket, coats, and towels piled between two rows of stacked rocks. Another circle of stones, all charred, had a grill top resting on them.

"Odd place to lay out your stuff," Lott said.

"It's a mattress."

Lott stared at the arrangement again and pointed to the blackened rocks. "Yeah, I see it now. That's his stove. We in someone's squat."

"Someone not a part of tent city."

"Means we on the right track."

"You ought to wipe your feet before entering a man's abode. It's just plain rude."

At the sound of the voice, King and Lott turned. Merle's slate gray eyes peered at them. His craggily auburn beard matched what wisps remained around his huge bald spot. Aluminum foil formed a chrome cap, which didn't quite fit atop his head. A black raincoat draped about him like a cloak.

"You stay here?" Lott asked.

"It's one place I stay, wayward knight, though not my secret place. You don't think I only spend my time with you lot. Sir Rupert craves the outdoors." A washcloth popped up, causing King to jump back. A squirrel peered left and then right, then dashed from beneath the cloth and scampered past his legs.

Lott could never shake the feeling that Merle never quite trusted him, like they shared a best forgotten secret only the crazy old man knew. He would chide himself for caring what the bum thought of him, though part of him feared it might be jealousy as Merle seemed to have King's ear in a way he didn't.

"Don't mean to bust your roll or nothing," King said, "but we on a mission."

"Oh? A quest? Is it that time already? Mayhaps we'll encounter a questing beast." Merle danced in a circle around King, hands spreading from his face in jazz hands wiggles as he cried out. "'A star appearing in the sky, its head like a dragon from whose mouth two beams came at an angle.' An egg shaped keystone, mayhaps a tower. A keystone illumination on the winter solstice. A sacred geometry. A date carved in stone. No wait, a stone unearthed from under a poplar tree, archaic names scribed into it along with strange symbols. A silver chalice, the Chalice of Antioch."

With that, Merle curtsied.

"You done?" King asked.

"It is finished," Merle said.

**KING'S WAR
BY MAURICE BROADDUS
COMING SOON**